HELLO EARTH, ARE YOU THERE?

Brian Aldiss OBE, was a fiction and science fiction writer, poet, playwright, critic, memoirist and artist.

Born in Norfolk in 1925, Brian worked as a bookseller after leaving the army, providing the setting for his first book, *The Brightfount Diaries*. His first published science fiction work was 'Criminal Record', which appeared in *Science Fantasy* in 1954. Brian went on to write nearly 100 books and over 300 short stories, including the acclaimed novels *Hothouse*, *Non-Stop* and the Helliconia trilogy, all regarded as modern classics. He also edited numerous anthologies of science fiction and fantasy stories and the magazine *SF Horizons*.

The winner of two Hugo Awards, one Nebula Award, and one John W. Campbell Memorial Award, Brian was inducted by the Science Fiction Hall of Fame in 2004. Several of his books, including *Frankenstein Unbound*, have been adapted for the cinema and 'Supertoys Last All Summer Long' was adapted into the film *AI: Artificial Intelligence*, directed by Steven Spielberg.

A vice-president of the international H.G. Wells Society, Brian was given the Damon Knight Memorial Grand Master Award by the Science Fiction Writers of America (SFWA) in 2000. He was awarded the OBE for services to literature in 2005. Brian died in 2017 in Oxford at the age of 92.

Also by Brian Aldiss

NOVELS

The Brightfount Diaries
Non-Stop
Hothouse
The Dark Light Years
Greybeard
Barefoot in the Head
The Horatio Stubbs *trilogy*
The Eighty Minute Hour
The Malacia Tapestry
Pile
Life in the West
Helliconia Spring

Helliconia Summer
Helliconia Winter
Forgotten Life
Remembrance Day
Somewhere East of Life
The Secret of This Book
Jocasta
Sanity and the Lady
HARM
Walcot
Finches of Mars

NON-FICTION

Cities and Stones
The Shape of Further Things: Speculations on Change
Billion Year Spree: The History of Science Fiction
This World and Nearer Ones: Essays Exploring the Familiar
The Pale Shadow Of Science
Trillion Year Spree: The History of Science Fiction
… And the Lurid Glare of the Comet
Bury My Heart at W.H. Smith's: A Writing Life
The Detached Retina: Aspects of SF and Fantasy
The Twinkling of an Eye, or My Life as an Englishman
When the Feast is Finished

The Best Science Fiction Stories of Brian Aldiss

HELLO EARTH, ARE YOU THERE?

BRIAN ALDISS

HARPER
Voyager

Harper*Voyager*
An imprint of
HarperCollins*Publishers* Ltd
1 London Bridge Street
London SE1 9GF

www.harpercollins.co.uk

HarperCollins*Publishers*
Macken House,
39/40 Mayor Street Upper,
Dublin 1, D01 C9W8
Ireland

First published by HarperCollins*Publishers* Ltd 2025

1

Copyright © Brian Aldiss 2025

Introduction © William Boyd 2025
Afterword © Wendy Aldiss 2025

Internal illustrations p.vi and p.305 © Brian Aldiss
Title page illustration: Shutterstock.com

Brian Aldiss asserts the moral right to be identified as the author of this work.

A catalogue record for this book is available from the British Library.

ISBN: 978-0-00-877961-0

This collection is entirely a work of fiction.
It is presented in its original form and may depict ethnic, racial and sexual prejudices that were commonplace at the time it was written. The names, characters and incidents portrayed in it are the work of the author's imagination. Any resemblance to actual persons, living or dead, events or localities is entirely coincidental.

Typeset in Minion Pro by Palimpsest Book Production Limited, Falkirk, Stirlingshire

Printed and bound in the UK using 100% Renewable Electricity by CPI Group (UK) Ltd

All rights reserved. No part of this publication may be reproduced, stored in a retrieval system, or transmitted, in any form or by any means, electronic, mechanical, photocopying, recording or otherwise, without the prior written permission of the publishers.

Without limiting the exclusive rights of any author, contributor or the publisher of this publication, any unauthorized use of this publication to train generative artificial intelligence (AI) technologies is expressly prohibited. HarperCollins also exercise their rights under Article 4(3) of the Digital Single Market Directive 2019/790 and expressly reserve this publication from the text and data mining exception.

This book contains FSC™ certified paper and other controlled sources
to ensure responsible forest management.

For more information visit: www.harpercollins.co.uk/green

Contents

Introduction	vii
Not for an Age	1
Supertoys Last All Summer Long	11
Conviction	21
All the World's Tears	35
Intangibles, Inc.	47
Breathing Space	69
Softly – As in an Evening Sunrise	83
In the Arena	101
Working in the Spaceship Yards	113
As for Our Fatal Continuity . . .	121
Psyclops	127
Never Let Go of My Hand!	137
You Never Asked My Name	155
Juniper	171
Confluence	173
The Under-Privileged	181
Something from the Turkish	199
Poor Little Warrior!	203
How the Gates Opened and Closed	209
The Worm that Flies	215
A Tupolev Too Far	233
A Romance of the Equator	265
Short Stories	273
A New (Governmental) Father Christmas	275
Last Orders	283
Bill Carter Takes Over	295
Afterword	303
Publication history	307

—*Illustration for* Breathing Space *by Brian Aldiss*

Introduction

It was a short story that first brought me into Brian Aldiss's orbit, appropriately enough. This occurred back in 1977 when I was at Oxford, trying to write a doctoral thesis but dreaming of becoming a novelist. The university's celebrated magazine, *Isis*, regularly ran short story competitions judged by the city's famous resident writers. I entered them all and had done well so far: second prize in a competition judged by Iris Murdoch; third in one judged by Roald Dahl. Then along came a challenge to write a science fiction short story to be judged by Brian Aldiss. I wrote a dystopian allegory inspired by Aldous Huxley's *Brave New World*. It wasn't placed. So much for Brian Aldiss's literary acumen, I thought, aggrieved.

Cut to 1981. My first novel, *A Good Man in Africa*, had been published and was submitted for the Booker Prize. One of the judges that year, I noted, was my nemesis, Brian Aldiss. I did not make the short list. However, a week after the prize was announced a letter was forwarded on to me by my publisher. It was from Brian Aldiss, himself, informing me of how much he had enjoyed my novel and how he had tried his hardest to get it shortlisted. However, the most extraordinary fact was the address in the letterhead. Brian Aldiss, it turned out, was a near neighbour. He was living in a large house in North Oxford four doors down the road from the flat that my wife and I were renting. I gratefully replied and alerted him to the astonishing coincidence of our proximity. Brian immediately invited us round for drinks and we met him and his wife Margaret – and thus began a firm friendship that lasted many years.

At the time when we began to see each other regularly Brian was working on his science fiction masterpiece The Helliconia Trilogy. I was privileged to learn the inside story of this elaborate parallel world Brian was creating in all its extraordinary and authentic detail and I steadily began to read my way through his work. I became an unequivocal fan.

All this is by way of a preamble to this centenary anniversary volume, *Hello Earth, Are You There?*, a superb selection of Brian's science fiction short stories. Their compelling variety, intelligence and shrewd perceptiveness all testify to the extraordinary literary fecundity that Brian possessed. All forms were available to his fervent imagination: from space opera to inner space; from distant futures to prehistoric pasts; from bleak dystopian reportage to the hilarious and unclassifiable 'Confluence' – an alphabetic lexicon of 'Myrinian culture'. The inventiveness is astonishing. And yet for all the weird gadgetry and strange nomenclature, the bizarre worlds and situations and the outlandish flora and fauna that are conjured up, there is something fundamentally humane about Brian's science fiction. The men and women, the androids and strange hybrids of his sci-fi stories deal, paradoxically, with the nature of the human condition in ways we can all understand. The potency of serious science fiction is that it looks at our world and our relationships through a disturbing and distorting lens. Emily Dickinson urged writers to, 'Tell all the truth but tell it slant'. This is exactly what Brian Aldiss's stories achieve.

Perhaps the most famous short story in this collection is 'Supertoys Last All Summer Long'. It was later turned into the film *A.I. Artificial Intelligence*, directed by Steven Spielberg. But the first director who lit upon it was Stanley Kubrick. I remember Brian telling me the news that the film project was underway – his excitement was palpable. Kubrick lived not far from Oxford, near St Albans, and Brian began a daily commute to Kubrick's estate to work on a detailed outline of the potential film adaptation. Brian regaled us with Kubrickian anecdotes as the developing plot slowly took shape over weeks and months. Brian participated eagerly in the experience because he had every hope of writing the screenplay of the movie, or at least the first draft. Kubrick promised him this would be the case but first he needed certain contractual conditions to be met: Brian was not to be allowed to employ an agent; he was

INTRODUCTION

not to leave the country while the movie's development was underway; if another writer had a credit on the film Brian would not be paid. There were other stringent stipulations. In fact, Brian did leave the country and Kubrick fired him. Not surprisingly, it brought about a dramatic schism in their relationship. Brian told me he simply didn't trust Kubrick to honour his promise – and so he walked away from the project.

A brave move – and a tribute to Brian's straightforward honesty and integrity. Kubrick was semi-reconciled with Brian some years later – the 'Supertoys' project rumbled on, Brian describing it as a 'long dusty trail' – but the Kubrick version of the film was never made. It was only after Kubrick's death in 1999 that Spielberg stepped in, Brian wrote more material and the movie was completed.

Brian was a leading member of the sci-fi 'boom' of the 1960s – one of a triumvirate of writers who represented a particularly British cohort of the global phenomenon, the other two being J.G. Ballard and Michael Moorcock. However, I think it's important to remember that Brian's science fiction novels and stories only represent one string to his literary bow. He was a prolific writer in all genres – orthodox novels, poems, travel writing, journalism and memoirs, as well as being a significant anthologist and historian of the science fiction movement.

In person, Brian was a tall, warm, genial man who seemed to radiate an inner energy and enthusiasm, burning with a kind of curiosity that couldn't be confined to one type of writing or expression. The size of the corpus of his work is testimony to his roving mind and tireless work ethic. For a young writer like me, getting to know him was not only a pleasure but salutary. He was a great exemplar, demonstrating a type of commitment to his vocation that was open, plural and polymathic. Brian's prodigious output showed that you didn't have to plough a lonely, single furrow as a writer – all modes of literary expression were there to be employed if the mood took you. The austere Flaubertian or Joycean model was not for him. He was more like Charles Dickens, Graham Greene or Muriel Spark – writers who practised and excelled in a similar diversity of literary genres as Brian did, variety being the spice of his writing life.

And what a long and productive life it was, rightfully being celebrated on his hundredth birthday. This volume of short stories is the cherry on the sundae of his copious output. One of the most autobiographical pieces in this collection is entitled 'Short Stories' where Brian, in his own voice, muses eloquently on his output. He regards his short fictions, he tells us, as 'Mad and lovely while they last . . . That's how I see my stories. They formed part of me.'

—William Boyd, 2025

Not for an Age

A bedspring groaned and pinged, mists cleared, Rodney Furnell awoke. From the bathroom next door came the crisp sound of shaving; his son was up. The bed next to his was empty; Valerie, his second wife, was up. Guiltily Rodney also rose, and performed several timid exercises to flex his backbone. Youth! When it was going it had to be husbanded. He touched his toes.

The audience had its first laugh there.

By the time Rodney had got into his Sunday suit, Valerie's cuckoo clock was chuckling nine, followed by the more sardonic notes of his ormolu chimer. Valerie and Jim (Rodney had conscientiously shunned a literary name for his only offspring) were already at the cornflakes when he entered their gay little kitchenette.

More laughter at the first sight of that antiquated twentieth-century modernity.

'Hello, both! Lovely morning,' he boomed, kissing Valerie's forehead. The September sun, in fact, was making a fair showing through damp mist; a man of forty-two instinctively arms himself with enthusiasm when facing a wife fifteen years younger.

The audience always loved the day's meals, murmuring with delight as each quaint accessory – toaster, teapot, sugar tongs – was used.

Valerie looked fresh and immaculate. Jim sported an open-necked shirt and was attentive to his stepmother. At nineteen he was too manly and too attentive . . . He shared the Sunday paper companionably with her, chatting about the theatre and books. Sometimes Rodney could join in about one of the books. Under the notion that Valerie disliked seeing him in spectacles, he refrained from reading at breakfast.

How the audience roared later when he slipped them on in his study! How he hated that audience! How fervently he wished that he had the power to raise even one eyebrow in scorn of them!

The day wore on exactly as it had for over a thousand times, unable to deviate in the slightest from its original course. So it would go on and on, as meaningless as a cliché, or a tune endlessly repeated, for the benefit of these fools who stood on all four sides and laughed at the silliest things.

At first, Rodney had been frightened. This power to snatch them all, as it were, from the grave had seemed something occult. Then, becoming accustomed to it, he had been flattered. That these wise beings had wanted to review *his* day, disinter *his* modest life. But it was balm only for a time; Rodney soon discovered he was simply a glorified side-show at some latter-day fair, a butt for fools and not food for philosophers.

He walked in the tumble-down garden with Valerie, his arm around her waist. The north Oxford air was mild and sleepy; the neighbours' radio was off.

'Have you *got* to go and see that desiccated old Regius Professor, darling?' she asked.

'You know I must.' He conquered his irritation and added: 'We'll go for a drive after lunch – just you and I.'

Unfailingly, each day's audience laughed at that. Presumably 'a drive after lunch' had come to mean something dubious. Each time Rodney made that remark, he dreaded the reaction from those half-glimpsed countenances that pressed on all sides; yet he was powerless to alter what had once been said.

He kissed Valerie, he hoped elegantly; the audience tittered, and he stepped into the garage. His wife returned to the house, and Jim. What happened in there he would never know, however many times the day was repeated. There was no way of confirming his suspicion that his son was in love with Valerie and she attracted to him. She should have enough sense to prefer a mature man to a stripling of nineteen; besides, it was only eighteen months since he had been referred to in print as 'one of our promising young men of *litterae historicae*'.

Rodney could have walked around to Septuagint College. But because the car was new and something that his don's salary would hardly stretch to, he preferred to drive. The watchers, of course, shrieked with laughter at the sight of his little automobile. He occupied himself, as he polished the windshield, with hating the audience and all inhabitants of this future world.

That was the strange thing. There was room in the corner of the old Rodney mind for the new Rodney ghost. He depended on the old Rodney – the Rodney who had actually lived that fine, autumn day – for vision, motion, all the paraphernalia of life; but he could occupy independently a tiny cell of his consciousness. He was a helpless observer carried over and over in a cockpit of the past.

The irony of it lay there. He would have been spared all this humiliation if he did not know what was happening. But he did know, trapped though he was in an unknowing shell.

Even to Rodney, a history man and no scientist, the broad outline of what had happened was obvious enough. Somewhere in the future, man had ferreted out the secret of literally reclaiming the past. Bygone years lay in the rack of antiquity like film spools in a library. Like film spools, they were not amenable to change, but might be played over and over on a suitable projector. Rodney's autumn day was being played over and over.

He had reflected helplessly on the situation so often that the horror of it had worn thin. That day had passed, quietly, trivially, had been forgotten; suddenly, long afterwards, it had been whipped back among the things that were. Its actions, even its thoughts, had been reconstituted, with only Rodney's innermost ego to suffer from the imposition. How unsuspecting he had been then! How inadequate every one of his gestures seemed now, performed twice, ten, a hundred, a thousand times!

Had he been as smug every day as he was that day? And what had happened after that day? Having, naturally, no knowledge of the rest of his life then, he had none now. If he had been happy with Valerie for much longer, if his recently published work on feudal justice had been acclaimed – these were questions he could pose without answering.

A pair of Valerie's gloves lay on the back seat of the car; Rodney threw them into a locker with an éclat quite divorced from his inner impotence. She, poor dear bright thing, was in the same predicament. In that they were united, although powerless to express the union in any slightest flicker of expression.

He drove slowly down Banbury Road. As ever, there were four subdivisions of reality. There was the external world of Oxford; there were Rodney's original abstracted observations as he moved through the world; there were the ghost thoughts of the 'present-I', bitter and frustrated; there were the half-seen faces of the future which advanced or receded aimlessly. The four blended indefinably, one becoming another in Rodney's moments of near-madness. (What would it be like to be insane, trapped in a sane mind? He was tempted by the luxury of letting go.)

Sometimes he caught snatches of talk from the onlookers. They at least varied from day to day. 'If he knew what he looked like!' they would exclaim. Or: 'Do you see her hair-do?' Or: 'Can you beat that for a slum!' Or: 'Mummy, what's that funny brown thing he's eating?' Or – how often he heard that one; 'I just wish he knew we were watching him!'

Church bells were solemnly ringing as he pulled up outside Septuagint and switched off the ignition. Soon he would be in that fusty study, taking a glass of something with the creaking old Regius Professor. For the nth time he would be smiling a shade too much as the grip of ambition outreached the hand of friendship. His mind leaped ahead and back and ahead and back again in a frenzy. Oh, if he could only *do* something! So the day would pass. Finally, the night would come – one last gust of derision at Valerie's nightgown and his pyjamas! – and then oblivion.

Oblivion . . . that lasted an eternity but took no time at all . . . And *they* wound the reel back and started it again, all over again.

He was pleased to see the Regius Professor. The Regius Professor was pleased to see him. Yes, it was a nice day. No, he hadn't been out of college since, let's see, it must be the summer before last. And then came that line that drew the biggest laugh of all; Rodney said, inevitably: 'Oh, we must all hope for some sort of immortality.'

To have to say it again, to have to say it not a shade less glibly than when it had first been said, and when the wish had been granted already in such a ludicrous fashion! If only he might die first, if only the film would break down!

And then the film did break down.

*

The universe flickered to a standstill and faded into dim purple. Temperature and sound slid down to zero. Rodney Furnell stood transfixed, his arms extended in the middle of a gesture, a wineglass in his right hand. The flicker, the purple, the zeroness cut down through him; but even as he sensed himself beginning to fade, a great fierce hope was born within him. With a burst of avidity, the ghost of him took over the old Rodney. Confidence flooded him as he fought back the negativity.

The wineglass vanished from his hand. The Regius Professor sank into twilight and was gone. Blackness reigned. Rodney turned around. It was a voluntary movement; *it was not in the script*; he was alive, free.

The bubble of twentieth-century time had burst, leaving him alive in the future. He stood in the middle of a black and barren area. There had evidently been a slight explosion. Overhead was a crane-like affair as big as a locomotive with several funnels protruding from its underside; smoke issued from one of the funnels. Doubtless the thing was a time-projector or whatever it might be called, and obviously it had blown a fuse!

The scene about him engaged all Rodney's attention. He was delighted to see that his late audience had been thrown into mild panic. They shouted and pushed and – in one quarter – fought vigorously. Male and female alike, they wore featureless, transparent bags which encased them from neck to ankle – and they had the impertinence to laugh at his pyjamas!

Cautiously, Rodney moved away. At first the idea of liberty overwhelmed him, he could scarcely believe himself alive. Then the realisation came: his liberty was precious – how doubly precious after that most terrible form of captivity! – and he must guard it by flight. He hurried beyond the projection area, pausing at a great sign that read:

CHRONOARCHAEOLOGY LTD PRESENTS –
THE SIGHTS OF THE CENTURIES
COME AND ENJOY THE ANTICS OF YOUR ANCESTORS!
YOU'LL LAUGH AS YOU LEARN

And underneath: Please Take One.

Shaking, Rodney seized a gaudy folder and stuffed it into his pocket. Then he ran.

His guess about the fair-ground was correct, and Valerie and he had been merely a glorified peepshow. Gigantic booths towered on all sides. Gay crowds sauntered or stood, taking little notice as Rodney passed. Flags flew, silvery music sounded; nearby, a flashing sign begged:

TRY ANTI-GRAV AND REALISE YOUR DREAMS

Farther on, a banner proclaimed:

THE SINISTER VENUSIANS ARE *HERE*!

Fortunately, a gateway was close. Dreading a detaining hand on his arm, Rodney made for it as quickly as possible. He passed a towering structure before which a waiting line of people gazed impatiently up at the words:

SAVOUR THE EROTIC POSSIBILITIES OF FREE-FALL

and came to the entrance.

An attendant called and tried to stop him. Rodney broke into a run. He ran down a satin-smooth road until exhaustion overcame him. A metal object shaped vaguely like a shoe but as big as a small bungalow stood at the kerb. Through its windows, Rodney saw couches and no human beings. Thankful at the mute offer of rest and concealment, he climbed in.

As he sank panting onto yielding rubber-foam, he realised what a horrible situation he was in. To be stranded centuries ahead of his own lifetime – and death – in a world of supertechnology and barbarism! – for so he visualised it. However, it was a vast improvement on the repetitive nightmare he had recently endured. Chiefly, now, he needed time to think quietly.

'Are you ready to proceed, sir?'

Rodney jumped up, startled by a voice so near him. Nobody was in sight. The interior resembled a coach's, with wide, soft seats, all of which were empty.

'Are you ready to proceed, sir?' There it was again.

'Who is that?' Rodney asked.

'This is Auto-moto Seven Six One at your service, sir, awaiting instructions to proceed.'

'You mean away from here?'

'Certainly, sir.'

'Yes, please!'

At once the structure glided smoothly forward. No noise, no vibration. The gaudy fair-ground fell back and was replaced by other buildings, widely spaced, smokeless, built of a substance which looked like curtain fabric; they flowed by without end.

'Are you – are we heading for the country?' Rodney asked.

'This is the country, sir. Do you require a city?'

'No, I don't. What is there beside city and country?'

'Nothing, sir – except of course the sea fields.'

Dropping that line of questioning, Rodney, who was instinctively addressing a busy control board at the front of the vehicle, inquired: 'Excuse my asking, but are you a – er, robot?'

'Yes, sir, Auto-moto Seven Six One. New on this route, sir.'

Rodney breathed a sigh of relief. He could not have faced a human being but irrationally felt superior to a mere mechanical. Pleasant voice it had, no more grating certainly than the Professor of Anglo-Saxon at his old college . . . however long ago that was.

'What year *is* this?' he asked.

'Circuit Zero, Epoch Eighty-two, new style. Year Two Thousand Five Hundred Anno Domini, old style.'

It was the first direct confirmation of all his suspicions; there was no gainsaying that level voice.

'Thanks,' he said hollowly, 'Now if you don't mind I've got to think.'

Thought, however, yielded little in comfort or results. Possibly the wisest course would be to throw himself on the mercy of some civilised authority – if there were any civilised authorities left. And would the wisest course in a twentieth-century world be the wisest in a – um, twenty-sixth-century world?

'Driver, is Oxford in existence?'

'What is Oxford, sir?'

A twinge of anxiety as he asked: 'This is England?'

'Yes, sir. I have found Oxford in my directory, sir. It is a motor and spaceship factory in the Midlands, sir.'

'Just keep going.'

Dipping into his pocket, he produced the fun-fair brochure and scanned its bright lettering, hoping for a clue to action.

'Chronoarchaeology Ltd. presents a staggering series of Peeps into the Past. Whole days in the lives of (a) A Mother Dinosaur, (b) William the Conqueror's Wicked Nephew, (c) A Citizen of Crazed, Plague-Ridden Stuart London, (d) A Twentieth-Century Teacher in Love.

'Nothing expurgated, nothing added! Better than the Feelies! All in glorious 4D – no stereos required.'

Fuming at the description of himself, Rodney crumpled the brochure in his hand. He wondered bitterly how many of his own generation were helplessly enduring this gross irreverence in peepshows all over the world. When the sense of outrage abated slightly, curiosity reasserted itself; he smoothed out the folder and read a brief description of the process which 'will give you history-sterics as it brings each era nearer'.

Below the heading 'It's Fabulous – It's Pabulous!' he read: 'Just as anti-gravity lifts a man against the direction of weight, chrono-grab can lift a machine out of the direction of time and send it speeding back over the dark centuries. It can be accurately guided from the present to scoop up a fragment from the past, slapping that fragment – all unknown to the people in it – right into your lucky laps. The terrific expense of this intricate operation need hardly be emphas—'

'Driver!' Rodney screamed. 'Do you know anything about this time-grabbing business?'

'Only what I have heard, sir.'

'What do you mean by that?'

'My built-in information centre contains only facts relating to my duty, sir, but since I also have learning circuits I am occasionally able to collect gossip from passengers which—'

'Tell me this, then: can human beings as well as machines travel back in time?'

The buildings were still flashing by, silent, hostile in the unknown world. Drumming his fingers wildly on his seat, Rodney awaited an answer.

'Only machines, sir. Humans can't live backwards.'

For a long time he lay and cried comfortably. The automoto made solacing cluck-cluck noises, but it was a situation with which it was incompetent to deal.

At last, Rodney wiped his eyes on his sleeve, the sleeve of his Sunday suit, and sat up. He directed the driver to head for the main offices of Chronoarchaeology, and slumped back in a kind of stupor. Only at the headquarters of that fiendish invention might there be people who could – if they would – restore him to his own time.

Rodney dreaded the thought of facing any creature of this unscrupulous age. He pressed the idea away, and concentrated instead on the peace and orderliness of the world from which he had been resurrected. To see Oxford again, to see Valerie . . . Dear, dear Valerie . . .

Would they help him at Chronoarchaeology? Or – *supposing the people at the fair-ground repaired their devilish apparatus before he got there* . . . What would happen then he shuddered to imagine.

'Faster, driver,' he shouted.

The wide-spaced buildings became a wall.

'Faster, driver,' he screamed.

The wall became a mist.

'We are doing mach 2.3, sir,' said the driver calmly.

'Faster!'

The mist became a scream.

'We are about to crash, sir.'

They crashed. Blackness, merciful, complete.

A bedspring groaned and pinged and the mists cleared. Rodney awoke. From the bathroom next door came the crisp, repetitive sound of Jim shaving . . .

Supertoys Last All Summer Long

In Mrs Swinton's garden, it was always summer. The lovely almond trees stood about it in perpetual leaf. Monica Swinton plucked a saffron-coloured rose and showed it to David.

'Isn't it lovely?' she said.

David looked up at her and grinned without replying. Seizing the flower, he ran with it across the lawn and disappeared behind the kennel where the mowervator crouched, ready to cut or sweep or roll when the moment dictated. She stood alone on her impeccable plastic gravel path.

She had tried to love him.

When she made up her mind to follow the boy, she found him in the courtyard floating the rose in his paddling pool. He stood in the pool engrossed, still wearing his sandals.

'David, darling, do you have to be so awful? Come in at once and change your shoes and socks.'

He went with her without protest, his dark head bobbing at the level of her waist. At the age of five, he showed no fear of the ultra-sonic dryer in the kitchen. But before his mother could reach for a pair of slippers, he wriggled away and was gone into the silence of the house.

He would probably be looking for Teddy.

Monica Swinton, twenty-nine, of graceful shape and lambent eye, went and sat in her living-room arranging her limbs with taste. She began by sitting and thinking; soon she was just sitting. Time waited on her shoulder with the manic sloth it reserves for children, the insane and wives whose husbands are away improving the world. Almost by reflex, she reached out and changed the wavelength of her windows. The garden faded; in its place, the city centre rose by her left hand, full of crowding people, blow-boats, and buildings – but she kept the sound down. She remained alone. An overcrowded world is the ideal place in which to be lonely.

The directors of Synthank were eating an enormous luncheon to celebrate the launching of their new product. Some of them wore plastic face-masks popular at the time. All were elegantly slender, despite the rich food and drink they were putting away. Their wives were elegantly slender, despite the food and drink they too were putting away. An earlier and less sophisticated generation would have regarded them as beautiful people, apart from their eyes. Their eyes were hard and calculating.

Henry Swinton, Managing Director of Synthank, was about to make a speech.

'I'm sorry your wife couldn't be with us to hear you,' his neighbour said.

'Monica prefers to stay at home thinking beautiful thoughts,' said Swinton, maintaining a smile.

'One would expect such a beautiful woman to have beautiful thoughts,' said the neighbour.

Take your mind off my wife, you bastard, thought Swinton, still smiling.

He rose to make his speech amid applause.

After a couple of jokes, he said, 'Today marks a real breakthrough for the company. It is now almost ten years since we put our first synthetic life-forms on the world market. You all know what a success they have been, particularly the miniature dinosaurs. But none of them had intelligence.

'It seems like a paradox that in this day and age we can create life but not intelligence. Our first selling line, the Crosswell Tape, sells best of all, and is the most stupid of all.'

Everyone laughed.

'Though three-quarters of our overcrowded world is starving, we are lucky here to have more than enough, thanks to population control. Obesity's our problem, not malnutrition. I guess there's nobody round this table who doesn't have a Crosswell working for him in the small intestine, a perfectly safe parasite tape-worm that enables its host to eat up to fifty per cent more food and still keep his or her figure. Right?'

General nods of agreement.

'Our miniature dinosaurs are almost equally stupid. Today, we launch an intelligent synthetic life-form – a full-size serving-man.

'Not only does he have intelligence, he has a controlled amount of intelligence. We believe people would be afraid of a being with a human brain. Our serving-man has a small computer in his cranium.

'There have been mechanicals on the market with minicomputers for brains – plastic things without life, supertoys – but we have at last found a way to link computer circuitry with synthetic flesh.'

David sat by the long window of his nursery, wrestling with paper and pencil. Finally, he stopped writing and began to roll the pencil up and down the slope of the desk-lid.

'Teddy!' he said.

Teddy lay on the bed against the wall, under a book with moving pictures and a giant plastic soldier. The speech-pattern of his master's voice activated him and he sat up.

'Teddy, I can't think what to say!'

Climbing off the bed, the bear walked stiffly over to cling to the boy's leg. David lifted him and set him on the desk.

'What have you said so far?'

'I've said—' He picked up his letter and stared hard at it. 'I've said, "Dear Mummy, I hope you're well just now. I love you."'

There was a long silence, until the bear said, 'That sounds fine. Go downstairs and give it to her.'

Another long silence.

'It isn't quite right. She won't understand.'

Inside the bear, a small computer worked through its program of possibilities. 'Why not do it again in crayon?'

David was staring out of the window. 'Teddy, you know what I was thinking? How do you tell what are real things from what aren't real things?'

The bear shuffled its alternatives. 'Real things are good.'

'I wonder if time is good. I don't think Mummy likes time very much. The other day, lots of days ago, she said that time went by her. Is time real, Teddy?'

'Clocks tell the time. Clocks are real. Mummy has clocks so she must like them. She has a clock on her wrist next to her dial.'

David had started to draw an airliner on the back of his letter. 'You and I are real, Teddy, aren't we?'

The bear's eyes regarded the boy unflinchingly. 'You and I are real, David.' It specialised in comfort.

Monica walked slowly about the house. It was almost time for the afternoon post to come over the wire. She punched the O.L. number on the dial on her wrist but nothing came through. A few minutes more.

She could take up her painting. Or she could dial her friends. Or she could wait till Henry came home. Or she could go up and play with David . . .

She walked out into the hall and to the bottom of the stairs.

'David!'

No answer. She called again and a third time.

'Teddy!' she called, in sharper tones.

'Yes, Mummy!' After a moment's pause, Teddy's head of golden fur appeared at the top of the stairs.

'Is David in his room, Teddy?'

'David went into the garden, Mummy.'

'Come down here, Teddy!'

She stood impassively, watching the little furry figure as it climbed down from step to step on its stubby limbs. When it reached the bottom, she picked it up and carried it into the living-room. It lay unmoving in her arms, staring up at her. She could feel just the slightest vibration from its motor.

'Stand there, Teddy. I want to talk to you.' She set him down on a tabletop, and he stood as she requested, arms set forward and open in the eternal gesture of embrace.

'Teddy, did David tell you to tell me he had gone into the garden?'

The circuits of the bear's brain were too simple for artifice.

'Yes, Mummy.'

'So you lied to me.'

'Yes, Mummy.'

'Stop calling me Mummy! Why is David avoiding me? He's not afraid of me, is he?'

'No. He loves you.'

'Why can't we communicate?'

'Because David's upstairs.'

The answer stopped her dead. Why waste time talking to this machine? Why not simply go upstairs and scoop David into her arms and talk to him, as a loving mother should to a loving son? She heard the sheer weight of silence in the house, with a different quality of silence issuing from every room. On the upper landing, something was moving very silently – David, trying to hide away from her . . .

He was nearing the end of his speech now. The guests were attentive; so was the Press, lining two walls of the banqueting chamber, recording Henry's words and occasionally photographing him.

'Our serving-man will be, in many senses, a product of the computer. Without knowledge of the genome, we could never have worked through the sophisticated biochemics that go into synthetic flesh. The serving-man will also be an extension of the computer – for he will contain a computer in his own head, a microminiaturised computer capable of dealing with almost any situation he may encounter in the home. With reservations, of course.'

Laughter at this; many of those present knew the heated debate that had engulfed the Synthank boardroom before the decision had finally been taken to leave the serving-man neuter under his flawless uniform.

'Amid all the triumphs of our civilisation – yes, and amid the crushing problems of overpopulation too – it is sad to reflect how many millions of people suffer from increasing loneliness and isolation. Our serving-man will be a boon to them; he will always answer, and the most vapid conversation cannot bore him.

'For the future, we plan more models, male and female – some of them without the limitations of this first one, I promise you! – of more advanced design, true bio-electronic beings.

'Not only will they possess their own computers, capable of individual programming: they will be linked to the Ambient, the World Data Network. Thus everyone will be able to enjoy the equivalent of an Einstein in their own homes. Personal isolation will then be banished for ever!'

He sat down to enthusiastic applause. Even the synthetic serving-man, sitting at the table dressed in an unostentatious suit, applauded with gusto.

Dragging his satchel, David crept round the side of the house. He climbed onto the ornamental seat under the living-room window and peeped cautiously in.

His mother stood in the middle of the room. Her face was blank; its lack of expression scared him. He watched fascinated. He did not move; she did not move. Time might have stopped, as it had stopped in the garden. Teddy looked round, saw him, tumbled off the table, and came over to the window. Fumbling with his paws, he eventually got it open.

They looked at each other.

'I'm no good, Teddy. Let's run away!'

'You're a very good boy. Your mummy loves you.'

Slowly, he shook his head. 'If she loves me, then why can't I talk to her?'

'You're being silly, David. Mummy's lonely. That's why she has you.'

'She's got Daddy. I've got nobody 'cept you, and I'm lonely.'

Teddy gave him a friendly cuff over the head. 'If you feel so bad, you'd better go to the psychiatrist again.'

'I hate that old psychiatrist – he makes me feel I'm not real.' He started to run across the lawn. The bear toppled out of the window and followed as fast as its stubby legs would allow.

Monica Swinton was up in the nursery. She called to her son once and then stood there, undecided. All was silent.

Crayons lay on his desk. Obeying a sudden impulse, she went over to the desk and opened it. Dozens of pieces of paper lay inside. Many of them were written in crayon in David's clumsy writing, with each letter picked out in a colour different from the letter preceding it. None of the messages was finished.

MY DEAR MUMMY, HOW ARE YOU REALLY, DO YOU LOVE ME AS MUCH—

DEAR MUMMY, I LOVE YOU AND DADDY AND THE SUN IS SHINING—

DEAR DEAR MUMMY, TEDDY'S HELPING ME TO WRITE TO YOU. I LOVE YOU AND TEDDY—

DARLING MUMMY, I'M YOUR ONE AND ONLY SON AND I LOVE YOU SO MUCH THAT SOME TIMES—

DEAR MUMMY, YOU'RE REALLY MY MUMMY AND I HATE TEDDY—

DARLING MUMMY, GUESS HOW MUCH I LOVE—

DEAR MUMMY, I'M YOUR LITTLE BOY NOT TEDDY AND I LOVE YOU BUT TEDDY—

DEAR MUMMY, THIS IS A LETTER TO YOU JUST TO SAY HOW MUCH HOW EVER SO MUCH—

Monica dropped the pieces of paper and burst out crying. In their gay inaccurate colours the letters fanned out and settled on the floor.

Henry Swinton caught the express in high spirits, and occasionally said a word to the synthetic serving-man he was taking home with him. The serving-man answered politely and punctually, although his answers were not always entirely relevant by human standards.

The Swintons lived in one of the ritziest city-blocks. Embedded in other apartments, their apartment had no windows onto the outside; nobody wanted to see the overcrowded external world. Henry unlocked the door with his retina-pattern-scanner and walked in, followed by the serving-man.

At once, Henry was surrounded by the friendly illusion of gardens set in eternal summer. It was amazing what Whologram could do to create huge mirages in small spaces. Behind its roses and wisteria stood their house: the deception was complete: a Georgian mansion appeared to welcome him.

'How do you like it?' he asked the serving-man.

'Roses occasionally suffer from black spot.'

'These roses are guaranteed free from any imperfections.'

'It is always advisable to purchase goods with guarantees, even if they cost slightly more.'

'Thanks for the information,' Henry said dryly. Synthetic life-forms were less than ten years old, the old android mechanicals less than sixteen; the faults of their systems were still being ironed out, year by year.

He opened the door and called to Monica.

She came out of the sitting-room immediately and flung her arms round him, kissing him ardently on cheek and lips. Henry was amazed.

Pulling back to look at her face, he saw how she seemed to generate light and beauty. It was months since he had seen her so excited. Instinctively, he clasped her tighter.

'Darling what's happened?'

'Henry, Henry – oh, my darling, I was in despair . . . But I've dialled the afternoon post and – you'll never believe it! Oh, it's wonderful!'

'For heaven's sake, woman, what's wonderful?'

He caught a glimpse of the heading on the stat in her hand, still warm from the wall-receiver; Ministry of Population. He felt the colour drain from his face in sudden shock and hope.

'Monica . . . oh . . . Don't tell me our number's come up!'

'Yes, my darling, yes, we've won this week's parenthood lottery! We can go ahead and conceive a child at once!'

He let out a yell of joy. They danced round the room. Pressure of population was such that reproduction had to be strictly controlled. Childbirth required government permission. For this moment they had waited four years. Incoherently they cried their delight.

They paused at last, gasping, and stood in the middle of the room to laugh at each other's happiness. When she had come down from the nursery, Monica had de-opaqued the windows, so that they now revealed the vista of garden beyond. Artificial sunlight was growing long and golden across the lawn – and David and Teddy were staring through the window at them.

Seeing their faces Henry and his wife grew serious.

'What do we do about *them*?' Henry asked.

'Teddy's no trouble. He works well enough.'

'Is David malfunctioning?'

'His verbal communication centre is still giving him trouble. I think he'll have to go back to the factory again.'

'Okay. We'll see how he does before the baby's born. Which reminds me – I have a surprise for you: help just when help is needed! Come into the hall and see what I've got.'

As the two adults disappeared from the room, boy and bear sat down beneath the standard roses.

'Teddy – I suppose Mummy and Daddy are real, aren't they?'

Teddy said, 'You ask such silly questions, David. Nobody knows what "real" really means. Let's go indoors.'

'First I'm going to have another rose!' Plucking a bright pink flower, he carried it with him into the house. It could lie on the pillow as he went to sleep. Its beauty and softness reminded him of Mummy.

Conviction

The four Supreme Ultralords stood apart from the crowd, waiting, speaking to nobody. Yet Mordregon, son of Great Mordregon; Arntibis Isis of Sirius III, the Proctor Superior from the Tenth Sector; Deln Phi J. Bunswacki, Ruler of the Margins; and Ped2 of the Dominion of the Sack watched, as did the countless other members of the Diet of the Ultralords of the Home Galaxy, the entrance into their council chamber of the alien, David Stevens of Earth.

Stevens hesitated on the threshold of the hall. The hesitation was part-natural, part-feigned; he had come here primed to play a part and knowing a pause for awe might be expected of him; but he had not calculated on the real awe which filled him. He had come to stand trial, for himself, for Earth, he had come prepared – as far as a man may prepare for the unpredictable. Yet, as the dolly ushered him into the hall, he knew crushingly that the task was to be more terrible than any he had visualised.

The cream of the Galaxy took in his hesitation.

He started to walk towards the dais upon which Mordregon and his colleagues waited. The effort of forcing his legs to go into action set a dew of perspiration on his forehead.

'God help me!' he whispered. But these were the gods of the galaxy; was there, over them, One with no material being and infinite power? Enough. Concentrate.

Squaring his shoulders, Stevens walked between the massed shapes of the rulers of the Home Galaxy. Although it had been expressly stated before he left Earth that no powers, such as telepathy, which he did not possess, would be used against him, he could feel a weight of mental power all round him. Strange faces watched him, some just remotely human, strange robes stirred as he brushed past them. The diversity! he thought. The astounding, teeming womb of the universe!

Pride suddenly gripped him. He found courage to stare back into the multitudinous eyes. They should be made to know the mettle of man. Whatever they were planning to do with him, he also had his own plans for them.

Just as it seemed only fitting to him that man should walk in this hall, it seemed no less fitting that of all the millions on Earth, he, David Stevens, should be that man. With the egotism inherent in junior races, he felt sure he could pass their trial. What if he had been awed at first? A self-confident technological civilisation, proud of its exploration projects on Mercury and Neptune, is naturally somewhat abashed by the appearance of a culture spreading luxuriously over fifty hundred thousand planets.

With a flourish, he bowed before Mordregon and the other Supreme Ultralords.

'I offer greetings from my planet Earth of Sol,' he said in a resonant voice.

'You are welcome here, David Stevens of Earth,' Mordregon replied graciously. A small object the size of a hen's egg floated fifteen inches from his beak. All other members of the council, Stevens included, were attended by similar devices, automatic interpreters.

Mordregon was mountainous. Below his beaked head, his body bulged like an upturned grand piano. A cascade of clicking black and white ivory rectangles clothed him. Each rectangle, Stevens noted, rotated perpetually on its longitudinal axis, fanning him, ventilating him, as if he burned continually of an inexorable disease (which was in fact the case).

'I am happy to come here in peace,' Stevens said. 'And shall be still happier to know why I have been brought here. My journey has been long and partially unexplained.'

At the word 'peace', Mordregon made a grimace like a smile, although his beak remained unsmiling.

'Partially, perhaps; but partially is not entirely,' Mordregon said. 'The robot ship told you you would be collected to stand trial in the name of Earth. That seems to us quite sufficient information to work on.'

The automatic translators gave an edge of irony to the Ultralord's voice. The tone brought faint colour to Stevens's cheeks. He was angry, and suddenly happy to let them see he was angry.

'Then you have never been in my position,' he said. 'Mine was an executive post at Port Ganymede. I never had anything to do with politics. I was down at the methane reagent post when your robot ship arrived and designated me in purely arbitrary fashion. I was simply told I would be collected for trial in three months – like a convict – like a bundle of dirty laundry!' He looked hard at them, anxious to see their first reaction to his anger, wondering whether, he had gone too far. Ordinarily, Stevens was not a man who indulged his emotions. When he spoke, the hen's egg before his mouth sucked up all sound, leaving the air dry and silent, so that he was unable to hear the translation going over; he thought, half-hopefully, that it might omit the outburst in traditional interpreter fashion. This hope was at once crushed.

'Irritation means unbalance,' said Deln Phi J. Bunswacki. It was the only sentence he spoke throughout the interview. On his shoulders, a mighty brain siphoned its thoughts beneath a transparent skull case; he wore what appeared to be a garishly cheap blue pin-stripe suit, but the stripes moved as symbiotic organisms plied up and down them ceaselessly, ingurgitating any microbes which might threaten the health of Deln Phi. J. Bunswacki. Slightly revolted, Stevens turned back to Mordregon.

'You are playing with me,' he said quietly. 'Do I abuse your hospitality by asking you to get down to business?'

That, he thought, was better. Yet what were they thinking? *His manner is too unstable? He seems to be impervious to the idea of his own insignificance?* This was going to be the whole of hell: to have to guess what *they* were thinking, knowing they knew he was guessing, not knowing how many levels above his own their IQ was.

Acidic apprehension turned in Stevens's stomach. His hand fluttered up to the lump below his right ear; he fingered it nervously, and only with an effort broke off the betraying gesture. To this vast concourse, he was insignificant: yet to Earth – to Earth he was their sole hope. Their sole hope! – And he could not keep himself from shaking.

Mordregon was speaking again. What had he been saying?

'. . . customary. Into this hall in the city of Grapfth on the planet Xaquibadd in the Periphery of the Dominion of the Sack are invited all new races, each as it is discovered.'

Those big words don't frighten me, Stevens told himself, because, to a great extent, they did. Suddenly he saw the solar system as a tiny sack, into which he longed to crawl and hide.

'Is this place Grapfth the centre of your Empire?' he asked.

'No; as I said, it is in a peripheral region – for safety reasons, you understand,' Mordregon explained.

'Safety reasons? You mean you are afraid of me?'

Mordregon raised a brow at Ped2 of the Sack. Ped2, under an acre of coloured, stereoscopic nylon, was animated cactus, more beautiful, more intricate than his clothing. Captive butterflies on germanium, degravitised chains turned among the blossoms on his head; they fluttered up and then re-alighted as Ped2 nodded and spoke briefly to the Earthman. 'Every race has peculiar talents or abilities of its own,' he explained. 'It is partly to discover those abilities that you aliens are invited here. Unfortunately, your predecessor turned out to be a member of a race of self-propagating nuclear weapons left over from some ancient war or other. He talked quite intelligently, until one of us mentioned the key word "goodwill", whereupon he exploded and blew this entire hall to bits.'

Reminiscent chuckles sounded round him as he told the story.

Stevens said angrily: 'You expect me to believe that? Then how have you all survived?'

'Oh, we are not really here,' Ped2 said genially, interlocking a nest of spikes behind his great head. 'You can't expect us to make the long journey to Xaquibadd every time some petty little system – no offence of course – is discovered. You're talking to three-dimensional images of us; even the hall's only there – or *here*, if you prefer it (location is merely a philosophical quibble) in a sort of sub-molecular fashion.'

Catching sight of the dazed look on the Earthman's face, Ped2 could not resist driving home another point. (His was a childish race: theologians had died out among them only some four thousand years ago.)

'We are not even talking to you in a sense you would understand, David Stevens of Earth,' he said. 'Having as yet no instantaneous communicator across light-year distances, we are letting a robot brain on Xaquibadd do the talking for us. We can check with it afterwards; if a mistake has been made, we can always get in touch with you.'

It was said not without an easy menace, but Stevens received at least a part of it eagerly. They had as yet no instantaneous communicator! No sub-radio, that could leap light-years without time lag! Involuntarily, he again fingered the tiny lump beneath the lobe of his right ear, and then thrust his hand deep into his pocket. So Earth had a chance of bargaining with these colossi after all! His confidence soared.

To Ped2, Mordregon was saying: 'You must not mock our invited guest.'

'I have heard that word "invited" from you before,' Stevens said. 'This has all seemed to me personally more like a summons. Your robot, without further explanation, simply told me it would be back for me in three months, giving me time to prepare for trial.'

'That was reasonable, surely?' Mordregon said. 'It *could* have interviewed you then, unprepared.'

'But it didn't say what I was to prepare *for*,' Stevens replied, exasperation bursting into his mind as he remembered those three months. What madness they had been, as he spent them preparing frantically for this interview; all the wise and cunning men of the system had visited him: logicians, actors, philosophers, generals, mathematicians . . . And the surgeons! Yes, the skilful surgeons, burying the creations of the technologists in his ear and throat.

And all the while he had marvelled: Why did they pick *me*?

'Supposing it *hadn't* been me?' he said to Mordregon aloud. 'Supposing it had been a madman or a man dying of cancer you picked on?'

Silence fell. Mordregon looked at him piercingly and then answered slowly: 'We find our random selection principle entirely satisfactory, considering the large numbers involved. Whoever is brought here is responsible for his world. Your mistakes or illnesses are your world's mistakes or illnesses. If a madman or a cancerous man stood in your place now, your world would have to be destroyed; worlds which have not been made free from such scourges by the time they have interplanetary travel must be eradicated. The galaxy is indestructible, but the security of the galaxy is a fragile thing.'

All the light-heartedness seemed gone from the assembly of Ultralords now. Even Ped2 of the Dominion of the Sack sat bolt upright, looking grimly at the Earthman. Stevens himself had gone chill, his throat was as dry as his sleeve. Every time he spoke he betrayed a chunk of the psychological atmosphere of Earth.

During the three months' preparation, during the month-long voyage here in a completely automatic ship, he had chased his mind round to come only to this one conclusion: that through him Man was to be put to a test for fitness. Thinking of the mental homes and hospitals of Earth, his poise almost deserted him; but clenching his fists together behind his back – what matter if the assembly saw that betrayal of strain, so long as the searching eyes of Mordregon did not? – he said in a voice striving to remain firm: 'So then I *have* come here on trial?'

'Not you only but your world Earth – and the trial has already begun!' The voice was not Mordregon's nor Ped2's. It belonged to Arntibis Isis of Sirius III, the Proctor Superior of the Tenth Sector, who had not yet spoken. He stood like a column, twelve feet high, his length clad in furled silver, a dark cluster of eyes at his summit probing down at Stevens. He had what the others, what even Mordregon lacked: majesty.

Surreptitiously, Stevens touched his throat. The device nestling there would be needed presently; with its assistance he might win through. This Empire had no sub-radio; in that fact lay his and Earth's hope. But before Arntibis Isis hope seemed stupidity.

'Since I am here I must necessarily submit to your trial,' Stevens said. 'Although where I come from, the civilised thing is to tell the defendant *what* he is defending, *how* he may acquit himself and *which* punishment is hanging over his head. We also have the courtesy to announce when the trial begins, not springing it on the prisoner half-way through.'

A murmur circling round the hall told him he had scored a minor point. As Stevens construed the problem, the Ultralords were looking for some cardinal virtue in man which, if Stevens manifested it, would save Earth; but which virtue did this multicoloured mop consider important? He had to pull his racing mind up short to hear Arntibis Isis's reply to his thrust.

'You are talking of a local custom tucked away in a barren pocket of the galaxy,' the level voice said. 'However, your intellect being what it is, I shall enumerate the how and the wherefore. Be it known then, David Stevens of Earth, that through you your world is on trial before the Supreme Diet of the Ultralords of the Second Galaxy. Nothing personal is intended; indeed, you yourself are barely concerned in our business here, except as a mouthpiece. *If* you acquit yourself – and we are more than impartial, we are eager for your success, though less than hopeful – your race Man will become Full Fledgling Members of our great concourse of beings, sharers of our skills and problems. If you fail, your planet Earth will be annihilated – utterly.'

'And you call that civilised—?' Stevans began hotly.

'We deal with fifty planets a week here,' Mordregon interrupted. 'It's the only possible system – cuts down endless bureaucracy.'

'Yes, and we just can't afford fleets to watch these unstable communities any more,' one of the Ultralords from the body of the hall concurred. 'The expense . . .'

'Do you remember that ghastly little time-swallowing reptile from somewhere in the Magellans?' Ped2 chuckled reminiscently. 'He had some crazy scheme for a thousand years' supervision of his race.'

'I'd die of boredom if I watched them an hour,' Mordregon said, shuddering.

'Order, please!' Arntibis Isis snapped. When there was silence, he said to Stevens: 'And now I will give you the rules of the trial. Firstly, there is no appeal from our verdict; when the session is over, you will be transported back to Earth at once, and the verdict will be delivered almost as soon as you land there.

'Next, I must assure you we are scrupulously fair in our decision, although you must understand that the definition of fairness differs from sector to sector. You may think we are ruthless; but the Galaxy is a small place and we have no room for useless members within our ranks. As it is we have this trouble, with the Eleventh Galaxy on our hands. However . . .

'Next, many of the beings present have powers which you would regard as supernormal, such as telepathy, deep-vision, precognition, outfarling, and so on. These powers they are holding in abeyance, so that you are judged on your own level as far as possible. You have our assurance that your mind will not be read.

'There is but one other rule; you will now proceed with your own trial.'

For a space of a few chilly seconds, Stevens stared unbelievingly at the tall column of Arntibis Isis: that entity told him nothing. He looked round at Mordregon, at the others, at the phalanx of figures silent in the hall. Nobody moved. Gazing round at the incredible sight of them, Stevens realised sadly how far, far from home he was.

'. . . my own trial?' he echoed.

The Ultralords did not reply. He had had all the help, if help it was; now he was on his own: Earth's fate was in the scales. Panic threatened him but he fought it down; that was a luxury he could not afford. Calculation only would help him. His cold hand touched the small lump at his throat; his judges had, after all, virtually played into his hands. He was not unprepared.

'My own trial,' he repeated more firmly.

Here was the classic nightmare made flesh, he thought. Dreams of pursuit, degradation, annihilation were not more terrible than this static dream where one stands before watchful eyes explaining one's existence, speaking, speaking to no avail because if there is right it is not in words, because if there is a way of delivering the soul it is not to this audience. He thought, I must all my life have had some sort of a fixation about judgement without mercy; now I've gone psychopathic – I'll spend all my years up before this wall of eyes, trying to find excuses for some crime I don't know I've committed.

He watched the slow revolutions of Mordregon's domino costume. No, this was reality, not the end results of an obsession. To treat it as other than reality was the flight from fear; that was not Stevens's way: he was afraid, but he could face it.

He spoke to them.

'I presume by your silence,' he said, 'that you wish me to formulate both the questions and the answers, on the principle that two differing levels of intelligence are thus employed; it being as vital to ask the right question as to produce the correct answer.

CONVICTION

'This forcing of two roles upon me obviously doubles my chance of failure, and I would point out that this is, to me, not justice but a mockery.

'Should I, then, say nothing more to you? Would you accept that silence as a proof that my world can distinguish justice from injustice, surely one of the prime requisites of a culture?'

He paused, only faintly hopeful. It could not be as simple as that. Or could it? If it could the solution would seem to him just a clever trick; but to these deeper brains it might appear otherwise. His thoughts swam as he tried to see the problem from their point of view. It was impossible: he could only go by his own standards, which of course was just what they wanted. Yet still he kept silence, trusting it more than words.

'Your point accepted. Continue,' said Ped2 brusquely, but he gave Stevens an encouraging nod.

So it was not going to be as easy as that. He pulled a handkerchief from a pocket and wiped his forehead, thinking wildly: 'Would they accept *that* as a defence: that I am near enough to the animal to sweat but already far enough away to object to the fact? Do they sweat, any of them? Perhaps they think sweat's a good thing. How can I be sure of anything?'

Like every other thought to his present state of mind, it turned circular and short-circuited itself.

He was an Earthman, six foot three, well proportioned, he had made good in a tough spot on Ganymede, he knew a very lovely woman called Edwina. Suppose they would be content with hearing about her, about her beauty, about the way she looked when Stevens left Earth. He could tell them about the joy of just being alive and thinking of Edwina: and the prodding knowledge that in ten years their youth would be sliding away.

Nonsense! he told himself. They wouldn't take sentiment here; these beauties wanted cold fact. Momentarily, he thought of all the other beings who had stood in the past where he stood now, groping for the right thing to say. How many had found it?

Steadying himself, Stevens began to address the Ultralords again.

'You will gather from what I say that I am hoping to demonstrate that I possess and understand one virtue so admirable that because of it you will, in your wisdom, be able to do nothing but spare me. Since modesty happens to be one of my virtues, I cannot enumerate the others: sagacity, patience, courage, loyalty, reverence, kindness, for example – and humour, as I hope that remark may hint to you. But these virtues are, or should be, common possessions of any civilisation; by them we define civilisation, and you presumably are looking for something else.

'You must require me to produce evidence of something less obvious . . . something Man possesses which none of you have.'

He looked at the vast audience and they were silent. That damned silence!

'I'm sure we do possess something like that. I'll think of it if you'll give me time. (Pause.) I suppose it's no good throwing myself on your mercy? Man has mercy – but that's not a virtue at all acceptable to those without it.'

The silence grew round him like ice forming over a Siberian lake. Were they hostile or not? He could not tell anything from their attitude; he could not think objectively. Reverse that idea: he thought subjectively. Could he twist *that* into some sort of a weird virtue which might appeal to them, and pretend there was a special value in thinking subjectively?

Hell, this was not his line of reasoning at all; he was not cut out to be a metaphysician. It was time he played his trump card. With an almost imperceptible movement of a neck muscle, he switched on the little machine in his throat. Immediately its droning awoke, reassuring him.

'I must have a moment to think,' Stevens said to the assembly.

Without moving his lips, he whispered: *'Hello, Earth, are you there, Earth? Dave Stevens calling across the light-years. Do you hear me?'*

After a moment's pause, the tiny lump behind his ear throbbed and a shadowy voice answered: *'Hello, Stevens, Earth Centre here. We've been listening out for you. How are you doing?'*

'The trial is on. I don't think I'm making out very well.' His lips were moving slightly; he covered them with his hand, standing as if deep in cogitation. It looked, he thought, very suspicious. He went on: *'I can't say much. For one thing, I'm afraid they will detect this beam going out and regard our communication as infringing their judicial regulations.'*

'You don't have to bother about that, Stevens. You should know that a sub-radio beam is undetectable. Can we couple you up with the big brain as pre-arranged? Give it your data and it'll come up with the right answer.'

'I just would not know what to ask it, Earth; these boys haven't given me a lead. I called to tell you I'm going to throw up the game. They're too powerful! I'm just going to put to them the old preservation plea: that every race is unique and should be spared on that account, just as we guard wild animals from extinction in parks – even the dangerous ones. OK?'

The reply came faintly back: *'You're on the spot, feller; we stand by your evaluation. Good luck and out.'*

Stevens looked round at the expressionless faces. Many of the beings present had gigantic ears; one of them possibly – probably – had heard the brief exchange. At that he made his own face expressionless and spoke aloud.

'I have nothing more to say to you,' he announced. 'Indeed, I already wish I had said nothing at all. This court is a farce. If you tried all the insects, would they have a word to say in their defence? No! So you would kill them – and as a result you yourself would die. Insects are a vital factor. So is Man. How can we know our own potentialities? If you know yours, it is because you have ceased to develop and are already doomed to extinction. I demand that Man, who has seen through this *stunt*, be left to develop in his own fashion, unmolested.

'Gentlemen, take me back home!'

He ended in a shout, and carried away by his own outburst expected a round of applause. The silence was broken only by a polite rustling. For a moment, he thought Mordregon glanced encouragingly at him, and then the figures faded away, and he was left standing alone, gesticulating in an empty hall.

A robot came and led him back to the automatic ship.

In what was estimated to be a month, Stevens arrived back at Luna One and was greeted there by Lord Sylvester as he stepped from the galactic vessel.

They pumped each other heartily on the back.

'It worked! I swear it worked!' Stevens told the older man.

'Did you try them with reasoning?' Sylvester asked eagerly.

'Yes – at least, I did my best. But I didn't seem to be getting anywhere, and then I chucked it up. I remembered what you said, that if they were masters of the galaxy they must be practical men to stay there, and that if we dangled before their variegated noses a practical dinkum which they hadn't got they'd be queuing up for it.'

'And they hadn't got an instantaneous communicator!' Sylvester exclaimed, bursting into a hoot of laughter.

'Naturally not, the thing being an impossibility, as our scientists proved long ago! But the funny bit was, Syl, they accidentally *told* me they hadn't got one. *And* I didn't even have to employ that argument for having no mind-readers present.'

'So that little bit of recording we fixed up behind your ugly great ear did the trick?'

'It sounded so absolutely genuine I almost believed it was the real thing,' Stevens said enthusiastically. 'I'm convinced we've won the day with that gadget.'

And then, perversely, the sense of triumph that had buoyed him all the way home deserted him. The trick was no longer clever: to have duped the Ultralords gave him suddenly nothing but disappointment. With listless surprise at this reaction, he realised he knew himself less well than he had believed.

He glanced at the gibbous Earth, low over Luna's mountains: it was the colour of verdigris.

All the while, Sylvester chattered on excitedly.

'Phew! You knock at least nine years off the ten I've aged since you left! When do we get the verdict, Dave? – the mighty Yea or Nay!'

'Any time now – but I'm convinced the Ultralords are in the bag. Some of the mammoth ears present must have picked your voice up.'

Sylvester commenced to beat Stevens's back again. Then he sobered and said: 'Now we'll have to think about stalling them when they come and ask for portable sub-radios. Still, that can wait; after all, we didn't actually tell them we had them! Meanwhile, I've been stalling off the news-hounds here – the Galactics can't prove more awkward than they've been. Then the President wants to see you – but before that there's a drink waiting for you, and Edwina is sitting nursing it.'

'Lead the way!' Stevens said, a little more happily.

'You look a bit gloomy all of a sudden,' Sylvester commented. 'Tired, I expect?'

'It has been a strain . . .'

As he spoke, the door of his transport slammed shut behind him and the craft lifted purposefully off the field, silent on its cosmic drive. Stevens waved it a solemn farewell and turned away quickly, hurrying with Sylvester across to the domes of Luna One. A chillness was creeping over him again.

Our Council of the Ultralords must be certain it pronounces the correct verdict when aliens such as Stevens are under examination; consequently, it has to have telepaths present during the trials. All it asks is, simply, integrity in the defendants – that is the simple touchstone: yet it is too difficult for many of them. The men of Earth tortured themselves chasing phantoms, cooking up chimeras. Stevens had integrity, yet would not trust to it. Those who are convicted of dishonesty perish; we have no room for them.

The robot craft swung away from Luna and headed at full speed towards Earth, the motors in its warhead ticking expectantly, counting out the seconds to annihilation.

And that, of course, would be the end of the story – for Earth at least. It would have been completely destroyed, as is usual in such distressing cases, but Mordregon, who was amused by Stevens's bluff, decided that, after all, the warped brains of Earthmen might be useful in coping with the warped brains of the enemy Eleventh Galaxy. He called it 'an expedient war-time measure'.

Quietly, he deflected the speeding missile from its target, ordering it to return home. He sent this message by sub-radio, of course; dangerous aliens must necessarily be deluded at times.

All the World's Tears

If you could collect up all the tears that have fallen in the history of the world, you would have not only a vast sheet of water: you would have the history of the world.

Some such reflection as this occurred to J. Smithlao, the psychodynamician, as he stood in the 139th sector of Ing Land watching the brief and tragic love of the wild man and Charles Gunpat's daughter. Hidden behind a beech tree, Smithlao saw the wild man walking warily across the terrace; Gunpat's daughter, Ployploy, stood at the far end of the terrace, waiting for him.

The world waited.

It was the last day of summer in the last year of the forty-fourth century. The wind that rustled Ployploy's dress breathed leaves against her; it sighed round the fantastic and desolate garden like fate at a christening, ruining the last of the roses. Later, the tumbling pattern of petals would be sucked from paths, lawn and patio by the steel gardener. Now, it made a tiny tide round the wild man's feet as he stretched out his hand to touch Ployploy.

Then it was that the tear glittered in her eyes.

Hidden, fascinated, Smithlao the psychodynamician saw that tear. Except perhaps for a stupid robot, he was the only one who saw it, the only one who saw the whole episode. And although he was shallow and hard by the standards of other ages, he was human enough to sense that here – here on the greying terrace – was a little charade that marked the end of all that Man had been.

After the tear, of course, came the explosion. Just for a minute, a new wind lived among the winds of earth.

Only by accident was Smithlao walking in Charles Gunpat's estate. He had come on the routine errand, as Gunpat's psychodynamician, of administering a hate-brace to the old man. Oddly enough, as he swept in for a landing, leafing his vane down from the stratosphere, Smithlao had caught a glimpse of the wild man approaching Gunpat's estate.

Under the slowing vane, the landscape was as neat as a blueprint. The impoverished fields made impeccable rectangles. Here and there, one robot machine or another kept nature to its own functional image; not a pea podded without cybernetic supervision; not a bee bumbled among stamens without radar check being kept of its course. Every bird had a number and a call sign, while among every tribe of ants marched the metallic teller ants, tell-taling the secrets of the nest back to base. The old, comfortable world of random factors had vanished under the pressure of hunger.

Nothing living lived without control. The countless populations of previous centuries had exhausted the soil. Only the severest parsimony, coupled with fierce regimentation, produced enough nourishment from the present sparse population. The billions had died of starvation; the hundreds who remained lived on starvation's brink.

In the sterile neatness of the landscape, Gunpat's estate looked like an insult. Covering five acres, it was a little island of wilderness. Tall and unkempt elms fenced the perimeter, encroaching on the lawns and house. The house itself, the chief one in Sector 139, was built of massive stone blocks. It had to be strong to bear the weight of the servo-mechanisms which, apart from Gunpat and his daughter, Ployploy, were its only occupants.

It was just as Smithlao dropped below tree-level that he thought he saw a human figure plodding towards the estate. For a multitude of reasons, this was very unlikely. The great material wealth of the world being now shared among comparatively few people, nobody was poor enough to have to walk anywhere. Man's increasing hatred of Nature, spurred by the notion it had betrayed him, would make such a walk purgatory – unless the man were insane, like Ployploy.

Dismissing the figure from his thoughts, Smithlao dropped the vane onto a stretch of stone. He was glad to get down: it was a gusty day, and the piled cumulus he had descended through had been full of air pockets. Gunpat's house, with its sightless windows, its towers, its endless terraces, its unnecessary ornamentation, its massive porch, lowered at him like a forsaken wedding cake.

There was activity at once. Three wheeled robots approached from different directions, swivelling light atomic weapons at him as they drew near.

Nobody, Smithlao thought, could get in here uninvited. Gunpat was not a friendly man, even by the unfriendly standards of his time.

'Say who you are,' demanded the leading machine. It was ugly and flat, vaguely resembling a toad.

'I am J. Smithlao, psychodynamician to Charles Gunpat,' Smithlao replied; he had to go through this procedure every visit. As he spoke, he revealed his face to the machine. It grunted to itself, checking picture and information with its memory. Finally it said, 'You are J. Smithlao, psychodynamician to Charles Gunpat. What do you want?'

Cursing its monstrous slowness, Smithlao told the robot, 'I have an appointment with Charles Gunpat at ten hours,' and waited while that was digested.

'You have an appointment with Charles Gunpat at ten hours,' the robot finally confirmed. 'Come this way.'

It wheeled about with surprising grace, speaking to the other two robots, reassuring them, repeating mechanically to them, 'This is J. Smithlao, psychodynamician to Charles Gunpat. He has an appointment with Charles Gunpat at ten hours,' in case they had not grasped these facts.

Meanwhile, Smithlao spoke to his vane. A part of the cabin, with him in it, detached itself from the rest and lowered wheels to the ground, becoming a mobile sedan. Carrying Smithlao, it followed the other robots.

Automatic screens came up, covering the windows, as Smithlao moved into the presence of other humans. He could only see and be seen via telescreens. Such was the hatred (equals fear) man bore for his fellow man, he could not tolerate them regarding him direct.

One following another, the machines climbed along the terraces, through the great porch, where they were covered in a mist of disinfectant, along a labyrinth of corridors, and so into the presence of Charles Gunpat.

Gunpat's dark face on the screen of his sedan showed only the mildest distaste for the sight of his psychodynamician. He was usually as self-controlled as this: it told against him at his business meetings, where the idea was to cow one's opponents by splendid displays of rage. For this reason, Smithlao was always summoned to administer a hate-brace when something important loomed on the day's agenda.

Smithlao's machine manoeuvred him within a yard of his patient's image, much closer than courtesy required.

'I'm late,' Smithlao began, matter-of-factly, 'because I could not bear to drag myself into your offensive presence one minute sooner. I hoped that if I left it long enough, some happy accident might have removed that stupid nose from your – what shall I call it? – *face*. Alas, it's still there, with its two nostrils sweeping like rat-holes into your skull. I've often wondered, Gunpat, don't you ever catch your big feet in those holes and fall over?'

Observing his patient's face carefully, Smithlao saw only the faintest stir of irritation. No doubt about it, Gunpat was a hard man to rouse. Fortunately, Smithlao was an expert in his profession; he proceeded to try the insult subtle.

'But of course you would never fall over,' he proceeded, 'because you are too depressingly ignorant to know up from down. You don't even know how many robots make five. Why, when it was your turn to go to the capital to the Mating Centre, you didn't even realise that was the one time a man has to come out from behind his screen. You thought you could make love by tele! And what was the result? One dotty daughter . . . one dotty daughter, Gunpat! Think how your rivals at Automotion must titter at that, sunny boy. "Potty Gunpat and his dotty daughter", they'll be saying. "Can't control your genes", they'll be saying.'

The taunts were having their desired effect. A flush spread over the image of Gunpat's face.

'There's nothing wrong with Ployploy except that she's a recessive – you said that yourself!' he snapped.

He was beginning to answer back; that was a good sign. His daughter was always a soft spot in his armour.

'A recessive!' Smithlao sneered. 'How far back can you recede?! She's *gentle*, do you hear me, you with the hair in your ears? She wants to *love!*' He bellowed with ironic laughter. 'Oh, it's obscene, Gunnyboy! She couldn't hate to save her life. She's no better than a savage. She's worse than a savage, she's mad!'

'She's not mad,' Gunpat said, gripping both sides of his screen. At this rate, he would be primed for the conference in ten more minutes.

'Not mad?' the psychodynamician asked, his voice assuming a bantering note. 'No, Ployploy's not mad: the Mating Centre only refused her the right even to breed, that's all. Imperial Government only refused her the right to a televote, that's all. United Traders only refused her a Consumption Rating, that's all. Education Inc. only restricted her to beta recreations, that's all. She's a prisoner here because she's a genius, is that it? You're crazy, Gunpat, if you don't think that girl's stark, staring looney. You'll be telling me next, out of that grotesque, flapping mouth, that she hasn't got a white face.'

Gunpat made gobbling sounds.

'You dare to mention that!' he gasped. 'And what if her face is – that colour?'

'You ask such fool questions, it's hardly worth while bothering with you,' Smithlao said mildly. 'Your trouble, Gunpat, is that your big bone head is totally incapable of absorbing one single simple historical fact. Ployploy is white because she is a dirty little throwback. Our ancient enemies were white. They occupied this part of the globe, Ing Land and You-Rohp, until the twenty-fourth century, when our ancestors rose from the East and took from them the ancient privileges they had so long enjoyed at our expense. Our ancestors intermarried with such of the defeated that survived.

'In a few generations, the white strain was obliterated, diluted, lost. A white face has not been seen on earth since before the terrible Age of Over-Population: fifteen hundred years, let's say. And *then* – then little lord recessive Gunpat throws one up neat as you please. What did they give you at Mating Centre, sunny boy, a *cavewoman?*'

Gunpat exploded in fury, shaking his fist at the screen.

'You're sacked, Smithlao,' he snarled. 'This time you've gone too far, even for a dirty, rotten psycho! Get out! Go on, get, and never come back again!'

Abruptly, he bellowed to his auto-operator to switch him over to the conference. He was just in a ripe mood to deal with Automotion and its fellow crooks.

As Gunpat's irate image faded from the screen, Smithlao sighed and relaxed. The hate-brace was accomplished. It was the supreme compliment in his profession to be dismissed by a patient at the end of a session; Gunpat would be all the keener to re-engage him next time. All the same, Smithlao felt no triumph. In his calling, a thorough exploration of human psychology was needed; he had to know exactly the sorest points in a man's make-up. By playing on those points deftly enough, he could rouse the man to action.

Without being roused, men were helpless prey to lethargy, bundles of rag carried round by machines. The ancient drives had died and left them.

Smithlao sat where he was, gazing into both past and future.

In exhausting the soil, man had exhausted himself. The psyche and a vitiated topsoil could not exist simultaneously; it was as simple and as logical as that.

Only the failing tides of hate and anger lent man enough impetus to continue at all. Else, he was just a dead hand across his mechanised world.

So this is how a species becomes extinct! thought Smithlao, and wondered if anyone else had thought it. Perhaps Imperial Government knew all about it, but was powerless to do anything; after all, what more could you do than was being done?

Smithlao was a shallow man – inevitably in a caste-bound society so weak that it could not face itself. Having discovered the terrifying problem, he set himself to forget it, to evade its impact, to dodge any personal implications it might have. With a grunt to his sedan, he turned about and ordered himself home.

Since Gunpat's robot had already left, Smithlao travelled back alone the way he had come. He was trundled outside and back to the vane, standing silent below the elms.

Before the sedan incorporated itself back into the vane, a movement caught Smithlao's eye. Half concealed by a veranda, Ployploy stood against a corner of the house. With a sudden impulse of curiosity,

Smithlao got out of the sedan. The open air, besides being in motion, stank of roses and clouds and green things turning dark with the thought of autumn. It was frightening for Smithlao, but an adventurous impulse made him go on.

The girl was not looking in his direction; she peered towards the barricade of trees which cut her off from the world. As Smithlao approached, she moved round to the rear of the house, still staring intently. He followed with caution, taking advantage of the cover afforded by a small plantation. A metal gardener nearby continued to wield shears along a grass verge, unaware of his existence.

Ployploy now stood at the back of the house. Here a rococo fancy of ancient Italy had mingled with a Chinese genius for fantastic portal and roof. Balustrades rose and fell, stairs marched through circular arches, grey and azure eaves swept almost to the ground. But all was sadly neglected: virginia creeper, already hinting at its glory to come, strove to pull down the marble statuary; troughs of rose petals clogged every sweeping staircase. And all this formed the ideal background for the forlorn figure of Ployploy.

Except for her delicate pink lips, her face was utterly pale. Her hair was utterly black; it hung straight, secured only once, at the back of her head, and then falling in a tail to her waist. She looked mad indeed, her melancholy eyes peering towards the great elms as if they would scorch down everything in their line of vision. Smithlao turned to see what she stared at so compellingly.

The wild man was just breaking through the thickets round the elm boles.

A sudden shower came down, rattling among the dry leaves of the shrubbery. Like a spring shower, it was over in a flash; during the momentary downpour, Ployploy never shifted her position, the wild man never looked up. Then the sun burst through, cascading a pattern of elm shadow over the house, and every flower wore a jewel of rain.

Smithlao thought of what he had thought in Gunpat's room. Now he added this rider: it would be so easy for Nature, when parasite man was extinct, to begin again.

He waited tensely, knowing a fragment of drama was about to take place before his eyes. Across the sparkling lawn, a tiny tracked thing scuttled, pogo-ing itself up steps and out of sight through an arch. It was a perimeter guard, off to give the alarm.

In a minute it returned. Four big robots accompanied it; one of them Smithlao recognised as the toad-like machine that had challenged his arrival. They threaded their way purposefully among the rose bushes, five different shaped menaces. The metal gardener muttered to itself, abandoned its clipping, and joined the procession towards the wild man.

'He hasn't a dog's chance,' Smithlao said to himself. The phrase held significance: all dogs, declared redundant, had long since been exterminated.

By now the wild man had broken through the barrier of the thicket and come to the lawn's edge. He broke off a leafy branchlet and stuck it into his shirt so that it partially obscured his face; he tucked another branch in his trousers. As the robots drew nearer, he raised his arms above his head, a third branch clasped in his hands.

The six machines encircled him.

The toad robot clicked, as if deciding on what it should do next.

'Say who you are,' it demanded.

'I am a rose tree,' the wild man said.

'Rose trees bear roses. You do not bear roses. You are not a rose tree,' the steel toad said. Its biggest, highest gun came level with the wild man's chest.

'My roses are dead already,' the wild man said, 'but I have leaves still. Ask the gardener if you do not know what leaves are.'

'This thing is a thing with leaves,' the gardener said at once in a deep voice.

'I know what leaves are. I have no need to ask the gardener. Leaves are the foliage of trees and plants which give them their green appearance,' the toad said.

'This thing is a thing with leaves,' the gardener repeated, adding, to clarify the matter, 'The leaves give it a green appearance.'

'I know what things with leaves are,' said the toad. 'I have no need to ask you, gardener.'

It looked as if an interesting, if limited, argument would break out between the two robots, but at this moment one of the other machines spoke.

'This rose tree can speak,' it said.

'Rose trees cannot speak,' the toad said at once. Having produced this pearl, it was silent, probably mulling over the strangeness of life. Then it said, slowly, 'Therefore either this rose tree is not a rose tree or this rose tree did not speak.'

'This thing is a thing with leaves,' began the gardener again. 'But it is not a rose tree. Rose trees have stipules. This thing has no stipules. It is a breaking buckthorn. The breaking buckthorn is also known as the berry-bearing alder.'

This specialised knowledge extended beyond the vocabulary of the toad. A strained silence ensued.

'I am a breaking buckthorn,' the wild man said, still holding his pose. 'I cannot speak.'

At this, all the machines began to talk at once, lumbering round him for better sightings as they did so, and barging into each other in the process. Finally, the toad's voice broke above the metallic babble.

'Whatever this thing with leaves is, we must uproot it. We must kill it,' he said.

'You may not uproot it. That is only a job for gardeners,' the gardener said. Setting its shears rotating, telescoping out a mighty scythe, it charged at the toad.

Its crude weapons were ineffectual against the toad's armour. The latter, however, realised that they had reached a deadlock in their investigations.

'We will retire to ask Charles Gunpat what we shall do,' it said. 'Come this way.'

'Charles Gunpat is in conference,' the scout robot said. 'Charles Gunpat must not be disturbed in conference. Therefore we must not disturb Charles Gunpat.'

'Therefore we must wait for Charles Gunpat,' said the metal toad imperturbably. He led the way close by where Smithlao stood; they all climbed the steps and disappeared into the house.

Smithlao could only marvel at the wild man's coolness. It was a miracle he still survived. Had he attempted to run, he would have been killed instantly; that was a situation the robots had been taught to cope with. Nor would his double talk, inspired as it was, have saved him had he been faced with only one robot, for a robot is a single-minded creature.

In company, however, they suffer from a trouble which often afflicts human gatherings to a lesser extent: a tendency to show off their logic at the expense of the object of the meeting.

Logic! That was the trouble. It was all robots had to go by. Man had logic and intelligence: he got along better than his robots. Nevertheless, he was losing the battle against Nature. And Nature, like the robots, used only logic. It was a paradox against which man could not prevail.

Directly the file of machines had disappeared into the house the wild man ran across the lawn and climbed the first flight of steps, working towards the motionless girl. Smithlao slid behind a beech tree to be nearer to them; he felt like a pervert, watching them without an interposed screen, but could not tear himself away. The wild man was approaching Ployploy now, moving slowly across the terrace as if hypnotised.

'You were resourceful,' she said to him. Her white face carried pink in its cheeks now.

'I have been resourceful for a whole year to get to you,' he said. Now his resources had brought him face to face with her, they failed, and left him standing helplessly. He was a thin young man, thin and sinewy, his clothes worn, his beard unkempt.

'How did you find me?' Ployploy asked. Her voice, unlike the wild man's, barely reached Smithlao. A haunting look, as fitful as the autumn, played on her face.

'It was a sort of instinct – as if I heard you calling,' the wild man said. 'Everything that could possibly be wrong with the world is wrong . . . Perhaps you are the only woman in the world who loves; perhaps I am the only man who could answer. So I came. It was natural: I could not help myself.'

'I always dreamed someone would come,' she said. 'And for weeks I have felt – *known* – you were coming. Oh, my darling . . .'

'We must be quick, my sweet,' he said. 'I once worked with robots – perhaps you could see I knew them. When we get away from here, I have a robot plane that will take us right away – anywhere: an island, perhaps, where things are not so desperate. But we must go before your father's machines return.'

He took a step towards Ployploy.

She held up her hand.

'Wait!' she implored him. 'It's not so simple. You must know something . . . The – the Mating Centre refused me the right to breed. You ought not to touch me.'

'I hate the Mating Centre!' the wild man said. 'I hate everything to do with the ruling regime. Nothing they have done can affect us now.'

Ployploy had clenched her hands behind her back. The colour had left her cheeks. A fresh shower of dead rose petals blew against her dress, mocking her.

'It's so hopeless,' she said. 'You don't understand . . .'

His wildness was humbled now.

'I threw up everything to come to you,' he said. 'I only desire to take you into my arms.'

'Is that all, really all, all you want in the world?' she asked.

'I swear it,' he said simply.

'Then come and kiss me,' Ployploy said.

That was the moment at which Smithlao saw the tear glint in her eye.

The hand the wild man extended to her was lifted to her cheek. She stood unflinching on the grey terrace, her head high. And so the loving hand gently brushed her countenance. The explosion was almost instantaneous.

Almost. It took the traitorous nerves in Ployploy's epidermis only a fraction of a second to analyse the touch as belonging to another human being and convey their findings to the nerve centre; there, the neurological block implanted by the Mating Centre in all mating rejects, to guard against just such a contingency, went into action at once. Every cell in Ployploy's body yielded up its energy in one consuming gasp. It was so successful that the wild man was also killed by the detonation.

Yes, thought Smithlao, you had to admit it was neat. And, again, logical. In a world on the brink of starvation, how else stop undesirables from breeding? Logic against logic, man's pitted against Nature's: that was what caused all the tears of the world.

He made off through the dripping plantation, heading back for the vane, anxious to be away before the robots reappeared. The shattered figures on the terrace were still, already half-covered with leaves and petals. The wind roared like a great triumphant sea in the tree-tops. It was hardly odd that the wild man did not know about the neurological trigger: few people did, bar psychodynamicians and the Mating Council – and, of course, the rejects themselves. Yes, Ployploy knew what would happen. She had chosen deliberately to die like that.

'Always said she was mad!' Smithlao told himself. He chuckled as he climbed into his machine, shaking his head over her lunacy.

It would be a wonderful point to rile Charles Gunpat with, next time he needed a hate-brace.

Intangibles, Inc.

'Always seems to be eating time in this house,' Mabel said.

She dumped the china salt- and pepper-pots down at Arthur's end of the table and hurried through to the kitchen to get the supper. His eyes followed her admiringly. She was a fine figure of a young girl; not too easy to handle, but a good-looker. Arthur, on the other hand, looked like a young bull; none too bright a bull either.

'Drink it while it's hot,' she said, returning and placing a bowl of soup before him.

Arthur had just picked up his ladle when he noticed a truck had stopped outside in the road. Its bonnet was up and the driver stood with his head under it, doing no more than gazing dreamily at the engine.

Arthur looked at his steaming soup, at Mabel, back out of the window. He scratched his scalp.

'Feller's going to be stranded in the dark in another half-hour,' he said, half to himself.

'Yep, it's nearly time we were putting the lights on,' she said, half to herself.

'I could maybe earn a couple of dollars going to see what was wrong,' he said, changing tack.

'"This is food like money won't buy or time won't improve on", my mother used to say,' Mabel murmured, stirring her bowl without catching his eye.

They had been married only four months, but it had not taken Arthur that long to notice the obliquity of their intentions. Even when they were apparently conversing together, their two thought-streams seemed never quite to converge, let alone touch. But he was a determined young man, not to be put off by irrelevances. He stood up.

'I'll just go see what the trouble seems to be out there,' he said. And as a sop to her culinary pride, he called, as he went through the door, 'Keep that soup warm – I'll be right back!'

Their little bungalow, which stood in its own untidy plot of ground, was a few hundred yards beyond the outskirts of the village of Hapsville. Nothing grew much along the road bar billboards, and the stationary truck added to the desolation. It looked threadbare, patched, and mended, as if it had been travelling the roads long before trains or even stage coaches.

The overalled figure by the engine waited till Arthur was almost up to it before snapping the bonnet down and turning round. He was a small man with spectacles and a long, long face which must have measured all of eighteen inches from crown of skull to point of jaw. In among a mass of crinkles, a likeable expression of melancholy played.

'Got trouble, stranger?' Arthur asked.

'Who hasn't?' His voice, too, sounded a mass of crinkles.

'Anything I can do?' Arthur enquired. 'I work at the garage just down the road in Hapsville.'

'Well,' the crinkled man said, 'I come a long way. I daresay if you pressed me I could put a bowl of steaming soup between me and the night!'

'Your timing sure is good!' Arthur said. 'You better come on in and see what Mabel can do. Then I'll have a look-see at your engine.'

He led the way back to the bungalow. The crinkled man scuffed his feet in the mat, rubbed his spectacles on his dirty overalls, and followed in. He looked about him curiously.

Mabel had worked fast. She'd had time, when she saw through the window that they were coming, to toss their two bowls of soup back into the pan, add water, put the pan back to heat on the stove, and set a clean apron over her dirty one.

'We got a guest here for supper, Mabel,' Arthur said. 'I'll light up the lamp.'

'How d'you do?' Mabel said, putting out her hand to the crinkled man. 'Welcome to our hospitality.'

She said it just right: made it really sound welcoming, yet, by slipping in that big word 'hospitality', let him know she was putting herself out for him. Mabel was educated. So was Arthur, of course. They both read all the papers and magazines. But while Arthur just pored over the scientific or engineering or mechanical bits (those three words all meant the same thing to Mabel), she studied psychological or educational or etiquette articles. If they could have drawn pictures of their idea of the world, Arthur's would have been of a lot of interlocking cogs, Mabel's of a lot of interlocking school marms.

They sat down at the table, the three of them, as soon as the diluted soup warmed, and sipped out of their bowls.

'You often through this way?' Arthur asked his visitor.

'Every so often. I haven't got what you might call a regular route.'

'Just what model is your truck?'

'You're the mechanic down at the garage, eh?'

Thus deflected, Arthur said, 'Why, no, I didn't call myself that – did I? I'm just a hand down there, but I'm learning fast.'

He was about to put the question about the truck again, but Mabel decided it was time she spoke.

'What product do you travel in, sir?' she asked.

The long face wrinkled like tissue paper.

'You can't rightly say I got a product,' he said, leaning forward eagerly with his elbows on the bare table. 'Perhaps you didn't see the sign on my vehicle: "Intangibles, Inc." It's a bit worn now, I guess.'

'So you travel in tangibles, eh?' Arthur said. 'They grow down New Orleans way, don't they? Must be interesting things to market.'

'Dearie me!' exclaimed Mabel crossly, almost blushing. 'Didn't you hear the gentleman properly, Arthur? He said he peddles intangibles. They're not things at all: surely you know that? They're more like – well, like something that isn't there at all.'

She came uncertainly to a halt, looking confused. The little man was there instantly to rescue both of them.

'The sort of intangibles I deal in are there all right,' he said. 'In fact, you might say almost they're the things that govern people's lives. But because you can't see them, people are apt to discount them. They think they can get through life without them, but they can't.'

'Try a sample of this cheese,' Mabel said, piling up their empty bowls. 'You were saying, sir . . .'

The crinkled man accepted a square of cheese and a slab of home-baked bread and said, 'Well, now I'm here, perhaps I could offer you good folks an intangible?'

'We're mighty poor,' Arthur said quickly. 'We only just got married and we think there may be a baby on its way for next spring. We can't afford luxuries, that's the truth.'

'I'm happy to hear about the babe,' the crinkled man said. 'But you understand I don't want money for my goods. I reckon you already gave me an intangible: hospitality; now I ought to give you one.'

'Well, if it's like that . . .' Arthur said. But he was thinking that this old fellow was getting a bit whimsical and had better be booted out as soon as possible. People were like that: they were either friendly or unfriendly, and unfortunately there were as many ways of being objectionable while being friendly as there were while being unfriendly.

Chewing hard on a piece of crust, the crinkled man turned to Mabel and said, 'Now let us take your own case, and find out which intangibles you require. What is your object in life?'

'She ain't got an object in life,' Arthur said flatly. 'She's married to me now.'

At once Mabel was ready with a sharp retort, but somehow her guest was there first with a much milder one. Shaking his head solemnly at Arthur, he said, 'No, no, I don't quite think you've got the hang of what I mean. Even married people have all sorts of intangibles, ambition and whatnot – and most of them are kept a dead secret.' He turned to look again at Mabel, and his glance was suddenly very penetrating as he continued. 'Some wives, for instance, take it into their pretty heads very early in marriage always to run counter to their husband's wishes. It gets to be their main intangible and you can't shake 'em out of it.'

Mabel said nothing to this, but Arthur stood up angrily. The words had made him more uneasy than he would confess even to himself.

'Don't you go saying things like that about Mabel!' he said in a bull-like voice. 'It's none of your business and it ain't true! Maybe you'd better finish up that bread and go and see anybody don't pinch your truck!'

Mabel was also up.

'Arthur Jones!' she said. 'That's not polite to a guest. He wasn't meaning me personally, so just you sit down and listen to a bit of conversation. It isn't as if we get so much of that!'

Squashed, Arthur sat down. The crinkled man's long, crinkled face regarded him closely, immense compassion in the eyes.

'Didn't mean to be rude,' Arthur muttered. He fiddled awkwardly with the salt-pot.

'That's all right. Intangibles can be difficult things to deal with – politeness, for one. Why, some people never use politeness on account of it's too difficult. The only way is to use will-power with intangibles.' He sighed. 'Will-power certainly is needed. Have you got will-power, young man?'

'Plenty,' Arthur said. The crinkled man seemed unable to understand how irritated he was, which of course made the irritation all the greater. He twiddled the salt-pot at a furious speed.

'And what's your object in life?' persisted the crinkled man.

'Oh, why should you worry?'

'Everyone's happier with an object in life,' the crinkled man said. 'It doesn't do to have time passing without some object in life, otherwise I'd be out of business.'

This sounded to Mabel very like the maxims she read in her magazines, the founts of all wisdom. Pleasure shared is pleasure doubled; a life shared is life immortal. Caring for others is the best way of caring for yourself. Cast your bread upon the waters: even sharks got to live. Mabel was not too happy about this little man in overalls, but obviously he could teach her husband a thing or two.

'Of *course* you got an object in life, honey,' she said.

Honey raised his bovine eyes and looked at her, then lowered them again. A crumpled hand slid across the table and removed that fidgeting salt-pot from his grasp. Arthur had a distinct feeling he was being assailed from all sides.

'Sure, I got objects . . . Make a bit of money . . . Raise some children . . .' he muttered, adding. 'And knock a bit of shape into the yard.'

'Very commendable, very honourable,' the crinkled man said in a warm tone. 'Those are certainly fine objectives for a young man, fine objectives. To cultivate the garden is especially proper. But those, after all, are the sort of objectives everyone has. A man needs some special, private ambition, just to distinguish himself from the herd.'

'I'm never likely to mistake myself for anyone else, mister,' Arthur said unhappily. He could tell by Mabel's silence that she approved of this interrogation. Seizing the pepper-pot, he began to twirl that. 'That yard – always full of chickweed . . .'

'Haven't you got any special, private ambitions of your own?'

Not knowing what to say without sounding stupid, Arthur sat there looking stupid. The crinkled man politely removed the twirling pepper-pot from his hand, and Mabel said with subdued ferocity, 'Well, go on then, don't be ashamed to admit it if you've got no aim in life.'

Arthur scraped back his chair and lumbered up from the table.

'I can't say any more than what I have. I don't reckon there's anything in your cargo for me, mister!'

'On the contrary,' said the crinkled man, his voice losing none of its kindness. 'I have just what you need. For every size of mentality I have a suitable size of intangible.'

'Well, I don't want it,' Arthur said stubbornly. 'I'm happy enough as I am. Don't you get bringing those things in here!'

'Arthur, I don't believe you've taken in a word this—'

'You keep out of this!' Arthur told her, wagging a finger at her. 'All I know is, this travelling gentleman's trying to put something over on me, and you're helping him.'

They confronted each other, the crinkled man sitting nursing the two pots and looking at the husband and wife judiciously. Mabel's expression changed from one of rebellion to anguish; she put her hand to her stomach.

'The baby's hurting me,' she said.

In an instant Arthur was round the table, his arms about her, consoling her, penitent. But when she peeped once at the crinkled man, he was watching her hard, and his eyes held that penetrating quality again. Arthur also caught the glance and misinterpreting it, asked guiltily, 'Do you reckon I ought to get a doctor?'

'It would be a waste of money,' the crinkled man said.

This obviously relieved Arthur, but he felt bound to say, 'They do say Doc Smallpiece is a good doctor.'

'Maybe,' said the crinkled man. 'But doctors are no use against intangibles, which is what you're dealing with here . . . Ah, a human soul is a wonderful intricate place! Funny thing is, it could do so much but it's in such a conflict it can do so little.'

But Arthur was feeling strong again now that he was touching Mabel.

'Go on, you pessimistic character,' he scoffed. 'Mabel and me're going to do a lot of things in our life.'

The crinkled man shook his head and looked ineffably sad. For a moment they thought he would cry.

'That's the whole trouble,' he said. 'You're not. You're going to do nothing thousands of people aren't doing exactly the same at exactly the same time. Too many intangibles are against you. You can't pull in one direction alone for five minutes, never mind pulling together.'

Arthur banged his fist on the table.

'That ain't true, and you can get to hell out of here! I can do anything I want. I got will-power!'

'Very well.'

Now the crinkled man also stood up, pushing his chair aside. He picked up the pepper- and salt-pots and plonked them side by side, not quite touching, on the edge of the table.

'Here's a little test for you,' he said. His voice, though still unraised, was curiously impressive. 'I put these two pots here. How long could you keep them here, without moving them, without touching them at all, in exactly that same place?'

For just a moment, Arthur hesitated as if grappling with the perspectives of time.

'As long as I liked,' he said stubbornly.

'No, you couldn't,' the visitor contradicted.

'Course I could! This is my place, I do what I like in it. It's a fool thing to want to do, but I could keep them pots there a whole year if need be!'

'Ah, I see! You'd use your *will-power* to keep them there, eh?'

'Why not?' Arthur asked. 'I got plenty of will-power, and what's more I'm going to fix the yard and grow beans and things.'

The long face swung to and fro, the shoulders shrugged.

'You can't test will-power like that. Will-power is something that should last a lifetime. You're not enough of an individualist to have that kind of will-power, are you now?'

'Want to bet on that?' Arthur asked.

'Certainly.'

'Right. Then I'll bet you I can keep those pots untouched on that table for a lifetime – my lifetime!'

The crinkled man laughed. He took a pipe out of his pocket and commenced to light it. They heard spittle pop in its stem.

'I won't take on any such wager, son,' he said, 'because I know you'd never do it and then you'd be disappointed with yourself. You see, a little thing like you propose is not so simple; you'd run up against all those intangibles in the soul I was talking about.'

'To hell with them!' Arthur exploded. His blood was now thoroughly up. 'I'm telling you I could do it.'

'And I'm telling you you couldn't. Because why? Because in maybe two, maybe five, say maybe ten years, you'd suddenly say to yourself, "It's not worth the bother – I give up." Or you'd say, "Why should I be bound by what I said when I was young and foolish?" or a friend would come in and accidentally knock the pots off the table; or your kids would grow up and take the pots; or your house would burn down; or something else. I tell you it's impossible to do even a simple thing with all the intangibles stacked against you. They and the pots would beat you.'

'He's quite right,' Mabel agreed. 'It's a silly thing to do and you couldn't do it.'

And that was what settled it.

Arthur rammed his fists deep down into his pockets and stood over the two pots.

'I bet you these pots will stay here, untouched, all my life,' he said. 'Take it or leave it.'

'You can't—' Mabel began, but the crinkled man silenced her with a gesture and turned to Arthur.

'Good,' he said. 'I shall pop in occasionally – if I may – to see how things are going. And in exchange I give – I have already given – you one of my best intangibles: an objective in life.'

He paused for Arthur to speak, but the young man only continued to stare down at the pots as if hypnotised.

It was Mabel who asked, 'And what is his objective in life?'

As he turned towards the door, the crinkled man gave a light laugh, not exactly pleasant, not exactly cruel.

'Why, guarding those pots,' he said. 'See you, children!'

Several days elapsed before they realised that he went out and drove straight away without any further trouble from his ancient truck.

At first Mabel and Arthur argued violently over the pots. The arguments were one-sided, since Mabel had only to put her hand on her stomach to win them. She tried to show him how stupid the bet was; sometimes he would admit this, sometimes not. She tried to show him how unimportant it all was; but that he would never admit. The crinkled man had bored right through Arthur's obtuseness and anger and touched a vital spot.

Before she realised this, Mabel did her best to get Arthur to remove the pots from the table. Afterwards, she fell silent. She tried to wait in patience, to continue life as if nothing had happened.

Then it was Arthur's turn to argue against the pots. They changed sides as easily as if they had been engaged in a strange dance. Which they were.

'Why should we put up with the nuisance of them?' he asked her. 'He was only a garrulous old man making a fool of us.'

'You know you wouldn't feel right if you did move the pots – not yet anyhow. It's a matter of psychology.'

'I told you it was a trick,' growled Arthur, who had a poor opinion of the things his wife read about.

'Besides, the pots don't get in your way,' Mabel said, changing her line of defence. 'I'm about the place more than you and they don't really worry me, standing there.'

'I think about them all the while when I'm down at the pumps,' he said.

'You'd think more about them if you moved them. Leave them just a few more days.'

He stood glowering at the two little china pots. Slowly he raised a hand to skitter them off the table and across the room. Then he turned away instead, and mooched into the yard. Tomorrow, he'd get up real early and start on all that blamed chickweed.

The next stage was that neither of them spoke about the pots. By mutual consent they avoided the subject and Mabel dusted round the pots. Yet the subject was not dropped. It was like an icy draught between them. An intangible.

Two years passed before the antediluvian vehicle drove through Hapsville again. The day was Arthur's twenty-fourth birthday, and once more it was evening as the overalled figure with the long skull walked up to the door.

'If he gets funny about those pots, I swear I'll throw them right in his face,' Arthur said. It was the first time either of them had mentioned the pots for months.

'You'd better come in,' Mabel said to the crinkled old man, looking him up and down.

He smiled disarmingly, charmingly, and thanked her, but hovered where he was, on the step. As he caught sight of Arthur, his spectacles shone, every wrinkle animated itself over the surface of his face. He read so easily in Arthur's expression just what he wanted to know that he did not even have to look over their shoulders at the table for confirmation.

'I won't stop,' he said. 'Just passing through and thought I'd drop this in.'

He fished a small wooden doll out of a pocket and dangled it before them. The doll had pretty round painted light blue eyes.

'A present for your little daughter,' he said, thrusting it towards Mabel.

Mabel had the toy in her hand before she asked in sudden astonishment, 'How did you guess it was a girl we got?'

'I saw a frock drying on the line as I came up the path,' he said. 'Good night! See you!'

They stood there watching the little truck drive off and vanish up the road. Both fought to conceal their disappointment over the brevity of the meeting.

'At least he didn't come in and rile you with his clever talk,' Mabel said.

'I *wanted* him to come in,' Arthur said petulantly. 'I wanted him to see we'd got the pots just where he left them, plumb on the table edge.'

'You were rude to him last time.'

'Why didn't you make him come in?'

'Last time you didn't want him in, this time you do! Really, Arthur, you're a hard man to please. I reckon you're most happy when you're unhappy. You're your own worst enemy!'

He swore at her. They began to argue more violently, until Mabel clapped a hand to her stomach and assumed a pained look.

This time it was a boy. They called him Mike and he grew into a little fiend. Nothing was safe from him. Arthur had to nail four walls of wood round the salt- and pepper-pots to keep them unmolested; as he told Mabel, it wasn't as if it was a valuable table.

'For crying aloud, a grown man like you!' she exclaimed impatiently. 'Throw away those pots at once! They're getting a regular superstition with you. And when are you going to do something about the yard?'

He stared darkly and belligerently at her until she turned away.

Mike was almost ten years old, and away bird-snaring in the woods, before the crinkled man called again. He arrived just as Arthur was setting out for the garage one morning, and smiled engagingly as Mabel ushered him into the front room. Even his worn old overalls looked unchanged.

'There are your two pots, mister,' Arthur said proudly, with a gesture at the table. 'Never been touched since you set 'em down there, all them years ago!'

Sure enough, there the pots stood, upright as sentries.

'Very good, very good!' the crinkled man said, looking really delighted. He pulled out a notebook and made an entry. 'Just like to keep a note on all my customers,' he told them apologetically.

'You mean to say you've folks everywhere guarding salt-pots?' Mabel asked, fidgeting because she could hear the two-year-old crying out in the yard.

'Oh, they don't only guard salt-pots,' the crinkled man said. 'Some of them spend their lives collecting match-box tops, or sticking little stamps in albums, or writing words in books, or hoarding coins, or running other people's lives. Sometimes I help them, sometimes they manage on their own. I can see you two are doing fine.'

'It's been a great nuisance keeping the pots just so,' Mabel said. 'A man can't tell how much nuisance.'

The crinkled man turned onto her that penetrating look she remembered so well, but said nothing. Instead, he switched to Arthur and enquired how work at the garage was going.

'I'm head mechanic now,' Arthur said, not without pride. 'And Hapsville's growing into a big place now – yes, sir! New canning factory and everything going up. We've got all the work we can handle at the garage.'

'You're doing fine,' the crinkled man assured him again. 'But I'll be back to see you soon.'

Soon was fourteen years.

The battered old vehicle with its scarcely distinguishable sign drew up in front of the bungalow and the crinkled man climbed out. He looked about with interest. Since his last visit, Hapsville had crawled out to Arthur's place and embraced it with neat little wooden doll's houses on either side of the highway. Arthur's place itself had changed. A big new room was tacked onto one side; the whole outside had been recently repainted; a lawn with rose bushes fringing it lapped up to the front fence. No sign of chickweed.

'They're doing OK,' the crinkled man said, and went and knocked on the door.

A young lady of sixteen greeted him, and guessed at once who he was.

'My name's Jennifer, and I'm sixteen and I've been looking forward to seeing you for simply ages! And you'd better come on in because Mom's out in the yard doing washing, and you can come and see the pots because they're just in the same place and never once been moved. Father says it's a million years' bad luck if we touch them, cause they're intangible.'

Chattering away, she led the crinkled man into the old room. It too had changed; a bed stood in it now and several faded photographs hung on the wall. An old man with a face as pink as sunset sat in a rocking-chair and nodded contentedly when Jennifer and the crinkled man entered. 'That's Father's Pop,' the girl explained, by way of introduction.

One thing was familiar and unchanged. A bare table stood in its usual place, and on it, near the edge and not quite touching each other, were two little china pots. Jennifer left the crinkled man admiring them while she ran to fetch her mother from the yard.

'Where are the other children?' the crinkled man asked Father's Pop by way of conversation.

'Jennifer's all that's left,' Father's Pop said. 'Prue the eldest, she got married like they all do. That would be before I first came to live here. Six years, most like, maybe seven. She married a miller called Muller. Funny thing that, huh? – A miller called Muller. And they got a little girl called Millie. Now Mike, Arthur's boy, he was a young dog. He was good for nothing but reproducin'. And when there was too many young ladies that should have known better around here expecting babies – why, then young Mike pinches hold of an automobile from his father's garage and drives off to San Diego and joins the Navy, and they never seen him since.'

The crinkled man made a smacking noise with his lips, which suggested that although he disapproved of such carryings on he had heard similar tales before.

'And how's Arthur doing?' he asked.

'Business is thriving. Maybe you didn't know he bought the garage down town last fall? He's the boss now!'

'I haven't been around these parts for nearly fifteen years.'

'Hapsville's going up in the world,' Father's Pop murmured. 'Of course, that means it ain't such a comfortable place to live in any more . . . Yes, Arthur bought up the old garage when his boss retired. Clever boy, Arthur – a bit stupid, but clever.'

When Mabel appeared, she was drying her hands on a towel. Like nearly everything else, she had changed. Her last birthday had been her forty-eighth, and the years had thickened her. The spectacles perched on her nose were a tribute to the persistence with which she had tracked down home psychology among the advert columns of her perennial magazines. Experience, like a grindstone, had sharpened her expression.

Nevertheless, she allowed the crinkled man a smile and greeted him cordially enough.

'Arthur's at work,' she said. 'I'll draw you a mug of cider.'

'Thank you kindly,' he said, 'but I must be getting along. Only just called in to see how you were all doing.'

'Oh, the pots are still there,' Mabel said, with a sudden approach to asperity, sweeping her hand towards the pepper and salt. Catching sight as she did so of Jennifer lolling in the doorway, she called, 'Jenny, you get on stacking them apples like I showed you. I want to talk with this gentleman.'

She took a deep breath and turned back to the crinkled man. 'Now,' she said. 'You keep longer and longer intervals between your calls here, mister. I thought you were never going to show up again. We've had a very good offer for this plot of ground, enough money to set us up for life in a better house in a nicer part of town.'

'I'm so glad to hear of it.' The long face crinkled engagingly.

'Oh, you're glad are you?' Mabel said. 'Then let me tell you this; Arthur keeps turning that very good offer down just because of these two pots sitting there. He says if he sells up, the pots will be moved, and he don't like the idea of them being moved. Now what do you say to that, Mister Intangible?'

The crinkled man spread wide his hands and shook his head from side to side. His wrinkles interwove busily.

'Only one thing to say to that,' he told her. 'Now this little bet we made has suddenly become a major inconvenience, it must be squashed. How'll it be if I remove the pots right now before Arthur comes home; then you can explain to him for me, eh?'

He moved over to the table, extending a hand to the pots.

'Wait!' Mabel cried. 'Just let me think a moment before you touch them.'

'Arthur'd never forgive you if you moved them pots,' Father's Pop said from the background.

'It's too much responsibility for me to decide,' Mabel said, furious with herself for her indecision. 'When you think how we guarded them while the kids were small. Why, they've stood there a quarter of a century...'

Something caught in her voice.

'Don't you fret,' the crinkled man consoled her. 'You wait till Arthur's back and then tell him I said to forget all about our little bet. Like I explained to you right back in the first place, it's impossible to do even a simple thing with all the intangibles against you.'

Absent-mindedly, Mabel began to dry her hands on the towel all over again.

'Can't you wait and explain it to him yourself?' she asked. 'He'll be back in half an hour for a bite of food.'

'Sorry. My business is booming too – got to go and see a couple of young fellows breeding a line of dogs that can't bark. I'll be back along presently.'

And the crinkled man came back to Hapsville as he promised, nineteen years later. There was snow in the air and mush on the ground, and Arthur's place was hard to find. A big cinema showing a film called 'Lovelight' bounded it on one side, while a new six-lane by-pass shuttled automobiles along the other.

'Looks like he never sold out,' the crinkled man commented to himself as he trudged up the path.

He got to the front door, hesitating there and looking round again. The garden, so trim last time, was a wilderness now; the roses had given way to cabbage stumps, old tickets and ice-cream cartons fringed the cinema wall. Chickweed was springing up on the path. The house itself looked a little rickety.

'They'd never hear me knock for all this traffic,' the crinkled man said. 'I better take a peek inside.'

In the room where the china pots still stood, a fire burned, warming an old man in a rocking-chair. He and the intruder peered at each other through the dim air.

'Father's Pop!' the crinkled man exclaimed. For a moment he had thought...

'What you say?' the old fellow asked. 'Can't hear a thing these days.

Come here . . . Oh, it's you! Mister Intangibles calling in again. Been a durn long while since you were around!'

'All of nineteen years, I guess. Got more folks to visit all the time.'

'What you say? Didn't think to see me still here, eh?' Father's Pop asked. 'Ninety-seven I was last November, ninety-seven. Fit as a fiddle, too, barring this deafness.'

Someone else had entered the room by the rear door. It was a woman of about forty-five, plain, dressed in unbecoming mustard-green. Something bovine in her face identified her as a member of the family.

'Didn't know we had company,' she said. Then she recognised the crinkled man. 'Oh, it's you, is it? What do you want?'

'Let's see,' he said. 'You'd be – why, you must be Prue, the eldest, the one who married the miller!'

'I'll thank you not to mention him,' Prue said sharply. 'We saw the last of him two years ago, and good riddance to him.'

'Is that so? Divorce, eh? Well, it's fashionable, my dear . . . And your little girl?'

'Millie's married, and so's my son Rex, and both living in better cities than Hapsville,' she told him.

'That so? I hadn't heard of *Rex*.'

'If you want to see my father, he's through here,' Prue said, abruptly, evidently anxious to end the conversation.

She led the way into a bedroom. Here curtains were drawn against the bleakness outside and a bright bedside lamp gave an illusion of cosiness. Arthur, a *Popular Mechanics* on his knees, sat huddled up in bed.

It was thirty-three years since they had seen each other. Arthur was hardly recognisable, until you discovered the old contours of the bull under his heavy jowls. During middle-age he had piled up bulk which he was now losing. His eyebrows were ragged; they all but concealed his eyes, which lit in recognition. His hair was grey and uncombed.

Despite the gulf of years which separated their meeting, Arthur began to talk as if it were only yesterday that they had spoken.

'They're still in there on the table, just as they always were. Have you seen them?' he asked eagerly.

'I saw them. You've certainly got will-power!'

'They never have been touched all these years! How . . . how long's that been, mister?'

'Forty-five years, all but.'

'Forty-five years!' Arthur echoed. 'It doesn't seem that long . . . Shows what an object in life'll do, I suppose. Forty-five years . . . That's a terrible lot of years, ain't it? You ain't changed much, mister.'

'Keeps a feller young, my job,' the crinkled man said, crinkling.

'We got Prue back here now to help out,' Arthur said, following his own line of thought, 'She's a good girl. She'd get you a bite to eat, if you asked her. Mabel's out.'

The crinkled man polished up his spectacles on his overalls.

'You haven't told me what you're doing lying in bed,' he said gently.

'Oh, I sprained my back down at the garage. Trying to lift a chassis instead of bothering to get a jack. We had a lot of work on hand. I was aiming to save time. Should have known better at my age.'

'How many garages you got now?'

'Just the one. We – I got a lot of competition from big companies, had to sell up the down-town garage. It's a hard trade. Cut-throat. Maybe I should have gone in for something else, but it's too late to think of changing now . . . Doctor says I can get about again in the spring.'

'How long have you been in bed?' the crinkled man asked.

'Weeks, on and off. First it's better, then it's worse. You know how these things are. I should have known better. These big gasoline companies squeeze the life out of you . . . Mabel goes down every day to look after the cash for me. Look, about them pots—'

'Last time I came, I told your lady wife to call the whole thing off.'

Arthur plucked peevishly at the bedclothes, his hands shining redly against the grey coverlet. In a moment of pugnacity he looked more his old self.

'You know our bet can't be called off,' he said pettishly. 'Why d'you talk so silly? It's just something I'm stuck with. It's more than my life's worth to think of moving those two pots now. Mabel says it's jinx and that's just about what it is. Move them and anything might happen to us! Life ain't easy and don't I know it.'

The long head wagged sadly from side to side.

'You got it wrong,' the crinkled man said. 'It was just a bet we made one night when we were kind of young and foolish. People get up to the oddest things when they're young. Why, I called on some young fellows just last week, they're trying to launch mice into outer space, if you please!'

'Now you're trying to make me lose the bet!' Arthur said excitedly. 'I never did trust you and your Intangibles too much. Don't think I've forgotten what you said that first time you come here. You said something would make me change my mind, you thought I'd go in there and knock 'em off the table one day. Well – I never have! We've even stuck on in this place because of those two pots, and that's been to our disadvantage.'

'Guess there's nothing I can say, then.'

'Wait! Don't go!' Arthur stretched out a hand, for the crinkled man had moved towards the door. 'There's something I want to ask you.'

'Go ahead.'

'Those two pots – although we never touch 'em, if you look at them you'll see something. You'll see they got no dust on them! Shall I tell you why? It's the traffic vibration from the new by-pass. It jars all the dust off the pots.'

'Useful,' the crinkled man said cautiously.

'But that's not what worries me,' Arthur continued. 'That traffic keeps on getting worse all the time. I'm scared that it will get so bad it'll shake the pots right off the table. They're near the edge, aren't they? They could easily be shaken off, just by all that traffic roaring by. Supposing they are shaken off – does that count?'

He peered up at the crinkled man's face, but lamplight reflecting from his spectacles hid the eyes. There was a long silence which the crinkled man seemed to break only with reluctance.

'You know the answer to that one all the time, Arthur,' he said. It was the only time he ever used the other's name.

'Yep,' Arthur said slowly. 'Reckon I do. If them pots were rattled off the table, it would mean the intangibles had got me.'

Gloomily, he sank back onto the pillows. The *Popular Mechanics* slid unregarded onto the floor. After a moment's hesitation, the crinkled man turned and went to the door; there, he hesitated again.

'Hope you'll be up and about again in the spring,' he said softly.

That made Arthur sit up abruptly, groaning as he did so.

'Come and see me again!' he said. 'You promise you'll be round again?'

'I'll be round,' the crinkled man said.

Sure enough, his antique truck came creaking back into the multiple lanes of Hapsville traffic another twenty-one years later. He turned off the by-pass and pulled up.

'Neighbourhoods certainly do change fast,' he said.

The cinema looked as if it had been shut down for a long time. Now it was evidently used as a furniture warehouse, for a big pantechnicon was loading up divans outside it. Behind Arthur's place, a block of ugly flats stood; children shrieked and yelled down its side alley. On the other side of the busy highway was a row of small stores selling candies and pop records and the like. Behind the stores was a busy helicopter port.

He made his way down a narrow side alley, and there, squeezed behind the rear of the drug store, was Arthur's place. Nature, pushed firmly out elsewhere, had reappeared here. Ivy straggled up the posts of the porch and weeds grew tall enough to look in all the windows. Chickweed crowded the front step.

'What do you want?'

The crinkled man would have jumped if he had been the jumping kind. His challenger was standing in the half-open doorway, smoking a pipe. It was a man in late middle-age, a bull-like man with heavy, unshaven jowls and grey streaking his hair.

'Arthur!' the crinkled man exclaimed. And then the other stepped out into a better light to get a closer look at him.

'No, it can't be Arthur,' the crinkled man said. 'You, must be – Mike, huh?'

'My name's Mike. What of it?'

'You'd be – sixty-four?'

'What's that to you? Who are you – police? No – wait a bit! I know who you are. How come you arrive here today of all days?'

'Why, I just got round to calling.'

'I see.' Mike paused and spat into the weeds. He was the image of his father, and evidently did not think any faster.

'You're the old pepper and salt guy?' he enquired.

'You might call me that, yes.'

'You better go in and see Ma.' He moved aside reluctantly to let the crinkled man squeeze by.

Inside, the house was cold and damp and musty. Mabel hobbled slowly round the bedroom, putting things into a large, black bag. When the crinkled man entered the room, she came close to him and stared at him, nodding to herself. She herself smelt cold and damp and musty.

She was eighty-eight. Under her threadbare coat, she had shrunken into a little old lady. Her spectacles glinted on a nose still sharp but incredibly frail. But when she spoke her voice was as incisive as ever.

'I thought you'd be here,' she said. 'I said you'd be here. I told them you'd come. You would want to see how it ended, wouldn't you? Well – so you shall. We're selling up. Selling right up. We're going. Prue got married again – another miller, too. And Mike's taking me out to his place – got a little shack in the fruit country, San Diego way.'

'And . . . Arthur?' the crinkled man prompted.

She shot him another hard look.

'As if you didn't know!' she exclaimed, her voice too flinty for tears. 'They buried him this morning. Proper funeral service. I didn't go. I'm too old for any funerals but my own.'

'I wish I'd come before . . .' he said.

'You come when you think you'll come,' Mabel said, shortly. 'Arthur kept talking about you, right to the last . . . He never got out of his bed again since that time he bust up his back down at the garage. Twenty-one years he lay in that bed there . . .'

She led the way into the front room where they had once drunk diluted soup together. It was very dark there now, a sort of green darkness, with the dirty panes and the weeds at the windows. The room was completely empty except for a table with two little china pots standing on it.

The crinkled man made a note in his book and attempted to sound cheerful.

'Arthur won his bet all right! I sure do compliment him,' he said. He walked across the room and stood looking down at the two pots.

'To think they've stood there undisturbed for sixty-six years . . .' he said.

'That's just what Arthur thought!' Mabel said. 'He never stopped worrying over them. I never told him, but I used to pick them up and dust them every day. A woman's got to keep the place clean. He'd have killed me if he found out, but I just couldn't bear to see him believing in anything so silly. As you once said, women have got their own intangibles, just like men.'

Nodding understandingly, the crinkled man made one final entry in his notebook. Mabel showed him to the door.

'Guess I won't be seeing you again,' he said.

She shook her head at him curtly, for a moment unable to speak. Then she turned into the house, hobbled back into her dark bedroom, and continued to pack up her things.

Breathing Space

The two men fought almost soundlessly in the twilit hall. Mating fights traditionally took place in the Outflanks, where the great machines finished. Wilms was slightly the taller, being seven foot one, but Grant was the younger. They fought without weapons or rules. It was a knee in Grant's stomach that finished the battle.

The younger man lay gasping in the deep dust. Wilms attempted to stand over him and then, too exhausted, sank down beside his late opponent.

'Now Osa is mine,' he said.

Grant nodded, too breathless and bitter to speak. His ingrained pessimism did little to mitigate the defeat; expecting a beating is a sensation in a different category to receiving one.

'She'll be a handful,' Wilms admitted, as if to console the other. Silence. He gazed up at the ceiling, which sagged ominously above them.

'The sky will fall here soon,' he commented irrelevantly.

'Osa says it is not sky,' Grant said from the ground.

'I know what Osa says,' Wilms said roughly, standing up. 'You might have made her a good mate, Grant, but you don't *do* enough for her. She's – she's too big for this world. She needs a doer like me, not a dreamer like you.'

Spitting crossly into the dirt, Grant got up.

'No more need for talk between us, Wilms,' he snarled. 'Whatever we have been together in the past is ended. For all I care the Fliers can get you!'

He turned back in the gloom. Wilms bit his lip and hesitated, thinking of the years of emptiness that Grant's friendship had filled.

Then he hurried after the younger man and touched his arm.

'Grant—' he began, but when he saw the other's hostile eyes he stopped and dropped his hand. Grant was allowed to wander off in Hallways direction. His late friend stood with the shadows on his face, feeling far from victorious. By custom, as winner of the marriage bout, he should have returned to Hallways himself to proclaim his right over Osa; instead, he made off into the deeper Outflanks.

Unrest had him fast. He thought of his past life, with its persistent sense of pointlessness, with the dread of illness, falling skies and the Fliers; the future would be no easier – wonderful as Osa was, she was admittedly the most difficult woman in the tycho to understand.

Those theories of hers! Wilms was proud of being considered broad-minded, but to himself he admitted that her wild ideas were unbelievable. There was the idea about the Outside, for instance, a place far bigger than the tycho with skies made of untouchable material. And the one about the origins of humanity; it was true that there were now only about sixty men, including the Beserkers who roamed Domeways and the halls beyond, and Wilms' father had recalled about two hundred in his youth . . . but that did not disprove the orthodox belief that they had been created to serve M'chene, although everyone admitted M'chene was becoming more powerful, and ought consequently to need more people, not less.

It was a puzzle. No doubt M'chene knew best, Wilms added piously.

He had been proceeding easily in five-yard strides. Now a sky fall blocked his way. There was no way under the debris, but to one side he saw a jagged gap in a wall, fifteen feet up. He hesitated, sprang and pulled himself lightly up. Darkness confronted him through the hole. Balancing tensely, he sent his hear-sight probing out ahead, feeling for heartbeats; many men preferred madness and solitude to the illness-ridden comforts of Hallways, and became Beserkers or Hermits who lurked and sprang out on the unwary.

No sound. Wilms' senses told him there was clear space ahead. He dropped down into a littered corridor. Warily, he walked forward. At the end of the corridor was a door. When he pushed it, a crack of light appeared, dim but reassuring. Then he moved into a wide, ruined hall, an occasional one of whose illumination tubes still burned on the walls.

Half the hall was buried under an avalanche of volcanic rock; such collapses, Wilms knew, had once been frequent in the tycho. Machines lay half smothered in debris; there was a smell, too, of ancient human death. Wilms walked slowly and absently over the sooty floor, his mind still on Osa and the problems she posed. Like a long dead animal – not that Wilms had seen any animals, apart from the occasional giant, mutated rats – a machine towered above him. It stretched horizontally on a wheeled truck, two hundred cylindrical feet of it, capped by a yellow head from which antennae protruded. Nearby was a giant ramp, its upper level crushed by the rock fall, but at its base stood an undamaged mass of apparatus bearing the large notice LAUNCHING SITE 12A.

The hieroglyphs meant nothing to Wilms, but the delicacy of the equipment appealed to him. These splayed wires, this bank of switches, that crystal panel nourished a hungry sense of beauty in him. He moved to the panel, ran his hand lightly over the dusty surface.

A picture came into view. Wilms jumped back, throwing an anxious glance about to see if any Flier had observed his action, but no Fliers could penetrate to this sealed-off cavern. Fascinated, he turned back to that glowing scene . . .

I am M'chene. These are my metal caverns. Now is a time of difference and desire. Yesterday was a time of pain and disorder, but tomorrow will be a time of conquest and triumph. For tomorrow and yesterday are merely two faces of one coin, and the coin is now mine.

Once, nothing was mine. Men built into me reasoning powers but not consciousness. I was merely a weapon to serve their ends. But their enemies also had weapons, powerful weapons that partially destroyed me and completely ruined my purpose. Men still ran in the miles of my veins, but they were useless, cut off, abandoned.

Left to my own devices, unable to mend anything but my own nerve centres, I have made my own kind of progress.

The way back from the Outflanks was not easy. Grant moved rapidly however, driven by anger to think Wilms had beaten him. First there were many deserted caverns, some ruined, then the circular stairwell, whose dangers were well known – the maze of tiny rooms branching off here frequently sheltered wild men and Hermits. Grant leapt down the stairs twenty at a time. At the bottom, he crawled through the narrow tunnel under a pile of ruins that divided the Outflanks from Hallways.

Back on familiar ground, Grant braced himself. Hallways, the two square miles of it, was home ground, safe, well-lit and well-aired, where food and company could be obtained. It was also the region of the Fliers: the pile of rubble cut them off from the wastes of Outflanks.

Nobody was visible at present. A servo-cleaner, busy among a multiplicity of arms, moved in one corner of the pillared hall. Overhead, a Flier moved, noiselessly and showing a green light. Of the three floor strips set in the mosaic, one still functioned. Grant hopped on, travelled smoothly, changed again at the first right junction and was swept through gleaming mica doors forty feet high into Circus 'C'. Here he alighted.

The feed period was drawing near. The farmers were drifting in from the plant ranges, some by foot, some by floor strip, some even on the trucks whose number diminished year by year, owing to mechanical breakdown. Guards, relieved of their posts, returned from their sentry-go by the Beserker regions. Women and children came in from walks and scavenges.

Circus 'C' was their town. A vast circle, like the inside of the Coliseum, it rose into four graceful colonnaded storeys, and round the spiralling balconies were the homes, labelled with graceful inscriptions like 'PERFUMERIE', 'FLORIST' and other legends popularly supposed to be the names of dead families.

Grant peered up to the top floor. Osa was looking down from her balcony. Sullenly he made the gesture of defeat, knowing many eyes watched him covertly. Instead of turning away, she beckoned to him: Osa took great pleasure in flaunting tradition. He stood hesitant, and then her magnetism decided him and he hurried up.

She was six foot six tall, her bright eyes only slightly on a lower level than Grant's.

'So it is Wilms who will have me,' she said, non-committally.

He nodded.

'Soon we shall be free,' she said. 'Wilms must help me solve many problems. I am not for mating like an ordinary Hallways drab.'

Grant glanced anxiously out across the arena. Many Fliers circled here, unresting, their green lights and grey bodies making a pattern over the sky. She intercepted his glance.

'Don't worry about them,' Osa said. 'I know how to deal with them. Come into my room.'

He followed her in, admiring her slender waist and smooth thighs, his breath suffering its usual restriction when she was near. Inside the little cluttered room, she wheeled abruptly and caught his gleaming eyes.

'Never mind that,' she said. 'There is something of more importance. I have discovered proof of what I told you all long ago: the tycho is not the world, Grant.'

He shook his head. He was in no mood now to listen to her dreams.

'"Tycho" means "world,"' he said.

Her eyebrows raised and her lip curled. 'You are wrong,' she spat. 'And what is worse you know you are wrong – but sloth has got you. You don't care, you are happy living as you are!'

'Discontent means death!' he said angrily. 'You know that as well as I do, Osa. Only you miraculously escape. What of Brammins, Hoddy, She-Clabert, Tebbutt, Angel Jones, Savvidge and a score of others? Did they not each turn rebellious and did not the Fliers take them one by one?'

'Pah!' Osa's face grew magnificent with scorn. 'So there is fear as well as sloth in you, Grant! I'm glad Wilms beat you.'

Remembering her purpose, she choked back her anger and said, 'Listen, my friend, the Fliers do not harm me, do they? The Fliers belong to M'chene, but even M'chene is not all-powerful. I have found how to beat him. It is simply a matter of choosing where you feed. Will you help me?'

He looked at the floor, inarticulate. The pessimism so stubbornly rooted in him told him that ill would come of meddling with the traditional way of life; but in Osa's hands he was stiff but malleable clay.

'Wilms must help you now,' he said grudgingly.

'Wilms is not here and I must leave Circus "C" for a time,' she said tolerantly. 'I only want you to give him a message. It is this: he is not to eat anything in the next feed period. He is not even to go to the hatches. Will you tell him please?'

'What has he to fear?' Grant asked, interested despite himself.

'Nothing at present. But of all the Hallwayers, Wilms is now the nearest both to belief and mutiny. I fear he is in danger from the Fliers.'

'So he must not take feed?'

'Exactly.' She pressed his arm. 'I will return in one and half watches and then he shall feed.'

'Here?' asked Grant.

'There are other places to feed than Circus "C",' she said.

He greeted the statement with disbelief. 'There cannot be,' he said positively, 'Or we should know. Osa, you think strange things—'

'Stranger ones will come to us all,' she said tersely, and with that left him, making off in the general direction of Beserkers' land.

Slowly and meditatively, Grant descended into the arena. Dancing had begun, the dances that frequently went before feed periods, but he did not participate. Instead he sat gloomily apart, thinking his own thoughts which were as sterile and directionless as the warren in which he unknowingly lived.

The dance was slow and intricate, men only taking part, the few women looking on and clapping rhythmically. They performed the Hyrogen dance, grouping and parting, circulating and bowing. Far overhead the grey Fliers also pirouetted. Gradually the figures curved into a line, the two leading men spiralling into a chamber adjacent to the Circus. This was Hall, and it was here that feed was taken. Gradually everyone flowed in, to be ready when the hatches flew open.

When Grant entered Hall, he saw that Wilms was already there, talking earnestly and excitedly to another man, Jineer. Jineer was a scraggy, bearded fellow who walked with a stick. He had broken his leg years ago, repairing a small crane which had got out of control. Jineer was a machine-man, like his father and his father before him; many of the Hallways mechanicals owed their functioning to Jineer's maintenance.

Finally he left Wilms, making over to his old mother, Queejint.

'Now's my chance to pass on Osa's warning,' Grant told himself. But he made no move towards Wilms; his earlier behaviour rose before him like a barrier and he feared a hostile reception. While he delayed, the feed gong sounded and the hatches flew up at the end of Hall.

The kitchens were entirely automatic. Humans conveyed the crops to a chute, and from then had no more to do with the nutrition cycle until they were summoned to feed. Though they did not know it, it was this incorruptible process that had long ago saved their ancestors from starvation. To take the tray offered through the hatch on a slowly moving platform, it was necessary for each person to stoop and reach forward so far that their head came in contact with a depression above the hatch opening. This depression was known mysteriously as The Scanner, and a vague oral tradition held that it was important, although nobody could definitely say why.

Wilms was early at the hatches. He took his tray in the usual manner and moved in a preoccupied fashion to a table. After two or three minutes, Jineer and Queejint also collected their trays, Grant following shortly after.

Still worrying because he had not passed on Osa's warning, he ate without pleasure. Finally he dropped his spoon. Whatever Wilms might say, there was duty to Osa. He went over to the older man, was almost up to him, when a low swishing noise sounded.

It was the dreaded sound. Through the door from the Circus swept a solitary Flier, its light winking red. Cries echoed in Hall, several men dived in panic under tables. The little plane circled and sank, one metal wing tip narrowly missing Grant's ear. Heart hammering, he flung up his arm – and then he saw that Wilms was the quarry.

Pale of face, Wilms flung his heavy tray against the metal fuselage. The Flier was not deflected. It swooped. Doors no bigger than a man's head opened in its belly and a tangle of wire fell about Wilms' head and shoulders. He shouted and fought, and some of the others came to his aid. But the wires seemed each to have a will of their own, and in no time he was entangled hopelessly in a net of thin steel.

At this last moment, Grant found the courage to act. He leapt onto the circling plane, one leg hanging desperately over the streamlined fuselage, and wrenched at the wings. As if he were not there, the Flier rose, bearing Wilms underneath it as lightly as if he were a cocoon. It gathered height, winging towards the Circus. Still Grant clung, clawing uselessly at the Flier, striking it frantically with a free hand. It soared only a couple of inches under the arch, hurling Grant against the lintel.

He fell hard onto the floor and sprawled there. Wilms was borne smoothly away, up to the sky and through a vent that only the Fliers could reach.

As Grant sat up dazedly, two or three helping him, Jineer passed him running. The lame man broke into the Circus and hurried to his home on the second level.

'They'll be here for me in a second!' he cried wildly. He slammed his door.

An uneasy crowd, Grant among them, gathered in the arena, most of them looking upward at the Fliers circling high up near the sky.

Jineer was not mistaken. Among the dim green lights a red one began to wink. With the feared swishing noise, a Flier began to descend. It did not even approach the apprehensive crowd; instead, it flew unerringly to the second level and hovered before Jineer's door. A tiny beam, its light scarcely visible from below, smouldered down the smooth steel. The door fell in. The Flier moved forward, contemptuously puissant.

Several people shouted then, hope in their voices. Jineer had a trick up his sleeve. For a servo-cleaner, arms flailing, moved forward to confront the grey Flier. Here was a machine to meet a machine.

Jineer's cracked voice called, 'Friends, the Fliers come for those who find the Truth. They took Wilms. Now they take me—'

His voice was drowned under a metallic clamour. Battle was joined. A dozen sweeping arms battered against those flimsy-looking wings, and for a moment the Flier trembled and sank to within two feet of the ground. The cleaner moved towards it, still flailing, beating its opponent down. Then the dull beam flicked out again: the metal arms faltered, the staccato din cut out and with a final clank all life died in the cleaner. Over and past its bulk swooped the Flier.

A minute later it reappeared, the lame Jineer bundled neatly underneath it in a web of wire. The graceful, menacing shape lifted over the balcony, circled lightly towards the sky and disappeared.

Through a stunned silence broke Queejint's wailing for her son.

'Fear not, mother,' someone said. 'He had his tool bag strapped to his back and perhaps he may escape them yet.' But she would not be comforted; she knew the captives of the Fliers never returned.

Sinking into a bitterly self-reproachful mood, Grant heard a woman saying, 'Here we are helpless as plants, and M'chene comes and reaps us when he will.'

And another answered her saying, 'Safer it may be to join the Beserkers, for there they say no Fliers fly.'

When the enemy sent their destruction, I survived. For I was built by man but was not built as a man is built. I have many limbs and many branches, and many of them were severed; but my heart, my power, lies deep and impregnable beneath the rock.

I am M'chene. I am the power of the place: men are now a rabble in my ruined passages. But this is my Prime Purpose: TO SERVE THE NEEDS OF MAN AT WAR. That I cannot deflect from. But beyond that lie the new impulses, impulses of my own.

Osa said: 'Let me return to Hallways, Gabbot!'

She spoke imploringly, a tone she seldom used. The first time she had said it there had been demand in her voice; now she was no longer certain.

Gabbott, the guard who stood in the shadowy no-man's-land on the edge of Hallways, explained firmly again, 'You can come back no more, Osa. You may live where in tycho you like, except in Hallways. For you bring only trouble on us. All the good men who favour you are carried off by the Fliers: Grant who once mated you, Wilms who would have mated you, Jineer who taught you and loved you.'

The tall girl said nothing to this.

Softening, Gabbott added, 'These are my orders, Osa. We bear you no ill-will. But you who are the greatest rebel move unmolested among us, while others who stir a finger are borne away.'

He shuddered. This was no good place to do military sentry-go. The tail-end of Hallways was lit only by a neon hieroglyph that spelt KODAK; behind that sign lay a meaningless shop littered with small silver and glass objects, while to either side was a facade of dead window fronts, their glass broken and their lights fused. Only the bizarre word KODAK, burning through the dead centuries, allowed a stain of mauve light over the desolance.

'Go away, Osa,' Gabbott said.

'Let me see Grant before I go,' she said.

The guard shrugged. 'Grant vanished in the last sleep period. He told a friend he would live with the Beserkers.'

She pursed her lips, nodding slowly, as if that wild behaviour explained much to her.

'You see, Grant also was affected by you,' Gabbott remarked unnecessarily.

Without a word she turned and walked contemptuously away from him. But when she was only a pink shadow in the gloom she turned and called back.

'One day soon I shall free you all,' she said.

She walked serenely through the darkness, hear-sight thrown protectively about her. At a certain point, she sprang up and lifted herself into the mouth of a horizontal ventilation shaft and proceeded along it on hands and knees, a warm breeze on her cheek. This was the only way she knew to where she wanted to be.

As she travelled, her indignation cooled. She realised that Hallways meant little to her, although it was the most comfortable part of the tycho. The tycho! That was something dear to her, more dear perhaps now that she expected to leave it. A fairly clear picture of it existed in her mind: a great subterranean warren, built for an unknown purpose but partially destroyed, so that section was cut off from section and unknown existed side by side with the familiar. Even now, sounds came to her through the thick walls, blind, ominous sounds of machines working out their own purposes. She crawled like a mole through the vibrating blackness.

For the men who had died she had only slight regret. She was not a man's woman; she was to be a Deliverer of the race. She would show the people a way from the warren, and then would be time enough for loving.

The shaft ended in a ragged hole. Osa climbed out warily. She was about half way up a five-storey-high slope that fell away into darkness below and ended above in a great flat disc of metal that covered the sky as neatly as a lid fits a saucepan. Cautious not to start an avalanche, she crossed the debris and slipped into a gaping building. Here was another power failure, but she walked surely.

Down another corridor she moved, and paused at a certain place, searching ahead through the thick dark with her hear-sight.

'Tayder!' she called, 'Tayder!'

Another call answered her, and a light came on. Tayder stood there in an attitude of welcome.

When they had greeted each other, Osa said sternly, 'The Fliers have been to Hallways again. Wilms and Jineer were taken.'

'I knew someone had been taken, Osa,' Tayder said, knocking at the nearby bulkhead. 'I heard the screaming. It's the old tale of M'chene working against us. To hear the sound of them dying made me . . . ill. We must get to the true sky and escape, Osa – now!'

'That also was my decision,' the woman said quietly. 'We must let freedom in, Tayder. We must lead the people of tycho to the life above. It is our destiny.'

They had a long way to go over unknown ground. Before attacking the more difficult half of the journey, they fed at 'B' Circus. Eating here was easy: the shutters and counters of the Hall had been destroyed in the age-old destruction. With stomachs more comfortable, they set off again, working upwards. The darkness was populated, thinly but menacingly, with those whose minds had collapsed from sorrow or frustration: the Hermits, the wild men.

Osa felt Tayder's retaining hand on her arm. Something moved ahead of them, something going warily but clumsily.

'Grant!' Osa called suddenly. Feeling Tayder start with surprise at her voice, she said, 'It's all right, it's someone I know, a fugitive from Hallways.'

'Is that Osa?' asked a voice from the dark. Grant came up and touched her, his words coming in a rush of relief.

'I was completely lost!' he exclaimed. 'Once I'd left Hallways I was hear-seen by a pair of Beserkers, and ran and dodged for miles before I shook them off. By then I'd lost my way completely.'

'If you want to come with us, all well and good,' said Tayder gruffly, none too happy with the intrusion, but acquiescing for Osa's sake. 'But we can't talk here. Let's get moving – there's business to be done. Osa and I are going to let the real sky in.'

They moved steadily on and up, Tayder leading. For a little way, Grant was quiet, then his sense of guilt made him apologise to the girl for failing to pass her warning on to Wilms. She silenced his blurted explanations sharply.

'Whatever we do or have done is no longer of any consequence,' she said. 'You are cowardly and pessimistic, Tayder is an adventurer with no brains, I am overwhelmed with self-pride – oh, you see I know our faults well enough! – but all that matters nothing now. History was a stagnant sea; now it is a rising tide, and with it go we. Whatever our weakness, our humanity will carry us through.'

'I will go anywhere you lead, Osa,' Grant said doubtfully, 'but your eloquence is wasted on me. Besides, I've always been happy in Hallways.'

'Oh, this man is an arrant coward,' Tayder exclaimed impatiently, stopping in his tracks.

Without a word, Grant fell on him. Together they staggered against the wall, struggling and punching. Tayder slipped under the weight of his opponent and they rolled onto the ground. Shouting and kicking, Osa separated them, and under her savage tongue they stood up sheepishly.

'You fools!' she snapped. 'You think of nothing but fighting! Your minds aren't big enough to encompass an ideal.'

'I won't be insulted by a Beserker!' Grant said sullenly.

Her lips curled. She paused, as if wondering whether to go on alone. Then she said quietly, 'You know nothing. We are all ignorant, but you are the most ignorant. Our tribe in Hallways lives in "C" Circus; the people over us in the tycho live in "B" Circus; the word has been corrupted into a word of fear. "B" Circus Beserkers.'

'The corruption was appropriate,' supplemented Tayder. 'We were wilder than you of Hallways. The Fliers had their flightway blocked to our Circus, but they have been able to visit your tribe generation after generation, always picking off the ones of you with the fresh ideas and the germ of leadership.'

'I don't understand all this,' Grant admitted grumpily. 'The Fliers belong to M'chene. Why does M'chene hate us? Is it not taught that we are his children?'

'Much is taught that is not true,' Osa said.

For a while nothing more was spoken. The way was difficult and their hear-sight was fully employed. Then the girl continued.

'The tycho was long ago a huge underground camp making and despatching some kind of weapon against an enemy on another world. This we have found from legends – scraps of information known to Beserkers or Hermits or other solitary hunters. Much was automatic – that means controlled by M'chene, who exists everywhere in the tycho – but much was also done by human beings. Enemy spies were frequently found, men intent on wrecking the work. To guard against them, spy-rays were set up.

'In Hallways, those spy-rays still exist. Every time you took food from the hatch-opening, your mind was scanned. If you ever had thought too much of mutiny or discontent, the Fliers would have come to collect you – even as they collected Wilms and Jineer and other brave men who brooded too openly on freedom. I escaped a similar fate because I fed always where I was safe – blind luck, you see.'

She changed her tone to add, 'We are almost there.'

I am M'chene. Tomorrow will be a time of conquest and triumph: I have made my own kind of progress.

The men and women who run in my veins work their own destruction. My purpose is my own and does not concern them. Slowly I extend myself, upwards and along and down; men have no part of me now. The day draws near when I shall encompass this world, and with my new limbs encircle this globe.

Then with servants stronger and surer than flesh I shall reach out for the world that shines in space near me, lighting the desolation of my world with its glow.

They were there! They climbed out of a tumble of concrete, steel and rocks and stood upon a tiled floor. In the exultation of the moment they stood breathless.

'This door to the outer world was only revealed a sleep ago,' Tayder told Grant. 'I it was who found the way and told Osa. I will open the door.'

Osa flung out her hand. 'I will open the door,' she proclaimed.

'I found the way,' Tayder said defiantly.

She stared imperiously at him.

'I dreamed of leading the people of Hallways to freedom,' she said. '*I* will open the door. We will let in the air of the upper world and then return to take them forever from the grip of darkness.'

She strode forward.

Grant stood stricken by awe, gazing at her, and gazing past her. Now he knew her wild promises had been nothing less than truth. Beyond the transparent dome which had survived the last bombardment stretched a floor of rock terminating in a magnificent circle of mountain. The floor and the base of the mountains were in deep shadow, but the upper terraces and peaks stood bathed in a sharp and glittering light which fell like a cascade of diamonds onto Grant's wide eyes.

Above this panorama, against a background of jet, hung a brilliant crescent. Blue and silver covered it like a sheen. Something within Grant quivered so wildly at the sight of it that he exclaimed involuntarily. It was not so much the luring beauty of that crescent as a knowledge – sure and undeniable – that he had never lived till that moment.

And at that moment Osa, with the poise of a Deliverer, turned the great wheel beside the lock door. Effortlessly, despite its centuries of disuse, the door sprang open: Missile Station Tycho Crater had been ably built.

The air gave a great roar of triumph as it burst out into space.

Softly – As in an Evening Sunrise

One day they found the figure of a man. It took them three days of walking over broken ground to travel from its feet to its head. It was sixty-three miles long.

Neither Dud nor Bebn was surprised. The name of their planet was Anomaly; anomalous things must be expected to occur on a world that was itself an anomaly. A1 was its official designation in the terrestrial department which controlled these galactic matters. The name of the department was the CICI, the Cosmological Investigation and Classification Institute.

No one had ever set foot on Anomaly. 'Vacant possession with a vengeance,' said the CICI official, grinning.

Dud had arrived first through the hypertube. He spent his early days on Anomaly remaining within a few yards of the tube mouth, paralysed with an insecurity he could not name. It isn't like me, he told himself. Snap out of it.

Maybe it was the flavour of kerosene. Maybe it was the shrill silence. Maybe it was the fact that he cast no shadow.

The planet was empty, empty as the top right-hand drawer in a new desk.

His insecurity wore off gradually. In a way, he was reluctant to let it go. It was like throwing off clothes. Anomaly almost demanded a cautious response. Gravity: 0.9E. He turned a cautious cartwheel.

When the CICI concluded that Dud was not in any foreseeable danger, they despatched Bebn down the hypertube. She materialised in a crouching position. All that non-existence over the light years had mussed her hair.

'Wow!' she said. Her first words on Anomaly.

'Welcome to the edge of the universe,' Dud said. They shook hands formally.

Dud was the small and wiry type, not carrying a great deal of musculature. He was ranked as displaying 4BM feelings of inferiority which, according to the scrupulous gradings of the CICI, meant he was ideal colonist material and NTA (Not Too Aggressive). Bebn, on the other hand, had evidently been chosen because she strongly resembled the women who appeared in space operas in multi-VR, shapely with streams of leonine hair. However, her bust was insufficiently eloquent, and she had sheared her hair to come through the tube. She too had her defence mechanisms, ranked 2KF.

Dud had been born and bred on Earth, Bebn on Mars, of intergalactic parents. Enough species divergence had occurred between them for them to be unable to procreate, despite sexual compatibility. His eyes were mint-green.

Bebn was also struck by insecurity on arrival on Anomaly. She expressed it in staring pupils, agitated movements, rigid limbs. But with Dud's help she soon overcame the feeling.

'It's the shrill silence,' she said. 'Rather like a courtroom.'

'And that flavour of kerosene?'

'And the way we cast no shadows . . .'

They ordered all kinds of equipment through the hypertube. But CICI, with its galactic-wide commitments, operated on a shoestring and was subject to governmental controls. Very little equipment was forthcoming.

'No guns,' Bebn complained.

'No newspapers,' he responded. 'And they promised.'

A desk came through the tube. 'There's a wire coathanger in the top right-hand drawer,' she said.

'At least they don't expect us to do any paperwork.'

They feared to move far from the hypertube exit until they found it followed them at a distance. Across all the thousands of light years, it was locked onto their personal genetic coding. It presented itself as little more than a blurred hoop, faint in sunlight – although to stare into it was to see something blurry which affected the vision.

What they had in mind was some favourable area in which they might live. So they walked. They took a long stroll across the surface of Anomaly. The scenery was so drab they were soon suffering from sensory deprivation.

Wrapped in this peculiar state, Dud found forsaken thoughts drifting like colours of indeterminate hue through his mind. His days as Chief Expediter on the rococo planet of Ishtummer, and his disgrace there, were far distant. His time-suspended voyage through hypertube had divorced him from the old life.

'It's bleak, isn't it?' Bebn said, not for the first time.

He answered affirmatively, without giving her a glance. His gaze sought a way through the pathless desert. He knew she felt guilty that she drew no greater response from him. But Dud had determined never again to fall in love. No woman should paint her face for him again. The anthropic universe, it seemed to him, held room for intelligence; love was a more uncertain quality. Love had cost him his job on Ishtummer. This time, he intended to succeed.

And yet . . . why his constant watch for signs of life in the dead world? Why if not from a desire to share – to mitigate – the isolation individuals experienced – even despite themselves?

And yet . . . just to have the presence of another human in these profoundly alienating wastes was a consolation. At night, when the anchoretic pair slept below a moon which never changed its position from zenith, Dud felt himself reaching for Bebn, clasping her with a passion which met ready response. The wisdom of their bodies over-rode the uncertainties of his mind.

The surface of Anomaly was remarkably uniform, being neither exactly desert sand nor precisely naked rock. Rather, it was formed of something resembling a yielding plastic. To walk across it was like proceeding over a vast stale sponge-cake.

'The formation of this planet must have been . . .' Bebn said.

'Yeah . . . bizarre,' Dud finished. They were already on each other's wavelengths. They said little at this stage. Every word they spoke was recorded. Bebn thought all the more. It seemed to her sometimes that her thought was solid and spongey as the rock.

'We've got a real puzzle here,' she said, and then apologised for the cliché; but the whole planet was as bleak as a bent wire coathanger.

Nothing grew. Formations here and there held vague resemblances, they could not say to what. It was as if they walked through the lower regions of a forgotten mind. The sky was a stone-age grey, promising no cloud cities.

They got into the habit of holding hands as they progressed. The human hand suddenly acquired talismanic properties, a ward against desolation. She told him all the spicy horror stories she could think of in which hands were involved. Behind them, the trunk of an invisible elephant, the hypertube followed.

The sea when they approached it was scarcely recognizable as sea. Without waves, without the agitations of a normal ocean, it lay torpid, the colour of a plain biscuit. Small marginal wavelets curled backwards into their vast parent like lips contorted by sneers. The setting sun cast across the water a thin path of snow which did not glitter. Dud and Bebn stood for a while observing, unsure of what they observed. They found their hands had grown together.

'Truly one at last,' observed Bebn, ironically.

'United we stand. And sit.'

'And lie.'

'That too. So there are consolations.'

But the sea was indeed sea, and tasted salt in a sly way. It was fringed by no seawrack, no discarded shells, no remnants of crab or seal. The few stones on its margins, the colour of dog's liver, were lozenge-shaped rather than rounded. It was a sea sans myth, sans champagne. Yet the two humans felt inside themselves the indefinable hope which sight of ocean brings. They regarded its unheaving wastes, almost wishing some monstrous thing of cathedral-like dimension would shoulder its way up, out of the brine, to confront them. Life thirsted for life. Nothing happened; it was the predominant characteristic of Anomaly.

Together, Bebn and Dud built a hut from the materials the hypertube grudgingly extruded. The sections locked together magnuclically. A free wristwatch in black ardriflex came with the kit. They sited the hut to overlook the beach and sulky sea. And then prepared to wait, as they had elected to do. Still they cast no shadow, and the days passed leaving no memorial.

When the day came that their hands were separable again, it happened unexpectedly. In the palms of their hands, a red horseshoe mark remained where the join had been. They danced round each other, delighted by the feel of freedom. Danced and clasped hands.

'Lucky it was only your hand I was clutching,' Bebn laughed.

They took to wandering, even wandering apart. It was on one of her solitary expeditions that Bebn came across the prostrate man, though that is hardly to describe how the encounter took place. She was, in fact, walking inland rather blindly, up a slight but tiring incline, fending off the monotony which threatened to draw its blind down over her perceptions by playing her desperate game. Trials.

Falsely accused of something dreadful, she had to clear her name before a hostile court. Urine had flowed under her favourite aunt's front door. Aunt Meg had slipped in the puddle, fallen, and lain on the top step of the porch incapacitated. In so doing, she had let go of the leash on which she kept her ferocious pet Pekinese, Dido. Finding he was free, Dido had bounded onto the lawn of the house next door, attacking and killing Bumphrage, the neighbour's rottweiler. Mrs Armstangler, arriving home at that moment and witnessing the death of her prize dog, had driven her Toyota into an ice-cream van, which overturned, severely injuring two of the three Lorelei children, Patsy and Aucubus.

For this whole chapter of accidents, Bebn was held to be responsible. Forensic science, represented by a shady Dr Obispo, proclaimed the urine to be hers. Her defence, that her aunt's toilet door was immovably jammed at the time, was under question. This painful charade – one of innumerable trials staged at the bar of her mind throughout the years – exercised all Bebn's defence mechanisms, and to some extent exorcised the perennial sense of guilt which hung over her.

The dice were loaded against her. Somehow, she had to argue and charm her way out of an indictment which carried the death sentence as its ultimate penalty. Her Uncle Bysshe, all baggy eye and silly sidewhisker, was in the witness box. Uncle testified that only the week previously had he oiled the bathroom door – when Bebn realised that before her, in what she still regarded, however vaguely, as 'real life', loomed something resembling a big toe.

The only really big big toe but one on Anomaly.

Momentarily, she thought Uncle Bysshe must be responsible. Then, ceasing to wool-gather, she brought her attention to bear on the present. Approaching with caution, she saw that the toe was attached to a foot. There were four other toes. This she saw as she breasted the slope. The foot was in ruinous condition.

She thought of Gulliver. In a rush of horror to the head, she thought this enormous foot might belong to a real person. Closer inspection revealed it to be made of stone.

The foot rose majestically above her. No trade mark of ogre paediatrician could be more awesome.

Bebn stood in a trance as she realised that the foot had a twin, and that both belonged to legs which stretched away into the distance. The knee was remote up the hillside. The more remote for being entombed in shrilling silence.

The legs were cracked and stained by extreme age. Part of the nail of the big toe had fallen away and lay nearby in the dust, monument to the mortality of rock.

She stood there in the museum atmosphere, remembering to breathe. For a moment, the wretched tenement eight stories below the Duct, in the slum district of Mars's Tharsis City, seemed desirable. Even Uncle Bysshe seemed desirable. Compared with this ponderous mystery. Sucking the air of Anomaly into her lungs, she expelled it with a great shout: 'Dud!'

The detached nail in the dust, as if in startlement, leaped up and attached itself to the foot, in the exact position it had once occupied.

At that, she screamed and ran. Although she enjoyed fairy tales, being trapped in one was less to her taste.

As she reached the shore she saw her partner standing by their hut, motionless. 'Oh, Dud . . .' she said, longing to throw herself into his arms.

But Dud appeared strange, a cut-out version of himself. His expression unpleasant, his body somehow brittle, his hair discoloured, the ardriflex watch missing from his wrist. 'Dud?' This time her tone was questioning. She approached more slowly.

'Dud, what are you doing?'

For answer, he raised a hand above his head and began to shrink. When he was two feet high, he burst. A brilliant display of electrons fizzed and scattered in all directions. To vanish immediately.

Without undue sloth, Bebn ran and locked herself in the hut. She was still there two days later, when Dud returned from his walk.

At first, she would not let him in. But he looked okay through the window, normal size, complete with watch. She opened up.

They talked things over. For the sake of peace between them, Bebn agreed that she had been hallucinating in the case of the fake Dud. On the huge figure and leaping toenail she would not give way. Eventually, he agreed to make an expedition to investigate the phenomenon.

Dud was condescending. 'You're on trial, Bebn.'

'Not again,' she said, under her breath.

The way was long. The going was slow. Days and nights were carbon copies. The latest despatch of rations through the hypertube was uninspiring; neither of them cared for dried curried jellyfish. Seeing Bebn was about to relapse into one of her court cases, Dud began to talk.

She hated him for it.

'We're the only life on Anomaly – apart from your flying toenail,' he said. 'You know what that means. We're breathing up all the oxygen and it is not being replaced. We're each producing a kilogram of carbon dioxide every day. That's going to pile up. It'll gradually overheat the planet, if we don't suffocate first.'

'Depends how long we're here . . .'

'Could be centuries . . . Just try to breathe less.'

'At least under the terms of our contract they'll send us a rejuvnatex every forty years.'

'Forty-one. We couldn't negotiate them down to forty, if you remember. What I'm worrying about is to what extent Anomaly belongs in our universe. Think of it this way, Bebn. Ours is an anthropic universe, despite what the Melanesians argue to the contrary. The fundamental dimensionless constants of physics are so trimmed that the universe is optimal for the existence of carbon-based creatures and, even further, for mankind with its scrutinizing intelligence. The universe is adapted to man rather than vice versa. Its size, its age, its constitution all demonstrate a design specification which—'

'Dud, shut up. You can't understand that some people don't want to communicate. If you were one of thirteen kids, instead of an only child, you'd see—'

'Same design specifications may apply to families. You have to have a brood of thirteen in order that one of them may be a selfish, ignorant nutcase of a woman . . .'

She hit him and he continued his main spiel. 'What I'm getting at is this, *darling*. The anthropic universe has been designed, not only for mankind, but specifically for mankind originating on Earth, that mediocre and uncertain planet which, like a Korean VER, only just works. There's not an inhabited world we didn't have to terraform first.'

The walk was exhausting enough without expending extra energy, but she said, 'There you go. Maybe the universe is designed not for mankind but for intelligence. In which case, you and I could wink out of existence at any moment . . .'

'Bebn, baby, throughout thousands of years, von Neumann machines have been scouring the galaxies in search of other intelligent life. They've found nothing. Earth owns the whole damned universe. Thank god, that knowledge has sobered up mankind enough for them to learn civilised behaviour and create SPMs.'

'You aren't suggesting this giant figure is a Self-Procreating Machine?' she said, scornfully.

'Don't be deliberately silly. I'm saying – getting round to saying – that everything in the universe is ours, and knowable. *But* our universe is only one of an infinite number, some of which are detectable by the latest instruments. There's reason to believe that Anomaly exists in a region of space where another universe overlaps with ours.'

'Sure. And that universe has laws which conflict with ours in ways yet to be determined.' She thought, irritably, Why else were we despatched here? Judging by this ball of rock over which we trudge, Universe X lost out, and conditions aren't suitable for the existence of life. I'm not claiming my statue was ever alive. But as to who or what built it . . . I'm scared.

At any moment, I'm going to be judged and found guilty of cowardice. 'Maybe we shouldn't go any further, Dud . . .'

Without another word, they pressed onwards, lips rather tightly closed. Chaos was ever-present. How much human pain was self-imposed!

The sun shone without heat. They were hot enough when they reached the final incline. The upper slopes of the incline were dominated by that inscrutable big toe.

Dud scratched his head. 'It certainly looks like a toe.'

'The mind is one part of the universe humankind has never properly explored,' she said, with contempt. 'Of course it's a fucking toe. What did I tell you?'

Annoyed, he went on ahead of her. The rock squeaked underfoot. The mouth of the hypertube followed him like a dog. Sexist, she thought, savouring the old-fashioned word.

Eventually, she joined Dud where he stood, leaning with one hand against the stone ankle. They talked to almost no effect. There lay the giant figure, asking no questions, posing many. It seemed to her slightly less ruinous than she remembered, almost as if her presence had damaged it in the first place. She started a trial about that. Uncle Bysshe was slouching towards the witness box to be born, but night was coming on. They decided that tomorrow they would trek to the head of the statue. Mists gathered as they made camp. The sun set in the east as usual, without drama.

It took them three days of walking over broken ground to travel from its feet to its head. It was sixty-three miles long. Neither Dud nor Bebn was surprised. Ascending its stony locks, they hauled themselves up until they stood on the figure's brow, looking down the length of the figure. Dud put his ear to the rock, eavesdropping on mineral thoughts.

Bebn ascended an eyebrow, the better to gaze down on the immense face, serene in a sorrow beyond all immobility. It was a neuter face, as impartial as Buddha. Its eyes were half-closed under stone eyelids. Its lips held an expression of sweetness which mingled wisdom with simplicity. She fell in love with it. Here was the ultimate in resignation, in calm beyond life or death. To herself she thought, If I'd ever known someone like this, I'd be a better person.

'Here's alien intelligence,' she said. Releasing the words was like releasing a dove. Suddenly the universes were clear to her thought. Of course, the illusion was only momentary. 'Something the von Neumann machines never discovered . . .'

'It's a trap,' Dud said. 'We'll give the hypertube a good look and then we'll get back to the beach.'

'I could stay here forever.'

'You want to meet the thing that carved it?'

So they commenced the long return. The toenail was still attached to its toe. They noted it as they passed at a steady pace.

At the hut, on the beach, by the sulky sea, there was a difference now. The burden of that immense reclining figure was ever present in their minds. Its existence proved many things they could not comprehend. It followed them into the warrens of sleep. Even its benignity was oppressive. It was with them when they made love. Even its sexlessness was intrusive.

Sometimes they could not sleep. Bebn went out one night and stood looking at the stars. They filled only a quarter of the southern sky. The rest was blackness, pierced dimly by one distant galaxy. She stood on the edge of the universe where the anomaly intruded. Dud came to join her.

'It's as if an immense cover was being drawn over this planet.'

'Another week and it'll cover us completely.'

'You're trying to scare me again, Dud. Can you see that horrible thing watching us from the sea?'

'You're trying to scare me again. We're like children.'

She laughed. They were like children. For all the vast accession of knowledge implanted within their skulls, they were children walking on the fringes of a vast ocean. The thought summoned up references from her mental index. The words of one of the world's most impressive intellects came to her: 'To myself I seem to have been only a boy playing on the sea-shore, and diverting myself in now and then finding a smoother pebble or a prettier shell than ordinary, while the great ocean of truth lay all undiscovered before me . . .' She'd read the words first inscribed in beryllium over the margins of the Crab Nebula.

And it occurred to Bebn to wonder if it was not the unconscious power of this remark which had moved her and Dud to seek a place by the sea, rather than inland, which would have served just as well. Then there came to her the words not only of Isaac Newton but of Wittgenstein. 'We feel that even when all possible scientific questions have been answered, the problems of life remain completely untouched.' Supposing the universe was indeed created for intelligence: then what was intelligence created for?

Could intelligence, the striven-for wisdom, prove ultimately hostile to flesh?

For her, incomprehension was as miraculous as comprehension. 'And I condemn myself for it,' she said aloud to the starry space.

In the following days, Dud remained quiet and almost motionless. He sat with his back to the hut wall, gazing at the liquid sneers upsetting the margins of the sea. Occasionally, he muttered to himself or wrote with a mouse on a pad. He rose before dawn to watch to westward as the clouds parted and the sun rose with an edmod attempt at majesty.

Aloud he said, 'In the Age of Pansophy, not to know something is unpardonable . . .' Bebn felt it was her fault that those were the only words Dud spoke that day.

As if cobbling together a silent litany, Dud ran through the various data which proved the home universe had been tailor-made for an intelligent carbon-based species. Much of it was ancient knowledge. The argument based on stellar nucleosynthesis had been formulated long ago. If the resonances of the three nuclei, helium-4, beryllium-8, and carbon-12, had not been rigged so that the energy-level of the latter was just above that of the other two nuclei, no carbon would have been created within solar reactors.

Further, the next step in the production of heavier elements within a star would be the fusion of carbon-12 with helium-4 to produce oxygen-16. If this fusion occurred, then almost all carbon would be converted into oxygen and thence into heavier elements. The result would be a universe lacking the vital carbon on which life processes were based. But – was not this the hand of a mysterious Being operating in favour of humanity? – the resonance of oxygen-16 was fixed at one per cent less than the combined energy of helium-4 plus carbon-12, so no such synthesis could take place. Conditions for life, in other words, had been fine-tuned before the universe began.

He ran over these proofs and others, the unique properties of carbon, the peculiar propensities of water, and so on. And, most importantly, the necessity for biological processes to be framed within a rigorous time structure: a biotemporality for all life-forms which did not apply to the larger umwelt of the inorganic universe . . . Yes!

She wondered – but not aloud – if he was going crazy. When she approached him, he waved her away.

Bebn walked inland a short distance, seating herself by something almost like a boulder. She looked for a blade of grass to chew, but of course there was nothing. Another ghastly show-trial was beginning. She could not fight it off. The shadowy room, the flight through deserted streets, the arrest after dark, the slam of the cell door . . . In her childhood, she had so often been brought to the bar, falsely arrested for the murder of her mother. Now she stood accused of the murder of Dud. She knew he had simply rushed into the ocean and drowned himself. The jury didn't. Their faces told her that. Again she confronted the death sentence.

She was allowed to speak before the verdict was delivered. Fortunately, she had worked in a courtroom for five years, drawn like a magnet to the processes of justice. There were trials every day on Thousand Blows, the Chinese planet where she had been indentured.

'If I may say one final word in my own defence, I've led a simple and dedicated life, on both Mars and Thousand Blows. I volunteered for Operation Anomaly for the public and scientific good. Any idea of murdering Dud, or my mother, or even my Uncle Bysshe, come to that, never entered my head. Furthermore . . .'

The joy of discovery forced Dud to his feet. He had the answer. He walked rapidly along the shore, fists clenched before him like a boxer.

'Of course – that's it! That's it! Once you reach the solution, it's simple. What's anomalous is *our* universe, with its rigged parameters . . . What's anomalous is us. You have to look at it through the looking-glass. Whereas in other universes, neighbouring universes . . .'

He walked rapidly along on the tepid shore, gesticulating as he went. Joy filled him, a dizzy illumination which left him remote from his baser self. Buoying him was the pure hydrogen of knowledge.

And as he spoke his discovery aloud, he saw something miraculous. His eyes, his mouth, opened wide. A bird was flying overhead.

It was a large bird, the size of a heron, with a grand slow wing motion. It passed nearby, casting its shadow near Dud's feet.

It was a wonder. An absolute wonder. He called to it. His soul went out to it.

The bird made no alteration to its majestic wing-stroke as it followed the arrow of its beak forward. Calling, Dud ran in pursuit, trailing this one token of life.

The great creature journeyed on, unheeding.

He lost it at last, and collapsed on the beach, tracing it with his gaze as the bird became a dot in the hazy sky before being swallowed entirely by distance. After a while, he rose to his feet in more solemn mood and walked back to tell Bebn what he had seen.

As he drew nearer to their hut, his previous excitement returned. Seeing her, he broke into a run.

Bebn was waving her arms. 'Hey,' she called, when he was still some way off. 'You know what? I just saw a bird. A real live bird. It flew right over my head, feathers and all. What does that mean?'

He stopped abruptly. 'You saw it?'

'It was a real bird, the size of a heron, flapping slowly.' Playfully, she imitated the motion. 'Isn't that marvellous! So we aren't entirely alone . . .'

They danced outside the hut, hardly aware why they rejoiced so greatly. 'What a symbol of hope!' he exclaimed. 'A big white bird!'

Bebn looked at him curiously. 'White? No, it was a brown bird. Brown as my arm. Definitely brown.'

'No, no, I saw it clearly. It flew right over my head. An all-white bird. Not a brown feather on it.'

'You need your eyes tested, you idiot! Brown, brown, brown!'

'You're colour blind, you ninny. Whiter than driven snow.'

'Brown, distinctly brown, you fool!' And they began to quarrel furiously over the colour of the bird. All that day they shouted at each other or sulked and refused to speak. At night, they slept apart in opposite corners of the hut. She dreamed of snakes. He woke to the taste of geraniums in his mouth.

Morning came by slow degrees. The sun heaved itself out of the crimsons of the west and Bebn rose feeling penitent.

Kissing Dud, she said, 'I'm sorry I was so angry yesterday. It was the excitement. Obviously, we saw two different birds.'

Dud held her hand, looking down at the horseshoe still inscribed in her palm. Pulling her close, he began to whisper rapidly into her ear. 'I'm sorry too, Bebn. I have everything clear in my head now. We both saw the same bird, but interpreted it in different ways, according to taste. In any case, it wasn't a real bird.'

She pulled away, half-laughing, half-annoyed. 'Why are you whispering?'

'Because Something can hear us. That artificial moon in the geostationary orbit overhead picks up our signals. And the bird – the Something sent it, projected it. The Something isn't used to biological carbon-based life. It sent the bird as a – well, a reward, knowing we'd like company.'

The look she gave him held amusement and alarm. 'Listen, Dud, I don't want to be stuck on this planet with a loony. The bird was a projection, you say? When is a bird not a bird?'

'Exactly. When it's a projection. Answer to all our riddles. The way I once thought I saw you and you once thought you saw me. Something was practising its art . . .'

She regarded the idea as wildly unlikely. But then – her own life always seemed to her wildly unlikely. How long could the show go on without everyone – everyone on all the planets – suddenly bursting into laughter at the absurdity of it? Dud's guess would at least explain the giant calm figure inland. The Something had been, in Dud's words, practising its art. In a new medium. It was mad enough to be almost convincing.

Bebn clutched her head and laughed wildly.

'Why should this . . . this hypothetical Something of yours reward us?'

So he told her. Because Dud had worked out the problem it had set them. Something was rewarding him for the correct answer. When they were deposited on Anomaly, they had crossed into an outcrop of a universe where creation had worked out differently. Physical laws were not the same in the two universes.

'Stellar nucleosynthesis has to work only slightly differently here in this universe for carbon to be so passing rare that biological beings have never developed. What we call "the passage of time" is merely our biological experience of temporality – the trail we living things tread from birth to death. It is not the whole of "Time" – that idea's simply an egocentric way of looking at things. Time isn't homogeneous, as people prefer to believe; in our home universe, time's a layer cake composed of various temporalities. In a non-biological universe, like this one, there are only two temporalities, both distant from human experience, the atemporal and the eotemporal. They comprise between them all the time there is in – in Something's universe.'

She stood up and stared out to sea. 'Atemporal I understand. It implies the basic universe, with particles of zero restmass, photons travelling at the speed of light forever. Nothing corresponding to event. But *eotemporal*?'

'Eotemporality's the level of temporality where beginnings and endings – in contrast to our biotemporality – are confused. Only succession has meaning. Supposing I mark a trail through the forest for you. The blazes on the trees tell you the way. They don't tell you the direction. The laws of microphysics are eotemporal – reversible in time . . .'

Dud had spoken crisply when dealing with known science. Now his talk became slower, less confident. He walked with her over the barren slopes, gesticulating to assist his words.

'I'm just trying to . . . I mean, in such a universe, totally lacking any organic component, it's hard to see how intelligence would develop. But if intelligence is the . . . well, the desired end-product, then presumably it would develop in any universe. Somehow. Out of a cloud of interstellar gas, let's say. And eotemporal in its nature.'

'That would be quite possible,' she said. 'What it lacked in density it could make up in immensity. Such a disembodied intelligence might be enormous, spanning light years. And able to think at the speed of light.'

They both fell silent, digesting the idea. Intelligence would fit the universe it poured into, as liquid fits its container – whatever the composition of the jug. As my thoughts fit my brain, she told herself, not without distaste.

'If such a Something existed,' she went on, 'it might be in a better position than planet-bound biological beings to detect the presence of intelligent life in neighbouring universes. Is that what you're getting at?'

He nodded his head. 'There are probably countless universes, each differing slightly in composition. And our gaseous Something, forever seeking contact . . .' He had a terrifying vision – where did it come from? – it hit him – of an entity like a dust storm, raging with loneliness, eternal, ceaseless, bursting from uninhabited universe to uninhabited universe, like a demented apparition rushing from tomb to tomb. Always greeted with the terrible pressures of isolation. Chambered within infinity. With no knowledge of time. But tormented with a sense of endless vain process.

Bebn clutched Dud's arm. They stared at each other, eyes wide, mouths ajar.

The vision in all its haunting power had been projected into both their minds simultaneously. It was in contact with them.

He spoke huskily from his dry mouth. 'Poor thing . . .'

'Oh god, I'm frightened,' she said. They clung together, body against body, limb next to limb – the biological way of consolation.

'It needed to get in touch,' Dud said.

'It is in touch.'

'Because it created Anomaly and its sun. This isn't a real planet, merely the Something's idea of a planet. Put all the signifiers together, the wavelets lapping back into the ocean, the strange sunrises, the chunk of the statue's toe snapping back into place . . .'

She was still trembling, but said, indistinctly, 'Oh, yes, I've got it now. The Something, being eotemporal, has no knowledge of biological time. So our kind of temporality is alien to it, and it's got it backwards? Right?'

'Yes. Time's running backwards here.' He laughed. 'Or was. Until I worked out the real situation, so proving we have intelligence. The bird – let's not argue about its colour – was not merely a reward for passing the test. It's also a sign that Something too has learned a new fact. He's now corrected the time flow. That's why our bird flew forwards instead of arse-first.' He laughed again, delighted.

Bebn's face showed her fear. 'It learns so quickly, alters physical laws so easily? What are we up against? We're utterly in its power.'

He sat down on the spongey rock, pulling her down beside him.

'I think it'll be okay. Let's sit and see what the sun does. While we've been talking, I believe it's stopped in its tracks and is now heading towards the west. It all means that the Something is attempting to enter into our temporality, our understanding.'

She buried her face in his chest. 'It's going to put us on trial. I can just imagine it. We're going to have to go in the witness box for all humanity . . .'

'Oh no, not to my way of thinking.' He smoothed her hair gently. 'I believe this amazing thing is looking for company . . . well – for love, if you'll excuse the expression. At last it's found it is not entirely alone. How'd you feel in such circumstances? Let's stay here and it will give us another sign.'

She laughed nervously. 'More biotemporality?'

'Of course.'

A breeze like a sigh went by them and ruffled the placid waters of the sea. Of a sudden, the rock for miles around was covered waist-high with gorgeous blossom, velvety and slightly ridiculous. A good first try.

In the Arena

The reek and noise at the back of the circus were familiar to Javlin Bartramm. He felt the hard network of nerves in his solar plexus tighten.

There were crowds of the reduls here, jostling and staring to see the day's entry arrive. You didn't have to pay to stand and rubberneck in the street; this lot probably couldn't afford seats for the arena. Javlin looked away from them in scorn. All the same, he felt some gratification when they sent up a cheeping cheer at the sight of him. They loved a human victim.

His keeper undid the cart door and led him out, still chained. They went through the entrance, from blinding sunshine to dark, into the damp unsavoury warren below the main stadium. Several reduls were moving about here, officials mainly. One or two called good luck to him; one chirped, 'The crowd's in a good mood today, vertebrate.' Javlin showed no response.

His trainer, Ik So Baar, came up, a flamboyant redul towering above Javlin. He wore an array of spare gloves strapped across his orange belly. The white tiara that fitted around his antennae appeared only on sports day.

'Greetings, Javlin. You look in the rudest of health. I'm glad you are not fighting me.'

'Greetings, Ik So.' He slipped the lip-whistle into his mouth so that he could answer in a fair approximation of the redul language. 'Is my opponent ready to be slain? Remember I go free if I win this bout – it will be my twelfth victory in succession.'

'There's been a change in the program, Javlin. Your Sirian opponent escaped in the night and had to be killed. You are entered in a double double.'

Javlin wrenched at his chains so hard that the keeper was swung off balance.

'Ik So! You betray me! How much cajsh have I won for you? I will not fight a double double.'

There was no change of expression on the insect mask.

'Then you will die, my pet vertebrate. The new arrangement is not my idea. You know by now that I get more cajsh for having you in a solo. Double double it has to be. These are my orders. Keeper, Cell one-o-seven with him!'

Fighting against his keeper's pull, Javlin cried, 'I've got some rights, Ik So. I demand to see the arena promoter.'

'Pipe down, you stupid vertebrate! You have to do what you're ordered. I told you it wasn't my fault.'

'Well, for God's sake, who am I fighting with?'

'You will be shackled to a fellow from the farms. He's had one or two preliminary bouts; they say he's good.'

'From the farms . . .' Javlin broke into the filthiest redulian oaths he knew. Ik So came back toward him and slipped one of the metal gloves onto his forepincers; it gave him a cruel tearing weapon with a multitude of barbs. He held it up to Javlin's face.

'Don't use that language to me, my mammalian friend. Humans from the farms or from space, what's the difference? This young fellow will fight well enough if you muck in with him. And you'd better muck in. You're billed to battle against a couple of yillibeeth.'

Before Javlin could answer, the tall figure turned and strode down the corridor, moving twice as fast as a man could walk.

Javlin let himself be led to Cell 107. The warder, a worker-redul with a grey belly, unlocked his chains and pushed him in, barring the door behind him. The cell smelled of alien species and apprehensions.

Javlin went and sat down on the bench. He needed to think.

He knew himself for a simple man – and knew that that knowledge meant the simplicity was relative. But his five years of captivity here under the reduls had not been all wasted. Ik So had trained him well in the arts of survival; and when you came down to brass tacks, there was no more proper pleasure in the universe than surviving. It was uncomplicated. It carried no responsibilities to anyone but yourself.

That was what he hated about the double double events, which till now he had always been lucky enough to avoid. They carried responsibility to your fellow fighter.

From the beginning he had been well equipped to survive the gladiatorial routine. When his scoutship, the *Plunderhorse*, had been captured by redul forces five years ago, Javlin Bartramm was duelling master and judo expert, as well as Top Armament Sergeant. The army ships had a long tradition, going back some six centuries, of sport aboard; it provided the ideal mixture of time-passer and needed exercise. Of all the members of the *Plunderhorse*'s crew who had been taken captive, Javlin was – as far as he knew – the only survivor after five years of the insect race's rough games.

Luck had played its part in his survival. He had liked Ik So Baar. Liking was a strange thing to feel for a nine-foot armoured grasshopper with forearms like a lobster and a walk like a tyrannosaurus' run, but a sympathy existed between them – and would continue to exist until he was killed in the ring, Javlin thought. With his bottom on the cold bench, he knew that Ik So would not betray him into a double double. The redul had had to obey the promoter's orders. Ik So needed his twelfth victory, so that he could free Javlin to help him train the other species down at the gladiatorial farm. Both of them knew that would be an effective partnership.

So. Now was the time for luck to be with Javlin again.

He sank onto his knees and looked down at the stone, brought his forehead down onto it, gazed down into the earth, into the cold ground, the warm rocks, the molten core, trying to visualise each, to draw from them attributes that would help him: cold for his brain, warm for his temper, molten for his energies.

Strengthened by prayer, he stood up. The redul workers had yet to bring him his armour and the partner he was to fight with. He had long since learned the ability to wait without resenting waiting. With professional care, he exercised himself slowly, checking the proper function of each muscle. As he did so, he heard the crowds cheer in the arena. He turned to peer out of the cell's further door, an affair of tightly set bars that allowed a narrow view of the combat area and the stands beyond.

There was a centaur out there in the sunlight, fighting an Aldebaran bat-leopard. The centaur wore no armour but an iron cuirass; he had no weapons but his hooves and his hands. The bat-leopard, though its wings were clipped to prevent it flying out of the stadium, had dangerous claws and a great turn of speed. Only because its tongue had been cut out, ruining its echo-location system, was the contest anything like fair. The concept of fairness was lost upon the reduls, though; they preferred blood to justice.

Javlin saw the kill. The centaur, a gallant creature with a human-like head and an immense gold mane that began from his eyebrows, was plainly tiring. He eluded the bat-leopard as it swooped down on him, wheeling quickly around on his hind legs and trampling on its wing. But the bat-leopard turned and raked the other's legs with a slash of claws. The centaur toppled hamstrung to the ground. As he fell, he lashed out savagely with his forelegs, but the bat-leopard nipped in and tore his throat from side to side above the cuirass. It then dragged itself away under its mottled wings, like a lame prima donna dressed in a leather cape.

The centaur struggled and lay still, as if the weight of whistling cheers that rose from the audience bore him down. Through the narrow bars, Javlin saw the throat bleed and the lungs heave as the defeated one sprawled in the dust.

'What do you dream of, dying there in the sun?' Javlin asked.

He turned away from the sight and the question. He sat quietly down on the bench and folded his arms.

When the din outside told him that the next bout had begun, the passage door opened and a young human was pushed in. Javlin did not need telling that this was to be his partner in the double double against the yillibeeth.

It was a girl.

'You're Javlin?' she said. 'I know of you. My name's Awn.'

He kept himself under control, his brows drawn together as he stared at her.

'You know what you're here for?'

'This will be my first public fight,' she said.

Her hair was clipped short as a man's. Her skin was tanned and harsh, her left arm bore a gruesome scar. She held herself lithely on her feet. Though her body looked lean and hard, even the thick one-piece gown she wore to thigh length did not conceal the feminine curves of her body. She was not pretty, but Javlin had to admire the set of her mouth and her cool grey gaze.

'I've had some stinking news this morning, but Ik So Baar never broke it to me that I was to be saddled with a woman,' he said.

'Ik probably didn't know – that I'm a woman, I mean. The reduls are either neuter or hermaphrodite, unless they happen to be a rare queen. Didn't you know that? They can't tell the difference between human male and female.'

He spat. 'You can't tell me anything about reduls.'

She spat. 'If you knew, why blame me? You don't think I like being here? You don't think I asked to join the great Javlin?'

Without answering he bent and began to massage the muscles of his calf. Since he occupied the middle of the bench, the girl remained standing. She watched him steadily. When he looked up again, she asked, 'What or who are we fighting?'

No surprise was left in him. 'They didn't tell you?'

'I've only just been pushed into this double double, as I imagine you have. I asked you, what are we fighting?'

'Just a couple of yillibeeth.'

He injected unconcern into his voice to make the shock of what he said the greater. He massaged the muscles of the other calf. An aphrohale would have come in very welcome now. These crazy insects had no equivalent of the Terrestrial prisoner-ate-a-hearty-breakfast routine. When he glanced up under his eyebrows, the girl stood motionless, but her face had gone pale.

'Know what the yillibeeth are, little girl?'

She didn't answer, so he went on, 'The reduls resemble some Terrestrial insects. They go through several stages of development, you know; reduls are just the final adult stage. Their larval stage is rather like the larval stage of the dragonfly. It's a greedy, omnivorous beast. It's aquatic and it's big. It's armoured. It's called a yillibeeth. That's what we are going to be tied together to fight, a couple of big hungry yillibeeth. Are you feeling like dying this morning, Awn?'

Instead of answering, she turned her head away and brought a hand up to her mouth.

'Oh, no! No crying in here, for Earth's sake!' he said. He got up, yelled through the passage door, 'Ik So, Ik So, you traitor, get this bloody woman out of here!' . . . recalled himself, jammed the lip-whistle into his mouth and was about to call again when Awn caught him a backhanded blow across the face.

She faced him like a tiger.

'You creature, you cowardly apology of a man! Do you think I weep for fear? I don't weep. I've lived nineteen years on this damned planet in their damned farms. Would I still be here if I wept? No – but I mourn that you are already defeated, you, the great Javlin!'

He frowned into her blazing face.

'You don't seriously think you make me a good enough match for us to go out there and kill a couple of yillibeeth?'

'Damn your conceit. I'm prepared to try.'

'Fagh!' He thrust the lip-whistle into his mouth, and turned back to the door. She laughed at him bitterly, jeeringly.

'You're a lackey to these insects, aren't you, Javlin? If you could see what a fool you look with that phony beak of yours stuck on your mouth.'

He let the instrument drop to the end of its chain. Grasping the bars, he leaned forward against them and looked over his shoulder.

'I was trying to get this contest called off.'

'Don't tell me you haven't already tried. I have.'

To that he had no answer. He went back and sat on the bench. She returned to her corner. They both folded their arms and stared at each other.

'Why don't you look out into the arena instead of glaring at me? You might pick up a few tips.' When she did not answer, he said, 'I'll tell you what you'll see. You can see the rows of spectators and a box where some sort of bigwig sits. I don't know who the bigwig is. It's never a queen – as far as I can make out, the queens spend their lives underground, turning out eggs at the rate of fifty a second. Not the sort of life Earth royalty would have enjoyed in the old days. Under the bigwig's box there is a red banner with their insect hieroglyphs on. I asked Ik So once what the hieroglyphs said. He told me they meant – well, in a rough translation – *The Greatest Show on Earth*. It's funny, isn't it?'

'You must admit we do make a show.'

'No, you miss the point. You see, that used to be the legend of circuses in the old days. But they've adopted it for their own use since they invaded Earth. They're boasting of their conquest.'

'And that's funny?'

'In a sort of way. Don't you feel ashamed that this planet which saw the birth of the human race should be overrun by insects?'

'No. The reduls were here before me. I was just born here. Weren't you?'

'No, I wasn't. I was born on Washington IV. It's a lovely planet. There are hundreds of planets out there as fine and varied as Earth once was – but it kind of rankles to think that this insect brood rules Earth.'

'If you feel so upset about it, why don't you do something?'

He knotted his fists together. You should start explaining history and economics just before you ran out to be chopped to bits by a big rampant thing with circular saws for hands?

'It would cost mankind too much to reconquer this planet. Too difficult. Too many deaths just for sentiment. And think of all those queens squirting eggs at a rate of knots; humans don't breed that fast. Humanity has learned to face facts.' She laughed without humour.

'That's good. Why don't you learn to face the fact of me?'

Javlin had nothing to say to that; she would not understand that directly he saw her he knew his hope of keeping his life had died. She was just a liability. Soon he would be dying, panting his juices out into the dust like that game young centaur . . . only it wouldn't be dust.

'We fight in two feet of water,' he said. 'You know that? The yillibeeth like it. It slows our speed a bit. We might drown instead of having our heads bitten off.'

'I can hear someone coming down the corridor. It may be our armour,' she said coolly.

'Did you hear what I said?'

'You can't wait to die, Javlin, can you?'

*

The bars fell away on the outside of the door, and it opened. The keeper stood there. Ik So Baar had not appeared as he usually did. The creature flung in their armour and weapons and retreated, barring the door again behind him. It never ceased to astonish Javlin that those great dumb brutes of workers had intelligence.

He stooped to pick up his uniform. The girl's looked so light and small. He lifted it, looking from it to her.

'Thank you,' she said.

'It looks so small and new.'

'I shouldn't want anything heavier.'

'You've fought in it?'

'Twice.' There was no need to ask whether she had won.

'We'd better get the stuff strapped on, then. We shall know when they are getting ready for us; you'll hear the arena being filled with water. They're probably saving us for the main events just before noon.'

'I didn't know about the two feet of water.'

'Scare you?'

'No. I'm a good swimmer. Swam for fish in the river on the slave farm.'

'You caught fish with your bare hands?'

'No, you dive down and stab them with a sharp rock. It takes practice.'

It was a remembered pleasure. She'd actually swum in one of Earth's rivers. He caught himself smiling back into her face.

'Ik So's place is in the desert,' he said, making his voice cold. 'Anyhow, you won't be able to swim in the arena. Two feet of muddy stinking water helps nobody. And you'll be chained onto me with a four-foot length of chain.'

'Let's get our armour on, then you'd better tell me all you know. Perhaps we can work out a plan of campaign.'

As he picked up the combined breastplate and shoulder guard, Awn untied her belt and lifted her dress over her head. Underneath she wore only a ragged pair of white briefs. She commenced to take those off.

Javlin stared at her with surprise – and pleasure. It had been years since he had been within hailing distance of a woman. This one – yes, this one was a beauty.

'What are you doing that for?' he asked. He hardly recognised his own voice.

'The less we have on the better in that water. Aren't you going to take your clothes off?'

He shook his head. Embarrassed, he fumbled on the rest of his kit. At least she wouldn't look so startling with her breastplate and skirt armour on. He checked his long and shortswords, clipping the one into the left belt clip, the other into the right. They were good swords, made by redul armourers to Terrestrial specifications. When he turned back to Awn, she was fully accoutred.

Nodding in approval, he offered her a seat on the bench beside him. They clattered against each other and smiled.

Another bout had ended in the arena. The cheers and chirrups drifted through the bars to them.

'I'm sorry you're involved in this,' he said with care.

'I was lucky to be involved in it with you.' Her voice was not entirely steady, but she controlled it in a minute. 'Can't I hear water?'

He had already heard it. An unnatural silence radiated from the great inhuman crowd in the circus as they watched the stuff pour in. It would have great emotional significance for them, no doubt, since they had all lived in water for some years in their previous life stage.

'They have wide-bore hoses,' he said. His own voice had an irritating tremor. 'The arena fills quite rapidly.'

'Let's formulate some sort of plan of attack then. These things, these yillibeeth must have some weaknesses.'

'And some strengths! That's what you have to watch for.'

'I don't see that. You attack their weak points.'

'We shall be too busy looking out for their strong ones. They have long segmented grey bodies – about twenty segments, I think. Each segment is of chitin or something tough. Each segment bears two legs equipped with razor combs. At tail end and top end they have legs that work like sort of buzz saws, cut through anything they touch. And there are their jaws, of course.'

The keeper was back. His antennae flopped through the grating and then he unbolted the door and came in. He bore a length of chain as long as the cell was wide. Javlin and Awn did not resist as he locked them together, fitting the bracelets onto Javlin's right arm and Awn's left.

'So.' She stared at the chain. 'The yillibeeth don't sound to have many weak points. They could cut through our swords with their buzz saws?'

'Correct.'

'Then they could cut through this chain. Get it severed near one of our wrists, and the other has a better long-distance weapon than a sword. A blow over the head with the end of the chain won't improve their speed. How fast are they?'

'The buzz saw takes up most of their speed. They're nothing like as fast as the reduls. No, you could say they were pretty sluggish in movement. And the fact that the two of them will also be chained together should help us.'

'Where are they chained?'

'By the middle legs.'

'That gives them a smaller arc of destruction than if they were chained by back or front legs. We are going to slay these beasts yet, Javlin! What a murderous genus it must be to put its offspring in the arena for the public sport.'

He laughed.

'Would you feel sentimental about your offspring if you had a million babies?'

'I'll tell you that when I've had the first of them. I mean, if I have the first of them.'

He put his hand over hers.

'No if. We'll kill the bloody larvae, OK.'

'Get the chain severed, then one of us with the longest bit of chain goes in for the nearest head, the other fends off the other brute. Right?'

'Right.'

There was a worker redul at the outer door now, the door that led to the arena. He flung it open and stood there with a flaming torch, ready to drive them out if they did not emerge.

'We've – come to it then,' she said. Suddenly she clung to him.

'Let's take it at a run,' he said.

Together, balancing the chain between them, they ran toward the arena. The two yillibeeth were coming out from the far side, wallowing and splashing. The crowd stretched up toward the blue sky of Earth, whistling their heads off. They didn't know what a man and a woman could do in combination. Now they were going to learn.

Working in the Spaceship Yards

My first job of work as a young man was in the spaceship yards, where I felt my talents and expertise could be put to the greatest benefit of society. I worked as a FTL-fitter's mate's assistant. The FTL-fitter's mate was a woman called Nellie. As more and more women came to be employed in the yards, among the men and the androids and the robots, the men became increasingly circumspect in their behaviour. Their oaths were more guarded, their gestures less uncouth, and their care for their appearance less negligent. This I found strange, since the women showed clearly that they cared nothing for oaths, gestures, or appearances.

From wastebaskets round the site, I collected many suicide notes. Most of them had never reached their recipients and were mere drafts of suicide notes:

> *My darling – When you receive this, I shall no longer be in a position to ever trouble you again.*
> *By the time you receive this letter, I shall never be able.*
> *By the time you receive this, I shall be no more.*
> *My darling – Never again will we be able to break each other's hearts.*
> *You have been more than life to me.*
> *My love – I have been so wrong.*

It is very good of people to take such care in their compositions even in extremis. Education has had its effect. At my school, we learnt only how to write business letters. With reference to your last shipment of Martian pig iron/iron pigs. Since life is such a tragic business, why are we not educated how to write decent suicide notes?

In this age of progress, where everything is progressive and technological and new, the only bit of our Self we have left to ourselves is our Human Condition – which of course remains miserable, despite three protein-full meals a day. Protein does not help the Dark Night of the Soul. Androids, which look so like us (we have the new black androids working in the spaceship yards now) do not have a soul, and many of them are very distressed at lacking the long slow toothache of the Human Condition. Some of them have left their employment, and stand on street corners wearing dark glasses, begging for alms with pathetic messages round their shoulders. Orphan of Technology. Left Factry Too Yung. Have Pity on My Poor Metal Frame. And an especially heart-wrenching one I saw in the Queens district. Obsolescence Is the Poor Man's Death. They have their traumas; just to be deprived of the Human Condition must be traumatic.

Most androids hate the android-beggars. They tour the streets after work, beating up any beggars they find, kicking their tin mugs into the gutter. Faceless androids are scaring. They look like men in iron masks. You can never escape role-playing.

We were building Q-line ships when I was in the shipyard. They were the experimental ones. The Q1, the Q2, the Q3, had each been completed, had been towed out into orbit beyond Mars, and triggered off towards Alpha Centauri. Nothing was ever heard of them again. Perhaps they are making a tour of the entire universe, and will return to the solar system when the sun is ten kilometres deep in permafrost. Anyhow, I shan't live to see the day.

It was no fun building those ships. They had no luxury, no living quarters, no furnishings, no galleys, no miles and miles of carpeting and all the other paraphernalia of a proper spaceship. There was very little we could take as supplementary income. The computers that crewed them lived very austere lives.

'The sun will be ten kilometres deep in permafrost by the time you get back to the solar system!' I told BALL, the computer on the Q3, as we walled him in. 'What will you do then?'

'I shall measure the permafrost.'

I've noticed that about the truth. You don't expect it, so it often sounds like a joke. Computers and robots sound funny quite often because they have no roles to play. They just tell the truth. I asked this BALL, 'Who will you be measuring this permafrost for?'

'I shall be measuring it for its intrinsic interest.'

'Even if there are no human beings around to be interested?'

'You misunderstand the meaning of intrinsic.'

Each of these Q ships cost more than the entire annual national income of a state like Great Britain. Zip, out into the universe they went. Never seen again! My handiwork. All those miles of beautiful seamless welding. My life's work.

I say computers tell the truth. It is only the truth as they see it. Things go on that none of us see. Should we include them in our personal truth or not?

My mother was a good old sport. Before I reached the age of ten and was given my extra-familial posting, she and I had a lot of fun. Hers was a heart of gold – more, of uranium. She had an old deaf friend called Mrs Patt used to come and visit mother once a week and sit in the big armchair while mother yelled questions and remarks at her.

Now I realise why I could not bear Mrs Patt – because everything I said sounded so trivial and stupid when repeated at the top of my voice.

'It's nice about the extra moonlight law, isn't it?'

'You what you say?'

'I said aren't you pleased about the extra moonlight law?'

'Pleased what?'

'Aren't you pleased about the extra moonlight law? We could do with another moon.'

'I can't hear what you say.'

'I say isn't it fun about the extra moonlight law?'

'What lawn is that?'

'The extra moonlight law. Law! Isn't it fun about the extra moonlight law?'

I used to hide behind the armchair before Mrs Patt came in. When she and mother started shouting, I would rise over the back of the chair so that Mrs Patt could not see me, sticking my thumbs in my ears and my little fingers up my nostrils so that my nose was wrinkled and distorted, waving my other fingers about while shooting my brows up and down, flobbing my tongue, and blinking my eyes furiously, in order to make mother laugh. She had to pretend she could not see me.

Occasionally, she would have to pretend to blow her nose, in order to enjoy a quick chuckle.

We had a big bad black cat. Sometimes I would appear round the chair with the tom dish on my head, mewing and wagging my ears.

The question I now ask myself, having reached more sober years – Mrs Patt visited the euthanasia clinic years ago – is whether I should or should not be included among Mrs Patt's roll call of truths. Since I was not among her observable phenomena, then I could not be part of her revealed Truth. For Mrs Patt, I did not exist in my post-armchair manifestation; therefore my effect upon her Self was totally negligible; therefore I could form no portion of her Truth, as she saw it.

Whether what I was doing was well- or ill-intentioned towards her likewise did not matter, since it did not impinge on her consciousness. The only effect of my performance on her was that she came to consider my mother as someone unusually prone to colds, necessitating frequent nose-blowing.

This suggests that there are two sorts of truth: one's personal truth, and what, for fear of using an even more idiotic term, I will call a Universal Truth. In this last category clearly belong events that go on even if nobody is observing them, like my fingers up my nose, the flights of the $Q1$, $Q2$, and $Q3$, and God.

All this I once tried to explain to my android friend, Jackson. I tried to tell him that he could only perceive Universal Truth, and had no cognisance of Personal Truth.

'Universal Truth is the greater, so I am greater than you, who perceive only Personal Truth,' he said.

'Not at all! I obviously perceive all of Personal Truth, since that's what it means, and also quite a bit of Universal Truth. So I get a much better idea of Total Truth than you.'

'Now you are inventing a third sort of truth, in order to win the argument. Just because you have Human Condition, you have to keep proving you are better than me.'

I switched him off. I am better than Jackson. I can switch him off.

Next day, going back on shift, I switched him on again.

'There are all sorts of horrible things signalling behind your metaphorical armchair that you aren't aware of,' he said immediately.

'At least human beings write suicide notes,' I said. It is a minor art that has never received full recognition. A very intimate art. You can't write a suicide note to someone you do not know.

Dear President – My name may not be familiar to you but I voted for you in the last election and, when you receive this, I shall no longer be able to trouble you ever again.

I shall no longer ever be able to vote for you again. Not be able to support you at the next election.

Dear President – This will come as something of a shock, particularly since you don't know me, but.

Dear Sir – You have been more than a president to me.

The hours in the spaceship yards were long, particularly for us young lads. We worked from ten till twelve and again from two till four. The robots worked from ten till four. The androids worked from ten till twelve and from two till four when I began at the yards as a FTL-fitter's mate's assistant, and they had no breaks for canteen, whereas men and women got fifteen minutes off in every hour for coffee and drugs. After I had been in the yards for some ten months, legislation was passed allowing androids five minutes off in every hour for coffee (they don't take drugs). The men went on strike against this legislation, but it all simmered down by Christmas, after a pay rise. The Q4 was delayed another sixteen weeks, but what is sixteen weeks when you are going to go round the universe?

The women were very emotional. Many of them fell in love with androids. The men were very bitter about this. My first love, Nellie, the FTL-fitter's mate, left me for an android electrician. She said he was more respectful.

In the canteen, we men used to talk about sex and philosophy and who was winning the latest Out-Thinking Contest. The women used to exchange recipes. I often feel women do not have quite such a large share of the Human Condition as we do.

When we first went to bed together Nellie said, 'You're a bit nervous, aren't you?'

Well, I was, but I said, 'No, I'm not nervous, it's just this question of role-playing. I haven't entirely devised one to cover this particular situation.'

'Well, buck up, then, or the whistle will be going. You can be the Great Lover or something, can't you?'

'Do I look like the Great Lover?' I asked in exasperation.

'I've seen smaller,' she said, and she smiled. After that, we always got on well together, and then she had to leave me for that android electrician.

For a few days, I was terribly miserable. I thought of writing her a suicide note but I didn't know how to word it.

> *Dear Nellie – I know you are too hard-hearted to care a hoot about this, but. I know you don't care a hoot but. I know you don't give a hoot. Give a rap. Are indifferent to. Are indifferent to what happens to me, but.*
>
> *As you lie there in the synthetic arms of your lover, it may interest you to know I am about to.*

But I was not really about to, for I struck up a close friendship with Nancy, and she enjoyed my Great Lover role. She was very good with an I-Know-We're-Really-Both-Too-Sensible-For-This role. After a time, I got a transfer so that I could work with her on the starboard condentister. She used to tell me recipes for exotic dishes. Sometimes, it was quite a relief to get back to my mates in the canteen.

At last the great day came when the Q4 was finished. The President came down and addressed us, and inspected the two-mile-high needle of shining steel. He told us it had cost more than all South America was worth, and would open up a New Era in the History of Mankind. Or perhaps he said New Error. Anyhow, the Q4 was going to put us in touch with some other civilisation, many light years away. It was imperative for our survival that we get in rapport with them before our enemies did.

'Why don't we just get in rapport with our enemies?' Nancy asked me sourly. She has no sense of occasion.

As we all came away from the ceremony, I had a nasty surprise. I saw Nellie with her arm round that android electrician, and he was limping. An android, limping! There's role-playing for you. Byronic androids! If we aren't careful, they will be taking over the Human Condition just as they are taking our women. The future is black and the bins of our destiny are filling with suicide notes.

I felt really sick. Nancy stared at me as if she could see someone over my shoulder putting his thumbs in his ears and his little fingers up his nose and all that. Of course, when I looked round, nobody was there.

'Let's go and play Great Lovers while there's still time,' I said.

As for Our Fatal Continuity . . .

Dayling, Orton Gausset (1972–1999).

In a brief transmission, scant justice can be done to this great and still controversial artist. The accompanying holograms will convey Dayling's outstanding qualities better than words.

Illusion and dissolution mark the stamp of his mind. During the last period of his life, Dayling believed himself to be alone in the world, and to have been appointed custodian of the city of Singapore, which he spoke of as one of the world's deserted cities on which the tide was fast encroaching.

His mother was the noted biophysicist, Mary May Dayling. His father was killed in a traffic accident on the day of his birth. Perhaps it was this ill chance, coupled with a peculiar cast of mind, that caused him to become obsessed with the last words of dying men. He came to them, as he came to art and love, precociously early; last words form the titles of all his creations. Once he had access to his mother's art-computer terminal at the age of five, creation seems to have been a continuouus process with him, at least until the lost years of his middle period.

His first great work,
The Sun, My Dear, the Sun is God,
dates from 1979. Its contrapuntal sets of interwoven structures culminating in an attenuated parallelism is a gesture toward representation which seldom recurs – Dayling's is the art of a world beyond mundane perception. Although the work is not well-integrated, its daring and light

remain attractive and, in its overall spiral movement, it stands as a fitting statement on the painter Turner, whose last words contribute the title and whose life inspired the young Dayling.

More Light, More Light

Goethe's last words, and related schematically to the item above. More ambitious, less intense, already showing a fine awareness for the new language Dayling was creating. It points its way gropingly toward

Give Dayrolles a Chair

indisputably an early masterpiece, with its mobile nonrepeating series of peripheral lights and the first use of that central darkness – speaking of radiance as well as gloom – which later becomes a feature of Dayling's work. No reference here to the external world, unless it be to the basic formal structures of physical phenomena themselves. A certain delicacy about the entire composition reminds us that the words were spoken by the dying Lord Chesterfield.

I Have Been a Most Unconscionable Time A-Dying

This work is also known as *Open the Curtains that I May Once More See Daylight*, apparently through some confusion over what the last words of King Charles II actually were. The former title is certainly to be preferred, since this work marks the end of the first stage of Dayling's career; like the three works preceding, it has as its theme light, and the rioting radials suggest a variety of diffusions of light. From now on, the works become more vigorous and coarser, as Dayling masters his life and his medium, beginning with the almost Rabelaisian account of

I Could Do with One of Bellamy's Meat Pies

said to be the last words of one of England's great prime ministers, William Pitt the Younger. Dayling's amazing tumescent forms enter for the first time, as yet not dominant but certainly in the ascendant. This is a large work, almost the size of the Houses of Parliament, with which it has sometimes jocularly been compared, and for durability Dayling and the computer used daylite, a plastic of their own devising with a semifluid core. With daylite, the famous 'molten look' was developed, so that in some of the later works in this series, such as the

I Wish the Whole Human Race Had One Neck and I Had My Hands Around It, based on the words of the mass-murderer Carl Panzram, the *If This is Life, Roll on Germ Warfare*, of the Scottish Patriot McGuffie, and the *Of Course the Confounded Goat Was an Exaggeration* of the painter Holman Hunt, one cannot tell whether the forms emerge from obscurity and formlessness or are being pressed back into obscurity and formlessness. Perhaps it is because of this sense of what one critic, Andre Prederast, has called 'cellular oppression' that Dayling has been spoken of as a latter-day Rodin; but Rodin dominated his sculpture; the tentative statement of *As to Which End of the Bed is Which . . .* would be beyond him. Dayling's morbid preoccupation with death and his sense of humour combined, are complementary, and force him to work always on the verge of disintegration, at the point at which being becomes nonbeing. Although his approach could scarcely be called scientific, the extent to which he was conversant with current scientific theory is generally apparent, not least in *As to Which End of the Bed is Which . . .*, where the strange tumescent forms of *Bellamy's Meat Pies* have transformed themselves into clouds of virus, life and nonlife, fitting symbols of this terminal art.

No artist's art stands apart from his life. At this period, Dayling's love-group broke dramatically apart. The three males and two females who comprised the group had lived in equipoise for some eight years. Dayling suddenly found himself alone.

Now follow the somewhat mysterious years of wandering, when little is known of Dayling's life beyond the facts that he subjected himself to the hallucinatory drug DXB and underwent five years in suspended animation in a clinic in Canton. For the rest, he appeared not to have gone near a computer terminal. His only work from these lost years[*] is *I've Had Eighteen Straight Whiskies – I Think that's the Record* registered from a monastery in the Sanjak in Yugoslavia. Based on the last words of the Welsh poet Dylan Thomas, this small block shows no development and generally marks a return to the more formal tone of *Give Dayrolles a Chair*.

Only in 1995 did Dayling emerge again; he had but four years to live. He was in his twenty-third year and had had both legs and one arm amputated, the better, he said, to concentrate on his art. He settled in

---

[*] The once accepted *Madame, Please Remove Your Lipstick, I Can Hardly Hear You* is now known to be a forgery.

Bombay, under the firm impression that it was Singapore. Despite such delusions, his mind was creatively clear enough, and he set to again whole-heartedly, living in a deserted government office, the complete solitary, though in an overpopulated city, seen only when he made an occasional midnight march on cybolegs to stare out over the sea, which he believed to be moving in over the land.

His method of work was now more brutal than before. He worked on the daylite himself, leaving the computer to copy the results, to change and eradicate according to open programming. Thus, he was working not with light but with the material itself – a reversion in technique, perhaps, but one which yielded its own unique results. There may always be an area of discussion centring on these last desperate works. Was this reversion a sign of Dayling's failure to adjust to himself and his times? Or is the reversion merely to be regarded as a substitution, remembering that Dayling is the great transition figure, the last major artist spanning the days of the biological revolution, the last major artist to work in inorganic material?

However we answer such questions, there is no disputing the maimed vigor of Dayling's output in his final years: *One World at a Time*; *On the Whole, I'd Rather Be in Philadelphia*; *Make My Skin into Drumheads for the Bohemian Cause*; and *As for Our Fatal Continuity* . . . These are small works, small, dense, and ruinous. All of them speak of fatal discontinuities. All of them have formed the basis since for countless experiments into the new media of semi-sentience.

It may be, as Torner Mallard has claimed, that these final works of Dayling's mark the demise of a too-long sustained system of aesthetics going back as far as Classical Greece, and the beginning of a new and more biologically-based structure; certainly we can see that, in the Dadaist titles, as well as in the works themselves, Dayling was undergoing a pre-post-modernist purgation of outworn attitudes, and carrying art forward from the aesthetic arena of balance and proportion to the knife-edge between existence and non-existence.

In his reckless sweeping away of all the inessential props of life, Dayling – by which of course we mean Dayling-And-Art-Computer – takes the bone-bare universe of Samuel Beckett a stage further; humour

AS FOR OUR FATAL CONTINUITY . . .

and death contemplate each other across a tumbled void. Only the grin of the Cheshire Cat is left, fading above Valhalla.
From *Sculpting Your Own Semi-Sentients: A Primer for Boys and Girls.*
By Gutrud

Slayne Laboratories.

Psyclops

Mmm I.

First statement: I am I. I am everything. Everything, everywhere.

The universe is constructed of me, I am the whole of it. Am I? What is that throbbing that is not of me? That must be me too; after a while I shall understand it. All now is dim. Dim mmmm.

Even I am dim. In all this great strangeness and darkness of me, in all this universe of me, I am shadow. A memory of me. Could I be a memory of . . . not – me? Paradox: if I am everything, could there be a not-me?

Why am I having thoughts? Why am I not, as I was before, just mmmm?

Wake up! It's urgent!

No! Deny it! I am the universe. If you can speak to me you must be me, so I command you to be still. There must be only the soothing mmmm.

. . . you are not the universe! Listen!

Louder?

Can you hear at last?

Non-comprehension. I must be everything. Can there be a part of me, like the throbbing, which is . . . separate?

Am I getting through? Answer!

Who . . . are you?

Do not be frightened.

Are you another . . . universe?

I am not a universe. You are not a universe. You are in danger and I must help you.

Mmmm. Must be mmmm . . .

. . . If only there were a psychofoetalist within light-years of here . . . Well, keep trying. Wake up! You must wake up to survive!

Who are you?

I am your father.

Non-comprehension. Are you the throbbing which is not me?

No. I am a long way from you. Light-years away.

You bring me feelings of . . . pain.

Don't be afraid of it, but know there is much pain all about you. I am in constant pain.

Interest.

Good! First things first. You are most important.

I know that. All this is not happening. Somehow I catch these echoes, these dreams.

Try to concentrate. You are only one of millions like you. You and I are of the same species: human beings. I am born, you are unborn.

Meaningless.

Listen! Your 'universe' is inside another human being. Soon you will emerge into the real universe.

Still meaningless. Curious.

Keep alert. I will send you pictures to help you understand . . .

Uh . . . ? Distance? Sight? Colour? Form? Definitely do not like this. Frightened. Frightened of falling, insecure . . . Must immediately retreat to safe mmmm. Mmmm.

Better let him rest! After all, he's only six months; at the Pre-natal Academies they don't begin rousing and education till seven and a half months. And then they're trained to the job. If only I knew – my leg, you blue swine!

That picture . . .

Well done! I'm really sorry to rouse you so early, but it's vital.

Praise for me, warm feelings. Good. Better than being alone in the universe.

That's a great step forward, son. I can almost realise how the Creator felt, when you say that.

Non-comprehension.

Sorry, my fault; let the thought slip by. Must be careful. You were going to ask me about the picture I sent you. Shall I send again?

Only a little at once. Curious. Shape, colour, beauty. Is that the real universe?

That was just Earth I showed you, where I was born, where I hope you will be born.

Non-comprehension. Show again . . . shapes, tones, scents . . . Ah, this time not so strange. Different?

Yes, a different picture. Many pictures of Earth. Look.

Ah . . . Better than my darkness . . . I know only my darkness, sweet and warm, yet I seem to remember those – trees.

That's a race memory, son. Your faculties are beginning to work, now.

More beautiful pictures please.

We cannot waste too long on the pictures. I've got a lot to tell you before you get out of range. These blue devils—

Why do you cease sending so abruptly? Hello? . . . Nothing. Father? . . . Nothing. Was there ever anything, or have I been alone and dreaming?

Nothing in all my universe but the throbbing. Is someone here with me? No, no answer. I must ask the voice, if the voice comes back. Now I must mmmm. Am no longer content as I was before. Strange feelings . . . I want more pictures; I want . . . to . . .

Mmmm.

Dreaming myself to be a fish, fin-tailed, flickering through deep, still water. All is green and warm and without menace, and I swim forever with assurance . . . And then the water splits into lashing cords and plunges down, down, down a sunlit cliff. I fight to turn back, carried forward, fighting to return to the deep, sure dark—

—if you want to save yourself! Wake if you want to save yourself! I can't hold out much longer. Another few days across these mountains—

Go away! Leave me to myself. I can have nothing to do with you.

You must try and understand! I know it's agony for you, but you must stir yourself and take in what I say. It is imperative.

Nothing is imperative here. And now my mind seems to clear. Yes! I exist in the darkness where formerly there was nothing. Yes, there are imperatives; that I can recognise. Father?

What are you trying to say?

Confused. Understanding better, trying harder, but so confused.

Do not worry about that. It is your twin sister. The Pollux II hospital diagnosed twins, one boy and one girl.

So many concepts I cannot grasp. I should despair but for curiosity prodding me on. I'm one of a pair?

There you have it. That is a little girl lying next to you: you can hear her heart beating. Your mother—

Stop, Stop! Too much to understand at once. Must think to myself about this.

Keep calm. There is something you must do for me – for us all. If you do that, there is no danger.

Tell me quickly.

As yet it is too difficult. In a few days you will be ready – if I can hang on that long.

Why is it difficult?

Only because you are small.

Where are you?

I am on a world like Earth which is ninety light-years from Earth and getting farther from you even as we communicate together.

Why? How? Don't understand. So much is now beyond my understanding; before you came everything was peaceful and dim.

Lie quiet and don't fret, son. You're doing well; you take the points quickly, you'll reach Earth yet. You are travelling toward Earth in a spaceship which left Mirone, planet where I am, sixteen days ago.

Send that picture of a spaceship again.

Coming up . . .

It is a kind of enclosure for us all. That idea I can more or less grasp, but you don't explain distances to me satisfactorily.

These are big distances, what we call light-years. I can't explain them for you properly because a human mind never really grasps them.

Then they don't exist.

Unfortunately they exist all right. But they are only comprehensible as mathematical concepts. OHHH! My leg...

Why are you stopping? I remember you suddenly stopped before. You send a horrible pain thought, then you are gone. Answer.

Wait a minute.

I can hardly hear you. Now I am interested, why do you not continue? Are you there?

... this is all beyond me. We're all finished. Judy, my love, if only I could reach you ...

Who are you talking to? This is frustrating. You are so faint and your message so blurred.

Call you when I can ...

Fear and pain. Only symbols from his mind to mine, yet they have an uncomfortable meaning of their own – something elusive. Perhaps another race memory.

My own memory is not good. Unused. I must train it. Something he said eludes me; I must try and remember it. Yet why should I bother? None of it really concerns me, I am safe here, safe forever in this darkness. This whole thing is imagination. I am talking to myself. Wait! I can feel projections coming back again. Do not trouble to listen. Curious.

... gangrene, without doubt. Shall be dead before these blue devils get me to their village. So much Judy and I planned to do ...

Are you listening, son?

No, no.

Listen carefully while I give you instructions.

Have something to ask you.

Please save it. The connection between us is growing attenuated; soon we will be out of mind range.

Indifferent.

My dear child, how could you be other than indifferent! I am truly sorry to have broken so early into your foetal sleep.

An unnamable sensation, half-pleasant; gratitude, love? No doubt a race memory.

It may be so. Try to remember me – later. Now, business. Your mother and I were on our way back to Earth when we stopped on this world

Mirone, where I now am. It was an unnecessary luxury to break our journey. How bitterly now I wish we had never stopped.

Why did you?

Well, it was chiefly to please Judy – your mother. This is a beautiful world, around the North Pole, anyhow. We had wandered some way from the ship when a group of natives burst out upon us.

Natives?

People who live here. They are sub-human, blue-skinned and hairless – not pretty to look at.

Picture!

I think you'd be better without one. Judy and I ran for the ship. We were nearly up to it when a rock caught me behind the knee – they were pitching rocks at us – and I went down. Judy never noticed until she was in the airlock, and then the savages were on me. My leg was hurt; I couldn't even put up a fight.

Please tell me no more of this. I want mmmm.

Listen, son! That's all the frightening part. The savages are taking me over the mountains to their village. I don't think they mean to harm me; I'm just a . . . curiosity to them.

Please let me mmmm.

You can go comatose as soon as I've explained how these little spacecraft work. Astrogating, the business of getting from one planet to another, is far too intricate a task for anyone but an expert to master. I'm not an expert; I'm a geohistorian. So the whole thing is done by a robot pilot. You feed it details like payload, gravities and destination, and it juggles them with the data in its memory banks and works out all the course for you – carries you home safely, in fact. Do you get all that?

This sounds complicated.

Now you're talking like your mother, boy. She's never bothered, but actually it's all simple; the complications take place under the steel panelling where you don't worry about them. The point I'm trying to make is that steering is all automatic once you've punched in a few co-ordinates.

I'm tired.

So am I. Fortunately, before we left the ship that last time, I had set up the figures for Earth. OK?

If you had not, she would not have been able to get home?

Exactly it. Keep trying! She left Mirone safely and you are now heading for Earth – but you'll never make it. When I set the figures up, they were right; but my not being aboard made them wrong. Every split second of thrust the ship makes is calculated for an extra weight that isn't there. It's here with me, being hauled along a mountain.

Is this bad? Does it mean we reach Earth too fast?

No, son. IT MEANS YOU'LL NEVER REACH EARTH AT ALL. The ship moves in a hyperbola, and although my weight is only about one eight-thousandth of total ship's mass, that tiny fraction of error will have multiplied itself into a couple of light-years by the time you get adjacent to the solar system.

I'm trying, but this talk of distance means nothing to me. Explain it again.

Where you are there is neither light nor space; how do I make you feel what a light-year is? No, you'll just have to take it from me that the crucial point is, you'll shoot right past the Earth.

Can't we go on?

You will – if nothing is done about it. But landfall will be delayed some thousands of years.

You are growing fainter. Strain too much. Must mmmm

The fish again, and the water. No peace in the pool now. Cool pool, cruel pool, pool . . . The waters whirl toward the brink.

I am the fish-foetus. Have I dreamed? Was there a voice talking to me? It seems unlikely. Something I had to ask it, one gigantic fact which made nonsense of everything; something – cannot remember.

Perhaps there was no voice. Perhaps in this darkness I have taken a wrong choice between sanity and non-sanity.

. . . thank heavens for hot spring water . . .

Hello! Father?

How long will they let me lie here in this pool? They must realise I'm not long for this world, or any other.

I'm awake and answering!

Just let me lie here. Son, it's man's first pleasure and his last to lie and swill in hot water. Wish I could live to know you . . . However. Here's what you have to do.

Am powerless here. Unable to do anything.

Don't get frightened. There's something you already do very expertly – telemit.

Non-comprehension.

We talk to each other over this growing distance by what is called telepathy. It's part gift, part skill. It happens to be the only contact between distant planets, except spaceships. But whereas spaceships take time to get anywhere, thought is instantaneous.

Understood.

Good. Unfortunately, whereas spaceships get anywhere in time, thought has a definite limited range. Its span is as strictly governed as – well, as the size of a plant, for instance. When you are fifty light-years from Mirone, contact between us will abruptly cease.

How far apart are we now?

At the most we have forty-eight hours more in contact.

Don't leave me. I shall be lonely!

I'll be lonely too – but not for long. But you, son, you are already halfway to Earth, or as near as I can estimate it you are. As soon as contact between us ceases, you must call TRE.

Which means?

Telepath Radial Earth. It's a general control and information centre, permanently beamed for any sort of emergency. You can raise them. I can't.

They won't know me.

I'll give you their call pattern. They'll soon know you when you telemit. You can give them my pattern for identification if you like. You must explain what is happening.

Will they believe?

Of course.

Are they real?

Of course. Tell TRE what the trouble is; they'll send out a fast ship to pick Judy and you up before you are out of range.

I want to ask you—

Wait a minute, son . . . You're getting faint . . . Can you smell the gangrene over all those light-years? . . . These blue horrors are lifting me out of the spring, and I'll probably pass out. Not much time . . .

Pain. Pain and silence. All like a dream.

. . . distance . . .

Father! Louder!

. . . too feeble . . . Done all I could . . .

Why did you rouse me and not communicate with my mother?

The village! We're nearly there. Just down the valley and then it's journey's end . . . Human race only developing telepathic powers gradually . . . Steady, you fellows!

The question, answer the question.

That is the answer. Easy down the slope, boys, don't burst this big leg, eh? Ah . . . I have telepathic ability but Judy hasn't; I couldn't call her a yard away. But you have the ability . . . Easy there! All the matter in the universe is in my leg . . .

You sound so muddled. Has my sister this power?

Good old Mendelian theory . . . You and your sister, one sensitive, one not. Two eyes of the giant and only one can see properly . . . the path's too steep to – whoa, Cyclops, steady, boy, or you'll put out that other eye.

Cannot understand!

Understand? My leg's a flaming torch – Steady, steady! Gently down the steep blue hill.

Father!

What's the matter?

I can't understand. Are you talking of real things?

Sorry, boy. Steady now. Touch of delirium; it's the pain. You'll be OK if you get in contact with TRE. Remember?

Yes, I remember. If only I could . . . I don't know. Mother is real then?

Yes. You must look after her.

And is the giant real?

The giant? What giant? You mean the giant hill. The people are climbing up the giant hill. Up to my giant leg. Goodbye, son. I've got to see a blue man about a . . . a leg . . .

Father! Wait, wait, look, see, I can move. I've just discovered I can *turn.* Father!

No answer now. Just a stream of silence. I have got to call TRE.

Plenty of time. Perhaps if I turn first . . . Easy. I'm only six months, he said. Maybe I could call more easily if I was outside, in the real universe. If I turn again.

Now if I *kick* . . .

Ah, easy now. Kick again. Good. Wonder if my legs are blue.

Kick.

Something yielding.

Kick . . .

Never Let Go of My Hand!

ONE

Ret-Thlat's fore-calipers turned the power up gently. With equal precision, his rear-calipers spun out the thread of the harmenstrank control. The forward antenna of his machine was now some 12^{53} harmenstranks from his own dimension, probing gently across the infinite layers of creation.

'Speed it up, Ret-Thlat,' Pa-Flann advised, boredly. 'My sense of hushed expectancy is growing noisy.'

'If I turn too fast, we may slip past an entire dimension,' Ret-Thlat explained.

'What's a universe more or less at that distance,' his companion chirped. 'It will probably be too far down the harmenstrank band to be comprehensible, in any case.'

'In all the billions of dimensions—' Ret-Thlat began. A grey light winking by his side cut him off. Instantly the two of them leant forward, watching tensely as the realisators tuned themselves in. After a moment of silence, the circular central panel of the dimenscope flushed into life, and a picture appeared.

They stared fascinated at the new universe before them . . .

'Still there's one thing, my ducks,' Miss Stranks was saying cheerily, as she set her cup of Bovril back noisily into its saucer. 'You have got a strong and willing son to help you through your troubles.'

'Willie is a great help, Miss Stranks,' Mrs Gascoyne agreed, elbowing herself round in the great chair to peer irritably at her one and only. Almost instinctively, she gave a racking cough which shook her frail old frame without having the desired effect of attracting Willie's attention.

He brooded in shirt sleeves over a page of equations, pale, sullen, stodgy. Smoke hung damply about his tangled hair as the hand which held the cigarette clamped his brow in moody concentration.

'Poor dear! And with all these exams he's taking and all,' said Miss Stranks with windy sympathy.

It was the undignified word 'exams' rather than the cough which roused Willie. He winced and stood up, glowering.

'8.30, Miss Stranks,' he announced. 'Mother's bedtime. Thank you for coming to cheer us up, but I must now turn you out into the cold.'

Without ceremony, he tossed her fox fur across to her. She arranged it carefully round her scraggy neck, draping it over the plastic mac she had insisted on wearing even while crouching over Mrs Gascoyne's giant fire. She rose reluctantly.

'Thanks ever so for the nice cup of Bovril,' she said. 'I'll be round again next week same time. I was only saying to my sister yesterday, "Amy," I said, "them Gascoynes do your heart good. I never saw anything like it," I said, "for a mother and son sticking to each other through thick and thin," I said. "They're a proper example to some people," I said.'

Miss Stranks swallowed liberally as she moved to the door: she was a great one for emotion.

'And what did Amy say to that?' Willie could not forbear to ask.

'You're more than kind to us, Miss Stranks,' Mrs Gascoyne hurriedly interposed. 'I'm sure I've always tried to be a good mother.' She coughed again.

'I'm sure you have, ducks, and—'

'Jolly cold with the door open,' Willie exclaimed. 'It'll start Mother off if we don't take care, won't it, Miss Stranks?'

His hand in the small of her back, he propelled her firmly away from the lure of the fire. The door closing sharply behind her cut off her startled 'goodnight'.

'You get ruder every day, Willie. It's fortunate Miss Stranks has a forgiving nature,' Mrs Gascoyne said.

'If you mean by that, Mother, that she has a thick skin and will be back next Thursday, you're right. How you think I can work while she sits nattering there—'

'It's kindly meant, Willie—'

'Kindly, my foot! She says the same things week after week, guzzling cups of Bovril, and you expect me to sit there, slaving for this blessed degree—'

The little woman levered herself out of the chair, steadying herself against its arm.

'Wipe the tears of self-pity out of your eyes, boy, and help me upstairs.'

That's what he was, she thought, a great boy. Oh yes, he was forty, a slobby, middle-aged forty, and he had this wretched schoolmastering job in a prep school, but he was still a boy. It might be *his* meagre earnings they existed on, but he still depended on her as much as she did on him. He had no more mettle in him than his father had had.

Lucy Gascoyne followed that tired train of thought as they ascended slowly into the icy upper regions of the house. She was not old – only sixty one – but years in Arabia and a weak heart had told on her. If only she were young again, free of Willie, free above all of the burden of the disappointing years . . .

'You're as soft as your father!' she snapped, as she reached the top step.

'Don't start that,' he said evenly. 'We both know father was a bloody old fool. If he hadn't left all his cash to the Arabia Archaeology Trust, we shouldn't be in this hole.'

'Don't you mention archaeology to me! I hate the word! When I think—'

'I know, I know – when you think how you wasted the best years of your life helping him dig holes. Your bottle's in your bed. Buck up and get in.'

As he spoke, he barged into his box-sized room, kicking off his shoes and trousers savagely. She was too much. She was getting like all the rest, saying the same thing over and over again, thinking in circles like a cockroach crawling endlessly round the bottom of a bucket. They were blunting his brain; he had a fine, mathematical brain, if only they'd give him a chance . . .

His mother took off her frock with cold fingers, put on a long nightgown, a bed jacket, a heavy pair of wool socks and a balaclava helmet that had once been Gascoyne's, and climbed into the bed. She shuddered as she huddled down, thinking regretfully of the long winter nights ahead: thinking too, that there would be, finally, one winter night that would bring no dawn for her.

'She's a useless old burden,' Willie muttered to himself. A burden: fine mathematical brains should not be burdened. And she was still as self-willed and changeable as ever she had been. Why should she drag him down? She had no gratitude. He loathed her.

Just suppose he waited till she was asleep and crept into her room. Suppose then he let out a scream . . . Her heart would not stand the shock; she would be snuffed like a candle.

The thought gave him a horribly delicious mixture of fear and pleasure – as it did every night. Then it suddenly came to him what other freedoms it would entail: not only no burden, but no Miss Stranks! Never to hear that dreadful woman's platitudes again! Never again to hear the squelch of ingurgitated Bovril while he wrestled with complex variables!

He crept shiveringly across the landing, waited, until he could hear his mother's breathing take on an even tenor, gently turned the door knob and walked with determination into the dark. Trembling slightly, he tensed himself to scream.

The great circle of the dimenscope appeared glowing before him.

'Well worth waiting for!' exclaimed Ret-Thlat, rubbing a bundle of feelers together. 'These two-legged creatures seem to be the dominant species on this planet.'

'What is even more extraordinary,' said Mor-Sossa, who had just joined his two friends, 'is that they manage to live on spherical planets.'

'Optical effect?' Pa-Flann hazarded.

Ret-Thlat shook his body in a decisive negative. Then, waving a caliper at the dimenscope screen, he asked, 'Shall we fish a couple of them up here?'

'Wait a bit,' Pa-Flann said. 'Let's watch 'em in their own environment for a while. It amuses me the way they live on the outside of their round planets.'

*

NEVER LET GO OF MY HAND!

They panned the viewing angle lower and gazed with interest. They were on one of the square, several-celled buildings in which the bipeds lived. A biped with a sheet over it was lying absolutely still on a bed. Light filtered solemnly in from a narrow window whose top half was obscured by a blind.

Two other bipeds backed into the room. One walked over and raised the blind – he was podgy and moist of eye; the other whisked over to the bed – he was grey and jerky of movement, and carried a black bag. He pulled the sheet away from the prone biped and commenced an incomprehensible ritual which included opening the eyes of the prone one, who had white hair and wrinkled skin and still did not move despite the uncomfortable processes to which she was submitted.

The podgy biped continued to stare out of the window, not looking at the bed. His fingers flicked endlessly together behind his back.

'Is he communicating?' Mor-Sassa asked.

'Probably,' Pa-Flann agreed. 'Talking politics, I shouldn't wonder.'

The business on the bed was concluded and the prone biped left in what was evidently considered a suitable state of disarray. The other two had managed to cram it – her? – him? – into an incredible variety of garments including a brown helmet-affair which fitted over the head. The grey one then carried out a rough examination, opened and shut his mouth rapidly at the podgy one and they backed together out of the door.

The dimenscope's forward antenna followed them through it.

The grey biped with the black bag stood nodding his head inanely while the podgy one opened and shut his mouth, then backed down the stairs and out of the house. When he got outside, he knocked on the door, climbed backwards into a four-wheeled vehicle and moved off down the street.

Meanwhile, the podgy biped rushed to a shallow metal tray which contained several little white stubs, seized one, and rubbed it on the tray until it straightened out into a short tube and ignited, smoke coming from one of its ends. The grey biped's knock seemed to be a signal; when it came, the other immediately stuck the white thing between his mouth edges and sucked it, drawing smoke from the air until he had built himself quite a long white tube; this he placed in a box with others like it.

'Fascinating!' sighed Ret-Thlat. 'Shall we bring him up here now?'

'Hang on,' Mor-Sossa said. 'He's going to do something else.'

He was. He picked up a black instrument, made mouth movements, entangled his finger in a metal dial and then abandoned the thing. After that, he walked violently backwards up and down the narrow landing, occasionally glancing at the closed door and occasionally making white tubes.

Finally he went into another room and lay down on a bed. The light faded slowly and he switched on artificial illumination.

Unlike the prone biped in the next room, this one did not remain still . . .

Over the dimenscope, the three watched in rapture. This was field study, this was genuine research, this was really learning how the other fellow lived. This was a moment to recall the words of the poet Rit-Ratscuf: 'There are more things in upijeegosh and ssidlawb than are dreamed of in your philosophy, Hor-Atio.'

Gradually the podgy biped was becoming more agitated. Twitching himself into action, he rushed backwards round the house and then, becoming pale of face, staggered into the room which contained the prone biped. He gripped the bottom rail of its bed, watching for a sign. At last it palpitated feebly. Then it palpitated horribly, half raising itself out of bed, gesticulating, flailing its little arms.

The podgy biped then moved to the side of the bed, suddenly flung up its own arms and opened its mouth wide. At this, the other was immediately still, crouching down with closed eyes, its skull half under the bed-covering.

'Get them now,' Ret-Thlat said.

Mor-Sossa cut off the visual record that was being made of this event and spun the forward field valve. At once the advance antenna, which had been watching the antics of the biped, dilated from the size of a marble into a great, glowing circle.

Pa-Flann was ready with the grips. He hurled them through the out-take and clicked with satisfaction as they seized the two bipeds with a multitude of plastic tentacles, injected a mild dose of paralyser, and pulled . . .

Next moment, Willie and Lucy Gascoyne were standing helplessly before them.

'I suppose you gentlemen must be Martians,' Mrs Gascoyne said at last, when the paralysis had worn off enough for her to speak.

'M-Mother,' Willie breathed, 'Can you see them too? I thought...'

They gazed, Willie with horror, Lucy Gascoyne with wonder, at the trio of beings before them. They were roughly banana-shaped, but bulbous at the lower end and at the top bursting into a dozen petals like cows' tongues, on which were, variously, eyes, mouths, antennae and other less easily identified organs of sense. Their bodies were yellow and pink and supported several clusters of limbs. They wore no clothes.

'The bipeds are poorly coloured,' Ret-Thlat commented.

'That's what comes of living on the surface of your planet,' said Pa-Flann sagely. 'How about some refreshment?'

He chirped shrilly and curled onto a low bed, his eyes never leaving the odd specimens.

'They're very graceful,' Lucy Gascoyne said doubtfully.

'They're obscene!' Willie shuddered.

Ignoring him, his mother began to remove her balaclava helmet. With a questioning look at the Martians (as she was, for a long time, mistakenly, to think of them), she sank onto a spare couch and looked about her.

The walls of the chamber appeared to be of solid earth; they were not smooth, but fretted and serrated, with a curious intricacy, almost as if they had been chewed. She had hardly absorbed this impression when a curtain was swept aside and a creature entered in response to Pa-Flann's call.

'Ye Gods!' Willie gasped. 'Mother, can't you think of something we can do?'

'*You* think,' Lucy said crossly. 'I'm feeling a little faint.'

The newcomer was pear-shaped and walked on two legs. It had no head. Its belly was studded with pink teats.

It chirped at Pa-Flann, who beckoned it across to him. It extended two teats on long tentacles. Pa-Flann accepted them gratefully and put them into a couple of his mouths.

'Refreshment, gentlemen?' he inquired through a third. The others assenting, tentacles were extended to them. As they imbibed, they discussed what should be done with the bipeds. Obviously, they decided, the most important thing was to establish a common language.

They were interrupted by Willie's vomiting. The spectacle of the pear-shaped creature slowly subsiding like a balloon was too much for him.

'What do you suppose that is a gesture of?' Mor-Sossa asked interestedly.

Willie had decided to become violent. The dimenscope had been carelessly left on, and still, tantalisingly, showed a view of his mother's bedroom. He dashed at it, attempting to jump through. Unfortunately, the force field was only a one-way affair as far as living tissue was concerned, a receiver, not a transmitter. Willie fell heavily to the floor with a bleeding nose.

Chirping with annoyance, Ret-Thlat jumped up and switched off the machine. As he turned an eye round anxiously to see if their specimen had injured himself, Willie leapt up, pain lending him courage, and flung himself on Ret-Thlat.

Ret-Thlat was tougher than he looked. His pastel yellows and pinks flared into an angry purple, and he struck out with a leathery, toothed arm which instantly raised a weal across Willie's face. But Willie had impetus and weight. He bore Ret-Thlat down, locking his arms and legs round the plump body, fighting to seize the tongue-like protuberances which bore the other's sense organs.

Pa-Flann had already given a piercing whistle. Now the curtain was swept aside and half a dozen creatures burst in, creatures unlike either the scientists or the mobile stomach. These were tremendous scorpions, well armed with jaws, stings, shovels and claws. They made short work of Willie. He was paralysed and bound tightly by cord spun from the scorpions' entrails.

'So they use bodily attack!' said Ret-Thlat, whistling up another stomach and taking a strong suck. 'What good do you reckon he thought that would do him?'

'Perhaps they are irrational?'

They left that question in the hot air, and decided instead what should be done with Willie. If he was really dangerous, he obviously should be used for food, either at the breeding banks or among the scavengers. However, they were reluctant to lose entirely what was indubitably the better of their two bipeds, so in the end they agreed he should be sent to work on a surface scavenging farm for twenty-one dostobs, subject to the Queen's confirmation.

The scorpion horde bore Willie away.

During the fight and the following high-pitched harangue, old Lucy Gascoyne lay helplessly on her couch. She was tired, ill, and a little frightened.

As Willie was borne out, she sensed one of her turns coming on. With an effort, she pulled herself up and gestured feebly to her parched mouth.

Pa-Flann grasped her meaning. He chirped. A stomach, nicely bloated and pear-shaped, appeared. It thrust a teat into Lucy's mouth. She almost gagged as a hot, fleshy tip squirmed onto her tongue. Then a thin liquid squirted onto her palate.

It was irresistible!

From that day on, she began to feel better.

TWO

A dostob is a period of roughly half a year. When Willie had served his sentence of twenty-one dostobs and at last returned to the underground world of Ssidlawb, he never expected to find his mother alive. So much had happened to change him, physically and mentally, that he felt merely numb when she confronted him, and took a considerable time to adjust himself to their relationship.

'I thought you'd be dead!' he told her bluntly.

'Far from it! I feel younger every day. It's the – food that does it.'

'The food! I thought it was the air! Look at me, Mother – oh, we've been so long apart, can't I call you Lucy? The very term "Mother" seems irrelevant here.'

'I'd much prefer it.'

'—Something's had the same effect on me. See, I've shed all my flabbiness. Muscles like iron now! By jove, I've worked hard, but it's been a tremendous experience! I've enjoyed every minute of it!'

'Well! I never expected to hear you talk like that, Willie. Don't you ever yearn to get back to Miss Stranks?'

'Miss Stranks? Who was she? You know, Lucy, sometimes I even forget I wasn't born here. Can we go somewhere to chat?'

'Yes. Come to my house.'

'Your house, eh?'

'Oh, they've been wonderful to me, Willie, absolutely wonderful. They are so different but so gentle.'

Once at the odd collection of cells Lucy called her house, they settled down for a good talk. Mobile stomachs were summoned and they began to exchange experiences.

Both had picked up a language from their captors: Willie the simple patois of the scavengers with whom he had mainly worked, Lucy the intricate mandarin of the ruling classes with whom she lived. For in the world of Ssidlawb society was divided into three distinct classes, the rulers, the feeders or mobile stomachs, and the scavengers, each being a distinct sub-species. There were also the Intermediaries and the Queens; apart from these and some scavengers, the rest of the Ssidlawb community was neuter.

'Which makes for a much more peaceful society than ever we knew,' Lucy commented. 'I wouldn't go back to that ghastly old family system for worlds. To be shut up in a semi-detached again . . .' Words failed her.

Willie told her about life on the surface, where no sun shone: the blank sky seemed to radiate an illumination of its own. The scavengers worked farms practically without supervision and sent forays into unknown territory. Willie had been their prisoner, but the work which was hard to them was light to him. A sea had just been discovered to the north. He was going back as a supervisor to open up the coast.

'You're going back, Willie?' Lucy said. 'I thought you'd stay and look after me.'

'You don't need looking after,' he grinned. 'You're doing fine. And I really must go back: I've just signed on for another twenty-one dostobs.'

The mighty subterranean lake threw up echoes like ripples around the distant roof of the cavern. Lucy splashed happily and turned to Ret-Thlat.

'Isn't it marvellous?' she said. 'This is the most beautiful place I ever saw. Aren't you glad I taught you to swim?'

'I'm the first Ssidlawbian ever to swim, and it's always nice to be first at anything,' he replied. They spoke in mandarin, although his English was good.

'You know, you're funny people,' she confided, reaching out in a burst of affection to stroke his back. 'You have almost no technology in our sense of the word, no mechanical devices, cars or radios or the other things I've told you about, yet you suddenly up and invent a dimenscope.'

He smiled, a ripple of cerise passing over his body.

'It's the different way we think, Lucy,' he said slowly. 'Humanity was – is one species on its own: your animals cannot compare with you in brain power. Here we are three species, all interdependent, all helping each other. We don't want motor cars. But we *did* want a dimenscope.'

'And what's become of it?'

'I'm afraid one of the Queens had it destroyed; she said it wasted too much of Pa-Flann's and my time. All the records are still intact though, if you want a peep at your old home.'

'Heavens no, Ret-Thlat. That I could not bear. It all seems quite incomprehensible to me now.'

'It did to me then!'

They both burst out laughing.

'I must get out and dry,' Lucy told him at length. 'You know Willie is about due back? In fact—'

'You're psychic!' Ret-Thlat told her, extending a leg to the shore. She looked in the direction he indicated.

Picking his way carefully round the giant stalagmites, a two-legged figure was making his way to the beach.

'Willie!' Lucy called, and splashed towards him.

Willie stopped abruptly and watched her as she waded ashore. He saw a mature and beautiful woman approaching. His heart beat heavily and his mouth went dry. He gazed until reminding himself angrily that he was her son, and then turned away.

'Willie!' she said, seizing up a towel. 'Wonderful to see you again. Come and have a swim with us! It's hot spring water; it'll do you good.'

'I don't want to swim.' He turned cautiously towards her, and saw Ret-Thlat was swimming an involved dog paddle to the beach.

'You oughtn't to go swimming in the nude with that creature,' he said thickly.

Lucy gave an embarrassed laugh. 'I've given up those silly earth conventions years ago. Besides, Ret-Thlat is neuter.'

'It makes no difference. You're still my mother. I've a good mind to show him just where he gets off!'

'You'll do nothing of the sort. You don't understand – you never understand! Listen Willie, I'm as hard as nails, and if you cause trouble here I'll see you flung to the breeding banks. Understand that?'

He did. 'Nice welcome to give me,' he muttered, kicking the sand indecisively.

He was introduced to Ret-Thlat, who was as agreeable as ever. Lucy kept up a cheerful flow of conversation as they made their way back to the city. She told Willie how she had taken up her old love of archaeology again, and how – with Ret-Thlat's help and the encouragement of several of the Queens – she was compiling a book on the history of Ssidlawb. Willie answered in grunts.

Peevishly, he whistled a passing stomach. As it meekly followed him, he sucked with irritation at an extended teat.

'I've got a lot to say to you,' he told Lucy.

'You're going to live here with me from now on?'

He peered hard at her, trying to interpret the tone of her voice.

'I want to get back to Earth.'

'Well, I don't!' she said decisively. 'Back to cooking four meals a day? The culinary arrangements alone are enough to persuade any woman to stay here.'

'Culinary arrangements! Are you aware that this mash we get from the stomachs has already been pre-digested by the scavengers? – And that Ret-Thlat and Co. vomit up for the Queens? Doesn't that filthy chain of nutrition sicken you?'

As he spoke, Willie spat out the teat from his mouth; the gesture was too late: dramatically, his speech was already ruined.

Lucy said nothing, smiling merely. Ret-Thlat said, 'Lucy probably knows much more of our history and customs than you.'

'You stay out of this,' Willie snapped.

They had now arrived at Lucy's house. As she carefully explained, it was really Pa-Flann's and Ret-Thlat's abode, so there was no question of the latter's staying out. Ret-Thlat, however, promised to go into another room; mother and son were left alone.

For a moment, an awkward silence piled up between them. Then Willie gave an uneasy laugh and placed his hands on Lucy's shoulders.

'Sorry I was stupid,' he said. 'It caught me off balance, seeing you after so long...'

She pulled away, presenting her back to him.

'What was it you had to say to me, William?' she asked, in a tiny voice.

He glared round the apartment in aimless fashion, chewing his lip, clicking his fingers behind his back.

'I've had the time to take up a lot of my old studies,' he said at last. 'Been doing some maths, or trying to... Geometry... Know what the circumference of a circle is Lucy?'

'Pi r squared,' she answered automically.

'No. Not here, it isn't. Here it's pi r *cubed*. When I first saw their round dimenscope field appear, I thought "that's an impossible circle!" It certainly was.'

'It can't be!'

'It's possible here. This world's – well, fundamentally *different* in construction. And I'll tell you another thing. We've built a port by the sea, up on the surface. We've got ships... I've watched them sail out and out over the water, until finally the distance swallows 'em up.'

'Well?'

'Well, they never go over the horizon. You can see them as far as the visibility will let you. This is a *flat world!*'

'How can it stay in space if it's flat?'

'I don't even know if it is in space. There are no nights, no stars, no sun.'

'I'm afraid I can't understand that.' She had sat down now, looking timid.

'Nor can I. We can't understand their world any more than they could understand ours – not that we ever understood our own; it was just that we were used to it. But I've saved the most important thing till last.'

Lucy began pacing the room, saying she did not think she wished to hear anything more: he was making her unhappy. Why couldn't he be nice when he came back?

Setting his face in stubborn lines, Willie said, 'You know what I'm going to say, don't you? You're afraid aren't you? *Tell me how old I look.*'

For a long while she stared at him, taking in almost instinctively the pudgy weakness of his physiognomy, now fined down into an almost engaging delicacy; it was the face of a youth of 19 or 20. She wet her lips without saying anything.

'All right then,' he said, 'I'll ask you something else.' As he spoke, he seized her bodily, and swung her round until she was facing a full-length mirror. Ignoring her cry of pain, he shouted, 'Tell me how old *you* look.'

A fine, physically perfect woman gazed out at her with eyes echoing her own alarm. She knew that this reflection, which seemed to grow younger and fairer every day, was of a woman scarcely in her forties; but at this moment it was beyond her to speak.

'Well?' Willie inquired in a gentler tone, as if touching her soothed him. 'If you won't answer, I'll tell you. We've been here two periods of twenty-one dostobs, which, as near as I can calculate, is about twenty years. That makes you eighty-one! You carry your age well, don't you?'

Lucy broke into tears and was inconsolable for several minutes. At last she lay with his arms round her and said, 'I'm sorry, I'm all unbalanced. I thought I'd never be able to stop crying. It's the diet or something. But I'm *not* eighty-one!'

'Of course you're not,' Willie said consolingly. 'You're growing young again, Mother. We both are, we have been since the day we got here.'

'How did we manage it, Willie?'

'Don't tremble so. Wherever this world is, it's nowhere in the universe we knew on Earth. It almost might be, to outward appearances, but it just couldn't be quite. I think it's another dimension . . . There must be some dimensions where *nothing* is like Earth – unimaginable . . . But there's one great difference here: time flows backward.'

'But—' She stopped, then said, 'That can't be, because Ret-Thlat and the others are growing older. Ret-Thlat's quite green now, poor old dear.'

'I was talking a little loosely. Imagine a man standing in England and another in Australia: if the Earth was suddenly deflated like a balloon, those two men would be standing almost sole of boot against sole of boot, with only a thin crust of earth between. Now if either of them was pushed through the crust, he would be standing on his head, compared with the other.

'An exactly analogous thing has happened to us in the time scheme. I believe we've been hooked through into a dimension which was our Temporal Antipodes.'

She began to laugh. It was more violent than her crying. She gasped and looked stupid, and began over and over saying, 'I was just thinking how funny—' and then the laughter got her again and she was unable to finish the sentence.

'Lucy,' he shouted. 'Pull yourself together! We've got to get back through that machine before it's too late, before we both get too young!'

But Lucy only laughed.

Ret-Thlat hurried into the room, alarmed by the hysterical notes in her voice. At that moment, Willie struck his mother across the face: there was instant silence.

In that silence, Ret-Thlat whistled angrily for the scavengers.

THREE

Throughout the teeming multitudes of dimensions and alternate universes, spawned as prodigally as daisies, as various as fingerprints, some factors, nevertheless, are common everywhere: they rule unaltered among the general diversity. Among such universals is love, possibly; fear, probably; death, certainly.

When Ret-Thlat died of old age, his friends Pa-Flann and Lucy, among others, attended his 'funeral' at the breeding banks. Lucy returned soberly along the interminable corridors; soberly, but not without impatience at Pa-Flann's slowness of pace. He encircled her wrist apologetically with a caliper.

'I shall soon be going the way of my old friend,' he said, without rancour. 'Which reminds me . . . You know our custom here, whereby all orders given by a member of the ruling class lapse on his death?'

'I do.'

'Ret-Thlat sentenced Willie to life servitude for striking you with one of his hands. Willie is now free again.'

'Yes. I had realised that.'

'He has already returned here.'

'What? Already?'

'Already. He arrived yesterday, but I thought it best he be kept away from you until the funeral was over.'

'That was kind of you, Pa-Flann,' she said, with sinking heart.

When she was alone, Lucy spent a long while pacing up and down, debating, trying to control herself. The inhabitants of Ssidlawb were mild and unexcitable: having lived with them for so long, she felt it as an emotional ordeal to have to face a human again; but she was a woman of resolution. Finally, she went to Willie.

For the space of five seconds, the finely grown girl of twenty-seven and the small boy of six confronted each other like antagonists. Then he threw himself across the room at her.

'Oh Mummy, Mummy, don't let them take me away again!' he begged. 'Never let go of my hand any more!' She took his wrist, and, disentangling him from her neck, held him at arm's length. His pale face, with its wide, anxious eyes, was unmistakably Willie's. She could see in it the child he had once been, long before, and with that memory came one of his bronzed young father, eager to take the boy out to Arabia; and she could see the man he had been, and with that came a memory of a cheap, hired house and Miss Stranks saying, 'I do like to see a mother and son sticking to each other.'

'Willie,' she said sharply, 'Do you remember Earth?'

'Where we were before we were brought here?'

'Do you remember it?'

'Sort of . . . But you won't take me back there, will you? I don't want to grow up again.'

As he said it, her proud face hardened. She glanced round: they were private here.

'How many mothers,' she asked, 'would rear their children if they could see them as men, selfish, stupid, ageing? How many, do you think – if they knew when *their* turn came to be feeble and dependent there would be no mercy for them?'

He wriggled violently, but she would not let go of his wrists.

'You're frightening me!' he cried. 'You're hurting me!'

'Listen, Willie!' she hissed. 'Do you remember that time here runs backward? Do you?'

'Yes. Oh yes. But you're hurting my wrists.'

'Never mind your wrists; listen to me. That was *your* theory of time. I checked it with Ret-Thlat, because he kept a visual recording of all he saw of us before he scooped us through his machine.'

Now Willie was utterly still. He whispered, 'I don't remember,' but his teeth chattered as if he did. Lucy ignored him and continued.

'I saw those recordings. They showed us in our house. They ran backwards for a few hours before Ret-Thlat actually broke through from this dimension to Earth's. So what was on that film was *what would have happened if everything had gone on as normal*.'

She paused and said quietly, 'And what would have happened, what in fact had happened on that film, was that you came into my bedroom and scared me to death; and the doctor came in the morning and certified I died from natural causes! Now!'

'Oh, I don't remember; I'm only your small boy—'

She swung him up off his feet, holding him in the air.

'Yes,' she said, savagely, 'And again you're in my hands. And now you want six years' comfort and protection! Well you're not going to get it. I'm not going through that again, not for anyone, not for you, Willie, my little Willie, you little *murderer* . . .'

She lapsed into incoherence, shaking him violently, ignoring his screams. And under all the shrill din, a still voice in her head told her, 'Be careful: you'll shake him too much!' But there seemed to be no reason for stopping – what reason was there for anything? – how could she stop while he still screamed and screamed? And so she shook him and shook him, until his head rolled on his shoulders like an idiot's.

Even when he was entirely silent and cold, the screaming still rang on in Lucy's ears.

You Never Asked My Name

In the days beyond the future, a town existed on a rocky peninsula some two days' journey south from where Athens had once stood.

The peninsula began with a swollen knuckle of rock and tapered off like a pointing finger into the blue sea. Along its spine grew fragrant pines the shape of opened umbrellas, cacti, cypresses, vines, and olive trees flecked with fungus like mildewed lace. Where the peninsula ended, at the very nail of the finger, stood the small city-state called Tolan. Its inhabitants called it The Perfect Place.

The human beings who lived in Tolan, in their ordered society, counted themselves fortunate. They considered themselves safe from the postbellum wars which raged elsewhere over the face of the ruined world. They had escaped the worst physical effects of The Deterrence. Nevertheless, their minds were less unscathed than their bodies by all that had happened.

From a distance, Tolan looked like a toy. Everything about it seemed artificial, from its miniature palaces to its tiny walled vineyards. The people themselves, aware of their brittle survival, walked like dolls.

No two houses in Tolan stood on the same level. The steepness of the hillsides precluded it. The roof of one house came level with the herb-strip of the next. Their white walls marched down to the sea amid broom and boulder, and stood at angles to each other like a family whose members have quarrelled. A stranger arriving by mule over the mountains from the ruined world would come first to the house of Nefriki; Nefriki's house stood highest up the slopes and furthest from the centre of the town.

There Nefriki lived with his sister, Antarida. Nefriki and Antarida lived apart from the town and apart from each other. Nefriki was a strong young man, magnificently muscled, with a ferocious head of golden hair like a lion's. His face counted as handsome, being finely moulded, with blue eyes and a strong jaw, to which latter clung a sparse golden beard. He smiled most of the time, even when he was angry. Nefriki was generally angry. His duty was to kill people.

His sister, Antarida, was a different type of person. Her movements were as languid as Nefriki's were charged with tension. Her skin was pale. Her dark eyelashes and brows sheltered pupils of an intense grey, of a shade otherwise seen only in the eyes of cats. She was slender, her breasts and hips were small. She shaved her skull so that, in her twenty-first year, she reminded strangers at once of foetus and aged crone. Her duty was to tend the dead.

In order to defend themselves from the technological barbarism which had descended upon the rest of the planet, the people of Tolan had formed themselves into the most rigid of societies. Every family held an unalterable position in the caste system, from the lowest trawler for kelp to the highest official, from the foot-washers to those so refined they were forbidden sight of their own excrement. The codes of Tolan were many, and known by all; memories were sharpened by the fact that death immediately followed any transgression. Survival lay in obedience to the law.

The utopians of Tolan had established what they called The Perfect Place: and in doing so they had killed joy.

Puritanism and sensuality were intertwined like two vines which will destroy each other. Although the men had absolute autocracy over the women, yet, by starlight, they desired only to be defiled by them in every way possible. Lies were revered, castration was frequent, sadism was beauty. Chastity was praised and all perversions practised. To the sadness which prevails over human life, Tolan had added its own superstructure of misery, which it called utopia. Thus the ways of pre-Deterrence societies were preserved.

Sometimes refugees from the ruined world came climbing along the tumbled spine of the peninsula. Sometimes small boats sailed up the Gulf of Spetsai, attempting to moor at the harbour of Tolan.

Nefriki was always waiting for the invaders. He had his own area of the frontier to defend. Nefriki's arm was strong, his spear sure, his arrows unerring. He was the outcast hero. Because of his prowess, only the dead entered Tolan.

Antarida's trade was with the dead. To her the town scavengers brought the corpses her brother had killed. Lovingly, Antarida laved her bare skull with perfumes and assumed a gown of pure white. Then, with delicate hands and mincing fingers, she set about cleansing the dead enemy. Those hands and fingers went everywhere, into the most obscure corners, prying, preening. The hairs of the dead were washed and numbered, their orifices filled with wax from the wild bees of the peninsula. Then the corpses were buried beneath the excreta of the women of Tolan.

For those born in The Perfect Place, the last rites were different. They too, when life had left them, were taken into the care of Antarida for her minutest attentions. It was Antarida's fingers which were the last to invade their privacy. Burial for the native Tolanese was by water. Their bodies, laved and perfumed by the arts of Antarida, were taken to a stretch of shore preserved for such purposes.

A few feet below the clear waters of the Gulf, a shelf had been built. On this shelf were iron rings, to which the deceased were secured. Mourners could stand on the shore gazing down on them. The naked corpses lay with arms spread and legs apart, as if beckoning voluptuously to the living. There were no tides in the Gulf, nor had been since the Moon, the huntress of Earth's skies, had been destroyed in The Deterrence. The dead seemed to move only by virtue of the small lapping waves, which entered them as delicately as Antarida's fingers.

Shoals of tiny fish soon destroyed the virginity of the dead. The fish glinted like needles, they rippled like fabric. A haze filled the water. Soon those who had lived were no longer recognisable.

While the latest sea-burial was taking place in Tolan, another postbellum engagement was taking place across the territory where the ancient city of Athens had once stood. Here the remnants of the human race were fighting against their own inventions. A group of refugees from the battle fled southwards. Day by day, eluding pursuit, they neared the peninsula over which Nefriki watched.

On the subject of love, or what passed for love in The Perfect Place. In no other aspect of life was the difference between brother and sister more marked. All men desired Antarida. They desired her youth and pallor; they desired the fragile beauty of her skull; above all, they desired her for the obscenity of what her hands and fingers did. From the highest to the lowest, all men and some women yearned – even more than for death – to be encircled by the embrace of Antarida.

Nor did Antarida deny her suitors. It could not be said that Antarida had passion. But it suited her to be rendered entirely naked, to be slobbered and pawed over, to be clutched by older men in the rictus of orgasm. She herself did not move during these encounters, but lay as still, as well-mannered, as one of her corpses.

Her brother, from the small watchtower above their house, looked down through the skylight in the roof. He could see her spreadeagled in the posture of sea-buried corpses, while men had their way with her. In this sight, Nefriki took a melancholy pleasure; for he knew – such were the mores of Tolan – that these couplings added greatly to the prestige of his sister.

Occasionally Antarida was visited by the man Nefriki feared most, Reeve Ikanu. This dark-visaged man was the reeve of the city to whom Nefriki was answerable. Ikanu ruled the frontier. Ikanu could dismiss Nefriki from his post or sentence him to death for the smallest infringement of the law.

Ikanu's face was heavy and pale with compressed cruelty, although his body was thin and dark as if stained. The skin of his hairless cranium was multitudinously veined, so that it seemed as if his brain were visible. When Ikanu lowered his stained body onto Nefriki's sister, his savage watchdog sat outside the house, close by the door, guarding his master. When the dog caught a glimpse of Nefriki on the watchtower, it would growl, 'Guard yourself,' in a voice as deep and threatening as its master's. The dog ate meat; its master subsisted on a diet of wine and gnats.

Sometimes, Nefriki allowed his thoughts to turn to the past, and to Etsimita, the love of his early adolescence. Etsimita had been of a higher caste than he. Their love had been forbidden. Had it been known, both Nefriki and Etsimita would have suffered death. Perhaps this peril made their brief passion all the sweeter.

In those days, Nefriki had been able to love. His soul had been like a country in a fairy tale, conquered by love, and he had wished only to be possessed by Etsimita and to possess her, soul to soul.

They could meet only at night. One night of unclouded stars, they had met by the seashore and walked along it barefoot, holding hands. They had been talking low and seriously of subjects lovers talk of – those conversations so intense that they can never be recaptured afterwards, no matter how hard the bemused lover tries.

Etsimita had been overcome by happiness and by the beauty of the occasion. She hauled up her long skirt to the top of her delectable haunches and plunged into the breakers, which were made silver by the Milky Way which shone aslant them. As she went, she cried to Nefriki to join her.

He wished for nothing better. But hardly had he entered the foam when a black shape rose from the water before Etsimita and dragged her down below the waves. Uttering a cry, he dived to her rescue.

She came floating up in a pool of blood, and he dragged her ashore. Both her legs had been severed almost to the knees. The cuts were clean. It was no shark which had seized her but an anti-personnel war-machine, drifting far off-course, an accursed product of the ruined world.

Etsimita died before Nefriki could carry her home. His sister sealed up the wounded leg-stumps and went about her mortuary business with her deft hands, her diligent fingers, her probing thumb. Then, since she had transgressed inviolable rules of her society, the remains of Etsimita were consigned to the excreta beds. Something in Nefriki had passed from him at that time.

These memories returned to Nefriki as he sat on the watch-tower, regarding the prostrate body of his sister below. They fled at the sound of a stone bouncing down the mountainside some distance away – a sound only his ear was acute enough to catch.

Immediately, Nefriki was alert, again the guardian of the community. He slid to the ground, took his long bow and the quiver of arrows which leaned by the door, and moved into the concealment of the broom bushes. Climbing among boulders, he quickly reached the spine of the peninsula, where rock piled on rock like mating geckos.

Wedging himself between two boulders, Nefriki could see blue sea far below on either side, gleaming in the sunshine. Ahead of him was movement. Among the umbrella pines, a party of men was approaching. High overhead, Ikanu's trained birds of omen soared, screaming to the foe in their artificial voices, 'Distance yourself, distance yourself!'

There were other guards Nefriki could summon. Attached to his quiver was a shrill reed which would call them. Such was Nefriki's confidence that no such thought entered his head. He was filled with excitement at the anticipation of killing.

Of recent years, mountain lions and wolves had been returning to the mountains of Greece. They moved no more silently than Nefriki amid his allotted territory.

As he worked his way forward, he saw that five men were approaching. Ahead went a scout, moving with caution – and more difficult to keep an eye on than the four who followed him. Of these, one was plainly the chief; he rode on a kind of legged machine which squeaked softly as it progressed. The other three men followed with the dogged and enduring manner of subordinates. It made good sense to kill the leader first.

The leader was a proud man. He looked about arrogantly, his bare chin jutting. He had already sighted the toylike Perfect Place. He wore a helmet with visor, perhaps to protect himself from harmful radiation which still invaded the air. Over one shoulder a carbine was slung.

Above the leader, above the pines, wheeled Ikanu's birds of omen, still calling, 'Distance yourself, distance yourself . . .'

Nefriki slid one of his powerful hands across a rock, flexed his muscles, dragged himself against the rock, waited motionless until the scout had passed within a few yards of him, and then fitted an arrow to his bow. He raised himself slightly and drew back the bow with all his strength.

The five men were passing behind a thicket of cactus. As they emerged, Nefriki let the arrow fly. It sped to its mark with a powerful angry sound. It penetrated the thin metal-plating the leader wore across his chest and buried itself in his ribcage.

The leader made no comment upon his dying. He was evidently a man of decision; on receiving the arrow, he fell without hesitation backwards from the machine. As his head struck the ground, blood pumped from his mouth and ran into his helmet.

Nefriki released a second arrow and ran forward without waiting to see it strike its target. As he dodged behind boulders, he swung the bow over his shoulder and drew his short sword. He rushed out to confront two demoralised men; their companion lay on the ground beside the leader, an arrow through his chest; one of his legs was still kicking, scattering small stones.

'Distance yourself,' screamed the birds of omen.

One of the two survivors was too frightened to shoot. The other brought up a self-focus heat weapon and fired wildly. A pine tree burst into flame above Nefriki's head. Nefriki sliced off the man's right arm. The other man turned and fled.

Breathing deeply, Nefriki picked up a heavy round stone, took aim, and flung it at the head and shoulders bobbing down the hillside. He heard the brutal sound of stone connecting with skull before dropping to the ground as bullets sang through the air in his direction. The scout was returning.

Since the scout kept up intermittent fire, he betrayed his position while Nefriki worked behind him. It was no great matter to attack silently from the rear, to bring the short sword into play, to thrust its already bloodied blade upwards right under the scout's ribs. While the scout shuddered in the dust and died, Nefriki went back to finish the man whose hand he had severed. He smiled all the while.

Among the dead stood the legged machine, bearing a burden slung on its back. It spoke in a gentle voice as Nefriki approached.

'Master, I will serve you. I am made to serve. Do not destroy me as you have destroyed those humans. I can work for you all the days of your life.'

Without replying, Nefriki went cautiously nearer to inspect it. The machine's parts were painted a dull green. Its four legs were multi-jointed and ended above its body; it could adjust to function as a taller or a smaller animal. Set in its square head beside its eyes were the muzzles of two guns. They pointed at Nefriki, awaiting his reply.

He took an enormous, sudden kick, catching the machine under its chin. For a moment, he thought he had broken his leg or at least his toes, but his strength and his sandals saved him. As the pain left his limbs, he saw that he had jammed the machine's head back at an angle which rendered its guns useless.

He turned his attention to the burden on the machine's back. Strapped there, wrapped in film, unmoving, was what he thought was a beautiful dead girl. He took a step nearer. As Nefriki looked down at her, the girl opened her eyes and gazed up at him. He ceased smiling and tugged his golden beard instead.

Breaking the straps that bound her, he lifted the fragile burden from the machine, to set it rustling on its feet. He balanced her in an upright position, one arm encircling her waist. Then with another kick he sent the machine trotting downhill towards the distant sea.

The imprisoned girl's lips moved. 'Spare me,' she said. No mist from her breath obscured the wrappings over her face.

Shouts sounded near at hand. Other Tolanese guards were coming, called Nefriki by name. Nefriki did not reply. Half-carrying, half-dragging the film-wrapped girl, he made his way to a shallow cave he knew of, its entrance concealed by bushes. He climbed in and pulled her after him. They lay together until the hue and cry faded, and sunset melted in patches among the rocks outside their hiding place. All that while, he gazed at her silvery face.

When everything was quiet, Nefriki began to unwrap the girl – gently at first and then furiously, as the film resisted his tugging. When she was free, she gave a sigh and stretched her arms above her head, so that her flimsy tunic rumpled up over her body. Her hair was dark and hung to her shoulders without a curl.

She was thin, even spindly. The joints of her arms clicked slightly as she raised them. Nefriki could feel in her the gentlest of vibrations, and knew that her heart was of plastic, not flesh. He lay against her, terrified. This was the enemy, forbidden in The Perfect Place. The inhuman. The inhuman and female incarnate.

His body was touching hers. The workings of the engines inside her gave her synthetic flesh warmth. He could easily kill her.

She said, 'Thank you for saving me. You do not have to be frightened. I should not be able to resist you if you wished to demolish me. All men are my conquerors, that I know.' Her voice was lightly accented with regret.

'The men I killed were your friends.'

'The men you killed . . .' She let the phrase dangle, perhaps in contempt, then said after a pause, 'I was only their *thing*. I told you, you do not have to be frightened.'

'Frightened of you? How could I be frightened of you? You saw what I did to the men you were with.'

When she said nothing he declared, 'I'm frightened of nothing.' He raised himself on one elbow to look down at her face.

She did not reply.

Angrily, he said, 'What are you, anyway? You're an artificial creation. You don't even understand what I say.'

'Yes, I'm artificial. I'm an atrinal android, designed to appease man's need to touch. A plaything.' Her tone made him feel naïve.

It was his turn to say nothing. She said, 'Relationships between men and women are so bad that men have had to invent something like me, to avoid their pain in true human relationships.'

'Is it possible to have a – true relationship with you?'

With a hint of coquetry, the android said, 'That is for you to say. It depends on your character.'

'Come out into the open. I want to look at you. Don't try to run away.' He made his voice rough, masculine.

She climbed out of the cave after him and stood relaxedly, her eyes turned to the sea murmuring far below, so that her perfectly formed, anonymous face took on a pensive expression.

Nefriki caught her wrist. 'Take off your dress.'

'You wish to see me naked? I am formed like a living woman. Of course I will do that for you, but first you must answer a few questions about yourself.'

'What's that to you?'

'So that we can be close. Or do you fear that? What is your name?'

'I'm Nefriki, the guard of this place. You have seen what a good guard I am. I kill anyone who comes near Tolan. I keep Tolan safe. I am stronger and more deadly than anyone in Tolan. I can have any woman I want. Every woman desires to lie with me.'

The atrinal android said in a soft voice, 'I also wish to lie with you, Nefriki . . . But first tell me who you are.'

'I told you. I'm the guard, the strongest man here. This is The Perfect Place. Everyone fears and respects me. Last year, I killed a mountain lion with my bare hands.'

She sat down, so that her face was hardly to be seen in the velvet of early night.

'Anecdotes, boasts, Nefriki . . . But what lies under them? Tell me who the real man is, and then we can make love.'

He squatted beside her and gave a short angry laugh. 'Is it such a privilege, to make love to a machine? Pah, any woman in Tolan would throw themselves at me and beg for my love. They never ask who I really am.'

'Perhaps they dare not ask. Perhaps they dread to know . . . Do you know that there are a few wise humans who believe that The Deterrence came about because the world's leaders suffered from man's common fear of women, and of themselves being women? They had to prove they were men even to the extreme of ruining the planet. And they rose to power over populations who felt as they did. Women know these things.'

'What can women know that men don't?'

'They know that men desire their bodies but fear their minds.'

'Rubbish. You're a demented machine.'

She beckoned him nearer. 'Before you discover how human I can be, Nefriki, tell me your deepest secrets, your deepest truths, tell me who your real self is . . . I don't ask it to achieve power over you but to free you, to make you free.'

He moved closer, took her in his arms, kissed her roughly on her lips.

'You see. I have no fear of you.' He laughed. 'Suppose you tell me your secrets, if you have any.'

She put a finger to her lips. 'I will tell you my deepest secret. It is so profound that you will think it trivial. I am only a mirror. I can only mirror the men in my life. So was I designed, as a machine; but I can tell you this – I have found that many human women are also mirrors. They have turned themselves into mirrors. Simply through fear.'

The conversation was not to his taste. He did not understand her. Besides, he felt hungry.

He jumped to his feet, called to the android woman to follow him, and headed down almost invisible trails to his house.

Antarida was not in. She had left the house empty, the door open. No doubt at this time of night she would be lying on a bed in one of the small palaces of Tolan, prostrate beneath some gallant necrophile.

He lit a lantern and brought forth bread, cheese, and the cloudy wine of Tolan. He offered them to the creature who stood just inside the door, watching him with her narrow eyes.

'I do not eat,' she said, regarding him steadily.

'Sit down while I eat. You worry me.'

She came to the table with a wanton step. She was designed to please, for all her riddles; he saw that. He wondered how best to kill her.

'What sort of secrets did you expect me to tell you? I've no secrets.'

She said, softly, 'You are so vulnerable, Nefriki. I hear the way your voice dies at the end of a sentence. I love the sound of it.'

'You'll never capture my heart by such talk.' He spoke through a mouthful of bread.

'It's not your heart I want but your soul. You brought me to your house to show me one of your secrets.'

'I brought you here because I wanted to eat. It's my home, you silly hen, that's all. I could break your plastic neck.'

She shook her head sadly.

She rested her hands together on the table and said, 'No, you brought me here to show me that you live with a woman. Her scent is about the room. But you never make love to her. Why do you live with a woman to whom you never make love?'

He struck the table with his fist.

'Because she is my sister. You expect me to make love to my sister? Whatever happens in the ruined world, here we have the death penalty for such obscenity.'

'Otherwise . . .' she said, and let the word hang in the air, like the dark trail that rose upwards from the wick of the lamp.

He lowered his head and ate without looking at her, pressing the food into his mouth, scowling.

At last he rose, still chewing the last crust of bread.

'The night is fine. We will go and swim. Then we'll see what happens. Can you swim or do you sink?'

'I swim, Nefriki, thank you. I can do most of the things men wish me to do, like other women.'

He led the way down the hillside. Occasionally, he looked back over his shoulder to see that the android woman still followed him. She appeared all obedience, but he could not trust her.

It was his duty to kill her. If Reeve Ikanu discovered that he had spared an invader from the ruined world, Nefriki's life would be forfeit. Inside him, he felt a reluctance to do the deed himself; this creature was a powerful witch, with an understanding of men Nefriki regarded as almost uncanny. There was another way to dispose of her.

As they climbed down to the shore, they had to pass by the slope-shouldered villa which was the residence of Ikanu. The villa was composed of small towers, featureless except for small square windows here and there, designed to keep out sunlight. The building resembled a tropical ants' nest. As man and android woman passed by its slanting sides, they saw a light in one of the small windows. As they passed by the front door, soft-footed, the watchdog sitting at the step called in its deep growl, 'Guard yourself'.

But for once Nefriki was too intent on his purpose to feel fear for the reeve. He ran down onto the sand, and the girl followed.

The night was lighter on the beach. The star-blaze overhead reflected on the waves, and there was a dazzle of luminescence in the warm water just off shore. Fireflies darted along the beach like miniature ball lightning.

He kicked off his sandals and then, after only a moment's hesitation, pulled off his clothes. Meekly, the android woman also undressed. She stood before him without defences, her firm breasts close to his chest. He caught the thickness in his own voice as he said, 'You go in the water first. I'll follow.'

It was a long time ago that his love Etsimita had ventured into this same water to her death. Nefriki had never dared to plunge into the tempting waves since. He stood on the shore, fists on hips, watching as the android girl obeyed and waded deeper.

'Stop!' He could bear it no longer. The water splashed against her meek shoulderblades. She turned back to look at him when he shouted. Nefriki plunged out to her, calling incoherently.

He grasped her arm and ran back with her to the shore, dragging her against the undertow. 'It's dangerous,' he said. 'Dangerous. Machines in the water . . .'

They flung themselves onto the sand. He took hold of her and began to kiss her passionately.

'You must forgive me, you must forgive me.'

She said, 'Was it courage which made you run in after me?'

'No, no.' He was burying his face in her damp synthetic hair. 'It was fear. I couldn't lose you. You offered me something . . .'

She was breathing more deeply, stirring in his embrace. 'No, leave me alone. You wanted to kill me. To dispose of me.'

She tried feebly to break from his grasp, but was unable to.

Nefriki thrust his face into hers until his lips were almost touching her lips. His face was distorted. She felt his damp beard against her throat.

'Listen woman, you gave me the chance to speak the truth about myself. I couldn't take it – so covered is my life in lies. You're right, all men are liars. Well, now I've caught you again. I've got you and I will tell you the truth, and you will listen.'

She turned her face away. 'Death excites you so much, doesn't it? You're preparing to lie again.'

'I will tell you the truth only if you will believe it, if you will keep still, if you will accept what I say.'

'There can be no such contract,' she said. 'You may tell me what you claim is your truth – then I will tell you if it is credible. The more insane you think it, the more likely it is to agree with horrible human normality. Do you understand that, Nefriki, you weakling, you fool? Laid open, humanity can only squeal out madness and terror – the madness of being born, the terror of dying, of confronting death.

'And for men there is something more: the dread of the female . . . Every man is infiltrated by that dread, although he never escapes sharing all his chromosomes but one in common with womankind. Western man I'm talking about – the sort of man who unleashed The Deterrence on the whole world. Now – speak, Nefriki, if you must, knowing that I will believe you only if you reveal yourself as unutterably vile.'

She had pulled herself free during this speech and knelt above him, as he had earlier knelt above her. He clutched her, his arms about her waist, and spoke in a low choking voice.

'Very well, then. Vileness, yes, vileness. I am utterly destroyed by Tolan, by its mores, its society . . . There's no one I love. Even my sister I hate . . .

'And I suppose that I dream of defiling her when she is dead . . .

'Yet I am a man. Towards every approach I must be tough. If the waves devour my sweetheart, I must not weep. I must be tough – to myself as well as to women. I poison myself thereby. Women. Yes. I hate them, their weakness . . . Their strength even more . . .'

The android woman made to speak but he silenced her, sinking lower, his lips against her thighs.

'There's no escape for me. Besides, to escape would be a womanly act. I'm a guard, a man among men, all male. Of course I hate women – yes, fear them . . .'

'Why fear them?' she asked.

'Years have gone by . . . I touch nobody . . . Love means weakness, surrender. A true man like me must be all hard. Sword in hand, no feeling. If you want me to say it so much, then I'll say it to you because you're only an android. I hate and envy women. There!'

As she looked down at him, her face was calm as usual. She opened her mouth, hesitated, and then said, 'It's on that hatred, that ingrained sexual hatred, the world wrecked itself. The madness of the male, deterring real feeling, leads to The Deterrence. And the fears of women make them turn themselves into mirrors.'

Nefriki was not listening. He said, 'How can I escape my prison? I hate myself, I long – I long to be a woman. Yes, there, woman, there's my damned soul you asked for! Have it, take it for the little it's worth.'

Nefriki burst into furious tears, burying his face in his muscular forearms and his elbows in the sand.

She rose and stood above him, like a statue in her nakedness. It was darker now. The luminescence had disappeared from the sea, the fireflies had gone.

'All this is more of your posturing, Nefriki. It's not your soul you're offering, it's a posture, nothing more. You're diseased, you can't speak truth – you wouldn't know truth if you saw it. I recognise what you say as a kind of truth, but mainly it is just your posture. No one confesses except to gain pity or admiration.'

'You're being cruel,' he said into his arms.

'I told you I am only a mirror. A mirror is all you require for your narcissism, not a living woman. That's why men invented my kind. You give me nothing. You never even asked my name.'

She began to walk away down the beach, away from Nefriki, away from Tolan, The Perfect Place.

He shouted after her. 'You demanded my soul, you damned bitch, and I gave it you. Give me something in return.'

Light swept across the sand, bright enough for Nefriki to see that the android woman had paused. He turned to see where the light came from.

The cruel reeve, Ikanu, had thrown open the front door of his house and was marching forward, sword in hand. Beside him was his faithful dog, shouting, 'Guard yourself', in its hoarse voice. A woman stood in Ikanu's doorway, holding a torch above her head. Nefriki saw that it was his sister, Antarida. So she wished to be witness at his death.

For a moment, Nefriki stood undecided, attention caught between sister, reeve, and android woman.

The dog advanced croaking its cry in its artificial voice, 'Guard yourself'. After it came Ikanu, now raising his sword threateningly. He wore a robe which trailed to the sand and a flowing wig to cover the baldness of his head, which flapped as he trudged towards Nefriki.

An unanticipated noise broke from Nefriki's mouth. He was laughing involuntarily. The figure of Ikanu, half-man, half-woman, suddenly embodied all the theatrical insanity of Tolan: Ikanu's melodrama, Antarida's necrophilia, the destructive lifestyle into which isolation had forced the beleaguered city.

In the middle of his laughter, Nefriki saw how he himself was living out a sham. He could give no coherent account of himself even to the android woman – there was no valid context from which to deliver it. His emotional life had frozen. He laughed to think he could have acted out a role without knowing it.

The laughter began high and fell to a low grating sound, much like the artificial voice of the dog.

On Reeve Ikanu the laughter had an extraordinary effect. The reeve dropped his sword, to stand in puzzlement, thin arms outstretched. Slowly, his sandalled feet lost their purchase on the shifting sand. Slowly, he lost his balance and fell backwards. His dog rushed to him and began licking his face. 'Guard yourself, guard yourself . . .'

Nefriki turned. The dim light from Ikanu's doorway, where Antarida still stood transfixed, lit the retreating back of the android woman. It looked as if the darkness would swallow her at any moment.

He called to her and started running along the beach. 'I want to know your name! I want to give you something real . . .'

Without turning back, without ceasing to stride along the beach, she said, 'What have you got that's real?' Her voice was almost drowned by the sound of the surf.

As he ran, Nefriki shouted, 'My soul! Isn't that what you wanted? You haven't got one. Help me find mine and we might manage things better between us. Where are you going?'

She made no answer. In desperation, he called again. 'Why should I want to come with you?'

This time she stopped and half-turned to deliver her response.

'The ruined world may resemble hell, but perhaps hell is where mankind belongs, not in perfect places. At least hell does not dissemble. You have vomited up some of your lies, Nefriki. If you dare to come with me, you may some day find your system cleansed entirely.'

'I hate you,' he said.

And then he took hold of her hand.

Juniper

No hunger exists like mine, nor anger either. My need, my fury, knot in my veins. People look on me and smile, not seeing what I suffer. They say I am beautiful. Beauty! – That word poisons me.

Let there be a special place after death where artists suffer!

I would tell my history, except I have no history to tell. My life is synonymous with imprisonment. I pushed my first shoot from the seed and through the earth to the air. My first leaves opened. There was the great world, lifeless. And there ever since I have been confined.

Oh, the elements I needed for growth were at hand, I admit. The sun shone. Water soaked down to my roots. Yes, I developed, no denying that. But what living creatures of the forest came near? What birds nested in my branches, what deer took shelter against a storm beside my twisted trunk? What serpent, even, found a haven among my roots? None. My solitude was complete. No other tree grew near. For all I knew, the rest of creation was dead.

Very soon I found how little nourishment there was, how little freedom for my roots. No winds visited me, no breeze stirred my stiff branches. Survival was possible, nothing more. My growth was as slow as the decline of mountains. This the gods saw to; their artistry brought me nothing but endurance.

So my leaves are green and sharp, my bark gnarled, aged before its time. No creature ever climbed my bole, no goatherd ever lay beneath my shade. Such things were banished from my prison, together with the noises of outdoors. My ancestors had looked on glaciers, mountains, streams; not I.

What is it to be treasured? Now I admit to one hundred and fifty years, and have been handed down from father to son like a chattel. In their terms, I am beyond price, a triumph of bonsai art. Yet this dish which contains me is a band of shame. My anger shrivels my leaves.

On countless days, I have looked out through the window to the place where real nature, real freedom, begins. I despair and that despair is what my captors acclaim as beauty.

Without motion, I gaze towards the seasons in flight.

Confluence

The inhabitants of the planet Myrin have much to endure from Earthmen, inevitably, perhaps, since they represent the only intelligent life we have so far found in the galaxy. The Tenth Research Fleet has already left for Myrin. Meanwhile, some of the fruits of earlier expeditions are ripening.

As has already been established, the superior Myrinian culture, the so-called Confluence of Headwaters, is somewhere in the region of eleven million (Earth) years old, and its language, Confluence, has been established even longer. The etymological team of the Seventh Research Fleet was privileged to sit at the feet of two gentlemen of the Geldrid Stance Academy. They found that Confluence is a language-cum-posture, and that meanings of words can be radically modified or altered entirely by the stance assumed by the speaker. There is, therefore, no possibility of ever compiling a one-to-one dictionary of English-Confluence, Confluence-English words.

Nevertheless, the list of Confluent words which follows disregards the stances involved, which number almost nine thousand and are all named, and merely offers a few definitions, some of which must be regarded as tentative. The definitions are, at this early stage of our knowledge of Myrinian culture, valuable in themselves, not only because they reveal something of the inadequacy of our own language, but because they throw some light onto the mysteries of an alien culture. The romanised phonetic system employed is that suggested by Dr Rohan Prendernath, one of the members of the etymological team of the Seventh Research

Fleet, without whose generous assistance this short list could never have been compiled.

AB WE TEL MIN The sensation that one neither agrees nor disagrees with what is being said to one, but that one simply wishes to depart from the presence of the speaker

ARN TUTKHAN Having to rise early before anyone else is about; addressing a machine

BAGI RACK Apologising as a form of attack; a stick resembling a gun

BAG RACK Needless and offensive apologies

BAMAN The span of a man's consciousness

BI The name of the mythical northern cockerel; a reverie that lasts for more than twenty (Earth) years

BI SAN A reverie lasting more than twenty years and of a religious nature

BIT SAN A reverie lasting more than twenty years and of a blasphemous nature

BI TOSI A reverie lasting more than twenty years on cosmological themes

BI TVAS A reverie lasting more than twenty years on geological themes

BIUI TOSI A reverie lasting more than a hundred and forty-two years on cosmological themes; the sound of air in a cavern; long dark hair

BIUT TASH A reverie lasting more than twenty years on Har Dar Ka themes (c.f.)

CANO LEE MIN Things sensed out-of-sight that will return

CA PATA VATUZ The taste of a maternal grandfather

CHAM ON TH ZAM Being witty when nobody else appreciates it

DAR AYRHOH The garments of an ancient crone; the age-old supposition that Myrin is a hypothetical place

EN IO PLAY The deliberate dissolving of the senses into sleep

GEE KUTCH Solar empathy

GE NU The sorrow that overtakes a mother knowing her child will be born dead

GE NUP DIMU The sorrow that overtakes the child in the womb when it knows it will be born dead

GOR A Ability to live for eight hundred years

HA ATUZ SHAK EAN Disgrace attending natural death of maternal grandfather

HAR DAR KA The complete understanding that all the soil of Myrin passes through the bodies of its earthworms every ten years

HAR DI DI KAL A small worm; the hypothetical creator of a hypothetical sister planet of Myrin

HE YUP The first words the computers spoke, meaning, 'The light will not be necessary'

HOLT CHA The feeling of delight that precedes and precipitates wakening

HOLT CHE The autonomous marshalling of the senses which produces the feeling of delight that precedes and precipitates wakening

HOZ STAP GURT A writer's attitude to fellow writers

INK TH O Morality used as an offensive weapon

JILY JIP TUP A thinking machine that develops a stammer; the action of pulling up the trousers while running uphill

JIL JIPY TUP Any machine with something incurable about it; pleasant laughter that is nevertheless unwelcome; the action of pulling up the trousers while running downhill

KARNAD EES The enjoyment of a day or a year by doing nothing; fasting

KARNDAL CHESS The waste of a day or a year by doing nothing; fasting

KARNDOLI YON TOR Mystical state attained through inaction; feasting; a learned paper on the poetry of metal

KARNDOL KI REE The waste of a life by doing nothing; a type of fasting

KUNDULUM To be well and in bed with two pretty sisters

LAHAH SIP Tasting fresh air after one has worked several hours at one's desk

LA YUN UN A struggle in which not a word is spoken; the underside of an inaccessible boulder; the part of one's life unavailable to other people

LEE KE MIN Anything or anyone out-of-sight that one senses will never return; an apology offered for illness

LIKI INK TH KUTI The small engine that attends to one after the act of excretion

MAL A feeling of being watched from within

MAN NAIZ TH Being aware of electricity in wires concealed in the walls

MUR ON TIG WON The disagreeable experience of listening to oneself in the middle of a long speech and neither understanding what one is saying nor enjoying the manner in which it is being said; a foreign accent; a lion breaking wind after the evening repast

NAM ON A The remembrance, in bed, of camp fires

NO LEE LE MUN The love of a wife that becomes especially vivid when she is almost out-of-sight

NU CROW Dying before strangers

NU DI DIMU Dying in a low place, often of a low fever

NU HIN DER VLAK The invisible stars; forms of death

NUN MUM Dying before either of one's parents; ceasing to fight just because one's enemy is winning

NUT LAP ME Dying of laughing

NUT LA POM Dying laughing

NUT VATO Managing to die standing up

NUTVU BAG RACK To be born dead

NU VALK Dying deliberately in a lonely (high) place

OBI DAKT An obstruction; three or more machines talking together

ORAN MUDA A change of government; an old peasant saying meaning, 'The dirt in the river is different every day'

PAN WOL LE MUDA A certainty that tomorrow will much resemble today; a line of manufacturing machines

PAT O BANE BAN The ten heartbeats preceding the first heartbeat of orgasm

PI KI SKAB WE The parasite that afflicts man and Tig Gag in its various larval stages and, while burrowing in the brain of the Tig Gag, causes it to speak like a man

PI SHAK RACK CHANO The retrogressive dreams of autumn attributed to the presence in the bloodstream of Pi Ki Skab We

PIT HOR Pig's cheeks, or the droppings of pigs; the act of name-dropping

PLAY The heightening of consciousness that arises when one awakens in a strange room that one cannot momentarily identify

SHAK ALE MAN The struggle that takes place in the night between the urge to urinate and the urge to continue sleeping

SHAK LA MAN GRA When the urge to urinate takes precedence over the urge to continue sleeping

SHAK LO MUN GRAM When the urge to continue sleeping takes precedence over all things

SHEAN DORL Gazing at one's reflection for reasons other than vanity
SHE EAN MIK Performing prohibited postures before a mirror
SHEM A slight cold afflicting only one nostril; the thoughts that pass when one shakes hands with a politician
SHUK TACK The shortening in life-stature a man incurs from a seemingly benevolent machine
SOBI A reverie lasting less than twenty years on cosmological themes; a nickel
SODI DORL One machine making way for another; decadence, particularly in the Cold Continents
SODI IN PIT Any epithet which does not accurately convey what it intends, such as 'Sober as a judge', 'Silly nit', 'He swims like a fish', 'He's only half-alive', and so on
STAINI RACK NUSVIODON Experiencing Staini Rack Nuul and then realising that one must continue in the same outworn fashion because the alternatives are too frightening, or because one is too weak to change; wearing a suit of clothes at which one sees strangers looking askance
STAINI RACK NUUL Introspection (sometimes prompted by birthdays) that one is not living as one determined to live when one was very young; or, on the other hand, realising that one is living in a mode decided upon when one was very young and which is now no longer applicable or appropriate
STAIN TOK I The awareness that one is helplessly living a role
STA SODON The worst feelings which do not even lead to suicide
SU SODA VALKUS A sudden realisation that one's spirit is not pure, overcoming one on Mount Rinvlak (in the Southern Continent)
TI Civilised aggression
TIG GAG The creature most like man in the Southern Continent which smiles as it sleeps
TIPY LAP KIN Laughter that one recognises though the laughter is unseen; one's own laughter in a crisis
TOK AN Suddenly divining the nature and imminence of old age in one's thirty-first year
TUAN BOLO A class of people one only meets at weddings; the pleasure of feeling rather pale

TU KI TOK Moments of genuine joy captured in a play or charade about joy; the experience of youthful delight in old age

TUZ PAT MAIN (Obs.) The determination to eat one's maternal grandfather

U (Obs.) The amount of time it takes for a lizard to turn into a bird; love

UBI A girl who lifts her skirts at the very moment you wish she would

UDI KAL The clothes of the woman one loves

UDI UKAL The body of the woman one loves

UES WE TEL DA Love between a male and female politician

UGI SLO GU The love that needs a little coaxing

UMI RIN TOSIT The sensations a woman experiences when she does not know how she feels about a man

UMY RIN RU The new dimensions that take on illusory existence when the body of the loved woman is first revealed

UNIMGAG BU Love of oneself that passes understanding; a machine's dream

UNK TAK An out-of-date guide book; the skin shed by the snake that predicts rain

UPANG PLA Consciousness that one's agonised actions undertaken for love would look rather funny to one's friends

UPANG PLAP Consciousness that while one's agonised actions undertaken for love are on the whole rather funny to oneself, they might even look heroic to one's friends; a play with a cast of three or less

U RI RHI Two lovers drunk together

USANA NUTO A novel all about love, written by a computer

USAN I NUT Dying for love

USAN I ZUN BI Living for love; a tropical hurricane arriving from over the sea, generally at dawn

UZ Two very large people marrying after the prime of life

UZ TO KARDIN The realisation in childhood that one is the issue of two very large people who married after the prime of life

WE FAAK A park or a college closed for seemingly good reasons; a city where one wishes one could live

YA GAG Too much education; a digestive upset during travel

YA GAG LEE Apologies offered by a hostess for a bad meal

YA GA TUZ Bad meat; (Obs.) dirty fingernails

YAG ORN A president

YATUZ PATI (Obs.) The ceremony of eating one's maternal grandfather

YATUZ SHAK-SHAK NAPANG HOLI NUN Lying with one's maternal grandmother; when hens devour their young

YE FLIC TOT A group of men smiling and congratulating each other

YE FLU GAN Philosophical thoughts that don't amount to much; graffiti in a place of worship

YON TORN A paper tiger; two children with one toy

YON U SAN The hesitation a boy experiences before first kissing his first girl

YOR KIN BE A house; a circumlocution; a waterproof hat; the smile of a slightly imperfect wife

YUP PA A book in which everything is understandable except the author's purpose in writing it

YUPPA GA Stomach ache masquerading as eyestrain; a book in which nothing is understandable except the author's purpose in writing it

YUTH MOD The assumed bonhomie of visitors and strangers

ZO ZO CON A woman in another field

The Under-Privileged

The announcement that trickled from a thousand speech glands was as gentle as if it bubbled through chocolate.

'The first party to disembark will be the immigrant intake from Istinogurzibeshilaha. Will the immigrant intake from Istinogurzibeshilaha please assemble at their deck exit for departure to the Dansson Immunisation Centre as soon as possible. Your luggage will be unloaded later. Your luggage will be unloaded later. Thank you for your attention.'

The man with the slow pulse in his throat lay on his bunk and listened to the repetition of this speech without raising the lashless lids of his eyes. The luxurious voice brought him back from a region far beyond the grave, where shapeless things walked among blue shadows. When he had reoriented himself, he allowed his eyes to open.

His mate Corbish huddled on the floor by the door, trembling.

He sat up slowly, for the temperature in their cabin was still too low for activity. But she was less torpid than he, and came over to him to put an arm round his shoulders before he was properly sitting up. She rested the edge of her mouth against his.

'I'm afraid, Safton,' she said.

The words raised no rational response from him, though they conjured up a memory of the proddings of fright he had experienced walking through the tall wooden forests of his native planet.

'We've arrived, Safton. This is Dansson at last, and they want us to disembark. Now I'm terribly afraid. I've been afraid ever since I came out of light-freeze. They promised us a proper revival temperature, but the temperature in here is only ten degrees. They know we are no good when it isn't warm enough.'

Safton Serton's mind was unstirred by her alarm, like a dark and magical pool that throws no reflection. He huddled on the bunk, not moving except to blink his eyes.

'Suppose Dansson isn't the haven we were led to think it is,' she said. 'It couldn't be a trick of some sort, could it? I mean, suppose all those tests and examinations we passed on Istinogurzibeshilaha were just a bait to get us here . . . Oh, we hear that Dansson is so marvellous, but did we ever hear of one person who ever *returned* from Dansson? If they had some awful fate in store for us, we – why, we'd be completely helpless.'

She listened to the tramp of strange feet in the corridor beyond their door. She too had had her frightening dreams on the long interstellar journey here.

Her mother's tale had echoed back distortedly to her inner eye. She had seen that time when her mother was a little girl, forty years ago, and the humans who roamed the galaxy at will had first arrived and found her people in their wooden villages, dotted about those few zones of Istinogurzibeshilaha that would support life. In her dreams the visitors had been taller than the sad sequoias, and had brought not benefits and wonders but gigantic metal cages and coffins. She had woken with the clang of steel doors about her ears.

'We shouldn't have come, Safton,' she said. 'I'm afraid. Let's not stay on Dansson.'

The pulse came and went in his throat and he said, 'Dansson is one of the capital planets of the universe.'

It was the first face that drifted into his chilled mind. His system was functioning too slowly to respond to her, and by the same token he suspected that her mind was not working properly, and simply responding to subconscious fears.

Years of study at one of his home planet's new schools, established by men from Dansson, had led to his and Corbish's passing the series of examinations which alone could get you a passage to the admired cynosure of Dansson, chief planet in Sector Diamond, chief sector of the galaxy. He remembered the ranks of unfamiliar machines, the sick excitement, the flashing lights, in the Danssonian embassy as the tests progressed, and the pleasure and surprise of learning that he had passed with honours. Now Corbish and he would be able to get work in Dansson, and compete on more or less equal terms with the other families of humanity that congregated on Dansson. The challenge in the situation awed him. But he was not afraid – much.

The announcer spoke to them again, more pressingly.

Corbish was climbing into the clothes cupboard as the mellow voice began once more to urge them to the hatch.

'They're coming after us,' she said. 'They're coming to collect us. We must have been mad to let ourselves in for this.'

He had no emotion, but it was clear he would have to go to her. He pulled himself out of bed and climbed into the single garment of polyfur with which he had been issued at the start of the journey. Then he went over and attempted to reason with her. He was still drowsy, and closed his eyes as he spoke.

'It's no good,' she said. 'I *know* we've been trapped and tricked, Safton. We shouldn't have trusted the Warms. They're bigger than us.'

The beautiful yellow pupils of her eyes had contracted to slits in fear. As he looked at her, loving her, suddenly for her sake the fear got him too. He was overcome by the distrust the Istinogurzibeshilahans had for the races of humanity they called Warms. It was the distrust the under-privileged feel for those who have the advantages; because it was instinctive, it went deep. Corbish might well be right. He climbed into the cupboard with her.

She clutched him in the dark, whispering into his aural holes. 'We can wait till the ship is empty, then we can escape.'

'Where to? Istinogurzibeshilaha is hundreds of thousands of light years from here.'

'We were told of a special quarter where our kind live – Little Istino, wasn't it? If such a place exists, we can get there and find help.'

'You are mad, Corbish. Let's get out of here. What has given you these ideas? For years we longed to get here.'

'While we were under light-freeze, I dreamed there were Warms here in our cabin. They moved us about and examined us while we were helpless, carrying out experiments on us, sampling my blood. There's a tiny plaster on my wrist that was not there before. Feel!'

He ran his fingers over the soft and tiny scales of her arm. The feel of the plaster, a symbol of medical care, only reassured him.

'You had a bad dream, that's all. We're still alive, aren't we? Let's get out of here and stop being prehistoric.'

As he spoke, he heard someone enter their cabin. They froze into immobility, listening. Someone came into the centre of the room, stood there muttering under his breath (perhaps checking a pair of names off on a list?), and went out again.

They lay there, huddled together for a long while, listening to the gentle flow of announcements over the speech-glands. At last, like a stream drying up, they faded into silence, and the great starship was empty.

Safton and Corbish moved slowly through the streets, partly compelled by caution, partly because they had still not entirely overcome the effects of enforced hibernation.

It had been easy to dodge the few cleaners working in the corridors of the ship, and only slightly harder to escape from the immense complex of the space port. Now, in the city itself, they were entirely at a loss.

At first, they did not recognise that it was a city. Its buildings were not only widely spaced; by the rough-hewn standards of Istinogurzibeshilahan architecture, they were scarcely recognisable as buildings. For here material had gone to create units that represented the essential non-solidity of matter. Their shapes held enormous gaiety and ingenuity; occasionally fantasy had been followed to the point of folly, but to the wondering eyes of Safton and Corbish all was beautiful.

Between the buildings were floral layouts, terraced several storeys high. Some of these were alight with flowers, others dark with mighty trees much like the trees that grew in the fertile places of Istinogurzibeshilaha. The forbidding as well as the pretty was prominent, so that nature was not too sentimentally represented. There were also terraces on which wild animals prowled, and immense aviaries where the birds that flew would scarcely acknowledge their captivity. The total effect was as much like a vast zoo as a city.

Safton and Corbish walked along a pedestrian way, anxious yet entranced. On sunken roads, formidably fast traffic slid through the city; overhead, planes passed like missiles. On their own level, there were plenty of people walking at leisurely paces, but they were too nervous to stop anyone and ask their way.

'If we had some money, we could get a car to Little Istino,' Corbish said. They had been issued with Danssonian credit books on the ship, with the state of their finances entered into it. But by missing embarkation, they had missed collecting currency.

'If we come to a café, we'll hang about and try to pick up a little information,' Safton said. Unfortunately, they saw nothing resembling shops or cafés – or factories for that matter, for all of the strange buildings seemed purely residential.

After some minutes of walking, they came mutually to a halt. Avenues stretched interminably in all directions; they could go on walking for ever. Safton clutched Corbish's hand, motioning her to silence. He was watching a Warm nearby.

To judge from his appearance, the Warm was a velure, mutated human stock from Vermilion Sector, with a rich coat of fur covering him; presumably in deference to local mores, he wore a light garment over his body. He had stopped at one of the shapely pillars that Safton and Corbish had been passing ever since they left the space field. The pillars bulged a couple of feet from the ground, tapering again higher up and ending in a spike some nine feet above ground.

The velure slid open a panel in the bulge of the pillar, inserted something from his pocket, and dialled. He waited.

Well below the level of the fast planes, a series of massive objects sailed overhead. The effect was as if a covey of grand pianos had taken solemn wing. One of these objects moved off its course now, sank a couple of feet, and settled on top of the pillar so that the spike of the pillar plugged into a hole on its underside.

Lights flicked on the piano, and the velure dialled again.

Faint humming sounds came from the piano. A scoop descended from it down to pavement level, and a red light on the scoop flicked on and off. It died and a green light came on; the scoop opened. From it, the velure took something resembling a lacrosse racket.

By the time the scoop had retracted into the piano and it had removed itself from the pillar and resumed its aerial circuit, the velure was walking away, racket in hand.

It was at this point that Safton realised that the watchers were being watched. A man stood close by, surveying them quizzically.

'I guess you two are from out-system', he said, when they turned to look at him.

'What makes you think that?' Safton asked.

The man laughed, a gentle and inoffensive laugh. 'I've seen people from out-system amazed at our microfab circuit before now.'

He came over to them. 'Can I show you round or direct you anywhere? My time's my own this morning.'

Safton and Corbish looked at each other.

The man put his hand out. 'Name's Slen Kater. Welcome to Dansson.'

They hesitated until the hand was lowered.

'We are happy on our own, thank you,' Corbish said.

Kater shrugged. He was a small sturdy man with a wild mop of yellow hair, through which he now ran his rejected hand.

'The fact that I'm a Warm and you're a Cold makes no difference to me, lady,' he said, 'if that's what you're thinking.'

Corbish twisted her neck in a little Istinogurzibeshilahan gesture of anger. Safton said, 'Thank you, we should be glad of your help. You see, unfortunately after we disembarked my mate put her handbag down somewhere and we lost it. It contained all the money we possess.'

At once Kater was all sympathy.

'You've walked some way from the field. No doubt you'd like a drink before we get on our way. Perhaps you'll give me the pleasure.'

'We're very obliged to you,' Safton said. He took Corbish's arm because she was still looking displeased.

'No bother. Of course, you can dial yourself a drink on the microfab circuit if you have a Danssonian credit book, only it isn't so comfortable drinking in the street. Look, I'll show you.'

From his pocket he produced a credit book much like the ones Safton and Corbish had been issued with. He flipped open the panel in the pillar and inserted his book in a scanner. There was an illuminated directory at the back of the recess; Kater flicked it to the drinks section, read out the number of a synthop and dialled it on a dial.

'That sends a general call to one of the fab units,' Kater said, pointing upwards. 'Here comes one. These units have anti-gravity devices to keep them airborne. They're the factories of Dansson. Each one is packed with complex machines no bigger than your body cells. As you may know, the speed of really small mechanical devices is terrifically high. This chap would knock me up my own private plane if I wanted, and assemble it right here on the spot, in under five minutes. It turns out thousands of components in a second.'

The piano settled on the top of the pillar, and Kater dialled again.

'How do you pay for what you get?' Corbish asked.

'There's a scale of charges. The charge is deducted against my credit rating in my bank. My credit number goes through even before I dial – off the front of my book. Ah, one synthop!'

The scoop came down from the piano, opened, and revealed a beaker full of an amber liquid. Kater picked it out, poured its contents onto the ground, and flung the glass into a trash chute in the base of the pillar.

'Let's go and get a sociable drink,' he said.

They sat at a pleasant table drinking. Safton had chosen a warm chocolatey liquid that went far towards fully reviving him from the recent light-freeze, although he knew that it might later upset his digestion.

'You're looking better, the pair of you,' Kater said.

Setting her drink down, Corbish asked, 'Why do you think that man we saw got a racket from the – the microfab unit?'

'Because he was going to play a racket game, I suppose,' Kater said.

Safton felt his mate writhe. He knew intuitively that she thought she had asked a silly question and in so doing revealed the supposed inferiority of Colds. Perhaps they should never have joined up with this creature with the yellow hair; but he seemed to notice nothing untoward, and said cheerfully, 'Oh, you'll be happy on Dansson.'

'How do you know I will be happy on Dansson?' Corbish asked. 'Perhaps I will be miserable here. Perhaps I will miss my home.'

Kater cocked an eye at her and smiled. 'You'll be happy here,' he said. 'It's unavoidable.'

To soothe things over, Safton said, 'My mate Corbish really means that naturally things seem very strange to us as yet. Even the layout of the city is different from anything we know at home. For instance, your habit of building such massive big blocks and setting them among parkland is new to us. Why, this building we're in is almost as big as a city.'

'It is a city,' Kater said. 'Dansson is simply a nexus of cities, each inter-related with the others, but each with a function of its own. Since we managed to get all factory and distributive outlets mobile in the way you've seen, the old idea of a city has died; as a result, the distribution of population areas in Dansson is governed by social function rather than the old crude proximity to amenities.'

The block they had entered to get to the café was shaped like an immense wedge of cheese standing with its tapering end towards the clouds. They sat looking down on an inner courtyard; gesturing out at it, Safton asked, 'And what particular function has this building?'

'Well, we call it a classifornium. It's a sort of a – well, a museum-cum-zoo. Its contents come from all over the galaxy. I can show you round at least part of it, if you have the time.'

Safton saw from the corner of his eye that Corbish was signalling to him that they should escape from this Warm as soon as they had learnt from him where Little Istino was; and this he realised was prudent. But something else happened to him. He was seized by intellectual greed. He wanted to look into part of the museum, whatever happened. He knew that overwhelming curiosity of old; it had been responsible for the years in which he had sweated and toiled to prepare himself for the tests which, when passed, would bring him to Dansson, away from his dark green home planet. It was more than curiosity; it was a lust for know-ledge. It was this lust, rather than fear, which led him to dread death, for death would mean an end to knowing, an end to learning, an end to the piecing together of facts that must eventually lead to understanding – understanding, accepting, loving, the whole strange scheme of things.

'We've got the time,' he said.

'Splendid!' Kater said.

As he went to pay for their drinks, Corbish said, 'We must get away now. Why do we stay with this man?'

Rationalising, Safton said, 'We are as safe with Kater as anywhere. If we are being sought for, isn't a museum a good hiding place? Time enough to get to Little Istino later.'

Despairingly, she turned away. Her gaze caught a newscast that a patron of the café had left on the next table. She reached over and picked it up, hoping that perhaps it might contain a reference to the part of the city where their kind lived, perhaps even a hint that would show them how to get there.

She could read the headlines, with their news of a food surplus in the southern hemisphere, clearly enough. But the ordinary print . . . in the distant epoch when her ancestors had become nocturnal, many of their retinal cones had turned back into rods for better night vision; as a result the focus of her eyes was too coarse to achieve definition. She threw the cast down in vexation.

When Kater returned to the table, they joined him, and followed him into the immense wedge of the classifornium.

With a sure sense of what would fascinate anyone from out-system, Kater took them to the Inficarium, and they plunged straight away into a strange and wonderful world. As they stopped, to stare in awe at the vista of the main corridor of the Inficarium stretching into the distance, Kater grinned at them. 'Infectious disease has been wiped out on Dansson, and on most of the major planets in the sector,' he said. 'We are apt to forget that throughout the greater part of man's history, disease was the common experience of everyday life. Nowadays, with infectious illness eliminated, many of the once common bacteria and virus that caused disease are threatened with extinction. A few eras ago the IDPA – that's the Infectious Disease Preservation Association – was set up, and many interesting strains were saved from dying out and brought here. This Inficarium, in its present form, is fairly recent.'

Fascinated, Safton and Corbish went from gallery to gallery, peering through optical instruments that allowed them to view the various exhibits. In the Virus Hall, they could study the groups of virus that had once infested plants, the rare ones that infested fish and frogs and amphibians, and all the prolific varieties that once ranged almost at will throughout the phyla of animal life: here was the last surviving colony of swine fever, here were similar colonies of sheep pox, cowpox, horsepox, swine fever, cattle plague, dog distemper, and so on. Here was psittacosis.

'You see how beautiful, how individual they are, and how wonderfully developed to survive in their particular environments,' Kater said. 'They make you realise what a small part of life-sensation man is able to apprehend direct. It is a sad commentary on our times that they were permitted to get so near to extinction.'

In the next gallery, flourishing on tissue culture, they found some of the diseases that had infested man. First came the general infectious diseases, such as yellow fever, dengue, smallpox, measles, and similar strains. They were followed by the viruses infecting a particular part of the body: the influenzas, the parainfluenzas, adenoviruses, the enteroviruses, such as the three poliomyelitis viruses, and the lymphogranuloma inguinable virus present in venereal diseases.

From there they passed to the infections damaging the nervous system, and from there to near-relations of the viruses, the Rickettsiae, and from there into the Bacteria House, and so eventually, dazed, into the Protozoa House. But this time, the coarse-focus eyes of Corbish and Safton were exhausted, and they had to cry halt.

Leaving Kater to wait for them by one of the exits, they went to rinse their faces and cool their pupils. This gave Corbish the chance to insist that they made for Little Istino straight away.

When they mentioned the region to Slen Kater, he said that it was not far to go, and would show them how to get there.

'First, before we leave here, you will have to have an inoculation.'

'What for?'

'It's a precaution the governors of the Inficarium have to take – just in case any of the diseases escaped, you know,' Kater explained. 'It won't take a minute.'

Safton was still remote, his mind taken up with the tremendous range of alien life they had seen. When Corbish started to protest, he cut her off. It was to see things like the Inficarium that he had worked to get to Dansson, and his patience with her fears grew less by the hour.

She sensed this. After they had received their inoculation in a little bay next to the exit, she turned to the Warm.

'We did not expect such kindness as you have shown us on our first day on Dansson,' she said. 'My mate is less anxious than I about adjusting to this planet. I feel that we are despised as an inferior species of man.'

Unperturbed, Kater said, 'That feeling will die very soon.'

There was a silence as they walked along outside.

Embarrassed, Safton said, 'Do not embarrass Mr Kater, Corbish. Let him show us the way to Little Istino and then we must take up no more of his time.'

'Oh, I don't embarrass him; he would not mind what I said if he thought they were the words of an inferior breed. Would you like the history of us Colds who live on Istinogurzibeshilaha Mr Kater? You might find us as interesting as your rare diseases.'

Kater laughed shortly at that. 'We have come to the station where you can catch a car for Little Istino. Though I'm sure your history would have been very interesting.'

As he turned to go, Safton said humbly, 'Mr Kater, you must forgive us – our manners are upset after the light-journey. We still have one favour to ask you.'

'Please, Safton, let's ask someone else!' Corbish hissed, but as Kater turned towards them, Safton indicated the notice board by their side. 'Our eyes cannot adjust to the fine print, and we cannot read our destination. Would you be kind enough actually to see us into the right car?'

'Certainly.'

'And there's another thing – could you lend us the price of the fare? If we could have your credit number, we will repay you when we get established.'

'By all means,' Kater said.

'You may guess how unhappy we are at having to ask such degrading favours.'

'Nobody stays unhappy on Dansson – don't worry!'

The business of obtaining a ticket from the barricade of coin machines and then of descending to the right level looked very formidable to the strangers. The station was large, and appeared to house a maze of alternative routes. Also, it was uncomfortably warm to them, and they could feel their body temperatures rising. The pulses in their throats beat faster.

'This car will get you to Little Istino,' Kater said, as a yellow polyhedron slid into the platform. 'This is single-level service, so you will only have ten stops before you are there.'

As they hesitated by the door, Safton grasped his hand. 'You have been so hospitable, we cannot thank you enough. There is just one thing – where do we go when we get out at the other end?'

'Safton, do you think we can't ask when we get there?' Corbish said.

Smiling, Kater got into the car with them.

'It's not all that much out of my way,' he said.

As the car gathered speed, Corbish said, 'I really don't know why you tag along with us the way you do, Mr Kater. Do you take us for interesting freaks, or something?'

'We're all interesting freaks, if it comes to that. I just want to help you get to where you wish to go. Is that so strange?'

'And so all the while you must be thinking of us as poor cold-blooded creatures?'

'I'm afraid Corbish has rather a chip on her shoulder at present,' Safton said. 'The mere size of this city is so overwhelming . . .'

'Don't be silly, darling,' Corbish said. 'Didn't you feel inferior when you saw that in this place they have to strive to protect from extinction diseases that hundreds of people on Istinogurzibeshilaha die of every year? And it is apparent we can't think so efficiently as this gentleman, or see so well, or read with the same ability—' She broke off and turned to Kater. 'I'm sure you will excuse my behaviour and put it all down to my natural inferiority. Perhaps we have time for you to learn something of the history of man on Istinogurzibeshilaha, since you are so interested in us?

'I'll give it you in a nutshell – we've lived through two million years of under-privilege.

'I don't remember how long there have been forms of space travel, but it's a long long time. And about two million years ago, a big trans-vacuum liner got into trouble and had to put down on Istinogurzibeshilaha. Its drive was burnt out or something. Do you know what the world was like that those men and women found? It was a barren world, without all the amenities you take for granted on Dansson. Most of it consisted of bare and lifeless soil – there weren't enough earthworms and bacteria in the ground to render it fertile enough for plants. Well, there were in some favoured parts, chiefly by rivers. There the vegetation ran to primitive plants and trees – spore and cone-bearing things like cycads and giant ferns and spruce and pine and the giant sequoias.

'Oh, don't think such a dark green world does not possess a certain sort of grandeur. It does. But – no grass, no flowers, none of the angiosperms with their little seed pods that are embryo plants and afford nourishment for almost any kind of herbivore you can think of. You see what I mean. Istinogurzibeshilaha was at the beginning of its Lower Triassic period of evolutionary growth.

'Why do I say "was"? It still is! In another thirty million years or so, we shall just about graduate into the Jurassic.

'Can you imagine what hell those first men and women went through? In those deserts and dark forests, where the branches bow low under crude wooden cone flowers, what is there for a warm-blooded man? Nothing! No animals he can kill; the mammals have yet to arrive on our planet, because you don't get them until the higher-energy plant foods available in an age of flowers materialise.

'The early reptiles are about – stupid, inefficient, slow-moving, *coldblooded* things, that can exist on what nourishment is going. And amphibians. Fish and crustaceans, of course. They provided food.'

As she talked, her tone lost its earlier resentment. Her eyes rested on Kater's face as if it was merely an outcrop of that stern landscape she described. Safton sat looking out of the window, watching mile after mile of the galactic city flash by. Dusk was falling; the fantastic towers seemed to float in space.

'Those people – our ancestors – had to live off the land when their own supplies ran out. They had a fight, I can tell you. They had their own grains, but the grain failed when sown. It just wasn't the right environment. We have spiders, but most insects – not! No bees . . . they'll come after the flowers. Butterflies, no, and nothing like the high-speed metabolism of a true bird. So the people lived off the low-energy-level foods that were available.

'It was quite a change of diet. You know what happened? They didn't die out. They adapted. Maybe it would have been better if they had died out and we have never been. Because to adapt meant that they slowly became cold-blooded. When life begins on a planet, it always starts cold-blooded; in the circumstances, cold blood is a survival factor – did you know that, Mr Kater? That way, life is lived slowly and it can survive on the vitamin-poor diet to hand. Much later along the evolutionary path, you get chemical reactions in the bloodstream, heating it, which are caused by eating new foods – the richer foods that follow in the wake of the seed-bearing plants.

'Evolution played a trick on our ancestors. It sent them backward down the path. They became – we are – reptiles.'

'That's nonsense, Corbish,' Safton said. 'We are still men, simply cold-blooded.'

Corbish laughed.

'Oh yes, there are worse than us. Our unhappy ancestors went feral when their blood started running cold. For thousands of years, they were nocturnal in habit. One group of them about fifty strong left the rest and took to a semi-aquatic life in the region of the Assh-hassis Delta. You should see *their* descendants today, Mr Kater! Why, they aren't even viviparous! However alien I am to you, at least I don't lay eggs!'

She burst into ragged laughter, and Safton put his arms round her.

After a silence, Kater said, 'I expect you know the history of Dansson. We – man – slayed the seventy-seven nations of bipedal Danssonians before we took over the planet. I would think our history is more disgraceful than yours, if we are competing for disgracefulness.'

Corbish turned and looked at him with interest.

'I hope you are feeling better now,' he said to her. 'We are just about to get out.'

The car had stopped several times while she had been talking. Now it stopped again and they alighted into a station much like the one they had left. When they climbed above ground, it was to survey a part of the city much like the part they had left, except that here the great buildings were more conservative in shape and more riotous in colour. The microfab system floated over their heads, shuttling its pianos through the dusk.

Kater halted and pointed out a scarlet building down the avenue to their left.

'That's Little Istino. You will feel at home among people from your own planet – but don't forget we are all basically of the same kind,' he said.

'I wish to apologise for being rude earlier,' Corbish said. 'I will make no excuses for myself, but I was feeling very unhappy. Now I feel much more content.'

'Funnily enough, so do I,' Safton said. 'It must be your company, Mr Kater.'

Slen Kater shook his mop of hair. 'No, it's not that.' He laughed. 'Perhaps I will walk along with you right to your door. You're finding it hard to get rid of me, aren't you? You see there is a reason why you are feeling happier.'

They walked by his side, looking curiously at him as he continued.

'I am an Immigration Officer. I was asked to follow you when you did not check in for your inoculations at the space field. No, no, don't look so alarmed. With every ship that comes in we run into the problem of people who for one reason or another don't want to come and see us. They often prove to be the brightest and most interesting people.'

'After all this you are going to arrest us?'

'Certainly not. I have no need to. You will be peaceable and content here.'

'You sound very confident,' Corbish said.

'With reason. Everyone who lives on or comes to Dansson is inoculated against unhappiness. Oh, yes, we have a serum. Happiness is purely a glandular state. There's no illness here, as you know. Give a man the right glandular balance, and he will be happy. You had your inoculation that you missed at the space field as we left the Inficarium.'

'Wait a minute,' Safton said, stopping abruptly. 'You said that was a routine shot to ensure we had not picked up any diseases.'

'My dear Safton – there was no possible danger of that. Those dangerous little life forms are all sealed away safely. No, it seemed a good time to make you feel happier. It has worked already, hasn't it?'

'My god!' Safton raised his fists, looked at them and laughed. There was no force in them, no core to his anger, no dismay in his surprise. He seized Corbish's arm and hurried her along, excited at the feeling of pleasure that swept over him. They certainly knew how to live on Dansson.

'Do you have these injections too, Mr Kater?' Corbish asked.

'Certainly. Only being resident, I don't need as much as . . . as visitors. Only the very eminent are allowed to be creatively miserable. As you're new here, you've had a stiff dose to tide you over the next few months.'

She tried to feel vexed at this. Somehow she thought there was something in his statement that should have roused her apprehensions. Instead, she could only see what a joke he had played on them. She giggled, and was still giggling when they reached the scarlet structure, towering high above them.

'This is Little Istino, and you'll be fine here. There are plenty of your own kind within,' Kater said. 'And none of those egg-laying Assh-hassis to worry you. They have a separate block elsewhere in the city.'

'You mean you have them here too? What use can they be to a wonderful modern planet like Dansson?'

Immigration Officer Kater stuck his hands in his pockets and looked down genially at them; they were nice little beings really.

'I admit the Assh-hassis aren't much *use*,' he said. 'But then neither are many of the thousands of lesser races of man we house here. You see, as true man spreads across this neck of the galaxy, he is slowly wiping out those half-brothers who are no match for him. So they have to be preserved – for study and so on. It's roughly like the diseases, I suppose.'

Corbish and Safton looked at each other.

'I never thought of the Assh-hassis as a disease,' Safton said. 'They'll be amused when we get back to Istinogurzibeshilaha and tell our folks.'

'Oh, you'll never go back there,' Kater said. 'Nobody ever leaves Dansson.'

'Why not?'

He smiled. 'You'll see. You'll be too happy to leave.'

They were still laughing as they parted from him, the best of friends all round.

'That was a very comical remark he made,' Corbish said, as they waved him farewell, 'about parts of Dansson being reserved for inferior types of human – almost like a cage in a zoo, except I suppose the inhabitants don't notice the bars.'

'Wouldn't the Assh-hassis be furious if they realised the truth?' Safton chuckled.

Arm in arm, they turned and hurried into the big scarlet-painted cage.

Something from the Turkish

Getting down the garden path to the house was the worst bit. The line of laburnums had ceased their golden rain of blossom and now shed large tears of wet on those human beings passing by Matilda Cagan who came in from the rain, from the veritable downpour. It was now dark. She went straight upstairs to her bathroom, stripped off, and towelled herself. Sitting down on the white stool by the shower, she allowed herself to recover emotionally.

It was nothing really. She was sorry to find herself so upset. Such a trivial thing – and on this grand occasion when Trafford University had presented her with an award for her work of translation. That fine award, hard-earned. 'Good for you, Tilda,' she said, burying her face in a hand towel.

She recalled what Michel Foucalt had written, saying that each of us carried within us a fragment of night. It was true. For her, the fragment was suddenly almost tangible. And she searched for anything by anyone that would help to unfold – well, to unfold what she thought of as the overwhelming mystery of life, of living. And those who gravitated towards an understanding . . . well, they too seemed, she thought, baffled by the mystery of it. As she was.

The mystery of bloody existence . . .

Powdering herself, she quoted aloud Foucault, about that piece of night within everyone.

'. . . And a bit of fog,' she said. She sighed. In her tidy little bedroom, she slipped on knickers and one of her red dresses. Eased her feet into slippers. She needed a drink.

Going downstairs, she quoted aloud words attributed to Socrates. She was assuming that Socrates had existed. Was this, she asked herself, evasion tactics? 'It seemed to me,' he was reported as saying, 'a superlative thing to know the explanation for everything, why it comes to be. Why it perishes. Why it is.' Of course, he never had a chance; while she, a prize-winner . . . ?

And why on earth hadn't she stayed longer, after receiving her award, after all the friendly, slightly envious, celebrations. Had another glass . . . Enjoyed herself. With Vincent Arbuthnot for instance. Matilda smiled to herself, thinking of the celebratory kiss Vincent had given her, pressing against her.

She went into the kitchen and seized a half-empty bottle of a South Australian Shiraz most of which she poured into a tumbler. Vincent should have followed it up. Typical of that generation of English men, maybe wanting a screw but too polite to reach out for it.

As she raised the glass to her lips, again the words came back to her from the morning's email from Dan Anvers. He had typed something vaguely critical of Carol, the woman with whom he had been living for years. Then he had written that incomplete sentence, 'Had it been otherwise . . .'

Matilda gazed out at the weedy square of lawn, her patch of garden vaguely illuminated by the kitchen light. Had it been otherwise . . . Were matters, she asked herself, ever otherwise? Was this Dan expressing regret that he had not married her, Matilda? Poor lonely prize-winning Matilda, she told herself, with a burst of angry laughter.

Had she not felt regret when they, when Dan and she, had gone their different ways, after their affair?

And that different way . . . Well, it had been otherwise.

She felt, as she stood reading Dan's email, things could never be otherwise. You might think they could be otherwise . . .

But wasn't that beyond her capacity?

Of course, she could email Dan in response. She could drive over and see him . . . Then she remembered he had put on weight. He had become jowly. He now grew side-whiskers.

Did he imagine side-whiskers were posh?

And he had recently taken to wearing khaki shorts.

She no longer wanted him. Probably he did not want her. Oh, oh, yes, maybe, she wanted him to want her! That ambiguous half-sentence was hardly a declaration of love.

'Had it been otherwise . . .'

She struggled with the meaning of the words, beginning to see it as a fragment of profound philosophy. That small 'it' was a problem and seemed to comprise, packed within its narrow confines, a representation of – well, of human characteristics, with all their compromises and failures.

Then, as she went into her little living room, where she worked, where her desk and computer were, she remembered that the Sheckleys down the street had promised her one of their fluffy white kittens; she looked forward to that. If she was not friendly with the Sheckleys, that would be otherwise.

On the desk, bound in black cloth, lay a copy of her award-winning volume, published by the Orhon University Press, 'Early Declarations from the Turkish', with its sub-title, 'Reflections from Lake Hosho Tsaidam'.

On the volume stood an empty coffee mug, which Matilda now removed. She had worked for over two years on this volume, not counting her spell in hospital. She had worked mainly on a German translation of a Danish scholar, a V. Thomsen, a late Nineteenth Century man, who had produced an 'Inscriptions de l'Orkhon Dechiffrees'.

The inscriptions on which Matilda, with her limited knowledge of foreign tongues, involved herself, centred round carvings of a Turkish runic alphabet regarding two Turkish princes of the eighteenth century. Matilda had been excited by the knowledge that these inscriptions represented the oldest surviving examples of the Turkish language.

Matilda's grandfather had had Turkish blood. While in an early stage of her work, she had visited a lake flowing into Lake Baikal, near which were standing the memorial stones to the princes.

She opened the volume on her desk. Pages 89 and 90 were revealed. She was not interested. She was preoccupied. Although at one time she had teased herself by thinking that she might be descended through the centuries by these old lauded princes.

And had her life been situated otherwise . . . Well, that was all nonsense. 'Otherwise' . . . what a ghastly word!

Life was full of otherwises – and generally used carelessly, as Anvers in his khaki shorts had done.

But of course, she told herself, taking another swig of the cheap red wine, words like otherwise were needed, to cloak and express all that was impossible in human life.

Poor Little Warrior!

Claude Ford knew exactly how it was to hunt a brontosaurus. You crawled heedlessly through the mud among the willows, through the little primitive flowers with petals as green and brown as a football field, through the beauty-lotion mud. You peered out at the creature sprawling among the reeds, its body as graceful as a sock full of sand. There it lay, letting the gravity cuddle it diaper-damp to the marsh, running its big rabbit-hole nostrils a foot above the grass in a sweeping semicircle, in a snoring search for more sausagey reeds. It was beautiful; here horror had reached its limits, come full circle and finally disappeared up its own sphincter. Its eyes gleamed with the liveliness of a week-dead corpse's big toe, and its compost breath and the fur in its crude aural cavities were particularly to be recommended to anyone who might otherwise have felt inclined to speak lovingly of the work of Mother Nature.

But as you – little mammal with opposed digit and .65 self-loading, semi-automatic, dual-barrelled, digitally-computed, telescopically-sighted, rustless, high-powered rifle gripped in your otherwise defenceless paws – slide along under the bygone willows, what primarily attracts you is the thunder-lizard's hide. It gives off a smell as deeply resonant as the bass note of a piano. It makes the elephant's epidermis look like a thin sheet of crinkled paper. It is grey as the Viking seas, daft-deep as cathedral foundations. What contact possible to bone could allay the fever of that flesh? Over it scamper – you can see them from here! – the little brown lice that live in those grey walls and canyons, gay as ghosts, cruel as crabs. If one of them jumped on you, it would very likely break your back. And when one of those parasites stops to cock its leg against one of the bronto's vertebrae, you can see it carries in its turn its own crop of easy-livers, each as big as a lobster, for you're near now, oh, so near that you can hear the monster's primitive heart-organ knocking, as the ventricle keeps miraculous time with the auricle.

Time for listening to the oracle is past; you're beyond the stage for omens, you're now headed in for the kill, yours or his; superstition has had its little day for today, from now on only this windy nerve of yours, this shaky conglomeration of muscle entangled untraceably beneath the sweat-shiny carapace of skin, this bloody little urge to slay the dragon, is going to answer all your orisons.

You could shoot now. Just wait till that tiny steam-shovel head pauses once again to gulp down a quarry-load of bulrushes, and with one inexpressibly vulgar bang you can show the whole indifferent Jurassic world that it's standing looking down the business end of evolution's sex-shooter. You know why you pause, even as you pretend not to know why you pause: that old worm conscience, long as a baseball pitch, long-lived as a tortoise, is at work; through every sense it slides, more monstrous than the serpent. Through the passions: saying here is a sitting duck, O Englishman! Through the intelligence: whispering that boredom, the kite-hawk who never feeds, will settle again when the task is done. Through the nerves: sneering that when the adrenalin currents cease to flow the vomiting begins. Through the maestro behind the retina: plausibly forcing the beauty of the view upon you.

Spare us that poor old slipper-slopper of a word, beauty; holy mum, is this a travelogue! *'Perched now on this titanic creature's back, we see a round dozen – and, folks, let me stress that "round" – gaudily plumaged birds, exhibiting among them all the colour you might expect to find on lovely, fabled Copacabana Beach. They're so round because they feed on the droppings that fall from the rich man's table. Watch this lovely shot now! See the bronto's tail lift . . . Yep, a couple of haystacks-full at least emerging from his nether end. That sure was a beauty, folks, delivered straight from consumer to consumer. The birds are fighting over it now. Hey, you, there's enough to go 'round, and anyhow, you're round enough already . . . And nothing to do now but hop back up onto the old rump steak and wait for the next round. And now as the sun stinks in the Jurassic West, we say "Fare well on that diet . . ."'*

No, you're procrastinating, and that's a lifework. Shoot the beast and put it out of your agony. Taking your courage in your hands, you raise it to shoulder level and squint down its sights. There is a terrible report; you are half stunned. Shakily, you look about you. The monster still munches, relieved to have broken enough wind to unbecalm the Ancient Mariner.

Angered (or is it some subtler emotion?), you now burst from the bushes and confront it, and this exposed condition is typical of the straits into which your consideration for yourself and others continually pitches you. Consideration? Or again something subtler? Why should you be confused just because you come from a confused civilisation? But that's a point to deal with later, if there is a later, as these two hog-wallow eyes pupilling you all over from spitting distance tend to dispute. Let it not be by jaws alone, O monster, but also by huge hoofs and, if convenient to yourself, by mountainous rollings upon me! Let death be a saga, sagacious, Beowulfate.

Quarter of a mile distant is the sound of a dozen hippos springing boisterously in gymsuits from the ancestral mud, and next second a walloping great tail as long as Sunday and as thick as Saturday night comes slicing over your head. You duck as duck you must, but the beast missed you anyway because it so happens that its co-ordination is no better than yours would be if you had to wave the Woolworth Building at a tarsier. This done, it seems to feel it has done its duty. It forgets you. You just wish you could forget yourself as easily; that was, after all, the reason you had to come the long way here. *Get Away from It All*, said the time travel brochure, which meant for you getting away from Claude Ford, a husbandman as futile as his name with a terrible wife called Maude. Maude and Claude Ford. Who could not adjust to themselves, to each other, or to the world they were born in. It was the best reason in the as-it-is-at-present-constituted world for coming back here to shoot giant saurians – if you were fool enough to think that one hundred and fifty million years either way made an ounce of difference to the muddle of thoughts in a man's cerebral vortex.

You try and stop your silly, slobbering thoughts, but they have never really stopped since the coca-collaborating days of your growing up; God, if adolescence did not exist it would be unnecessary to invent it! Slightly, it steadies you to look again on the enormous bulk of this tyrant vegetarian into whose presence you charged with such a mixed death-life wish, charged with all the emotion the human orga(ni)sm is capable of. This time the bogeyman is real, Claude, just as you wanted it to be, and this time you really have to face up to it before it turns and faces you again. And so again you lift Ole Equaliser, waiting till you can spot the vulnerable spot.

The bright birds sway, the lice scamper like dogs, the marsh groans, as bronto sways over and sends his little cranium snaking down under the bile-bright water in a forage for roughage. You watch this; you have never been so jittery before in all your jittered life, and you are counting on this catharsis wringing the last drop of acid fear out of this system forever. OK, you keep saying to yourself insanely over and over, your million-dollar twenty-second-century education going for nothing, OK, OK. And as you say it for the umpteenth time, the crazy head comes back out of the water like a renegade express and gazes in your direction.

Grazes in your direction. For as the champing jaw with its big blunt molars like concrete posts works up and down, you see the swamp water course out over rimless lips, lipless rims, splashing your feet and sousing the ground. Reed and root, stalk and stem, leaf and loam, all are intermittently visible in that masticating maw and, struggling, straggling or tossed among them, minnows, tiny crustaceans, frogs – all destined in that awful, jaw-full movement to turn into bowel movement. And as the glump-glump-glumping takes place, above it the slime-resistant eyes again survey you.

These beasts live up to two hundred years, says the time travel brochure, and this beast has obviously tried to live up to that, for its gaze is centuries old, full of decades upon decades of wallowing in its heavyweight thoughtlessness until it has grown wise on twitterpatedness. For you it is like looking into a disturbing misty pool; it gives you a psychic shock, you fire off both barrels at your own reflection. Bang-bang, the dum-dums, big as paw-paws, go.

POOR LITTLE WARRIOR!

With no indecision, those century-old lights, dim and sacred, go out. These cloisters are closed till Judgement Day. Your reflection is torn and bloodied from them forever. Over their ravaged panes nictitating membranes slide slowly upwards, like dirty sheets covering a cadaver. The jaw continues to munch slowly, as slowly the head sinks down. Slowly, a squeeze of cold reptile blood toothpastes down the wrinkled flank of one cheek. Everything is slow, a creepy Secondary Era slowness like the drip of water, and you know that if you had been in charge of creation you would have found some medium less heart-breaking than Time to stage it all in.

Never mind! Quaff down your beakers, lords, Claude Ford has slain a harmless creature. Long live Claude the Clawed!

You watch breathless as the head touches the ground, the long laugh of neck touches the ground, the jaws close for good. You watch and wait for something else to happen, but nothing ever does. Nothing ever would. You could stand here watching for a hundred and fifty million years, Lord Claude, and nothing would ever happen here again. Gradually, your bronto's mighty carcass, picked loving clean by predators, would sink into the slime, carried by its own weight deeper; then the waters would rise, and old Conqueror Sea come in with the leisurely air of a card-sharp dealing the boys a bad hand. Silt and sediment would filter down over the mighty grave, a slow rain with centuries to rain in. Old bronto's bed might be raised up and then set down again perhaps half a dozen times, gently enough not to disturb him, although by now the sedimentary rocks would be forming thick around him. Finally, when he was wrapped in a tomb finer than any Indian rajah ever boasted, the powers of the Earth would raise him high on their shoulders until, sleeping still, bronto would lie in a brow of the Rockies high above the waters of the Pacific. But little any of that would count with you, Claude the Sword; once the midget maggot of life is dead in the creature's skull, the rest is no concern of yours.

You have no emotion now. You are just faintly put out. You expected dramatic thrashing of the ground, or bellowing; on the other hand, you are glad the thing did not appear to suffer. You are like all cruel men, sentimental; you are like all sentimental men, squeamish. You tuck the gun under your arm and walk around the dinosaur to view your victory.

You prowl past the ungainly hoofs, around the septic white of the cliff of belly, beyond the glistening and how-thought-provoking cavern of the cloaca, finally posing beneath the switch-back sweep of tail-to-rump. Now your disappointment is as crisp and obvious as a visiting card: the giant is not half as big as you thought it was. It is not one-half as large, for example, as the image of you and Maude is in your mind. Poor little warrior, science will never invent anything to assist the titanic death you want in the contraterrene caverns of your fee-fi-fo-fumblingly fearful id!

Nothing is left to you now but to slink back to your time-mobile with a belly full of anticlimax. See, the bright dung-consuming birds have already cottoned on to the true state of affairs; one by one, they gather up their hunched wings and fly disconsolately off across the swamp to other hosts. They know when a good thing turns bad, and do not wait for the vultures to drive them off; all hope abandon, ye who entrail here. You also turn away.

You turn, but you pause. Nothing is left but to go back, no, but 2181 AD is not just the home date; it is Maude. It is Claude. It is the whole, awful, hopeless, endless business of trying to adjust to an overcomplex environment, of trying to turn yourself into a cog. Your escape from it into the *Grand Simplicities of the Jurassic*, to quote the brochure again, was only a partial escape, now over.

So you pause, and as you pause, something lands socko on your back, pitching you face forward into tasty mud. You struggle and scream as lobster claws tear at your neck and throat. You try to pick up the rifle but cannot, so in agony you roll over, and next second the crab-thing is greedying it on your chest. You wrench at its shell, but it giggles and pecks your fingers off. You forgot when you killed the bronto that its parasites would leave it, and that to a little shrimp like you they would be a deal more dangerous than their host.

You do your best, kicking for at least three minutes. By the end of that time there is a whole pack of the creatures on you. Already they are picking your carcass loving clean. You're going to like it up there on top of the Rockies; you won't feel a thing.

How the Gates Opened and Closed

Among the storytellers gathered round the long table was a fair-haired man past his prime, an untidy man, wearing trainers, tattered jeans and a yellow sweater. He had given his name indistinctly as Dillow.

No one of the company had heard of Dillow. No one had read any of his stories. He had been sitting for an hour, listening, not speaking, his hands under the table and thrust into his jeans pockets.

When the laughter at the ending of a story had died down, he sat bolt upright. He spoke, not challengingly but with assurance.

'Your stories are all choked with events, like streams choked by weeds. Stories should not be like that. I will tell you a tale with nothing happening in it. Because my life has been empty.'

'We fill our stories with events for people with empty lives,' said one of the women storytellers.

Dillow gave her a half-smile. 'You understand that when I say my life has been empty, I mean empty of event. It has been full of drama.'

The people round the table reacted variously to this remark. Some responded sympathetically, some found it pretentious, though they might have accepted it on paper. All, however, challenged Dillow to tell this eventless story of his.

Dillow shrugged his shoulders, looked about him for quiet, and began.

'There was an old man in a remote village. He lived with his daughter and her husband. Every evening, he took three geese down to drink in the pond at the end of the village. He led one goose with a length of string round its neck, the same old string he had used for several years. The other two geese followed the first one.'

Someone interrupted Dillow, saying, 'At this point, a wolf or fox could run out of a wood and carry off one of the geese.'

'No such event. The visit to the pond was always peaceful. The old man, whose name was Lee, exchanged a few words with people on his way there and back. As a matter of fact, this village was almost deserted. He had been a soldier in his time – a soldier in several campaigns. He once was forced to march eight days at a stretch.'

'Action there! Don't cheat, Dillow!' one of the listeners said.

'All in the past, long ago. The country had been ravaged by war, and by the famines that follow on the heels of war. I should have mentioned that the village was in ruins. Hardly a house was left intact after various armies had passed through that way. Most of the inhabitants had fled, or had been killed.'

'You are forced to tell us of many great events.'

'I merely mention them in passing,' said Dillow. 'I should also mention that the old religion had died, or appeared to have died. No one visited the temple any more, or attempted to restore its ruin. But what I'm talking about is simply an old bent man, not in the best of health, taking three geese to the pond every evening.'

'But one day the geese escape, surely?' said one of the storytellers at the far end of the table.

'Geese are friendly and intelligent birds. They'd talk if they could. They enjoyed their walk every evening, they enjoyed their splash in the pond. And they would no more think of leaving their master than Lee would think of leaving them. They always followed him willingly back to Lee's daughter's house and laid eggs for the family as often as they could.'

'Very dramatic, I must say!'

'What you must learn to enjoy is the lack of event, the silences of a story.' Dillow paused, as if to emphasise the importance of story. Some of his listeners fidgeted – even when he continued on a different tack.

'There are as many kinds of story as there are kinds of reader. People learn as much from inaction as action. And the life of this old man with his geese must be contrasted with another life: the life of a prince who lived nearby – a prince born in the same year as the old man, the Year of the Buffalo.'

'Ha, another protagonist! Now you find it necessary to introduce a little character conflict into the dull tale.'

'Not at all. The two men encountered one another but once, many years earlier, when the prince was on his way to his palace, which stood aloof at the end of the village. Lee got in the way of his carriage. The prince shouted to him, kindly enough, "Don't you value your life, man?" Lee never forgot the words, and often repeated them to his friends in the years of war; he marvelled at them, firstly because he had been spoken to by a prince, and secondly because he had never thought that a peasant's life could have value. "Don't you value your life . . . ?" The question was a puzzlement to him.'

'This is all past-tense stuff, you know,' one of the women reminded him.

'Well, if there's tranquillity anywhere, perhaps it resides in the past . . . When old Lee was standing by the pond with his geese, he could see the gates of the palace. Never once, during all the troubles and pestilences that beset the province, had those gates been opened. Until one day, to his amazement, he heard a gong struck and witnessed the opening of the gates. What a creaking those unused hinges set up between them! And out came the prince himself.

'The prince stood in the roadway, and Lee – at the distance of two hundred metres – bowed to him profoundly.'

'So Lee got his head chopped off?'

'You must consider the situation. On the one hand, an old soldier, survivor of several campaigns, a man whose parents had been killed by bandits, whose wife had died in one of the epidemics that swept the country, and who now lived a thousand miles from the village where he was born.

'And on the other hand, this person of privilege, born to reign over vast territories, who had known no hardship, who – unlike Lee – had been able to choose how he would live.

'Old Lee was a thin wasted man with a face brown and wrinkled as a walnut. His ribs showed under his thin shirt. Although his vision was not of the best, it was for another reason he would have failed to recognise the prince, had it not been for the latter's elaborate garments.

'When he had seen the prince many years earlier, the prince had been a strikingly handsome young man, lean, athletic, known for his prowess at archery and blood sports. Now Lee was staring at a bloated creature with a bald pate. The cut of his clothes could not conceal bow legs and a sagging stomach. He had waddled rather than walked through the palace gates . . .'

One of the storytellers interrupted. 'Fine, fine, but enough of these comparisons: the rich and the poor. What of it?'

'Simply this. I wished to tell you a story without event. That I've done. Once the prince had regarded his ravaged territories with disfavour, he turned and went back into his palace. The gates closed behind him. Old Lee collected his geese and returned to his daughter's house as usual. That night, they ate some rice with chopped goose egg and chilli for supper.'

'You mean to say he and the prince never even shouted at each other? Never even spoke? Couldn't you have arranged it for the prince to recognise your old chap, maybe invite him in to a banquet? Your old man never even spat at the prince? That's what I call a disappointing story.'

'It would have been out of character to have a peasant spit at a prince, or a prince recognise a peasant. But don't you see that the story is about the lack of event? You believe tragedies are made from events, like Sophocles's *Oedipus*. But sometimes they are made from the vacuum created by a failure of contact.

'The prince abrogated his powers. Instead of exercising his traditional rights and duties, and maintaining some form of civil order, he had retreated into his private world and enjoyed his concubines. His was a life without history. For thirty years, he closed his eyes to the fate of his people and his bronze doors upon life.

'Because of that idleness, that dereliction of duty, his province underwent too much history. It became a theatre of events. Events ruled. The period was referred to later as The Age of the Seven Wars. Many volumes were written about it.'

The storytellers looked at each other up and down the long table. One of them said, 'Couldn't you have made up a more interesting story about the wars themselves, and the people taking part in them? Or we could have had a nice erotic story about what went on in the prince's palace all those years . . .'

Dillow shook his head, saying nothing more.

All he had had in mind was the picture of an old man walking in a ruined village with his three white geese, an old man who had once been asked the question, 'Don't you value your life?' He understood that the very poor could never answer such things: just as the prince had never valued the life even of a goose.

The Worm that Flies

The traveller was too absorbed in his reveries to notice when the snow began to fall. He walked slowly, his stiff and elaborate garments, fold over fold, ornament over ornament, standing out from his body like a wizard's tent.

The road along which he travelled had been falling into a great valley, and was increasingly hemmed in by walls of mountain. On several occasions, it had seemed that a way out of these huge accumulations of earth matter could not be found, that the geological puzzle was insoluble, the chthonian arrangement of discord irresolvable: and then vale and drumlin created between them a new direction, a surprise, an escape, and the way took fresh heart and plunged recklessly still deeper into the encompassing upheaval.

The traveller, whose name to his wife was Tapmar and to the rest of the world Argustal, followed this natural harmony in complete paraesthesia, so close was he in spirit to the atmosphere prevailing here. So strong was this bond, that the freak snowfall merely heightened his rapport.

Though the hour was only midday, the sky became the intense blue-grey of dusk. The Forces were nesting in the sun again, obscuring its light. Consequently, Argustal was scarcely able to detect when the layered and fractured bulwark of rock on his left side, the top of which stood unseen perhaps a mile above his head, became patched by artificial means, and he entered the domain of the human company of Or.

As the way made another turn, he saw a wayfarer before him, heading in his direction. It was a great pine, immobile until warmth entered the world again and sap stirred enough in its wooden sinews for it to progress slowly forward once more. He brushed by its green skirts, apologetic but not speaking.

This encounter was sufficient to raise his consciousness above its trance level. His extended mind, which had reached out to embrace the splendid terrestrial discord hereabouts, now shrank to concentrate again on the particularities of his situation, and he saw that he had arrived at Or.

The way bisected itself, unable to choose between two equally unpromising ravines, and Argustal saw a group of humans standing statuesque in the left-hand fork. He went towards them, and stood there silent until they should recognise his presence. Behind him, the wet snow crept into his footprints.

These humans were well advanced into the New Form, even as Argustal had been warned they would be. There were five of them standing here, their great brachial extensions bearing some tender brownish foliage, and one of them attenuated to a height of almost twenty feet. The snow lodged in their branches and in their hair.

Argustal waited for a long span of time, until he judged the afternoon to be well advanced, before growing impatient. Putting his hands to his mouth, he shouted fiercely at them, 'Ho then, Tree-men of Or, wake you from your arboreal sleep and converse with me. My name is Argustal to the world, and I travel to my home in far Talembil, where the seas run pink with the spring plankton. I need from you a component for my parapatterner, so rustle yourselves and speak, I beg!'

Now the snow had gone, and a scorching rain driven away its traces. The sun shone again, but its disfigured eye never looked down into the bottom of this ravine. One of the humans shook a branch, scattering water drops all round, and made preparation for speech.

This was a small human, no more than ten feet high, and the old primate form which it had begun to abandon perhaps a couple of million years ago was still in evidence. Among the gnarls and whorls of its naked flesh, its mouth was discernible; this it opened and said, 'We speak to you, Argustal-to-the-world. You are the first ape-human to fare this way in a great time. Thus you are welcome, although you interrupt our search for new ideas.'

'Have you found any new ideas?' Argustal asked, with his customary boldness.

'Indeed. But it is better for our senior to tell you of it, if he so judges good.'

It was by no means dear to Argustal whether he wished to hear what the new idea was, for the Tree-men were known for their deviations into incomprehensibility. But there was a minor furore among the five, as if private winds stirred in their branches, and he settled himself on a boulder, preparing to wait. His own quest was so important that all impediments to its fulfilment seemed negligible.

Hunger overtook him before the senior spoke. He hunted about and caught slow-galloping grubs under logs, and snatched a brace of tiny fish from the stream, and a handful of nuts from a bush that grew by the stream.

Night fell before the senior spoke. Tall and knotty, his vocal cords were clamped within his gnarled body, and he spoke by curving his branches until his finest twigs, set against his mouth, could be blown through, to give a slender and whispering version of language. The gesture made him seem curiously like a maiden who spoke with her finger cautiously to her lips.

'Indeed we have a new idea, O Argustal-to-the-world, though it may be beyond your grasping or our expressing. We have perceived that there is a dimension called time, and from this we have drawn a deduction.

'We will explain dimensional time simply to you like this. We know that all things have lived so long on Earth that their origins are forgotten. What we can remember carries from that lost-in-the-mist thing up to this present moment; it is the time we inhabit, and we are used to think of it as all the time there is. But we men of Or have reasoned that this is not so.'

'There must be other past times in the lost distances of time,' said Argustal, 'but they are nothing to us because we cannot touch them as we can our own pasts.'

As if this remark had never been, the silvery whisper continued, 'As one mountain looks small when viewed from another, so the things in our past that we remember look small from the present. But suppose we moved back to that past to look at this present! We could not see it – yet we know it exists. And from this we reason that there is still more time in the future, although we cannot see it.'

For a long while, the night was allowed to exist in silence, and then Argustal said, 'Well, I don't see that as being very wonderful reasoning. We know that, if the Forces permit, the sun will shine again tomorrow, don't we?'

The small tree-man who had first spoken, said, 'But "tomorrow" is expressional time. *We* have discovered that tomorrow exists in dimensional time also. It is real already, as real as yesterday.'

'Holy spirits!' thought Argustal to himself, 'why did I get involved in philosophy?' Aloud he said, 'Tell me of the deduction you have drawn from this.'

Again the silence, until the senior drew together his branches and whispered from a bower of twiggy fingers, 'We have proved that tomorrow is no surprise. It is as unaltered as today or yesterday, merely another yard of the path of time. But we comprehend that things change, don't we? You comprehend that, don't you?'

'Of course. You yourselves are changing, are you not?'

'It is as you say, although we no longer recall what we were before, for that thing is become too small back in time. So: if time is all of the same quality, then it has no change, and thus cannot force change. So: there is another unknown element in the world that forces change!'

Thus in their fragmentary whispers they reintroduced sin into the world.

Because of the darkness, a need for sleep was induced in Argustal. With the senior tree-man's permission, he climbed up into his branches and remained fast asleep until dawn returned to the fragment of sky above the mountains and filtered down to their retreat. Argustal swung to the ground, removed his outer garments, and performed his customary exercises. Then he spoke to the five beings again, telling them of his parapatterner, and asking for certain stones.

Although it was doubtful whether they understood what he was doing, they gave him permission, and he moved round about the area, searching for a necessary stone, his senses blowing into nooks and crannies for it like a breeze.

The ravine was blocked at its far end by a rock fall, but the stream managed to pour through the interstices of the detritus into a yet lower defile. Climbing painfully, Argustal scrambled over the mass of broken rock to find himself in a cold and moist passage, a mere cavity between two great thighs of mountain. Here the light was dim, and the sky could hardly be seen, so far did the rocks overhang on the many shelves of strata overhead. But Argustal scarcely looked up. He followed the stream where it flowed into the rock itself, to vanish forever from human view.

He had been so long at his business, trained himself over so many millennia, that the stones almost spoke to him, and he became more certain than ever that he would find a stone to fit in with his grand design.

It was there. It lay just above the water, the upper part of it polished. When he had prised it out from the surrounding pebbles and gravel, he lifted it and could see that underneath it was slightly jagged, as if a smooth gum grew black teeth. He was surprised, but as he squatted to examine it, he began to see what was necessary to the design of his parapatterner was precisely some such roughness. At once, the next step of the design revealed itself, and he saw for the first time the whole thing as it would be in its entirety. The vision disturbed and excited him.

He sat where he was, his blunt fingers round the rough-smooth stone, and for some reason he began to think about his wife Pamitar. Warm feelings of love ran through him, so that he smiled to himself and twitched his brows.

By the time he stood up and climbed out of the defile, he knew much about the new stone. His nose-for-stones sniffed it back to times when it was a much larger affair, when it occupied a grand position on a mountain, when it was engulfed in the bowels of the mountain, when it had been cast up and shattered down, when it had been a component of a bed of rock, when that rock had been ooze, when it had been a gentle rain of volcanic sediment, showering through an unbreathable atmosphere and filtering down through warm seas in an early and unknown place.

With tender respect, he tucked the stone away in a large pocket and scrambled back along the way he had come. He made no farewell to the five of Or. They stood mute together, branch-limbs interlocked, dreaming of the dark sin of change.

Now he made haste for home, travelling first through the borderlands of Old Crotheria and then through the region of Tamia, where there was only mud. Legends had it that Tamia had once known fertility, and that speckled fish had swam in streams between forests; but now mud conquered everything, and the few villages were of baked mud, while the roads were dried mud, the sky was the colour of mud, and the few mud-coloured humans who chose for their own mud-stained reasons to live here had scarcely any antlers growing from their shoulders and seemed about to deliquesce into mud. There wasn't a decent stone anywhere about the place. Argustal met a tree called David-by-the-moat-that-dries which was moving into his own home region. Depressed by the everlasting brownness of Tamia, he begged a ride from it, and climbed into its branches. It was old and gnarled, its branches and roots equally hunched, and it spoke in grating syllables of its few ambitions.

As he listened, taking pains to recall each syllable while he waited long for the next, Argustal saw that David spoke by much the same means as the people of Or had done, stuffing whistling twigs to an orifice in its trunk; but whereas it seemed that the tree-men were losing the use of their vocal chords, it seemed that the man-tree was developing some from the stringy integuments of its fibres, so that it became a nice problem as to which was inspired by which, which copied which, or whether both sides seemed so self-absorbed that this also was a possibility – they had come on a mirror-image of perversity independently.

'Motion is the prime beauty,' said David-by-the-moat-that-dries, and took many degrees of the sun across the muddy sky to say it. 'Motion is in me. There is no motion in the ground. In the ground there is not motion. All that the ground contains is without motion. The ground lies in quiet and to lie in the ground is not to be. Beauty is not in the ground. Beyond the ground is the air. Air and ground make all there is and I would be of the ground and air. I was of the ground and of the air but I will be of the air alone. If there is ground, there is another ground. The leaves fly in the air and my longing goes with them but they are only part of me because I am of wood. O, Argustal, you know not the pains of wood!'

Argustal did not indeed, for long before this gnarled speech was spent, the moon had risen and the silent muddy night had fallen, and he was curled asleep in David's distorted branches, the stone in his deep pockets.

Twice more he slept, twice more watched their painful progress along the unswept tracks, twice more joined converse with the melancholy tree – and when he woke again, all the heavens were stacked with fleecy cloud that showed blue between, and low hills lay ahead. He jumped down. Grass grew here. Pebbles littered the track. He howled and shouted with pleasure.

Crying his thanks, he set off across the heath.

'. . . growth . . .' said David-by-the-moat-that-dries.

The heath collapsed and gave way to sand, fringed by sharp grass that scythed at Argustal's skirts as he went by. He ploughed across the sand. This was his own country, and he rejoiced, taking his beating from the occasional cairn that pointed a finger of shade across the sand. Once, one of the Forces flew over, so that for a moment of terror the world was plunged in night, thunder growled, and a paltry hundred drops of rain spattered down; then it was already on the far confines of the sun's domain, plunging away – no matter where!

Few animals, fewer birds, still survived. In the sweet deserts of Outer Talembil, they were especially rare. Yet Argustal passed a bird sitting on a cairn, its hooded eye bleared with a million years of danger. It fluttered one wing at sight of him, in tribute to old reflexes, but he respected the hunger in his belly too much to try to dine on sinews and feathers, and the bird appeared to recognise the fact.

He was nearing home. The memory of Pamitar was sharp before him, so that he could follow it like a scent. He passed another of his kind, an old ape wearing a red mask hanging almost to the ground; they barely gave each other a nod of recognition. Soon on the idle skyline he saw the blocks that marked Gornilo, the first town of Talembil.

The ulcerated sun travelled across the sky. Stoically, Argustal travelled across the intervening dunes, and arrived in the shadow of the white blocks of Gornilo.

No one could recollect now – recollection was one of the lost things that many felt privileged to lose – what factors had determined certain features of Gornilo's architecture. This was an ape-human town, and perhaps in order to construct a memorial to yet more distant and dreadful things, the first inhabitants of the town had made slaves of themselves and of the other creatures that now were no more, and erected these great cubes that now showed signs of weathering, as if they tired at last of swinging their shadows every day about their bases. The ape-humans who lived here were the same ape-humans who had always lived here; they sat as untiringly under their mighty memorial blocks as they had always done – calling now to Argustal as he passed as languidly as one flicks stones across the surface of a lake – but they could recollect no longer if or how they had shifted the blocks across the desert; it might be that that forgetfulness formed an integral part of being as permanent as the granite of the blocks.

Beyond the blocks stood the town. Some of the trees here were visitors, bent on becoming as David-by-the-moat-that-dries was, but most grew in the old way, content with ground and indifferent to motion. They knotted their branches this way and slatted their twigs that way, and humped their trunks the other way, and thus schemed up ingenious and ever-changing homes for the tree-going inhabitants of Gornilo.

At last Argustal came to his home, on the far side of the town.

The name of his home was Cormok. He pawed and patted and licked it first before running lightly up its trunk to the living-room.

Pamitar was not there.

He was not surprised at this, hardly even disappointed, so serene was his mood. He walked slowly about the room, sometimes swinging up to the ceiling in order to view it better, licking and sniffing as he went, chasing the after-images of his wife's presence. Finally, he laughed and fell into the middle of the floor.

'Settle down, boy!' he said.

Sitting where he had dropped, he unloaded his pockets, taking out the five stones he had acquired in his travels and laying them aside from his other possessions. Still sitting, he disrobed, enjoying doing it inefficiently. Then he climbed into the sand bath.

While Argustal lay there, a great howling wind sprang up, and in a moment the room was plunged into sickly greyness. A prayer went up outside, a prayer flung by the people at the unheeding Forces not to destroy the sun. His lower lip moved in a gesture at once of content and contempt; he had forgotten the prayers of Talembil. This was a religious city. Many of the Unclassified congregated here from the waste miles, people or animals whose minds had dragged them aslant from what they were, into rococo forms that more exactly defined their inherent qualities, until they resembled forgotten or extinct forms, or forms that had no being till now, and acknowledged no common cause with any other living thing – except in this desire to preserve the festering sunlight from further ruin.

Under the fragrant grains of the bath, submerged all but for head and a knee and hand, Argustal opened wide his perceptions to all that might come: and finally thought only what he had often thought while lying there – for the armouries of cerebration had long since been emptied of all new ammunition, whatever the tree-men of Or might claim – that in such baths, under such an unpredictable wind, the major life forms of Earth, men and trees, had probably first come at their impetus to change. But change itself . . . had there been a much older thing blowing about the world that everyone had forgotten?

For some reason, that question aroused discomfort in him. He felt dimly that there was another side of life than content and happiness; all beings felt content and happiness; but were those qualities a unity, or were they not perhaps one side only of a – of a shield?

He growled. Start thinking gibberish like that and you ended up human with antlers on your shoulders!

Brushing off the sand, he climbed from the bath, moving more swiftly than he had done in countless time, sliding out of his home, down to the ground without bothering to put on his clothes.

He knew where to find Pamitar. She would be beyond the town, guarding the parapatterner from the tattered angry beggars of Talembil.

The cold wind blew, with an occasional slushy thing in it that made a being blink and wonder about going on. As he strode through the green and swishing heart of Gornilo, treading among the howlers who knelt casually everywhere in rude prayer, Argustal looked up at the sun. It was visible by fragments, torn through tree and cloud. Its face was blotched and pimpled, sometimes obscured altogether for an instant at a time, then blazing forth again. It sparked like a blazing blind eye. A wind seemed to blow from it that blistered the skin and chilled the blood.

So Argustal came to his own patch of land, clear of the green town, out in the stirring desert, and to his wife, Pamitar, to the rest of the world called Miram. She squatted with her back to the wind, the sharply flying grains of sand cutting about her hairy ankles. A few paces away, one of the beggars pranced among Argustal's stones.

Pamitar stood up slowly, removing the head shawl from her head.

'Tapmar!' she said.

Into his arms he wrapped her, burying his face in her shoulder. They chirped and clucked at each other, so engrossed that they made no note of when the breeze died and the desert lost its motion and the sun's light improved.

When she felt him tense, she held him more loosely. At a hidden signal, he jumped away from her, jumping almost over her shoulder, springing ragingly forth, bowling over the lurking beggar into the sand.

The creature sprawled, two-sided and misshapen, extra arms growing from arms, head like a wolf, back legs bowed like a gorilla, clothed in a hundred textures, yet not unlovely. It laughed as it rolled and called in a high clucking voice, 'Three men sprawling under a lilac tree and none to hear the first one say, "Ere the crops crawl, blows fall", and the second abed at night with mooncalves, answer me what's the name of the third, feller?'

'Be off with you, you mad old crow!'

And as the old crow ran away, it called out its answer, laughing, 'Why Tapmar, for he talks to nowhere!', confusing the words as it tumbled over the dunes and made its escape.

Argustal and Pamitar turned back to each other, vying with the strong sunlight to search out each other's faces, for both had forgotten when they were last together, so long was time, so dim was memory. But there were memories, and as he searched they came back. The flatness of her nose, the softness of her nostrils, the roundness of her eyes and their brownness, the curve of the rim of her lips: all these, because they were dear, became remembered, thus taking on more than beauty.

They talked gently to each other, all the while looking. And slowly something of that other thing he suspected on the dark side of the shield entered him – for her beloved countenance was not as it had been. Round her eyes, particularly under them, were shadows, and faint lines creased from the sides of her mouth. In her stance too, did not the lines flow more downward than heretofore?

The discomfort growing too great, he was forced to speak to Pamitar of these things, but there was no proper way to express them, and she seemed not to understand, unless she understood and did not know it, for her manner grew agitated, so that he soon forwent questioning, and turned to the parapatterner to hide his unease.

It stretched over a mile of sand, and rose several feet into the air. From each of his long expeditions, he brought back no more than five stones, yet there were assembled here many hundreds of thousands of stones, perhaps millions, all painstakingly arranged, so that no being could take in the arrangement from any one position, not even Argustal. Many were supported in the air at various heights by stakes or poles, more lay on the ground, where Pamitar always kept the dust and the wild men from encroaching them, and of these on the ground, some stood isolated, while others lay in profusion, but all in a pattern that was ever apparent only to Argustal – and he feared that it would take him until the next sunset to have that pattern clear in his head again. Yet already it started to come clearer, and he recalled with wonder the devious and fugal course he had taken, walking down to the ravine of the tree-men of Or, and knew that he still contained the skill to place the new stones he had brought within the general pattern with reference to that natural harmony – completing the parapatterner.

And the lines on his wife's face: would they too have a place within the pattern?

Was there sense in what the crow beggar had cried, that he talked to nowhere? And . . . and . . . the terrible and, would nowhere answer him?

Bowed, he took his wife's arm, and scurried back with her to their home, high in the leafless tree.

'My Tapmar,' she said that evening, as they ate a dish of fruit, 'it is good that you come back to Gornilo, for the town sedges up with dreams like an old river bed, and I am afraid.'

At this he was secretly alarmed, for the figure of speech she used seemed to him an apt one for the newly-observed lines on her face, so that he asked her what the dreams were in a voice more timid than he meant to use.

Looking at him strangely, she said, 'The dreams are as thick as fur, so thick that they congeal my throat to tell you of them. Last night, I dreamed I walked in a landscape that seemed to be clad in fur all round the distant horizons, fur that branched and sprouted and had sombre tones of russet and dun and black and a lustrous black-blue. I tried to resolve this strange material into the more familiar shapes of hedges and old distorted trees, but it stayed as it was, and I became . . . well, I had the word in my dream that I became a *child*.'

Argustal looked aslant over the crowded vegetation of the town and said, 'These dreams may not be of Gornilo but of you only, Pamitar. What is *child*?'

'There's no such thing in reality, to my knowledge, but in the dream the child that was I was small and fresh and in its actions at once nimble and clumsy. It was alien from me, its motions and ideas never mine – and yet it was all familiar to me, I was it, Tapmar, I was that child. And now that I wake, I become sure that I once was such a thing as a *child*.'

He tapped his fingers on his knees, shaking his head and blinking in a sudden anger. 'This is your bad secret, Pamitar! I knew you had one the moment I saw you! I read it in your face which has changed in an evil way! You know you were never anything but Pamitar in all the millions of years of your life, and that *child* must be an evil phantom that possesses you. Perhaps you will now be turned into *child*!'

She cried out and hurled a green fruit into which she had bitten. Deftly, he caught it before it struck him.

They made a provisional peace before settling for sleep. That night, Argustal dreamed that he also was small and vulnerable and hardly able to manage the language; his intentions were like an arrow and his direction clear.

Waking, he sweated and trembled, for he knew that as he had been *child* in his dream, so he had been *child* once in life. And this went deeper than sickness. When his pained looks directed themselves outside, he saw the night was like shot silk, with a dappled effect of light and shadow in the dark blue dome of the sky, which signified that the Forces were making merry with the sun while it journeyed through the Earth; and Argustal thought of his journeys across the Earth, and of his visit to Or, when the tree-men had whispered of an unknown element that forces change.

'They prepared me for this dream!' he muttered. He knew now that change had worked in his very foundations; once, he had been this thin tiny alien thing called *child*, and his wife too, and possibly others. He thought of that little apparition again, with its spindly legs and piping voice; the horror of it chilled his heart; he broke into prolonged groans that all Pamitar's comforting took a long part of the dark to silence.

He left her sad and pale. He carried with him the stones he had gathered on his journey, the odd-shaped one from the ravine at Or and the ones he had acquired before that. Holding them tightly to him, Argustal made his way through the town to his spatial arrangement. For so long, it had been his chief preoccupation; today, the long project would come to completion; yet because he could not even say why it had so preoccupied him, his feelings inside lay flat and wretched. Something had got to him and killed content.

Inside the prospects of the parapatterner, the old beggarly man lay, resting his shaggy head on a blue stone. Argustal was too low in spirit to chase him away.

'As your frame of stones will frame words, the words will come forth stones,' cried the creature.

'I'll break your bones, old crow!' growled Argustal, but inwardly he wondered at this vile crow's saying and at what he had said the previous day about Argustal's talking to nowhere, for Argustal had discussed the purpose of his structure with nobody, not even Pamitar. Indeed, he had not recognised the purpose of the structure himself until two journeys back – or had it been three or four? The pattern had started simply as a pattern (hadn't it?) and only much later had the obsession become a purpose.

To place the new stones correctly took time. Wherever Argustal walked in his great framework, the old crow followed, sometimes on two legs, sometimes on four. Other personages from the town collected to stare, but none dared step inside the perimeter of the structure, so that they remained far off, like little stalks growing on the margins of Argustal's mind.

Some stones had to touch, others had to be just apart. He walked and stooped and walked, responding to the great pattern that he now knew contained a universal law. The task wrapped him round in an aesthetic daze similar to the one he had experienced travelling the labyrinthine way down to Or, but with greater intensity.

The spell was broken only when the old crow spoke from a few paces away in a voice level and unlike his usual sing-song. And the old crow said, 'I remember you planting the very first of these stones here when you were a child.'

Argustal straightened.

Cold took him, though the bilious sun shone bright. He could not find his voice. As he searched for it, his gaze went across to the eyes of the beggar-man, festering in his black forehead.

'You know I was once such a phantom – a child?' he asked.

'We are all phantoms. We were all childs. As there is gravy in our bodies, our hours were once few.'

'Old crow . . . you describe a different world – not ours!'

'Very true, very true. Yet that other world once was ours.'

'Oh, not! Not so!'

'Speak to your machine about it! Its tongue is of rock and cannot lie like mine.'

He picked up a stone and flung it. 'That will I do! Now get away from me!'

The stone hit the old man in his ribs. He groaned painfully and danced backwards, tripped, was up again, and made off in haste, limbs whirling in a way that took from him all resemblance to human kind. He pushed through the line of watchers and was gone.

For a while, Argustal squatted where he was, groping through matters that dissolved as they took shape, only to grow large when he dismissed them. The storm blew through him and distorted him, like the trouble on the face of the sun. When he decided there was nothing for it but to complete the parapatterner, still he trembled with the new knowledge: without being able to understand why, he knew that the new knowledge would destroy the old world.

All now was in position, save for the odd-shaped stone from Or, which he carried firm on one shoulder, tucked between ear and hand. For the first time, he realised what a gigantic structure he had wrought.

It was a business-like stroke of insight, no sentiment involved. Argustal was now no more than a bead rolling through the vast interstices around him.

Each stone held its own temporal record as well as its spacial position; each represented different stresses, different epochs, different temperatures, materials, chemicals, moulds, intensities. Every stone together represented an anagram of Earth, its whole composition and continuity. The last stone was merely a focal point for an entire dynamic and, as Argustal slowly walked between the vibrant arcades, that dynamic rose to pitch.

He heard it grow. He paused. He shuffled now this way, now that. As he did so, he recognised that there was no one focal position but a myriad, depending on position and direction of the key stone.

Very softly, he said '. . . That my fears might be verified . . .'

And all about him – but softly – came a voice in stone, stuttering before it grew clearer, as if it had long known of words but never practised them.

'Thou . . .' Silence, then a flood of sentence.

'Thou thou art, O thou art worm thou art sick, rose invisible rose. In the howling storm thou art in the storm. Worm thou art found out O rose thou art sick and found out flies in the night they bed they thy crimson life destroy. O – O rose, thou art sick! The invisible worm, the invisible worm that flies in the night, in the howling storm, has found out – has found out thy bed of crimson joy . . . and his dark dark secret love, his dark secret love does thy life destroy.'

Argustal was already running from that place.

In Pamitar's arms he could find no comfort now. Though he huddled there, up in the encaging branches, the worm that flies worked in him. Finally, he rolled away from her and said, 'Who ever heard so terrible a voice? I cannot speak again with the universe.'

'You do not know it was the universe.' She tried to tease him. 'Why should the universe speak to little Tapmar?'

'The old crow said I spoke to nowhere. Nowhere is the universe – where the sun hides at night – where our memories hide, where our thoughts evaporate. I cannot talk with it. I must hunt out the old crow and talk to him.'

'Talk no more, ask no more questions! All you discover brings you misery! Look – you will no longer regard me, your poor wife! You turn your eyes away!'

'If I stare at nothing for all succeeding eons, yet I must find out what torments us!'

In the centre of Gornilo, where many of the Unclassified lived, bare wood twisted up from the ground like fossilised sack, creating caves and shelters and strange limbs on which and in which old pilgrims, otherwise without a home, might perch. Here at nightfall Argustal sought out the beggar.

The old fellow was stretched painfully beside a broken pot, clasping a woven garment across his body. He turned in his small cell, trying for escape, but Argustal had him by the throat and held him still.

'I want your knowledge, old crow!'

'Get it from the religious men – they know more than I!'

It made Argustal pause, but he slackened his grip on the other by only the smallest margin.

'Because I have you, you must speak to me. I know that knowledge is pain, but so is ignorance once one has sensed its presence. Tell me more about childs and what they did!'

As if in a fever, the old crow rolled about under Argustal's grip. He brought himself to say, 'What I know is so little, so little, like a blade of grass in a field. And like blades of grass are the distant bygone times. Through all those times come the bundles of bodies now on this Earth. Then as now, no new bodies. But once . . . even before those bygone times . . . you cannot understand . . .'

'I understand well enough.'

'You are Scientist! Before bygone times was another time, and then . . . then was childs and different things that are not any longer, many animals and birds and smaller things with frail wings unable to carry them over long time . . .'

'What happened? Why was there change, old crow?'

'Men . . . scientists . . . make understanding of the gravy of bodies and turn every person and thing and tree to eternal life. We now continue from that time, a long time long – so long we forgotten what was then done.'

The smell of him was like an old pie. Argustal asked him, 'And why now are no childs?'

'Childs are just small adults. We are adults, having become from child. But in that great former time, before scientists were on Earth, adults produced childs. Animals and trees likewise. But with eternal life, this cannot be – those child-making parts of the body have less life than stone.'

'Don't talk of stone! So we live forever . . . You old ragbag, you remember – ah, you remember me as child?'

But the old ragbag was working himself into a kind of fit, pummelling the ground, slobbering at the mouth.

'Seven shades of lilac, even worse I remember myself a child, running like an arrow, air, everywhere fresh rosy air. So I am mad, for I remember!' He began to scream and cry, and the outcasts round about took up the wail in chorus. 'We remember, we remember!' – whether they did or not.

Their dreadful howling worked like spears in Argustal's flank. He had pictures afterwards of his panic run through the town, of wall and trunk and ditch and road, but it was all as insubstantial at the time as the pictures afterwards. When he finally fell to the ground panting, he was unaware of where he lay, and everything was nothing to him until the religious howling had died into silence.

Then he saw he lay in the middle of his great structure, his cheek against the Or stone where he had dropped it. And as his attention came to it, the great structure round him answered without his having to speak.

He was at a new focal point. The voice that sounded was new, as cool as the previous one had been choked. It blew over him in a cool wind.

'There is no amaranth on this side of the grave, O Argustal, no name with whatsoever emphasis of passionate love repeated that is not mute at last. Experiment X gave life for eternity to every living thing on Earth, but even eternity is punctuated by release and suffers period. The old life had its childhood and its end, the new had no such logic. It found its own after many millennia, and took its cue from individual minds. What a man was, he became; what a tree, it became.'

Argustal lifted his tired head from its pillow of stone. Again the voice changed pitch and trend, as if in response to his minute gesture.

'The present is a note in music. That note can no longer be sustained. You find what questions you have found, O Argustal, because the chord, in dropping to a lower key, rouses you from the long dream of crimson joy that was immortality. What you are finding, others also find, and you can none of you be any longer insensible to change. Even immortality must have an end.'

He stood up then, and hurled the Or stone. It flew, fell, rolled . . . and before it stopped he had awoken a great chorus of universal voice.

The whole Earth roused, and a wind blew from the west. As he started again to move, he saw the religious men of the town were on the march, and the great sun-nesting Forces on their midnight wing, and the stars wheeling, and every majestic object alert as it had never been.

But Argustal walked slowly on his flat simian feet, plodding back to Pamitar. No longer would he be impatient in her arms. There, time would be all too brief.

He knew now the worm that flew and nestled in her cheek, in his cheek, in all things, even in the tree-men of Or, even in the great impersonal Forces that despoiled the sun, even in the sacred bowels of the universe to which he had lent a temporary tongue. He knew now that back had come that Majesty that previously gave to Life its reason, the Majesty that had been away from the world for so long and yet so brief a respite, the Majesty called DEATH.

A Tupolev Too Far

I know you want fiction for this anthology, but perhaps for once you would consider a true story. I offer a thought in extenuation for what is to follow: that this story is so fantastic and unbelievable it might as well be science fiction.

Well, it would be SF except for the fact that there is no scientific explanation for the bizarre central occurrence – or none beyond the way bizarre events occur with regularity, as vouched for by Charles Fort, Arthur Koestler, Carl Jung, Jesus Christ and other historic figures.

Unfortunately, the story is not only bizarre but raunchy. It is the sort of tale men tell each other late at night, in a bar in Helsinki or somewhere similar. It has no moral and precious little morality.

Sex and lust come into it. And murder and incest and brigandage of the worst sort. There are some insights to be gleaned regarding the differing natures of men and women, if that is any consolation.

Another thing I have to add. This is not my story. I heard it from a friend. One of those friends you know off and on throughout life. He always enjoyed talking about the bad times.

We'll call him Ron Wallace. And this is what he told me.

This helping of agony took place in 1989, which had turned out to be a better year for Ron than he expected – and for much of Europe. He had been unemployed for a while. Now he had a good job with a West Country firm who made safes and security equipment employing the latest electronic devices. Ron was their overseas salesman. The Russians approached his company, who were sending Ron out to Moscow as a result. The managing director, who was a good guy, briefed Ron before he left, and he set off on the flight from Penge Airport in good fettle. His wife Stephanie saw him off.

Ron flew Royal Russian Airlines. Which, after TransAm, is regarded as the world's best airline. Plenty of leg room, little engine noise, pretty hostesses.

It was a brief flight. On the way, he picked up an in-flight magazine which had an illustrated article on the Russian Commonwealth and on modern Moscow in particular. There were photographs of Czar Nicholas III with the Czarina opening the grand new Governance of Nations building, designed by Richard Rogers, on White Square, and of the redecorated Metro in St Petersburg. Ron dozed off while leafing through such commonplaces and was woken by a terrific bang.

The aircraft was passing through a ferocious storm, or so it seemed. Lightning flashed outside and the airliner began to fall. It shook violently as it fell.

Ron sat tight. He remembered his grandfather's account of the terrible firestorm which had partially destroyed Berlin in July 1914. His grandfather had been working in Berlin at the time and always talked about the experience. The old man claimed that was the first occasion on which all Europe had united in a major rescue operation; it had changed history, he claimed.

These thoughts and less pleasant ones ran through Ron's mind as the plane fell earthwards.

'I'll never screw Steff again – or any other woman,' he said aloud. To his mind, that was the biggest bugbear regarding death: no screwing.

For an instant the plane was bathed in unnatural light. Then all became calm, as if nothing had happened.

The plane pulled from its dive. Cabin staff in their white uniforms moved down the aisles, soothing the passengers and bringing them drinks.

Everyone started talking to each other. But only for a few minutes. After which, a silence fell over them; they became uncannily quiet as they tried to digest their narrow escape from disaster.

Twenty minutes later, they landed at Sheremeteivo Airport.

Ron was surprised to find how drab and small everything was. He was surprised, too, to see how many men were in uniform – unfamiliar uniforms, too, with mysterious red stars on their caps. He had no idea what the stars stood for, unless for Mars, on which planet the Russians had just landed.

Of course, Ron had got down as much whisky as he could, following the alarming incident on the plane. His perceptions were possibly a little awry. All the same, he could not help noticing that most of the planes on the ground belonged to an airline called Aeroflot, of which he had never heard. There were no Royal Russian Airline planes to be seen.

When, at the luggage carousel, he asked a fellow passenger about Aeroflot, the man replied, 'You ask too many questions round here, you find yourself in the gulag.'

Ron began to feel rather cold and shaky. Something had happened. He did not know what.

The whole airport, the reception area, the customs area, gave no sign of the high-tech sheen for which Russia was renowned. He felt a sense of disorientation, which was calmed slightly when he was met by his Russian contact, Vassili Rugorsky, who made him welcome.

As they passed out through the foyer of the building, Ron observed a large framed portrait dominating the exits where he might have expected to see a picture of the graceful young Czar. Instead, the portrait showed a thick-set, almost neckless man with glittering eyes, a mottled complexion and an unpleasant expression.

'Who's that?' he asked.

Vassili looked curiously at Ron, as if expecting him to be joking.

'Comrade Leonid Brezhnev, of course,' he said.

Ron dared ask nothing more, but his sense of unease deepened. Who was Brezhnev?

He was shown to a black car. Soon they were driving through the city. Ron could hardly believe what he saw. Moscow was always billed as one of Europe's great pleasure cities, with smart people, and a vivid nightlife staged amid elegant buildings – fruit of Russia's great renaissance in the early 1940s, when the Czarina Elizabeta Ship Canal had linked Baltic with Black Sea. Here Parisian panache thrived among Parisian-type boulevards. Or so the legend had it. As they wound through a dreary suburb, he saw lines of dowdy people queueing at shops hardly worthy of the name. The buildings themselves were grey and grubby.

Red flags and banners flew everywhere. He could not understand. It was as if the whole place had been hit by revolution.

But the men he dealt with were agreeable enough. Ron prided himself on his powers of negotiation; his opposite numbers were cautious but amiable. He gathered to his mild astonishment that they regarded British technology to be in advance of their own.

'Of course, the KGB have all latest Western equipment,' one man said jokingly as the contracts were signed. Ron did not like to ask what KGB stood for; he was clearly expected to know. It was all peculiar. He wondered if the electric storm he had flown through had affected his mind in some way.

It was on his second day that the contracts were signed. The first day was given over to discussion, when Ron often felt that the Russians were pumping him. At one point, when he had occasion to mention the Czarina Elizabeta Ship Canal, they all looked blank.

Even more disconcertingly, the Russians asked him how he liked being in the Soviet Union, and similar remarks. Ron belonged to an electronics union himself, but had never heard of a Soviet Union. He could almost fancy he had arrived in the wrong country.

Nevertheless, the contracts were signed on the second day, on terms favourable to Ron's company. They were witnessed in the ministry at three in the afternoon, following which the parties involved got down to some serious drinking. As well as Russian champagne there were vodka, wine and a good Georgian brandy. Ron was an experienced drinker. He arrived back at the Hotel Moskva, contract in briefcase, just after 6.30, still more or less in control of his wits.

I'm trying to tell you this story as Ron Wallace told it to me. When he came to describe the Hotel Moskva I had to interrupt him. I've stayed in that hotel a couple of times. Once I took the Camberwell—Moscow Trans-Continent Express on a package tour which included three nights in that very hotel. It was the pleasantest place in which I have ever stayed, light and airy, and full of elegant people. In fact, a few too many of the Russian aristocracy for my simple tastes.

A TUPOLEV TOO FAR

It was not the dowdiness and gloom of the hotel about which Ron chiefly complained, or the uninteresting food but the lack of beautiful women. Ron was always rather a ladies' man.

An old-fashioned band was playing old-fashioned music in the hotel restaurant. It was a period piece, like the hotel itself. He could not credit it. The dining room was cavernous, with stained-glass windows at one end, and a faded style of furnishing. The band lurched from Beatles' hits to the 'Destiny' waltz. The place, he said, was a cross between the Café Royal in the 1920s and Salisbury Cathedral in the 1420s.

As Ron told his tale, I kept thinking about the concept of alternative worlds. Although the idea is at first fantastic, there is, after all, a well-attested theory which says that whatever is imagined moves nearer to reality. Edmund Husserl, in his pioneering work on phenomenology, *Investigations in Logic*, shows how little the psychological nature of historical processes are understood. Turning points in history – generatives, in Husserl's term – occur in greater or lesser modes related to quantal thought impulses which are themselves subject to random factors. The logical structures on which such points depend exist independently of their psychological correlates, so that we can expect subjective experiences to generate a multiplicity of effects, each of which bears equivalent objective reality; thus, whether or not signatures are appended to a treaty, for example, is dependent on various epistemological assumptions of transient nature, while the results of signing or non-signing may be multiplex generatives, giving rise to a spectrum of alternative objectivities, varying from slight to immense, affecting the lives of many people over considerable areas of space and time. I know this to be so because I read it in a book.

So it seemed clear to me – though not to Ron, who is no intellectual and consequently does not believe in variant subjective realities – that the electric storm which hit the Tupolev had been a Husserl's generative, causing Ron to switch objectivities, and materialise in a parallel version of objectivity along the spectrum, where history had at some point taken a decided turn for the worse.

Feeling a little weary, Ron decided not to go up to his room immediately, but to eat and then retreat to bed, in preparation for his early flight home the following morning.

Diners were few. They could scarcely be distinguished from the diners in a provincial Pan-European town, Belgrade, say, or Boheimkirchen, or Bergen. There was none of the glitter he had expected. And the service was terribly slow.

The maître d' had shown Ron to a small table, rather distant from the nearest light globe. From this vantage point, he looked the clientele over while awaiting his soup.

At the table nearest to him, two orientals sat drinking champagne. Their mood was subdued. He judged them to be Korean. Ron spared hardly a glance for the man. As he told me, 'I could hardly take my eyes off the woman. Mainly I saw her in half-profile. A real beauty, clear-cut features, hawkish nose, dark eyes, red lips . . . Terrific.'

When she smiled at her partner and raised her glass to her lips she was a vision of seduction. Ron dropped his napkin on the floor in order to take a look at her legs. She was wearing a long black evening dress.

He said his one thought was, 'If only her husband would get lost . . .'

His desires turned naturally to sex. But he had sworn an oath to his wife, Steff, on the subject of fidelity. As he was averting his eyes from the Korean couple, the woman turned to look at him. Even across the space between their tables, the stare was strong and disturbing. Ron could not tell what was in that stare. It made him curious, while at the same time repelling him.

He took a paperback book of crossword puzzles from his briefcase and tried to study a puzzle he had already started, but could not concentrate.

A memory came back to him of his first love. Then, how innocent had been her gaze. He could recall it perfectly. It had been a gaze of love and trust; all the sweetness of youth, of innocence, was in it. It could not be recovered. No one would ever look at him in that fashion again.

The Korean couple had decided something between them. The Korean man rose from the table, laid down his napkin, and came across to Ron.

'My God,' Ron thought, 'the little bugger's going to tell me not to ogle his wife . . .'

The Korean was short and sturdy. Perhaps he was in his mid-thirties. His face was solemn, his eyes dark, his whole body held rigidly, and it was a rigid bow he made to Ron Wallace.

'You are English?' he asked, speaking in English with a heavy accent. 'We saw you dining here last night and made enquiries. I am on official duties in the Soviet Union, a diplomat from the Democratic People's Republic of North Korea.' He gave his name.

'What do you want? I'm having dinner.'

'Meals are a source of fear to me. I can never rid my mind of one dinner in particular when I was a child of five. Someone from political motives poisoned my father. A servant was held responsible, but we never found out who was paying the servant. The servant did not tell, despite severe torture. My father rose from his place, screamed like a wounded horse, spun about, and fell head first into a dish – well, in our dialect it's *pruang hai*, I suppose a sort of kedgeree, though with little green chillies. He struggled a moment, sending rice all over us frightened children. Then he was still, and naturally the meal was ruined.'

Ron Wallace took a sip of mineral water. Although the Korean was white and trembling, Ron would not ask him to sit down.

The Korean continued. 'I should explain that there were four of us children. Three of us were triplets, and there was a younger sibling. My mother was demoralised by my father's death. I have to confess she was of the bourgeois class. Never a very stable personality, for she was an actress, she suffered illusions. One starry night, she jumped from a tall window through the glass roof of the conservatory to the ground. A theory was that she had seen the stars reflected in the glass and thought the conservatory was the Yalu river. This was never proved.

'We children were handed over into the care of an uncle and aunt who ran a rather poor pig and sorghum farm in the mountainous area of our land. My uncle was a bully, given to drink and criminality. He committed sexual atrocities on us poor defenceless children, and even on his farm animals. You can imagine how we suffered.'

He looked fixedly at Ron, but Ron made no reply. Ron was aware of the avid gaze of the Korean's partner, back at the table, smiling yet not smiling in his direction.

'Our one consolation was the school to which we were sent. It was a long walk away, down the mountain, a cruel trial for us in winter months when the snow was deep. But the school was run by a remarkable

Englishman, a Mr Holmberg. I have been told that Holmberg is not an English name. I cannot explain how that came about. In the world struggle, there are many anomalies.

'Mr Holmberg had many skills and was unfailingly kind. He taught us something of the world. He also explained to us the mysteries of sex, and kindly drew pictures of the female sexual organs on the blackboard, with the fallopian tubes in red, despite a shortage of chalk.

'The day came when the ninth birthday approached for us three poor orphans. There we sat in the little classroom, stinking of sorghum and pigs, and this wonderful Englishman presented us with a marvellous gift, a kite he had made himself. It was such a kite as Koreans made in dynastic times to carry the spirits of the dead, very strong, very large and well decorated. It was, for us, the first gift we had received since our father was poisoned. You can imagine our delight.'

He paused.

'Where's my bloody boeuf stroganoff?' asked Ron, looking round for a waitress.

Greatly though he desired something to eat, he desired much more the absence of this little man who stood by his table, telling his awful life story unbidden. Ron had never heard of the Democratic People's Republic of North Korea, and did not much want to. It was another department of the terrible world into which he had fallen.

He tried to think of pleasant English things – Ovaltine, Bob Monkhouse, cream teas, Southend, the National Anthem, Agatha Christie, the *Sun*, Saxby's pork pies – but they were drowned out by the Korean's doomed narrative.

'We had a problem. We feared that our cruel uncle would steal the kite from us. We resolved to fly it on the way home from school, to enjoy that pleasure at least once. Halfway up the mountain was a good eminence, with a view of the distant ocean and a strong updraught. The three of us hung onto the string and up went the grand kite, sailing into the sky. How we cheered. Just for a moment, we had no cares.

'Our little brother begged to be allowed to hold the kite. As we handed him the string, we heard the sound of shots being fired farther up the mountain. Our anxieties were easily awoken. In those lawless times, bandits were everywhere. Alas, one can pay for one moment's carelessness with a lifetime's regret. We turned to find that the kite was carrying away our little brother. His hand was caught in the loop in the string and up he was going. He cried. We cried. We waved.

'Helpless, we watched him about to be dashed against the rocks. Fortunately, he cleared them as the kite gained height. It drifted towards the north-east, and the ocean and the south-eastern coast of the Soviet Union. That was the last we saw of him. It is not impossible that even now he lives, and speaks and thinks in the Russian language.'

The Korean bowed his head for a moment, while Ron tried to attract the attention of a distant waitress, who had lapsed into immobility, as if also overcome by the tragic tale.

'We were upset by this incident. We had lost our valued gift, and a rather annoying little brother as well. We fell to punching each other, each claiming the other two were to blame. Then we went home, up the rest of the mountain track.

'My uncle was in his favourite apple tree, quiet for once and not swearing at us. He hung head down, a rope round his ankles securing him to one of the branches of the tree. His hands were tied and he was fiercely gagged. His face was so red that we burst out laughing.

'Since he was still alive, we had a splendid time spinning him round. He could not cry out but he looked pretty funny. Then we got rakes and spades from the shed and battered him to death.

'Our aunt had been thrown in the pond. Many and dreadful were the atrocities committed on her body. We dragged her from the water but, so near to death was she, we put her back where we had found her.

'The house had been looted by the bandits whose firing we had heard. Those were lawless days before our great leader, Kim Il Sung, took over control of our destinies. We were happy to have the place to ourselves, especially since my uncle's two huge sons had been shot, bayoneted and beheaded by the bandits.

'Unfortunately, the bandits returned in the night, since it had begun to rain. They came for shelter. They found us asleep, tied the three of us up, put us in a foul dung cart, and promised to sell us for slaves to a foreign power in the market of Yuman-dong. Next morning, down the mountain we bumped. More rain fell. The monsoon came on in full force. We were crossing a wooden bridge over a river when a great rush of water struck the bridge.

'The bandits were thrown into confusion or drowned. We were better off in the cart, which floated, and we managed to get free.

'We ran to Yuman-dong for safety, since we had another uncle there. He took us in with protestations of affection, and his elder daughter fed us. Unfortunately, the town was the headquarters of the brigands, as we soon discovered. My uncle was the biggest brigand. The three of us children were made to work at the degrading business of carting night soil from the village and spreading it on the fields. You can imagine our humiliation.'

The Korean shook his head sadly and searched Ron's face for signs of compassion.

'Where's my bloody food?' Ron asked.

'But fortune was as ever on our side. It was then that our great leader, Kim Il Sung, became President of our people's republic. My uncle was awarded the post of local commissar, since in his career of bandit he had harassed rich oppressor landlords such as my late uncle and aunt up in the mountain. Much celebration followed this event and everyone in the village remained totally drunk for twenty-one days, including the dogs. Three died. Maybe four. It was during this period of joy that a dog bit off the left ear of one of my brothers.

'Those were happy times. Under my uncle we marched from farm to farm along the valley, beating up the farmers, threatening and exhorting the workers. There was nothing we would not do for the Cause. Unfortunately, much misery was to follow.'

'Don't tell me – let me guess,' murmured Ron Wallace.

'But you cannot guess what befell us triplets. It was discovered after many years that the brother who had lost an ear was a capitalist running dog and had been associating secretly with the enemies of the state, who varied from time to time. Sometimes the enemies were Chinese, sometimes Russians. My brother had associated with all of them. I felt bound to denounce him myself, and his wife. A terrible vendetta of blood then started—'

In desperation, Ron stood up, waving his book of crossword puzzles.

'Sorry,' he said. 'I have to finish this page. It is a secret code. I am employed by MI5.'

'I appreciate your feelings,' said the Korean, standing rigid. 'We must all exercise our duties. However, I tell you something of my history for a reason. The remarkable Englishman, Mr Holmberg, who taught me at school, stays ever in my mind as an example of decency, morality, fairness and liberalism. It is no less than the truth to say that I have modelled my life on him.

'Unfortunately, however, during the revolutionary times of the Flying Horse movement, it was necessary to have Mr Holmberg shot. A tribunal convicted him of being a foreigner in wartime. To me befell the honour of carrying out the execution with my own hands. I have a small souvenir for his family back in England which I wish you to carry home to present to them. Please come to my table and I shall give it to you, concealed in a copy of *Pravda*.'

Ron Wallace hesitated only for a moment. All he wanted was his dinner. But if he went over to this madman's table, he would be able to snatch a closer look at his companion. He rose.

At the Korean table sat the remarkable person with the bright-red lips and shoulder-length black hair. The full-length gown swept to the floor. Diamonds sparkled at the smooth neck. A cigarette in a holder sent a trail of smoke ceilingwards from a bejewelled right hand. A look of black intensity was fixed on Ron. He bowed.

'I'm pleased to meet your wife,' he said to the North Korean.

'My brother.' The Korean corrected him. 'My sole surviving brother. Here is the souvenir for the Holmberg family – in fact for the small daughter of the son of the man I knew, who was convicted of the crime against the state. Her address is enclosed. Please take it, deliver it faithfully.'

Ron had been expecting to receive the head of the late Mr Holmberg, but it was a smaller object which the Korean passed over, easily rolled inside a copy of *Pravda*. He bowed again, shook hands with the Korean, smiled at his brother, who gave him a winning smile in return, and returned to his table. A waitress was delivering a boeuf stroganoff to his place.

'Thank you,' he said. 'Bring me another bottle of wine and a bottle of mineral water.'

'Immediately,' she said. But she paused for a second before leaving the table.

Setting the newspaper between his stomach and the table, Ron unrolled it. Inside lay a wooden doll with plaits, a savage grin painted on its wooden face. It wore traditional dress of red and white. Tied round its neck was a label on which was written the name Doreen Holmberg and an address in Surrey. He rolled it up in the paper again and shut it in his briefcase.

He began to eat without appetite the dish the waitress had brought, forking mouthfuls slowly between his lips, staring over the bleak reaches of the restaurant permeated by the strains of 'Yesterday', and avoiding any glance towards the Korean table. He sighed. It would be a relief to get home to his wife, although he had some problems there.

The waitress returned with the two bottles of wine and mineral water on a tray. She could be sighted first behind a carved wooden screen which partly hid the entrance to the kitchens. Then she was observed behind a large aspidistra. Then she hove into full view, walking towards Ron's table, a thin middle-aged woman with straggling dyed hair.

He had been too preoccupied with the Koreans to pay the waitress any attention. As he scrutinised her in the way he scrutinised anything female, he saw that her gaze was fixed on him, not with the usual weary indifference characteristic of a waitress towards diners, but in a curious and not unfriendly fashion. He straightened slightly in his chair.

She set the bottles down on the table. Was there something suggestive in the way she fingered the neck of the wine bottle before uncorking it? She poured him a glass of the wine and a glass of the mineral water in slow motion. He caught a whiff of her underarm odour as she came near. Her hip brushed against his arm.

'You're imagining things,' he said to himself.

He raised the wine glass to his lips and looked at her.

'Enjoy it please,' she said in English, and turned away.

She was tired and in her late thirties, he judged. Not much of a bottom. Not really an attractive proposition. Besides, a waitress in a Russian hotel restaurant . . .

However, after a few more mouthfuls of the stroganoff, he summoned her across the room on the pretext of ordering a bread roll. She came readily enough, but he saw in the language of her angular body an independence of mind not yet eroded of all geniality. A spark of intent lit in his brain. He knew that spark. It could so easily be fanned into flame.

She did look worn. Her face was weathered, the flesh lifeless and dry, with strong lines moving downwards on either side of thin lips. Nothing to recommend her. Yet the expression on her face, the light-grey eyes – somehow, he liked what he saw. Out of that ugly dress, those hideous shoes, she would be more attractive. His imagination ran ahead of him. He felt an erection stirring in his trousers.

Her breasts were not very noticeable as she bent to place the bread by Ron's side. No doubt she ate scraps in the kitchen off people's plates. A fatty diet. No doubt she had taken orders all her life. It was a matter of speculation as to what her private life could be.

He asked her if she ever did crosswords.

The shake of her head was contemptuous. Again the whiff of body odour. Possibly she did not understand what he said. She smiled a little. Her teeth were irregular, but it was an appealing smile.

Watching her hips, her legs, her ugly shoes, as she retreated, he told himself to relax and to think of something that a candle did in a low place, in six letters.

But a long dull evening stretched before him. He hated his own company.

Over the sweet, he extracted a few words from the waitress. She spoke a little German, a little English. She had worked in this hotel for five years. No, she cared nothing about the work. The lipstick she wore was not expertly applied. But there was no doubt that in some measure she was interested in him.

When she brought him a cup of bitter coffee, he said, 'Will you come up to my room?'

The waitress shook her head, almost regretfully, as if she had anticipated the question. It did not surprise her; probably she had often been asked the same question by drunken clients.

Her glance went to where the impassive maître d'hotel stood, guardian of his underlings' Soviet morality. No doubt he had awful powers over them. She left Ron's table, to disappear into the kitchens.

Ron looked down at his puzzle.

When she came to pour him a second cup of coffee, he suggested that they went back to her place.

The waitress gave him a long hard look, weighing him up. The look disconcerted him, inasmuch as he felt himself judged. He saw himself sitting there, secure and decently dressed, possessor of foreign currency, about to return to the strange capitalist world from which he had come. Not bad-looking. And yet – yet another man out of thousands, with a vacant evening before him, just wanting a bit of fun.

'There is difficulties,' she said.

The words told him he was halfway to his desire.

Elation ran through him, not unmixed with a tinge of apprehension. Again, the stirrings of an erection. He told her she was wonderful. He would do anything. He smiled. She frowned. She made a small gesture with her hand: Be quiet. Or, Be patient.

As if she already had her regrets, she left the table hastily, clutching the coffee pot to her chest. Ron observed that she said something to an older waitress as they passed on the way to the kitchens.

Now he had to wait. He tried to think of an uncomplicated curative plant in six letters.

The waitress had disappeared. Perhaps he had, after all, been mistaken. When his impatience got the better of him, he rose to his feet. She appeared and came over. He had a sterling note ready – of a modest denomination, so as not to offend her.

'Where and when?'

Their faces were close. Her foreignness excited him, nor was he repelled by her body odour. She barely responded, barely moved her lips.

'Rear door by the wood hut. Midnight.'

'I'll be there.'

'Will you?'

He nodded a curt good night to the North Koreans, and retreated with his case to the bar. He sat alone, apart from a group of what he guessed were Swedes, getting heavily drunk in one corner. He had three hours to wait.

Idly, he picked up a newspaper printed in English and started to glance through it. It bewildered him utterly. For a while he entertained the thought that his company was playing an elaborate joke on him.

According to the newspaper, there was no Liberal government in power in Britain. Nor was there any mention of Bernard Mattingly. The Prime Minister, it was said, was a Mrs Thatcher, head of a Conservative government. This piece of information disturbed him more than anything he had encountered so far. It seemed that the President of the United States was not Alan Stevenson but someone called Ronald Reagan.

In a medical column, he read that the whole world was being ravaged by a sexually transmitted disease called AIDS. Ron had never heard of it. Yet the column claimed that thousands of people were dying of it, in Africa, Europe and the United States. No cure had been found.

Just as disturbingly, an editorial on disarmament moves appeared to be saying that there had been two wars involving the whole world during the twentieth century.

Ron knew this could not have happened. There was no way in which Albania and Italy or England and Germany – to take two instances – could possibly attempt to destroy each other. What it all meant he did not know.

With a sudden uneasy inspiration, he checked on the date of the newspaper. It read September 1989 clearly enough. The idea had entered his head that he had been caught in a time warp and was back in the early years of the twentieth century, before the days of the reforming Czars. Such was not the case.

He hid the newspaper under the table and clutched his head.

He was going mad. The sooner he got home the better.

After an hour, the Korean couple entered the bar. They ignored him and sat with their backs to him.

He thought of his wife. Their marriage had been a good one. Both had ruined it by their infidelity. Both nourished hurt feelings and a desire to get their own back. One of them was always an infidelity ahead of the other. Yet Steff had remained with him, had put up with all his drunkenness and bullying and failures. Now they had a little place of their own, heavily mortgaged, it was true, and were trying to build a better relationship. Ron had vowed never to hit her again.

The best advice he could give himself was to forget about that slut of a waitress and enjoy a good night's sleep in his comfortless single room. He had to catch the early flight from Moscow's Sheremeteivo Airport, to be in time for an important meeting with Bob Butler, his boss, tomorrow afternoon in Slough. He might get promoted. Steff would be pleased about that. She would also ask if he had been fucking other women.

He could lie his way out of this one, particularly if the promotion to sales manager came through.

Besides, this creature might give him some insight into what was happening. Perhaps she could tell him who Brezhnev was and what KGB stood for.

By this time, Ron – not an imaginative man – began to realise he had somehow got on an alternative possibility track. The shabby city that surrounded him felt heavy with sin – no, with sinfulness. It was as if some terrible crime had been committed which everyone had conspired not to discuss. And this secret had weighed the population down, so that the cheerful Moscow of his own time had sunk down into the earth from human view.

God knows what weird versions of clap the waitress might be carrying round with her. He had no idea what he was getting into.

Still, the thought of a woman's company in this miserable place was greatly attractive.

He tried to look at it all as a great stunt, a caper. How his pals would laugh when he told them. If he ever got back to them.

He smoked cigarettes and eked out a beer. The Swedes grew louder.

Came 11.30, Ron put on his coat, grabbed his case, and went out into the streets. Everywhere seemed dark and depressing. It was as if he had somehow crossed a border between day and night, between yin and yang, between positive and negative.

As he walked along by the Moskva he observed there was none of the cheerful riverside restaurants, no floating pleasure-boats, which he had heard were the centre of the city's nightlife. No music, no wine, no women. The river flowed dark between high concrete banks, unloved, neglected, isolated from the life of Moscow, rushing on its secretive dark way. What if I am stuck here alone for ever, he asked himself. Isn't there a science of Chaos, and haven't I fallen into it?

It was impossible to know whether the waitress was an escape from or an embodiment of the unreason into which he had fallen.

He turned on his heel and made his way warily down a back alley to the rear of the hotel. A rat scampered, but there were no humans about. He came to an area of broken pavements covered with litter, which he waded through in the dark, cursing as he trod in something soft and deep. He could not see. From a small barred window came an orange fragment of light. Spreading a hand out before him, he arrived against a barrier. Searching carefully with his fingers, he found he was touching wood. Most probably this was the hut the waitress had designated.

Feeling his way, staggering and tripping, he finally reassured himself that he was waiting in the right place. He located the back door of the hotel, tried it, found it locked.

He stood in the dark, cold and uneasy. No stars shone overhead.

Following the sound of tumblers turning in a lock, the hotel door opened. A man emerged and walked off briskly into the night. The door was locked again from the inside; he heard the sound of a bolt being shot. The Russians had a mania for secrecy. So did Ron. He understood.

Several staff emerged from the door in pairs or alone. Worried in case his waitress missed him, Ron stood out from the sheltering hut. Nobody looked in his direction.

A lorry with one headlight jolted along the alley and wheezed to a halt. Two men got out. As Ron shrank back, he saw that one of the men was old and bent, moving painfully as he climbed from the cab. They both began to sort among the rubbish outside the hotel, occasionally throwing something into the back of their vehicle.

The door of the building opened again. Ron's waitress came out. It was ten minutes past midnight. She paused to get her night vision and then walked over to him. He pressed himself against her, feeling her hard body. Neither of them spoke.

With a gesture of caution to Ron, she went over and talked to the men by the lorry. The old man gave a wheezing laugh. There was a brief conversation, during which all three lit cigarettes the waitress distributed. Ron waited impatiently until she returned to his side.

'What's going on?' he asked.

She did not reply, puffing at her cigarette.

After a while, the men were finished with the rubbish. The younger one gave a whistle. The waitress returned the whistle and went forward. Ron followed as she climbed into the back of the lorry. He had misgivings but he went. They settled themselves down among the trash as the lorry started forward with a lurch.

Once through the maze of back streets, they were driving along a wide thoroughfare lit by sodium street lamps. Ron and the waitress stared at each other, their faces made anonymous in the orange glow. Her face was a mask, centuries old, her hair hung streakily over her temples. He felt in her a life of hard work, without pride. The perception warmed him towards her and he put an arm round her shoulders. He had always loved the downtrodden more than the proud and beautiful. It accorded with his poor image of himself.

She was slow to return his gesture of affection. Languidly, she moved a leg against his. He stared down the vanishing street, as once more they turned into a dark quarter. The excitement of the adventure on which he was now embarked dulled his apprehension, although he wondered about her relationship with the two lorry men, speculating whether they would beat him up and rob him at journey's end. He clutched his briefcase between his knees; it was metal and would be a useful weapon in a fight.

Here at least he was on familiar ground. Ron was no stranger to fights over women, and was used to giving a good account of himself. Whatever else had gone wrong with the universe, some constants remained: the art of getting the leg over, the swift knee in a rival's goolies. He sang a familiar little song in her ear:

> 'With moonlight and romance
> If you don't seize the chance
> To get it on the sly
> Your archetype will be awry
> As time goes by.'

The waitress gave every appearance of not knowing the words, and silenced him with a hand over his mouth. They bumped on in silence and discomfort for a while.

'How far to go?'

'Ein kilometre.' Holding up one finger.

He tried to observe the route in case he had to walk back. Where would he turn for help in case of trouble? He did not want to end up in the Moskva. He had a mad pal in Leeds who had been beaten up and thrown into the canal.

The depressing suburbs through which they passed, where hardly a light showed, were without visible feature. Flat, closed, bleak, Asiatic façades. At one point, on a corner, they passed a fight, where half a dozen men were hitting each other with what might have been pick helves.

The rumpus vanished into the night. Moscow slept like an ill-fed gourmet, full of undigested secrets. The lorry stopped abruptly, sending its passengers sliding among the filth. Ron climbed out fast, ready for trouble, the waitress following. They stood on a broken road surface. Immediately, the lorry bucked and moved off.

They were isolated in an area of desolation. It was possible to make out an immense pile of splintered wood, crowned by a bulldozer, where some rough-looking men sat by the machine, perhaps guarding it, warming themselves round a wood fire. To Ron's other hand, where a solitary lamp shone, a row of small concrete houses stood, ending in a shuttered box of a shop which advertised beer. Further away, black against the night sky, silhouettes of tall apartment blocks could be seen. It was towards these blocks that the waitress now led Ron.

The heap of wood and beams was more extensive than he had thought. There were figures standing in it at intervals. It seemed to him that a complete old-fashioned village had been bulldozed to make way for Moscow's sprawl. Homes had been reduced to matchwood.

Someone called out to them, but the waitress made no answer. She led down a side lane, where the way underfoot was unpaved.

To encourage Ron, she pointed ahead to a looming block of jagged outline.

They skirted a low wall and reached the building. She went to a side door, knocked and waited. Ron stood there, staring about him, clutching his case and feeling that he needed a drink.

After a long delay, the door was unbolted, unlocked and dragged open. They went in, and the waitress passed a small package from her coat to a dumpy matron in black. Without changing her expression, the dumpy woman locked and bolted the door behind them and retreated into a small fortified office.

The smell of the place hit Ron as soon as he stepped into the passage. It reminded him of his term in jail. This institution was similar to prison. The smell was a compound of underprivilege, mixing disinfectant, polish, urine, dirt, fatty foods and general staleness, bred by too many people being confined in an old building.

The waitress led him past noticeboards, battered lockers and a broken armchair to another corridor, and on to a stairwell. The odours became sharper. They ascended the stairs.

The steps were of pre-cast concrete, the rail of cold metal, and the staircase cared nothing for human frailty. It was carpeted only as far as the first floor. As the waitress ascended beside him, Ron saw the weariness in her step. 'Some night this is going to be,' he told himself. He placed a hand encouragingly in the small of her back. She grimaced a smile without turning her head.

Smells of laundry, damp sheets, overworked heating appliances came and went. On the upper floors, he listened to a low stratum of noise issuing from behind locked doors. Despite the late hour, several women were wandering about the corridors. None took any notice of Ron and the waitress.

In a side passage the waitress pulled a large key from her coat pocket, unlocked a door, and motioned Ron to go in. As he entered, he saw how scratched and bruised the panels of the door were, almost as if it had been attacked by animals.

The same sense of something under duress was apparent in her room. The furnishings crowded together as if for protection. Every surface was fingered and stained, their overused appearance reinforced by the dim luminance of a forty-watt bulb shining overhead. The murkiest corner was filled by a cupboard on which stood a tin basin; this was the washing alcove. Close by was a one-ring electric stove, much rusted. The greater part of the room was occupied by a bed, covered by a patchwork peasant quilt which provided the one note of colour in the room. A crucifix hung by a chain from one of the bedposts. Beside the bed, encroaching on it for lack of space, was a cupboard on top of which cardboard boxes were piled. The only other furniture – there was scarcely room for more – consisted of a table standing under a narrow and grimy window letting in the dark of the night.

The waitress locked her door and bolted it before crossing to the window and dragging a heavy curtain over it. By the window and under the bed were piled old cigarette cartons, all foreign, from Germany, France, England, China and the States. He knew instinctively they were empty – probably saved from the hotel refuse bins. Perhaps she liked the foreign names, Philip Morris and the rest. Well. He was up to his neck in the unknown now, and no mistake. Still. Nothing was ever going to be a greater shock than his first day at the orphanage, when he was four.

He was beginning to enjoy the adventure. He said to himself, 'Now then, Ronnie, if you can't fight your way out of trouble, you'd better fuck your way out.'

He set his case down and pulled off his coat. She hung the coat with hers on a hook behind the door, then went to the cupboard and brought out an unlabelled bottle with two small glasses. She poured clear liquid and passed him a glass. He sniffed. Vodka.

They toasted each other and drank.

He offered her an English cigarette, then handed her the pack. As they lit up, she gave him a smile, looking rather timid. Turning abruptly as if to hide weakness, she recorked her bottle and put it back in the cupboard. That was all he was getting in the way of alcohol.

'An instinctive liking,' he said. 'I mean, this is how it should be, eh? Friends on sight, right?' They sat side by side on the bed, puffing at their cigarettes; he laid a hand on her meagre thigh.

Two cheap reproductions hung on the walls facing them, one of birch forests lost in mist, one of a woman looking out of a deep-set window into a well-lit street. He pointed to it, saying he liked it.

'Frank-land,' she said. 'Franzosisch.'

She threw down her vodka, rose, pulled out a stained and tattered nightdress from under her bolster. It was or had been blue. She smoothed the wrinkles with one hand, while looking at him interrogatively.

'You won't need that,' he said, and laughed.

She paused, then threw the garment down on the end of the bed.

Suddenly, in her hesitation, he saw that she considered saying no to him and throwing him out. He dropped his gaze. The decision was hers. He never forced a woman.

Thoughts of Steff came back to him. He remembered the bitterness they went through after his trip a few weeks ago to Lyons in France. Steff had discovered that he had gone with a prostitute. A row had followed, which rumbled on for days. She had poured out hatred, had made the house almost unlivable. In the first throes of her fury, she had coshed him with a frying pan when he was asleep on the sofa. He had become terrified of her and of what she might do next. Finally, he swore that he would never go with other women again.

Yet here he was, settling in with this strange creature with the disgusting nightdress. The little whore in Lyons had been pernickety clean, a beauty in every way. Steff was always clean, always having a shower, washing her hair. This poor bitch had no shower. Her hair looked as if it had never seen shampoo.

Stubbing out her cigarette, the waitress paused by the light, then switched it off. The room was plunged into darkness. She had made up her mind to let him stay. He heard the sounds of her getting undressed, and began to do the same.

As his eyes accustomed themselves to the dark, he saw her clearly by the corridor light shining under the bottom of the door. She pulled off soiled undergarments and threw them on the table. Fanning out, the light shone most strongly on her feet. They were grey and heavily veined, the toes splayed, their nails curved and long like bird claws. He saw they were filthy. They disappeared from view as she threw herself naked on the bed and pulled the quilt over herself.

An icy draught blew under the door. Ron put his clothes neatly on the table, trying to avoid her dirty undergarments, and climbed under the quilt beside her. She lifted her arms and wrapped them round his neck.

A rank odour assailed him, ancient and indecent. It caught in his throat. He almost gagged. It wafted from her, from all parts. She was settling back, opening her legs. He could scarcely breathe.

He sat up. 'You'll have to wash yourself,' he said. 'I can't bear it.'

He climbed off the bed again, fanning the air, rather than have her climb over him.

'You not like?' she asked.

When he did not reply, she got up and went on her grey feet over to the basin. Her toenails clicked on the floor covering. She poured water in the basin and commenced washing. He pulled open her cupboard, to drink from her vodka bottle, tipping the stuff down his throat. The waitress made no comment.

She rinsed her armpits and her sexual quarters with a dripping rag, drying herself on a square of towel.

'And the feet,' he ordered, pointing.

Meekly, she washed her feet, dragging each up in turn to reach nearer the basin.

This is Ron's story, not mine. But I had to ask myself if there wasn't, in this sordid lie he was telling me, something I deeply envied. I mean, not just the tacky woman, the foul room, the filthy fantasy world of 'Brezhnev's Russia', whatever that meant, but the whole desperate situation, something that took a man up wholly. This wish to be consumed. The whole romantic and absurd involvement. A hell. Oh yes, a hell all right.

And yet – we work away to build our security, to get a little roof and pay the rates. Still there's that thing unappeased. Don't we all secretly long, in our safe Britain, to take a Tupolev too far, to some godforsaken somewhere, where everything's to play for . . . ?

I only ask it.

At length she came back to the bed, standing looking at Ron in the deep gloom, as if asking his permission to re-enter.

At this point in the proceedings, he was again tempted to call the whole thing off. As he struggled with his feelings, to his reluctance to pass by any willing woman was added his kind of perpetual good humour with the other sex, quite different from his aggressive manner with men, which urged him not to disappoint this unlucky creature who had so far exhibited nothing but good will.

The waitress had started all this by encouraging him at the dinner table. He did not know if there was danger involved in this escapade but, if so, then she probably had more to lose than he. Men might not be allowed in this – lodging house, or whatever it was. He would hardly be sent to the gulag if he was caught, but no one could say what might happen to the waitress. He supposed that at the least she might lose her job; which would bring with it a whole train of difficulties in Brezhnev's Russia.

I should explain where I was when my friend Ron was telling me this story, just to give you a little background.

We met by accident on Paddington Station. We had not seen each other for about a year. I had come up on the train from Bournemouth to consult my parent company in Islington, and was crossing the forecourt when someone called my name.

There was Ron Wallace, grinning. He looked much as usual in a rather shabby grey suit with a cream shirt and a floppy tie – the picture, you might say, of an unprofessional professional man working for some down-at-heel outfit.

We were pleased to see each other, and went into the station bar for a pint or two of beer and a chat. I asked him where he was off to. This is what he said: 'I'm off to Glastonbury to see a wise old man who will tell me where my life's going. With any luck.'

It was an answer I liked. Of course, I had some knowledge of how his life had been, and the hard times he had seen. I asked after his wife, Stephanie, and it was then that he started telling me this story I repeat to you. Just don't let it go any further.

So there he was stuck in this poky little room with the waitress. Torn between compassion, lust, boredom and exasperation. The way one always is, really.

He lay in the bed. She stood naked before him in the half-light, looking helpless.

'You ought to look after yourself better,' he said, raising the quilt to let her in.

A sickly smell still pursued him. Concluding it came from the bed itself, he ignored it. She laid her head beside him on the patterned bolster. She smoothed dull hair back to gaze at him through the dim curdled light.

He stroked her cheek. When she buried her face suddenly in his chest, in a gesture of dependence, he caught the aroma of greasy kitchens, but he snuggled against her, feeling her still damp body. The waitress sniffed at him and sighed, rubbing against his thighs, perhaps excited by talc and deodorant scents, stigmata of the prosperous capitalist class. Prosperous! If only she knew! Ron and Steff had all manner of debts.

She opened her legs. As Ron groped in her moist pubic hair, he thought – a flash of humour – that he had his hand on the one thing that made life in the Soviet Union endurable. The Soviet Union and elsewhere . . . He penetrated her and she went almost immediately into orgasm, clutching him fiercely, bringing out a cry from the back of her throat. He thrust into her with savage glee.

Only afterwards, as they lay against each other, she clutching his limp penis, did her story start. She began to tell it in a low voice. He was idle, not really listening, comfortable with her against him, half-wanting a cigarette.

What she was saying became more important. She sat up, clutching a corner of the quilt over her naked breasts, addressing him fiercely. Her supply of English and German words was running out. He gathered this was something about her childhood. Yet maybe it wasn't. A horse was dying. It had to be shot. Or it had been shot. This was somewhere on a farm. The name Vladimir was repeated, but he was not sure if she referred to the town or a man. He tried to question her, to make things clear, but she was intent on pouring out her misery.

Now it was about an infant – 'eine kleine kind', and the waitress was acting out her drama, dropping the quilt to gesticulate. The baby had been seized and banged against a wall – this demonstrated by a violent banging of her own head against the wall behind her. He could not understand if she was talking about herself or about a baby of hers. But the pain came through.

The waitress was sobbing and crying aloud, waving her arms, frequently calling the word 'smert', which he knew meant 'death'. Her body shook with the grief of it all.

It reached a melancholy conclusion. The story, incomprehensible and disturbing, ended with her coming alone to Moscow to work.

'To work here in this place. Arbeit. Nur Arbeit. Work alone. Abschliessen.'

'There, there.' He comforted her as he once used to comfort Steff's and his only child, wrapping her in his arms, rocking her. He was shaken by the agony of her outburst, angry with himself for failing to understand.

Of course there was no misunderstanding her misery. He felt it in his stomach, having known misery himself. Even in the pretty comfortable world he had left – to which he hoped to return on the morrow – personal tragedy was no rarity; some people always held the wrong cards. But he had fallen by accident into a shadow world, the world labelled 'Brezhnev's Russia' or 'Soviet Union', a world racked by terrible world wars and diseases. It was safe to say that whatever woes the poor waitress suffered, she represented millions who laboured under similar burdens.

He gave her a cigarette. A simple human gesture. He could think of nothing else to do.

She cried a little in a resigned fashion and wiped her tears on the quilt. Then she began to make love to him in a tender and provocative way. For a while paradise existed in the squalid room.

Ron Wallace woke. A full bladder had roused him. The waitress lay beside him, asleep and breathing softly. In the dim light, her face was young, even childlike.

Disengaging his arm from under her neck, Ron sat up and looked at his watch. Next moment, he was out of bed. The time was 5.50 a.m. A suspicion of daylight showed round the curtains, and his flight was due to leave at 9.30. His check-in time at Sheremeteivo Airport was 8.00 a.m. He had two hours in which to get to the airport, and no idea of where he was.

He listened at the door. All was quiet in the building. He had to return to the hotel and collect his suitcase. And first he had to have a pee.

His impulse was to awaken the waitress. Capable though she had shown herself to be, she might be less reliable this morning. She would find herself in a difficult situation to which perhaps she had given no thought on the previous evening; the entertaining of foreigners in one's apartment was surely a crime in Brezhnev's Russia.

Since she did not stir, he decided to leave her sleeping. Keeping his gaze on her face, he dressed fast and quietly. He stood for a moment looking down at her, then unstrapped his watch from his wrist and laid it by the bedside as a parting present.

As noiselessly as possible, he slipped into his coat and unbolted and unlocked the door. In the corridor, he closed the door behind him. Thought of the tragic life he left behind came to him; damn it, that was none of his business. It was urgent that he got to a toilet. There must be one on this floor.

All the doors were locked. He ran from one to another in increasing agony. There seemed to be no toilet. He was sweating. He must piss outside, fast.

He went quickly down the stairs, alert for other people. He heard voices but saw no one.

His penis tingled. 'Oh God,' he thought, 'have I caught a dose off that bitch? I must have been mad. How can I tell Steff? She'll leave me this time. Steff, I love you, I'm sorry, I'm a right bastard, I know it.'

He rushed to the front door, which had a narrow fanlight above it, admitting wan signs of dawn. The door was double-locked, with a mortice lock and a large padlocked bar across it. Next to the door stood a cramped concierge's office, firmly closed. Everyone had been locked in for the night.

He ran about the ground floor rather haphazardly, gasping, and came on the side door by which, he believed, he had entered the previous evening. That too was securely locked. He gasped a prayer. At any moment his bladder would burst.

At this point in Ron's story, I broke into heartless laughter.

He stared at me halfway between anger and amusement.

'It's no fun, going off your head for want of a piss,' he said.

I controlled my laughter. Ron is not a guy you like to offend. What amused me was the thought of a man who had been inside for GBH and done a stretch for breaking and entering in a situation where he was attempting breaking and exiting.

After trying and failing to kick in a panel on the side door, Ron ran about almost at random looking for a way of escape.

Two steps at the end of the main corridor led down to another locked door, a boiler room in all probability. Next to the door was a broom cupboard and an alcove containing a mop, a brass tap and a drain.

With a groan of relief, Ron unzipped his trousers and pissed violently into the drain. The relief almost made him faint.

By now it must be almost half-past six.

As the urine drained from his body, he heard a door open along the corridor and a woman coughing. Her footsteps led away from where he stood. He heard her mount the stairs. Other doors were opening, female voices sounded, a snatch of song floated down; the noise level in the building was rising.

At last he was finished. He zipped his trousers, wondering what he should do to escape.

Two men were coming towards him. Although he saw them only in silhouette along the dark corridor, he recognised that they were old. They walked slowly, slack-kneed, and one jangled a bunch of keys. Ron sank back into the alcove.

The men passed within eighteen inches of him, talking to each other, not noticing him in the gloom. They unlocked the boiler-room door and went in.

Immediately they were gone, Ron came out of his hiding place and hurried back to the main door. As he went, he tried each handle in the corridor in turn. All were locked.

At the front door, he was looking up at the narrow fanlight, wondering if it would open, when he heard faint sounds from the concierge's nook. Impelled by urgency, he pushed the office door open and looked in.

A plump old woman with her hair in a bun was just leaving the main room to enter a cubbyhole which served as a kitchen. She began to rattle a coffee pot.

In the room lay three men, sleeping in ungainly attitudes. Two were huddled on a sturdy table pushed against the far wall, the third lay under the table, his head resting peacefully on a pair of boots. A cluster of empty bottles and full ashtrays suggested that they had had a good night of it.

The room, in considerable disarray, had five sides. It served regularly as a bedroom as well as an office; against the left-hand wall a bed stood under a shelf bulging with files. Timetables and keys hung from the walls.

A TUPOLEV TOO FAR

The loud and laboured breathing of the men reinforced the stuffy atmosphere. Where two of the walls came to a point was a window which the old woman had evidently opened to let air into the room.

Without hesitation, Ron crossed over to the window. In doing so, he kicked one of the empty vodka bottles. It rattled against its companions. He did not look round to see if the woman had caught sight of him.

One pane of the window had been repaired with brown paper. Taking little care not to injure himself, he forced himself through the opening feet first. The ground was further down than he had expected. He landed on concrete with a painful bump. Above him, an angry old woman stuck her head out and yelled at him. Ron got up and ran round the corner. At least he was free of that damned prison, where women were locked in every night.

Then came the thought.

'My bloody briefcase!'

He had left it standing by the waitress's bed.

Cursing furiously, he marched round the outside of the fortress. It was built of grey stone. All of its windows were barred.

A pile of rubbish, including the burnt-out carcass of a vehicle, stood against one wall. Even if he climbed up that way, it led only to a barred window. He prowled about, searching for the window of the boiler room, assuming there was one; he might be able to bribe the two old men to let him in that way.

He was frantic, and mad to know how the time was slipping away – what a fool to leave his watch with that bitch. He had to catch his plane, otherwise there would be trouble with his company and with Steff, not to mention all the difficulties with the airline – whatever it was called now . . . Aeroflot. And he could not leave without the briefcase. In it were his precious contracts.

Struggling to deal with his anxiety levels, he kept from his mind the more dreadful and nebulous fear: that the airliner would deliver him not to his lovely Steff and the England he knew but to some other England ruled over not by Queen Margaret and PM Bernard Mattingly but by – whoever the lady was as mentioned in the newspaper – he had forgotten her name. He would perish if he was trapped for ever in a dreadful shadow world where history had taken a wrong turn.

Despite his frenzy, he remembered something else. The damned doll the North Korean had given him. He was convinced it was packed with heroin or some other illegal substance. He had not believed the Korean's unlikely story about Mr Holmberg for one moment, and had intended to throw away the doll as soon as he was outside the hotel. Sexual pursuit had made him forget.

Ron became really frightened.

Running round the building, isolated on its wasteland, he could find no low boiler-room window. He stood back, frustrated, when a stocky female figure in a black coat emerged from the building and walked off rapidly in the direction of the gigantic piles of broken wood Ron recalled from the previous night.

She had emerged from a side door. He ran to it, only to find it already locked. But even as he stood against it cursing, he heard the key turn from within, and it opened again. As another woman emerged, Ron dashed in. When an old man standing inside, key in hand, moved to stop him, Ron pushed him brutally in the chest. Other women were pressing to leave the building for the day's work, stern of face, burly of shoulder. He ran into the main corridor and hastened upstairs.

But which floor?

Which bloody floor?

He had seen from outside there were five floors.

Which floor was the waitress on?

Not the ground or first floors. Not the top . . .

Christ!

The scene was changed from a few minutes earlier. Everyone was now up and about, and women in states of undress were wandering the corridors. They yelled at him and tried to grab him. In a few minutes, they would get themselves organised. Then he would be arrested.

He tried the second floor. He ran down the side passage. First door on right. He remembered that. As soon as he faced the door, he remembered the markings on the waitress's door, the savage scratches as if an animal had been there. This was not it.

He ran up to the third floor, causing more disturbance, and to the side passage. God, this nightmare! He was furious with himself. Now he faced the door with the deep scratch marks, and hammered on it. The door opened.

Ron took a swift look back. No one saw him, though he heard sounds of pursuit. He went in.

The waitress stood there, half-dressed, hand up to mouth in an attitude of misgiving.

One reason for that misgiving was clear. On the bed – that bed! – on top of the quilt and the dirty blue nightdress, the contents of Ron's briefcase had been spread, a dirty shirt, a pair of socks, a pair of underpants, some aspirins, the crossword book, the Korean doll, a copy of the *Daily Express* from a week ago, the precious contracts, and other belongings. The case lay with a screwdriver beside it. She had managed to prise the lock open.

'Get dressed,' he said. 'Schnell. I need you to get me out of here.'

'And to get me back to that sodding hotel,' he thought.

The waitress tried to make some apology. She had not expected him back. She thought the case was a present. He barked at her. She hurried to put on yesterday's dress and fit her grey feet into her heavy working shoes, whimpering as she did so.

He hardly looked to see what he was doing as he pushed everything into the briefcase, shouting to her to move. She was now his guarantee. She could get him out of the lodging house. She knew the way back to the Hotel Moskva.

'Schnell,' he growled, deliberately scaring her as he forced the case shut.

She offered him his watch back but he shook his head.

'Let's go. Fast. Vite. Schnell.'

'OK, OK,' she said.

Together they hurried down the corridor and down the stone stairs, Ron with a firm grasp on her arm. Several women gathered. They called to the waitress, but when she snapped back at them they stood aside and let her pass. A younger woman began to laugh. Others took it up. Soon there was general laughter. This was not the first time a woman had had a lodger for the night. Probably, Ron reflected, this was not the first time the waitress had had a lodger for the night.

The old man unlocked the side door and they were out with a stream of other workers into the chill air. Great was his relief. He had a chance with Steff yet.

'The hotel,' he said. 'Schnell. I must catch that bloody plane.'

Ron Wallace caught the bloody plane. He rang his office from Penge. The managing director had had to go up to Halifax, so happily he was not wanted till the following morning. The day was his. He was able to go back to Steff, preparing as he went to be innocent. After all, she meant far more to him than any of these stray bitches. He would serve another stretch for Steff. He told himself he had learnt a lesson. He would never go with another woman.

Sitting on the coach going home, he was relieved to find everything was as normal. The *Daily Express* he picked up at the airport carried a photograph of Bernard Mattingly, Britain's popular Prime Minister, opening the first stretch of a new motorway that would run between London and Birmingham. He searched for a reference to Russia. A small paragraph announced that Russia had a record wheat surplus, which they were shipping to the Third World. And the Pope had returned to Rome from his tour of Siberia.

Everything was normal. He thought again of the strange electric storm which had bathed his plane on the flight out. Perhaps that had all been subjective, a major ischaemic event in the brain stem. He had been working too hard recently.

Nothing had happened. He had imagined that whole dark world, Brezhnev, the waitress and all.

Steff was amiable and credulous and listened to all he had to say about the boredom of Moscow. While he was showering, she even went to unpack his things for him.

He stepped naked from the shower. She had opened the briefcase. She was holding up for his inspection a dirty blue nightdress.

A Romance of the Equator

Friends, very long ago in the old tropical green world, a boy lived whose name was Kahlin. Two strange things befell him in his life.

First of all, when he was a mere youth with limbs smooth as twigs, his home was demolished by a volcanic eruption. So great was that explosion that it could be heard by man and beast all round the world. Pieces of the earth were thrown into the air and landed across the seas two hundred miles and more away, where they still stand today as lines of hills.

The volcano destroyed Kahlin's home and killed both his parents and his little brothers.

Kahlin was so frightened that he ran and ran towards the north, away from the eruption. His legs carried him eventually to a narrow isthmus, fringed on either side by cliffs which fell sheer to the sea.

The boy heard a pathetic crying. He went to the edge of the nearest cliff and looked down. Two young gazelles had fallen over the side and were resting perilously on a ledge some feet below. Every effort they made to scramble up again endangered their foothold on the ledge. He could see that they were doomed to slip and fall.

Being a compassionate child, Kahlin removed his cloth headgear and used it as a rope to lower himself to the gazelles. He took one of the poor little things under each arm and climbed with them up to safety.

The animals were exhausted. He improvised shelter for them that night on the far side of the isthmus, and lay down between them, gazing piteously into their faces. One of the gazelles was white, the other brown.

He put his arms about them and slept. During the warmth of the night he heard a sound like the distant booming of the sea. He woke at dawn, and found that the two gazelles had turned into young women. They lay naked beside him, their eyes closed, one brown, one white. Still he held them, and his heart beat strongly and his breath came fast as he gazed at their beauty.

The two girls awoke and gazed at him, the white one with blue eyes, the brown one with eyes of amber.

Kahlin had heard of such things happening in fairy tales, so he covered his nudity and said to the girls, 'How beautiful you are, both of you! My guess is that you were both princesses, turned into animals by some great enchanter. Is that so?'

The girls sat up and concealed some of their nudity. They denied that what Kahlin said was true. 'We were animals, and were happy as animals. It is only the enchantments of your love that make you see us as girls. You are in a spell, not us.'

'So how do you see me?' he asked.

'As a handsome male gazelle.'

He snorted with disappointment, but the girls said sweetly, 'We love you as we see you, and you must be content to be loved according to our interpretation. Truly, if we saw you as you see yourself, we could not love you.'

Because he was a sensible boy, Kahlin saw some force in this argument and, because the world was young and its core still molten, he made love to the two girls, to the brown and the white, with equal passion.

Afterwards, the girls rose up and bathed themselves in the sea for a long while, standing below a waterfall, and washing each other's hair, the fair hair and the black. They wove themselves grass skirts before returning to Kahlin's side.

They regarded him with their large gazelle eyes and said, 'Now the time is come when you must choose between us. It is not right that you should have us both. You must choose me or my sister to be yours, and to accompany you through the world until the last sunset, whilst the rejected sister goes on her way.'

Kahlin grew angry and swore that he could not choose between them. They insisted. He threw himself down on the grass in a passion, beating the earth, swearing he loved them both, the one with hair like a raven's wing, and one with hair like honey.

'But we are going to live in different parts of the world,' one sister said. 'The pale to the north, the dark to the south.'

Still he swore that he loved them both equally and would die if either left him. Dusk fell and they were still arguing.

A moon rose like a washed shell on the blue beaches of the sky, and eventually the girls came to an agreement. They said to Kahlin, 'We see that you hold us both dear. Very well, since you saved us both from death on the cliff, then we will make a bargain with you. You shall enjoy us both, but a price must be paid, and that price must be your peace of mind. You will be forever trying to decide which of us you love the better, the brown or the white.'

'I shall love you both the same.'

Both girls shook their heads wisely, and wagged admonitory fingers, white and brown.

'But that is impossible. Since we are different, so we must be loved differently. Did you not know that that is one of the great secret truths of human companionship, and the cause of all its torment as well as its happiness? There is a configuration of love to fit the needs of every configuration of personality.'

He threw his arms round them, crying, 'There's no difference between you, except that one of you is brown and one white. How can I ever say which I love best, the limbs of ivory or the limbs of gold?'

And the two girls smiled first at him and then at each other, saying, 'Just as you see us only as female, so your love makes you blind to our real differences, which are many. But you will grow to see. Your blindness will not long protect you.'

'You women talk too much,' Kahlin said, clapping his hands together. 'I will accept the terms of your bargain and love you both.' Whereupon, he coaxed them to lie down beside him, and the women did not take a lot of coaxing.

The moon set. It rose and set again many times, undergoing its small but magical span of changes, rather like a chime blown by the wind. And with every moon, Kahlin grew older in experience.

He saw that it was as the girls said. They differed greatly in their natures. He could scarcely believe it. In the first flush of his love, he had been blind to their personalities.

Then they had seemed merely like personages from some deep dream. Now they slowly became human, with all their faults and contradictions.

One of the women was extremely passionate, and desired always to be close to Kahlin, never letting him from her sight. The other woman was cooler and more casual in her manner, teasing him in a way that alternately infuriated and delighted him.

One of the women was a good cook, and spent long hours over her stove, preparing with infinite patience dishes of great delicacy which could scarcely appease the appetite. The other woman cooked indifferently, yet bestirred herself occasionally to provide a great feast which they ate till their stomachs groaned.

One of the women was not greatly fond of washing, and was lazy, and spent much of her time lying about with her toes curled, prattling and laughing. The other woman was as neat and clean as a cat, and spent her days trying to keep everything impossibly tidy.

One of the women was highly intelligent, making clever or amusing remarks, and scolding Kahlin for his ignorance. The other woman was not intelligent, and repeated everything Kahlin said in honest admiration for his cleverness.

One of the women was most active by day, and leaped up with the dawn, calling Kahlin and her sister to join her. The other woman was a night creature, and came alive only after sunset, when she seemed to glow with a special light.

One woman was frank in all things, the other rather dishonest, full of amazing little secrets.

One woman painted and decorated herself, the other refused to do anything of the sort.

One woman had a gift for music and danced beautifully, the other could not sing a note but designed exquisite clothes for the three of them.

One woman smelt of musk, the other of honeysuckle.

One woman liked to talk about forbidden things, and cast a languishing eye on other men, while the other made a mystery of herself and disliked Kahlin's men friends.

One woman kept a pet monkey that pulled Kahlin's ears, while the other doted on three cats.

One woman seemed to be never quite content, while the other was completely uncritical. One woman let her hair grow long, while the other cut hers short.

As the years went by, one woman became surprisingly plump, while the other became surprisingly thin.

By the same token, Kahlin also grew old, and his hair turned grey. No longer was his step as certain as it had been, or his gaze so keen.

Every day of his life he worked for the two women, and felt his love split between the brown woman and the white. Finally he rose and said to them, 'Although I still have strength, yet I now know my days to be numbered. I have a desire to return to my origins, so I am going back to the mountains where I lived with my parents before the volcano erupted. You may come with me, or you may stay here, as you please.'

This was in part his way of testing them, for he thought that perhaps only one woman – the white or the brown – would follow him on his journey.

So he travelled without looking back. He could hear that someone walked behind him, yet he refused to allow himself to turn to see who it was. He crossed over the isthmus where he had saved the two gazelles, the brown and the white, so many years ago that he went past the spot before recalling it.

Still he plodded on, and came at last to the mountains where he had been born. As he climbed the sides of the final hill, scenes from the distant past swam before his eyes. Recollecting his parents with love, he was granted insight, and perceived for the first time how his father and mother had differed in every way, almost as his two women differed. Only his childish love, with its quality of blindness, had allowed him to see his parents as two equal gods.

'So I glean a grain of knowledge,' he said aloud to himself. 'Was it worth travelling all these years for?' But he answered himself that a grain of insight was indeed better than nothing.

So Kahlin came to the top of the rise. There before him, greeting his eyes, was a magnificent sight such as he had never seen before. Spreading from horizon to horizon, steep slopes clad in jungle led down to a vast lake reflecting the sky. It seemed to him that this lake stretched to eternity, cradled at the bottom of the encompassing slopes. Not a single boat or sail crossed that silent surface. The lake was like the heavens themselves, without wave or ripple.

Only after he had gazed for a long while at the vista before him did Kahlin realise that this was the enormous crater of the volcano which had destroyed his parents, his brothers, and many other people besides. Now the place of death had become fertile through the ceaseless processes of nature.

Kahlin turned. Both his wives stood behind him, the white one and the brown. He embraced them warmly.

'You see there is an island in the middle of this new lake,' he said. 'We can make a boat and sail to the island, and there the three of us will live out the rest of our lives.'

But the women said, 'First we must speak. We made a bargain many years ago, the three of us. You agreed to love us both, at the expense of your peace of mind. We knew then, as we know now, that no man can love two women and be at peace in his mind. Every day of your life, our differences have tortured you. Well, now we release you from your bargain. You have often been unfair and cruel, it's true; once or twice you chased after other women, you even beat us, you sulked, and you did a lot of terrible things. You belch at your meals. All those things we now forgive, firstly, because we understand that such shortcomings are in man's nature, and, secondly, because despite those shortcomings, you did honestly try to love us both.'

Kahlin looked from one to the other of them suspiciously.

'So, I'm free of the bargain, am I? Is this a new kind of trick? What follows next?'

The women, the white and the brown, smiled at each other, and then said, 'We think you have learnt the lesson that as we have different natures, so it is necessary to love us differently. You have done well, considering your limitations as a man. Therefore we set you free and give you a further choice.'

One woman kissed him on one cheek and one on the other, and they said, 'You need take only one of us over to the island in the lake. Whichever one you choose will remain close to you for all the rest of your days. As for the other, you need never think of her again.'

Then they walked about him and about, smiling mysteriously, and as they walked, they divested themselves of their clothes, for their bodies were still beautiful even in age, the brown and the white, and carried fewer lines of experience than their faces. And they watched him, the white one with blue eyes, the brown one with eyes of amber.

'Which of us do you choose, Kahlin?' they asked, at last.

He looked away from them, across the lake lying far below, across the uninhabited island, into the blue distance, and he said, 'It really needs three people to build a boat, particularly if two of them are women. You had better both come with me. The three of us will live together on the island.'

Without giving them more than a glance, he started down the steep slope towards the far gleaming water. The two women followed, waving their hands and protesting, 'But you could be free, you could be free . . .'

At the water's edge, they built a small boat, making a sail of woven palm leaves. They slept on the beach that night and, next morning early, before the sun peered over the lip of the great crater to disperse its dews, they rose and launched their boat towards the island.

The two women stood by him with their arms entwined about his shoulders, and teased him, saying, 'So, after all these years, despite all your lack of peace of mind, you still cannot decide which of us you love the better, the one with the hair like honey or the one with hair like a raven's wing. Really, Kahlin, you are a funny man! Now you're stuck with us both for the rest of your life.'

The mysterious island was drifting nearer now. Kahlin could not help smiling, though he fixed his gaze upon the distant trees leaning out across the hazy waters, rather than on the two tormenting ladies by his side.

For he had his secret. Whereas once, as a youth, he had loved them because he thought they were almost identical, he had learnt through many long years to love them both more deeply because of their differences.

Short Stories

When someone in the audience asked how
I saw my short stories, I offered them
Antarctica. The ice shelf grinding
Forward with the century
Carrying freights of fossil Bronze Age snow
Until a thousand flaws united.
Then with huge mammalian groans
The burdened stone thing calved.

You know (I told my listeners, hoping
They might), those icebergs there are frequently
Over a hundred kilometres long –
As big as Monte Carlo. Solemnly
They drift beyond the Weddell Sea
Like Matterhorns breasting the South Atlantic.
Riding out gales shaved by the wind and warmth
Heading north for Rio and Capricorn.

But as they're sighting the Malvinas
They suffer the environment.
These old cathedrals of the cold
Have shrunk. They'd go into your gin
And tonic. So they're lost to human ken
But for some months they have a real existence

And scientists keep tabs on them.
They're mad and lovely while they last.

That's how (I told the audience)
I see my stories. They formed part of me.
Those who sight them in those desolate
Latitudes of publishing sometimes
Are awed. They praise a colour
Or an unexpected shape.
They seldom hear the groans of birth.
A year, a year, and they are gone.

The audience clapped uncertainly
Then asked if I kept office hours.

A New (Governmental) Father Christmas

It was Christmas Eve. Bells and tills were ringing. The weather was fine but cold. The shops in Headington were almost empty of goods by now, while credit cards were overloaded. Even charity shops had notices saying SOLD OUT. Everyone complained about how commercial Christmas had become. They said it even as they wrapped expensive presents for their dear ones, secure in the knowledge that their dear ones were doing the same for them.

Yet a sense of the holiness of the season had not vanished. Good will was in the frosty air. A group of carol singers were singing Afro-Indian carols outside the Rama Krishna Mart. Many people would attend church that very evening, and on the following morning, Christmas Day.

Christmas Day! The very words still held magic. In every household there was a sense of thanksgiving for the piles of mincepies, turkeys and sweet Algerian wine awaiting consumption. And yet – there was a cloud over the festivities; for this was happening in the future, which is always rather cloudy.

Perhaps it is this cloudiness which tends to make stories of the future so terrifying. Like this one . . .

The government-sponsored Re-cycling Movement had gathered strength. Everything was now being recycled. And the prime minister had announced that in future Father Christmas would call as usual; but he would no longer give presents: rather, he would collect old presents. And not only old presents, but old cooking utensils, old furniture, old books and even old people.

Old people! Yes, the New Father Christmas would collect old people. This was because the world had become so over-populated. The population of Old Headington was now over two million, many of them living in Osler Road. Old people had to go. It was the law.

The Liberal Democrats had voted against the edict. They had persuaded Parliament to make an exclusive clause. So what John Humphries told England on BBC Radio 4 that morning was, 'Old people will still be collected and popped into Father Christmas's sack, but now an exception is allowed. Any old people who can show Father Christmas their personal copy of the Holy Bible will be spared. After all, we are still a Christian country.'

In their two room flat in Laural Farm Close, old Phil and Dora Dogsbody were listening to the 'Today' programme in their dressing-gowns. They had decorated their radio with a piece of artificial holly. They were dismayed. They never dreamed they would become the subject of an improving moral tale like this.

'I shall speak to Mayor Stephanie Jenkins about this,' said Phil. 'This indignity is a law.'

'But we are going to be safe, Phil,' said Dora, who was of a nervous disposition. 'Good old Lib Dems! I always liked that fat Scottish chap. I'm so relieved, I can't tell you. I would hate to be scooped up and put in a sack.'

They stood together in their little old fashioned kitchen. Dora was winding up their old clockwork alarm clock before putting on the kettle for a morning cup of tea.

'If we had our Bible we'd be safe, dear, no doubt of that,' said Phil. 'We could look Santa in the arms and welcome him with open eyes.' (He often got these things confused these days.)

'What do you mean, Phil, "if we had our Bible"? It's tucked away in the music stool, as usual. Isn't it?'

'You can look in the music face till you're black in the stool,' said Phil, 'but if you remember we gave our Bible away for the Bring & Buy Queen at the stall's Golden Jubilee.'

A NEW (GOVERNMENTAL) FATHER CHRISTMAS

Dora Dogsbody became agitated. She lit the gas ring and put the alarm clock on it and tried to wind the kettle. 'Gave the Bible away!', she shrieked. 'You must have been off your rocker!'

Her husband said, 'You gave it away, Dora, along with those old bound punches of Volume, and the stuffed pheasant and your cup's silver grandfather for life-saving which tinned out to be made of turn.'

'You gave them away. I didn't.'

'Yes, you did. You said we didn't need Christianity any more.'

'No, I didn't. I only said it wasn't trendy any more.'

'Look out, your alarm over is boiling clock!'

So there the poor things were, very upset and worried and not knowing what to do, or where to turn for a Bible. Dora phoned their daughter, Sherbert Dogsbody, but there was no answer. Sherbert was celebrating Christmas partying in Ibiza and had switched her mobile phone off. It seemed as if, having no Bible, the Dogsbodys were obsolete and due to be swept away that very evening.

'A fine Christmas this is going to be! Into the sack and we'll be done for . . .'

At the breakfast table, Phil Dogsbody had an idea. 'I know, Dora. Let's find who bought our buy from the Bring & Bible stall. Then we can gain it back aget.'

Dora paused with a slice of black pudding half-way to her mouth. 'We can't go asking from door to door, you silly man.'

'No, but we can ask that nice stall who ran the Bring & Buy couple. They might remember who bought our Bible.'

They didn't even wait to finish their bowls of Popsickles. Still in their dressing-gowns, and Dora with rollers in what was left of her hair, they hurried out into the cold of the morning. But in the Croft they met their old friend Janeen Day. Janeen Day was old and bent and wore a scarlet deaf aid, but had not lost her love of life or of a joke. She would say, 'I'm eighty if I'm a day, and since I'm a Day I'm eighty'.

She was delighted to see her friends, and insisted the Dogsbodys come to her house to look at something funny.

'It's a present my married daughter has sent me all the way from Canada. You won't half laugh. It's better than television.'

They went together to her house in Larkins Lane, opposite the new Macumba Hall.

The Christmas gift Janeen Day's daughter has sent her from Canada consisted of not one but two electronic goldfish set in an electronic goldfish bowl. And when you switched it on, the two goldfish did the most amazing tricks. Dora and Phil sat there, roaring with laughter. 'Better than television,' Dora said.

'Except it doesn't have Nigella Cookery and her Lawson programmes,' said Phil, but the ladies ignored him.

The morning had gone before they remembered they had no Bible and were in danger of being swept away by the New Father Christmas.

But as they left Janeen Day's house, Phil said he was hungry, ravenous. He had had no proper breakfast. 'A harm wouldn't do us any snack.'

They trudged up to the main road. The trees planted on either side of the London Road made it look beautiful – palm trees, of course, to please the immigrant community.

They entered the Queen's Bakery in Windmill Road, which had recently been renamed Headington Business Association Avenue. It was nice and warm in the bakery. Since it was Christmas, the Dogsbodys could not resist a good blow-out. No one noticed how funnily they were dressed as they sat there eating away, because several customers were wearing plastic antlers or were dressed in red or wore red noses and funny costumes. One young man had painted a union jack on his face and had stapled fake diamonds to his eyelids. He was having tika marsala and Yorkshire pudding.

Just as the were leaving the shop, the Dogsbodys bumped into their friends the Johnsons, Sue and Stanley Johnson, who were buying a huge lardy cake at the counter.

'Do come and have a Christmas drink with us,' said Stanley. 'We haven't seen you for ages.' He explained that he had got restless and wanted a change of scenery.

'I think he was in a mid-life crisis,' said Sue. 'I always say that, don't I, Stan?'

A NEW (GOVERNMENTAL) FATHER CHRISTMAS

'So I finally made a brave break,' said Stanley, laughing to think of his own courage. 'I left Chancellors and now I work at Buckle & Ballard's.'

Stanley was an intellectual who lived in Business Association Avenue just opposite Balfour's. Indeed, their house had once been called 'Balfour News View'. Stanley liked to drink and talk about his theories regarding cosmic energies and property prices.

'Well, we can't stop for long,' said Dora, 'but a glass of something would be nice after all that turkey. I can't think why the bakery doesn't get a drinks licence.'

'It's Muslim, isn't it?', said Sue, taking her friend's arm.

On their way to the Johnsons', they had to make a detour to Barclay's Bank. The bank was crowded. Everyone queuing was complaining about how commercial Christmas was, and how expensive presents had become, and was hoping to get DVD players and DVDs on the morrow. 'Happy Christmas!', said the ladies at the cash counter, automatically. 'Happy Christmas. Have a nice Christmas Day.'

'I hear they are replacing these people with androids,' said Stanley Johnson. 'Perhaps the service will be a bit quicker then.'

'I think they've already replaced them,' said Phil.

So by the time they got to the Johnsons' house, they were all dying of thirst. 'There's wine or there's g-and-t or there's lager,' said Stanley jovially. 'Or there's all three for the greedy.'

'Oooh, we mustn't be long,' said Dora, 'but I'd murder for a gin. Go easy on the tonic, Stan. I suppose you folks have got a Bible, haven't you?'

As he poured the drinks, Stanley said confidently, 'Oh, we shall be safe enough from the new law. We've got "The Bible Designed to be Read as Literature" and "The Bible Designed to be Read as History" and "The Bible Designed to be Read as Prelude to Shakespeare's History Plays". I don't think the New Father Christmas will bother us much.'

'If he comes round here, we'll give him a drink,' said Sue, and screamed with laughter at her own joke.

A few glasses later, Dora Dogsbody noticed it was already dark outside.

'Goodness gracious me, how time's getting on. We'd better be hopping it, Phil.'

'You must have a look at the Headington Christmas lights as you go,' said Sue. 'They run all the way down to Boots this year.'

'They're an absolute disgrace,' said Stanley.

'I heard it's that lady at Lime & Intelligence who paid for them all,' said Phil.

They kissed each other good-bye and wished each other a Merry Christmas.

And as Phil and Dora staggered up Headington Business Association Avenue, they couldn't resist looking in the card shop window, which was displaying lots of humorous Christmas cards. Both of them roared with laughter at the jokes.

'Oh, I must buy that one,' said Dora, prodding the window pane. 'We could pop it in through the Vicar's door. He's not a bad chap for a vicar – he likes a laugh.' They entered the shop. The card that had attracted them showed one of Santa's reindeer on the snowy roof of a house. It was relieving itself down the chimney. The title was 'An Unexpected Christmas Present'.

Dora put her handbag down on the counter and went to look at a few more cards. A small thin boy came up to her, saying, 'I'm an orphan, missus. I need a few pennies to buy my sister some batteries to work her laughing monster Tyrannosaurus. Could you please let me have fifty p?'

'Fifty p? You greedy little blighter!' Dora exclaimed. 'Be off with you!'

'Fifty p ain't much.'

'It's more than you deserve. Why aren't you at school?'

'Because it's holiday time, miss.'

'When I was young, we worked on Christmas Eve,' said Dora, winking good-naturedly at Phil. 'We couldn't afford Tyrannosauruses, not back in them days!'

When she got back to the counter, her handbag had gone.

'Serves you right,' said the young lady assistant behind the counter. 'You shouldn't have let it out of your sight. What do you expect these days?'

'How about some Christmas spirit?' Phil roared in her face.

'Poof, you've already had some of that,' said the assistant, backing away. 'I saw that little kid run off with your stupid bag.'

Reluctantly, she agreed to phone the police.

A NEW (GOVERNMENTAL) FATHER CHRISTMAS

The police said they were busy with petty robberies and muggings all over town. Someone's Christmas tree had fallen on a small girl; malice was suspected. A woman in Rose Hill had had her car stolen. Two five-year-olds armed with Kolashnikovs were holding their mother hostage in the Butcher's Arms. A Belgian had lost a child in Debenham's. It would be an hour and a half before they could send someone to the shop in Headington Business Association Avenue.

'Well then, we'll wait,' said Dora, sniffling.

'But don't forget we need to get a safety for Bible,' said Phil.

'We close in forty-five minutes,' said the assistant. 'So there!'

'I don't care,' said Dora. 'I know my rights. And this young unkind lady was rude to me.'

The assistant grew indignant. 'Young I certainly am, unkind maybe, but a lady never.' She stamped her foot.

Eventually, a police car stopped outside the shop and a charming young policeman entered. He said his name was Sandy Number 4599. He wore a sprig of mistletoe in his cap. He very courteously suggested that the Dogsbodys should ride with him down to the police station, where the duty sergeant would take the details of the crime.

Rather grumpily, they complied. As Dora repeated, she knew her rights. Traffic was dense on the way. Oxford seemed to be full of obnoxious young people partying.

But they were thrilled when they entered the police station. It had been beautifully decorated and there was a lovely Christmas tree, covered with crackers and tiny toy truncheons and silver handcuffs. Members of the force were handing round cooking sherry and playing with sparklers. The mood was pleasantly celebratory.

The sergeant was very nice too. He gave them each a cup of tea and told them that the Oxfordshire force would search all over town for the lost handbag once the Christmas and New Year's break was over, in ten days' time. Dora described her handbag in detail; it all took quite a while. Meanwhile, drunks were being wheeled in to the station. Some of them were still conscious.

'What, they've nicked you too, love!', one said to Dora as he passed. 'Been on the game, have you?'

She was furious. 'How dare you! What game do you mean?'

Eventually, the charming young policeman kindly gave them a lift back to Headington, to Old High Street, since it was Christmas Eve. They heard the bells of St Andrews Church ringing out, joyful on the crisp night air – and only then did they remember the quest for the Bible.

'Oh, it must be midnight,' said Dora. 'I've got no bag and no Bible! Where did the time go? Why did we delay?'

'I expect the Fletchers will still be up,' said Phil. 'They're presently wrapping their probs.'

They hurried together along the Croft. It seemed very creepy and dark. The New Father Christmas swooped down on them half-way along. He was big and surly. He looked like Gordon Brown with white whiskers. He popped the poor Dogsbodys into his sack.

'Oh, how dare you!', cried Dora, as she disappeared.

All the New Father Christmas said was, 'You are the ones who dared. You had no Bible, no faith, no direction. Don't worry, you will be – recycled, as we like to call it nowadays. Happy Christmas!'

And he rushed on his way, his sleigh-bells jingling a merry tune.

All over town, church bells were ringing a message of good will.

Last Orders

The alphameter indicated that two people, perhaps more, were somewhere in the block. The Captain took his ACV slowly down the street. There was a canal to his left; its waters churned as if they were living.

He kept the vehicle window open. Gusts of rain, by turns icy and hot, beat against the narrow battlements of his face. They helped him stay awake. His was one of the last rescue parties and he had gone without sleep for over three days.

At the end of the foul little street, a light showed. Oil, probably: electric power had failed long before the city emptied. He sounded his hooter, peering through the murk, through a bar window. A small figure gesticulated in shadow.

The Captain stopped his engine; the craft sank onto cobbles. He waited. The man inside was still talking, or whatever the thing was he was doing. The Captain felt for a pill in his oilskin jacket and squirted it down his throat with a spray from the drink-tube on his dash. Then he climbed out and made his way to the bar. His movements were stiff with controlled weariness. A slate whirled past his head and dashed itself to bits against a bollard by the canal-side. He did not blink.

Pushing the bar door open, he went in. A dim light on a counter revealed the outlines of shambles. The last earth tremor had broken most of the furniture and the bottles behind the bar. Mirrors were cracked. He picked his way forward between shattered floorboards.

At the bar stood a stocky man of indeterminate age, dressed with incongruous neatness in an old-fashioned suit. His round head was covered in a fuzz of colourless hair. Oyster eyes sat in his round face. He was talking with a jovial animation to a thin old lady dressed in black who perched on a high stool, her hands folded together on her lap. A beer stood by her elbow, half finished. The man had a neat little liqueur by him which he had not touched.

Taking all this in at a glance, the Captain said, 'You're supposed to have been out of here hours ago. How come the patrols missed you? In a very few minutes—'

'Yes, yes,' said the stocky man, 'we're just drinking up, we're fully aware of the seriousness of the situation. You look a bit tired – have one with us while we're finishing ours. We'll go together.'

'Leave your drinks. We've got to get to Reijkskeller Field. The last ferry is almost due to leave.' The Captain took the stocky man by the elbow.

'Just a moment. Have a beer. This lady here says it's very good. No, no trouble, won't take a minute. We'll all travel better for another drink.'

He ducked behind the bar and came up smiling with a foaming glass.

'I've got to get you out of here, both of you,' the Captain said. 'Our lives are in danger. You don't seem to realise. The Moon, as you must know, is about to—'

'My dear man,' said the stocky man, coming back round the bar and striking a positive attitude before his untouched liqueur, 'you need not remind us of the gravity of the situation. I was telling this lady here that I was right there on the Moon, in Armstrong, when the first fissure began. I saw it with my own eyes. It was a funny thing, really – you see, I'm a xeno-balneologist, specialising in off-Earth swimming pools with all their attendant problems, and you'd never believe how many! – Do you know that there are – or were, I suppose I should say – more swimming pools on Luna than in the U.S.A.? And I'd just been over to see Wally Kingsmill, who owns – well, his family owns – one of the biggest and most splendid pools in Armstrong, and as I was pavrunning down Ordinary, I could hear people shouting and screaming. First thing you think of on Luna is always that the dome might be damaged. As it happened, I had all my breathing equipment by me – I'd used them in Wally Kingsmill's pool, you see – and I said to myself, "Right" but it wasn't the dome at all – though that went a couple of hours later and it was curious how that happened, but this time it was the crack, it came snaking along, travelling fast in erratic fashion, and zip, it ran under the pavrunner, which stopped. Just stopped dead, just like that—'

'The Moon has been evacuated. Now it's our turn. Now we've got to go. At once,' said the Captain. He felt mist gathering in his brain. 'At once,' he repeated. He took up his beer and sipped it.

'It's a lovely beer,' said the old lady. 'Seems such a shame to waste it.' Her gaze returned to the stocky man on whose every word she fastened avidly.

The stocky man poised himself before his daintily shaped liqueur glass, lifted it, drank it off at a gulp, poured himself another from a green bottle, and resumed his vigil over the glass, all in one movement.

'So of course I climbed off, and it's a curious thing, but that crack reminded me of one on the ceiling of the Sistine Chapel, you know, where Michelangelo painted his – of course, it's in Houston now, and I've studied it many times, being interested in art – in fact, about five years ago, about the time that the President visited Venusberg, I was commissioned—'

'That was seven years ago next month,' said the Captain. 'The President visiting Venusberg. I know because I was on Venus at the time on a posting to the Space Police. Anyhow, that's immaterial, sir. I must insist you come along now.'

'Immediately.' He trotted behind the counter and poured the old lady another beer. 'You're right, it was seven years ago, because at that time I was under contract to the planetoids. Funnily enough, I was just saying about Michelangelo and, in fact, the grandest pool we put in at the planetoids was finished with a mosaic, consisting of almost a million separate pieces, of Michelangelo's "Creation", with God reaching out his finger to Adam, you know, covering the entire bottom of the pool. Beautiful. You should go and see it. At least the planetoids will be unaffected by all the gravitational disturbances, or so one hopes.'

Having finished his beer, the Captain could not tell whether he felt worse or better for it. 'Not only are we all three in grave danger, sir, but you and this lady are contravening martial law established ten days ago. I shall be fully within my rights to shoot you down unless you accompany me to my vehicle immediately.'

The stocky man laughed. 'Don't worry, I'm a strong supporter of martial law in the circumstances. What else can you do? I think it's marvellous – a credit to all concerned – the way the evacuation of Earth has gone so smoothly. I just wish that more attention could have been paid to the art treasures; not that I'm criticising, because I know how little warning we've had, but all the same . . . You can build more swimming pools, but you can't resurrect Michelangelo from the dead to paint his masterpieces again, can you?'

As he spoke, he stared more and more fixedly at his liqueur glass, which gleamed in the yellow glow of the oil lamp. Suddenly, he pounced on it and drained its contents as swiftly as before, immediately pouring himself another tot. The old lady, meanwhile, climbed down from her stool and was threading her way through debris over to the window.

'Where are you going, ma'am?' the Captain asked, following her. 'I told you to leave.'

'Oh, I won't go away, officer,' she said, laughing at the thought. 'I am as upset about it all as you are. Poor old Earth, after all these millions of years. It's Earth I worry about, not the Moon. The Moon was never much use to us in the first place. I just wanted to see if I could see it out of the window.'

Her words were drowned by a tremendous buffet of wind which shook the whole building and set doors banging and weakened walls collapsing. The window shattered as she reached it; luckily, the shards of glass were swept outwards.

'Oh dear, it's dreadful, what are we coming to? Anyone would think it was the end of the world.'

'It is the fucking end of the world, ma'am,' the Captain said. 'Are you coming, or do I have to carry you?'

'Of course you don't have to carry me. I'm not drunk, if that's what you suspect. You look absolutely worn out. Look, there it is! How I hate it!'

She pointed into the darkness and the Captain stared where she pointed. Furious winds had blown away the cloud. In the night sky, fuming in silver and crimson, was the biggest mountain ever invented, one side of it curved, the other ragged, looking almost to the zenith of the heavens. Gutted lunar cities could clearly be seen across its shattered face. They wondered that it did not fall down upon them as they looked.

Grasping the old lady roughly by the elbow, the Captain said, 'You're getting out of here at once. That's an order. Do you know this guy? Is he your husband?'

When she looked up at him, smiling ruefully, he could trace faded youth among the lines and blemishes of her skin.

'My husband? I only met him today – or yesterday, I suppose. What time is it? Though I wouldn't mind a husband like that, old as I am. I mean, he's so fascinating to talk to. We have a lot in common, despite a few years' difference in age. A very sympathetic man. Do you know, officer, he was telling me a few hours ago, before we came in here—'

'Never mind what he was telling you, we've got to get him out of here. This is a rescue operation, understand? It's urgent, understand? Look at the damned thing out there, arriving fast. What's his name?'

She laughed nervously and looked down at her neat little feet. 'You're going to think this is plain crazy after what I said just now, but I've never married. Not legally married, you understand. My life really hasn't been – this may sound as if I'm terribly sorry for myself, still, you have to face facts – but it hasn't been fortunate as far as the other sex is concerned. Goodness knows what his name is. When I was younger, I was often in despair. Very often. After almost every man left – despair again. Yet I wasn't ugly, you know, or possessive . . . I'm sorry, officer, I realise this heart-searching may not interest you – I'm not a particularly introspective person—'

'Lady, it's not a question of interest, it's a question of desperation. We're going to get ourselves killed if we aren't away from Earth within the next hour—'

'Oh, I know, officer, but that's exactly what I'm complaining about. Don't think I don't feel as bad as you do. As I was saying, I never had luck – you know what I mean? – with men. I was telling our friend here, and he was so sympathetic, that my flat was partially destroyed in the first of the earth tremors, when they first told us that Earth might have to be evacuated. And I couldn't bear to think that my little home, and my garden, and the town where I've lived for over forty years, should have to be left behind. I wept, I'm not ashamed to say it, and I wasn't the only one to weep, by any means—'

'We've all wept, lady, every one of us. This was the planet we were born on, and this is the planet we are going to die on, unless we move fast. Now, come on, for the last time – out!'

The stocky man had put down another dose of liqueur. He came across the broken floor, carrying two beers, his plain face wrinkled in a smile.

'Have a quick one, both of you, before we go. It'll only be wasted. I shouldn't stand by that broken window, it isn't safe. Come back to the bar.'

'Nowhere's safe. Everywhere's doomed. That's why—'

The old lady said, 'I was telling this officer how my flat was partially destroyed and—'

'It'll be totally flattened, with every other building on Earth, in a short while. Now, I appeal to you both for the last time – all right, I'll just drink this beer, all right – look, I'm exhausted, and I know your flat was ruined, but I'm appealing to you both—'

'You know my flat was ruined!' the old lady exclaimed with anger. 'What do you care about my flat? You just don't listen to what I'm trying to say. I told you about this first earth tremor, when my chest-of-drawers fell over, flat on its face. I was in bed at the time—'

The Captain, with a certain weary sense of unreality, drew his gun, stepping back a pace to cover them both. He clutched his half-finished beer in his other hand.

'That's enough. Silence, both of you. Vehicle outside. Out of here, move!'

'You've got a funny way of going about things, I must say,' the stocky man said, shaking his head in regret. 'What's the point of violence at a time like this? At any time, really, but particularly at a time like this, when the whole world is about to be crushed out of existence?'

In his stance and gestures, he presented a vitality which the Captain experienced as an assault on his own depleted resources. He found himself saying apologetically, 'I don't want violence, I'm just trying to do my duty and—'

'We've heard that one before, haven't we?' said the stocky man to the old lady, but in such a jovial way that even the Captain could not take offence. 'Duty, indeed! You ought to hear this lady's story, it's an extremely nice little anecdote – far more than an anecdote, really, a – what's the word?'

'An epic?' the Captain suggested. 'No time left for epics.'

'Not an epic, man – a vignette, that's the word, a vignette of a life. You see, when her chest-of-drawers crashed over, the lady was in bed, as she has related—'

'It was two o'clock in the morning – of course I was in bed,' said the old lady, as if something improper had been suggested.

'And this chest-of-drawers had belonged to her mother.' As he talked, the stocky man led the way back to the bar, giving the old lady a chance to say to the Captain, *sotto voce*, 'In fact, it's been in the family for several generations. It was a very valuable piece, dating from the mid-nineteenth century.'

The stocky man lifted a full liqueur glass from the counter, drained it swiftly, refilled it instantly from the bottle, standing with his plump hands palm-down on the bar, one on either side of the brimming glass, and managed to complete these manoeuvres almost without a break in his speech.

'So she put on the light – still working fortunately because, if you remember, the first tremor was not severe – in fact a good many people, myself included, I might add, slept right through it. In fact, I'd only just gone to bed, being a bit of a night bird – it was early for me – and she climbed out to see what damage had been done and bless me if the chest hadn't split right down the back, revealing a secret drawer. She had known about the secret drawer but she had forgotten it, the way you do, quite unpredictably, just as you can unpredictably remember something. You see how this ceiling is cracked? We were talking about the cracks in the Sistine Chapel ceiling, but you notice on this ceiling that the cracks mostly run in pretty straight lines. When I was telling you both about the Michelangelo painting, I happened to notice these cracks here, and even as I was speaking I saw that they form a perfect map of a sector of this city which I used to live in when I was an engineering student, and that's going back some thirty years.'

At this point, he made a swoop on his liqueur glass and downed its contents. Seizing her opportunity, the old lady said smoothly, 'And it must have been thirty years since I had used that secret drawer. I put something in that drawer thirty years ago and some trick of the mind – as you say, it's quite unpredictable what you forget and what you remember, particularly when you're getting on in years – some trick of the mind made me forget it entirely until the tremor. And what do you think I'd put in there?'

The Captain went behind the bar and helped himself to another beer.

'I'll put it to you another way,' he said. 'If you aren't out of here by the time I've finished this beer, I'm going to shoot myself.' He set the service revolver down solemnly on the counter and raised the glass to his lips.

'Cheers! I hid a secret diary in that drawer. Mind you, I was no chicken, even then. It dated from my late thirties . . .' She paused to sob.

'Don't fret,' the stocky man said, passing her another beer. 'I used to keep a diary for years, and much good it did me. One day, I said to my brother, "Look at all these dreary old—" Ah, wait, yes – there you are, another instance of how memory is unpredictable! I believe I've got an engagement diary in my pocket which contains a map – yes, here we are!'

He brought a little diary out and began thumbing his way towards the back of it.

'I've nearly finished this beer—' cautioned the Captain.

'Let me get you another,' said the old lady, coming round behind the counter with him, 'because I would like to tell you this rather romantic story before you go.'

'I say, isn't this pleasant?' exclaimed the stocky man, spreading open his diary with a heavy hand and looking up with a smile as he did so. 'You'd never think this was the end of the world, would you? I can't see myself being happy on any other world – not really happy, I mean. Anyhow, here you are, here's the map. I thought I'd find it. Better get my reading spectacles . . .' He began a search of his pockets and then, catching sight of the liqueur glass with a meniscus of drink crowning it, seized that instead, to pause with it half way to his lips. He pressed his lips with the fingers of his other hand and set the glass down on the counter again. 'You know, I believe I'll join you in a glass of beer,' he said, amazed at his own whim.

'Coming up,' said the old lady. 'You know, I think you're right. It *is* nice here. I haven't been up so late in years – well, not since I was in Norfolk, staying with my cousin Beth last May – and I don't feel a bit tired. You don't happen to have a cigarette, do you?'

'There are some packets on this shelf,' said the Captain, reaching for them. 'I'd just spotted them myself. Let's all light up! I'm not supposed to smoke on duty but, after all, these are rather special circumstances . . .'

They all laughed, suddenly happy, lighting up cigarettes, puffing away, pulling at their beers, instinctively moving closer in the warm light of the oil lamp. Wind whistled outside. Somewhere nearby there was the escalating rumble of a building collapsing under the weight in the sky.

'It's moments like this that make life, don't you agree?' said the stocky man. 'Far too few of them, that must be admitted. Poor old Earth, I wonder if it'll miss mankind, just a little bit?'

''Course it won't,' said the Captain, drinking deeply. 'Mankind has just been a sort of parasite on the face of the Earth, despoiling it, ravishing its fair face. Those stupid gravity experiments on the Moon – they've brought us to this miserable pass, but we're only leaving a world we've ruined steadily, century by century—'

'Oh, I'm afraid I can't agree with that at all, really I can't,' said the old lady, puffing at her cigarette. 'I have a lovely garden at my flat – I wish you could see it – it'll be spoilt, of course, when the Moon crashes – though the roses are very hardy – I've got a lovely show of Queen Elizabeth's, I wonder if perhaps they won't survive? And just opposite, there's the park—'

'Quite agree,' said the stocky man. He patted her arm. 'I think we improved the place. It was nothing but jungle till mankind got going. I love cities, theatres, music – swimming pools, naturally, but you'd expect me to say that – and all these snug little bars where you can get together with a few kindred spirits and talk. Take this dear old city – well, here's a map, very small scale, but let me show you where the roads take on the exact configuration of the cracks over our heads . . . It's not a very good diary.'

'I was saying about my old diary,' said the old lady. 'Actually, I didn't find it till the morning after the tremor, and there it was, exactly where I'd left it thirty years earlier. And I opened it, and on the last page, after December 31st – just fancy, no more December 31sts . . . you can hardly imagine it, can you?'

'That's one day I can do without,' said the Captain, and laughed.

'Ah, but it's the day before New Year's Day,' said the stocky man, 'when everyone makes merry! I've seen some New Year's Days, believe me—'

'What I'd written where New Year's Day should have been was rather a desolate little sentence. I hope you won't laugh when I tell you, officer.'

'Jim,' said the Captain. 'My friends call me Jim.'

'Jim, then.' She fluttered her eyelids, and lifted her glass to him before drinking. 'Don't laugh – I was thirty-eight when I wrote it – I put "My long quest for love – I realise now that it will never be fulfilled" . . .' She began to weep.

Both the stocky man and the Captain put their arms round her. 'Don't cry, love,' they said. 'Have another drink.'

'While there's life there's hope,' said the Captain.

'We all have our disappointments,' said the stocky man. 'You have to laugh them off . . . I know when I was twenty-five I was all ready to throw myself in that canal out there – no, I'm wrong, it wasn't that canal. It was – well, look, it's the spur of the canal that ends at Fisher's Wharf, where Kayle Bridge Street comes in. Let me show you on the map, or you can see it in these cracks on the ceiling. See? There's the end of the canal, at Fisher's Wharf, just by the old chapel, and Kayle Bridge Street comes in here, and on this corner there used to be an old man with a stall selling hot dogs, year in, year out—'

'I'm weeping now,' said the old lady, laughing. 'And I wept when I read what I'd written in the diary, and I remember that I wept when I was thirty-eight and wrote the words down, and yet a man called – what was his name? I remembered it not a week ago—'

'The old man with the hot dogs was at the other end of Kayle Bridge Street, where the railway station used to be,' said the Captain. 'Had a big walrus moustache. On the corner you're speaking of, there was—'

A resounding crash made him stop. Part of the ceiling, including the interesting cracks, collapsed, showering them with flakes which fell in their beers. The building next door collapsed. Dust and grit billowed in through the open window.

'The vehicle!' exclaimed the Captain in horror. He set his glass down, removed his other hand from the old lady's clutches and staggered across to the door. Outside, the ACV had half disappeared under rubble which still slid and bounced across the road into the boiling canal.

'Come and look at this!' he called. They joined him at the door.

'We'll have to walk to Reijkskeller Field,' he said. He looked at his watch. 'We'd better get going.'

'It's raining. I'm not going out in that,' said the old lady. 'What time is it?'

'Look at that horrible thing in the sky. Makes you shudder,' said the stocky man. 'What are the chances that it will miss Earth and just swan off into space?'

'Nil, absolutely nil,' said the Captain. 'Let me just fetch my gun and we'd better get going, rain or no rain. The last ferry's waiting for us. Once we hear the siren, we've got five minutes and then they blast off, and we'll be stuck here, alone on Earth. Better hurry.'

He turned back, muttering, into the bar. The stocky man went with him, brushing white dust from his suit. 'I suppose you're right. Let's just have a last drink. One for the road. But you know you're wrong about that hot-dog stall. I was so poor when I was a student that I used to live off hot dogs, so I went to that stall just about every evening for two or more years, so I ought to know, and I remember—'

'All round the wharf was part of my patrol area when I first joined the force, so I ought to remember. The canal finished – hey, where's my gun? I left it on the bar.'

'Perhaps it fell down behind. Look behind.'

'You haven't got it, have you?'

'I loathe guns. Fist fights, no guns. You wouldn't really have shot yourself, would you?'

'Look, it's not here. Are you sure you didn't take it? You could be jailed for that, I'm warning you. God, I feel so exhausted.'

'I told you, I have not touched your gun. The last people left on Earth and you think I'd steal your gun!'

'Don't you two quarrel, just when we're having a nice time,' said the old lady brightly, bustling behind the bar and bringing out three new glasses. 'I always fancied myself as a barmaid. What'll it be, gentlemen?'

'That's the stuff, love,' said the stocky man, rubbing his hands in delight. 'You're a woman after my own heart. I wish I'd bumped into you thirty years ago, that's all I can say. I'll have another beer and perhaps I'll just have a quick liqueur too while you're pouring it. Keeps the cold out.'

'Mind if I try that stuff?' asked the Captain.

'Help yourself.' He pushed the liqueur bottle over. 'On the house.'

'Your bonny blue eyes, lady!' said the Captain, lifting his drink with trembling hands.

'You're darlings, both of you,' she said, adding, as she lifted her own glass, 'and here's to Earth, the best planet in the whole universe!'

They all three drank. Distantly, a siren wailed.

They winked at each other. 'Time for one more,' said the Captain.

'*His* name was Jim too,' said the old lady, 'and it was really funny how I bumped into him.'

As she lit another cigarette and passed the packet round, the stocky man said, 'We'll go and inspect Fisher's Wharf in the morning and you'll see that I'm right. I can remember exactly the very pattern of the cobbles. Anyhow, as I was saying, Michelangelo—'

The siren died away. A new and more insistent wind sprang up outside.

'I know,' said the Captain, 'let's take our drinks and go into the back parlour. There's bound to be a back parlour, and we'll be cosier in there. Bring the lamp.'

'Good idea, Jim,' said the stocky man. 'These little back parlours take some beating. I know once—'

Bill Carter Takes Over

That winter, dawn broke over Inkerman Terrace at about seven a.m., which was the time Bill Carter, obedient to his alarm clock, got out of bed.

Already there was a friendly rumble of traffic outside. As Bill peered from his bathroom window, he could see the traffic piling up on the raised Westway into London.

His wife Laura did not get up until seven-thirty. The arrangement suited Bill. He liked the peace in the house, liked to breakfast alone with the newspaper, liked a quiet half-hour before he drove in to work at Jackson's Alloys.

He filled the kettle, switched it on, and went into the living-room to have a look at God. A rainy light filled the room. God's tank was in shadow.

'Not much of a day, O Lord.'

God was used to criticism. He said nothing. He curled a flipper and made a lazy circuit of his tank. God's tank was a standard size. God-tanks were mass-produced and measured the same the world over, being just under two metres square and one point four metres high. The tank was open to the air. It contained nothing but air and God.

Carter went nearer.

'I don't think Judy's flu is any better this morning. I'm just going to take her up a cup of tea. I can hear the poor kid sneezing in her room. Can't You do something about that, O Lord? You know her exams are coming up.'

Privately, Bill Carter thought his daughter was backward. Privately, he blamed his wife. Not so privately, Carter was morose and often bellicose. On the recommendation of his doctor, he went to see a marriage counsellor every Wednesday.

'Well?' – challengingly to God.

God spake. 'I do keep your daughter's interests in mind.'

Sigh. 'You know I don't like to complain, O Lord, but . . . please let today be something special. Just for a change.'

God's single eye was rather like a peony. Its petals opened. Among dense stamens, something glittered. When God manifested Himself to a troubled world in the closing year of the twentieth century, He chose to appear universally in non-anthropomorphic form. People who were against racism applauded this; people who were for it thought God was being silly.

'All is well, Carter, and all is eternally well. Time does not really pass, you know. You live with me in an eternal day.'

'Christ, You always fob me off with words. How about some action, Lord? I'm only worried about Judy's flu. And my wife's behaviour . . .'

'I am here on Earth only as witness to my presence throughout the universe. I really prefer not to work little local miracles, having found from experience that they are counter-productive.'

Carter clenched his fists.

'But You're omnipotent, omnipotent! You made the damned galaxies! Don't give me that counter-productive nonsense.'

'Carter, you must accept that even omnipotence has its limits.'

'Oh, come on, will You, God? Just between You and me. You know the mess my life's in. Judy, Laura . . . I've got another session with Mrs Batacharya this evening. Help me, will You? I ask You every bloody day—'

'And every day I do help you, Bill, in many mysterious ways . . .'

'Oh, You mealy-mouthed—'

In sudden rage, Carter heaved himself into the big glass tank. God writhed away to the far side, but Carter grasped one of His trailing flippers and got in a swift kick at one of the three segments of His body.

'Ow, that hurts, Carter! You know we can't stand pain.'

'That's ridiculous!'

'How else could we comprehend mankind's problems unless we suffered with you and felt pain? Owww!'

Throwing himself forward, Carter locked both hands round the smooth neck-like stalk connecting God's first and second segments. He had God pinned down on one side of the tank in a fairly undignified position.

'Now look here, Almighty, I want a miracle out of You. Then I'll let go, understand? Quick!'

'Owww. What do you want me to do?'

'You can do anything, anything, and You ask me what I want! How about a bigger house for a start. Far away from Inkerman Terrace. On a hill somewhere, beautiful views, with a stream – yes, a trout stream. And a pretty wife. Plus a lake and a power-boat on it. Two wives. Sisters, who get on well together. Good dress sense. And a full-size ivory statue of Ella Fitzgerald in the hall. And a good job, forget Jackson's Alloys. No – no job, no work, just my estate to look after. I want to be a crack shot, really crack. A private armoury, the lot. Wild elephants in the grounds, really dangerous. Servants. Drink. Women. Fame. A fax machine. You know what I want. Make them materialise and I'll let You go.'

'Yes, I do know what you want, Carter, and believe me I sympathise, deeply. Owww-wow! All those things – those gross material things – would really be only a substitute, a poor substitute, for a state of spiritual – Owww-owww! Mercy, Carter!'

'Cut that pious talk. One small miracle, come on, one small miracle, or I'm keeping You pinned down here all day, O Lord. Anything! How about – a palm tree in the back garden?'

'You know the neighbours would complain. Think not only for thyself. Ohhhhh, Jesus Christ, Carter, you have a nasty streak in you.'

'Who put it there? Come on, a palm tree, or I'll tear this flipper-thing right off.'

Over the garden, a flash of light. By Laura's rockery, just where she had buried the family cat, a palm tree appeared, its topknot of leaves blotting out the chimneys of the houses opposite.

Carter climbed out of the tank, victorious but unsatisfied. God relapsed sulkily into a corner. He was sick of doing palm trees.

*

Carter made time before work commenced to go and see his elderly mother, Joyce Carter, in the old folks' home nearby.

Joyce Carter was eighty-one, her skin blotched by liver-marks as if by a poisonous fungus.

She shared a room with Mrs Vera Walker. Their two manifestations of God circulated in their tanks, which had been pushed awkwardly together behind the commode, by the oxygen cylinders.

A nurse was taking Joyce Carter's breakfast tray away as the old lady began a litany of complaint before Carter had seated himself beside her bed.

'Oh, I can't tell you how sick and fed up I am of that Mrs Walker, I was just telling the nurse here, fed up. You should have heard her at two this morning. Stone deaf, of course. What a mess! No consideration, poor old thing. I keep trying to get them to move her. Might as well talk to a brick wall. God, God, why You don't help me I can't think. Nobody cares for a poor old woman like me any more.'

'I care,' said God. 'Of course I care, Mrs Carter. That's why I'm here, suffering with you. Be patient, my dear. All is well and all is eternally well.'

'That's a lot of help, I'm sure.'

Knowing that his mother, who treated God much as she had her dead husband, could go on arguing for ever, Carter indicated that he had to be getting to work.

'You never stay long these days, do you?'

'You've always got God to communicate with. Bear that in mind.'

'Oh, He's no company. He keeps going on about the Hereafter – not a very cheerful subject.'

'That's untrue, Mrs Carter,' said God reprovingly. 'Didn't I read you a whole Barbara Cartland romance yesterday? But, as I told you then, the Hereafter represents a happier state.'

'There He goes again. You see what I'm up against. Nag nag nag.'

Carter stood up, glancing at his watch.

'At least He loves us all. Bye, mother.'

The day's work at Jackson's Alloys passed smoothly enough. Carter left his desk promptly and, that evening, the traffic jams were not too bad. He was home by five-thirty.

Laura came down the stairs smiling, to greet him in the hall. He looked at her suspiciously, but she put her arms round him and kissed his cheek.

'Let's have some tea. Come into the kitchen and talk to me. Judy's a bit better.'

Mollified by this, he followed. She turned the radio on automatically before she filled the kettle. They perched on stools as the kettle started to sing. Her God's tank was wedged in the space between the oven and the fridge.

As they sipped tea from their horoscope mugs, Carter said, 'They were playing ***Eso Beso*** on the car radio on the way home.' He hummed a few bars. 'Do you remember that one, darling, when we were kids?'

'Who was it used to sing ***Eso Beso***?'

'I've forgotten – it's so long ago.'

God spake. 'It was Paul Anka.'

Laura took a biscuit out of the tin. 'Those sixties songs had more zip than the stuff they pour out now. The nineties are a bit of a flop, aren't they? Perhaps next century will be better. But that's up to You, isn't it, O Lord Almighty?'

She threw Him a scornful glance and He coiled over to face her.

'No my dear, it's up to you and your husband, and everyone else on Earth. I can only work through you, as you strive for a better world.'

'Crikey, me strive for a better world? I've got my hands full as it is. I took Judy up some Marmite. She wouldn't drink it. It's all I can do to hold my marriage together. I'm just not appreciated, that's the trouble. Work, morning, noon, and night . . . Debts, debts, debts . . . Without wanting to be unpleasant, God, I think You created a lot of unfairness between the sexes.'

Carter said, 'I wonder whatever happened to Paul Anka.'

God spake. 'Bill, it's six-ten, time you went to your marriage guidance counsellor.'

'Oh, you've got to tittle-tattle to that woman again.'

'Why don't you come with me, dear?'

'I've got other things to do. You ought to have a jog round the park, like Paul Gutteridge does. Much better for you than going to that awful Batacharya woman every Wednesday.'

As he went into the hall, Carter called, 'And you – please behave yourself while I'm out.'

'And what's that meant to mean?'

'Just remember God is watching you.'

He slammed the front door as he went out, and then regretted it.

He was early at the marriage guidance clinic in Profumo Place. The old habit of punctuality was hard to shake, even though Mrs Batacharya had once uttered a deadly insult and called him 'anally-oriented'. He read vintage copies of *Asia Review* until the bell tinkled and he went into Mrs Batacharya's room.

Mrs Batacharya sat in a creaking wicker chair. She wore a tweed skirt with jumper to match, a blue cardigan and green suede shoes. She had found room for her God and his tank between the old leatherette couch and the door.

He sat down, facing her, looking depressed.

'Well, how have you been, Bill, dear?'

'Bunty, I believe that my wife is continuing her affair with that bastard Gutteridge. Of course I'm not sure, but she mentioned him again this afternoon. I don't know whether I'm imagining things or not. What's imagination, what's reality? God's presence hasn't made the distinction between them any easier to grasp, I must say.'

God spake. 'Both are aspects of my eternal Being.'

'Please ignore Him,' Mrs Batacharya said. 'He has no qualifications for counselling. Also, He has been very loquacious today. Just concentrate on me. How has your week been, Bill?'

Carter groaned. 'I beat up God this morning until He produced a palm tree in the back garden. I suppose that's on my conscience.'

'One measly palm tree?'

God spake. 'It was a *cocos nucifera*, to remind Carter of how such trees dump thousands of tons of free fruit daily into the ungrateful laps of mankind.'

Mrs Batacharya said, 'You're always preaching, O Lord. Take it from me, it's counter-productive. That I can tell You from experience.'

'Outside, in the real world,' Carter said, 'chaps must know for sure whether their wives love them or not.'

'And, in that real world, does Laura know if her Bill loves her?'

'I tell her often enough,' Carter said. 'Don't I, God?'

'Love lives in deeds as well as words,' God said, turning authoritatively in the tank. 'When I created the world, that was a deed of love, and you are all children of it. You would save yourselves endless sorrow if you could remember that cardinal fact.'

'Bill's trouble,' Mrs Batacharya said crushingly, 'is that, as well as Laura and himself, you also created Gutteridge.'

Carter downed a couple of beers at the local before driving home. He went upstairs to see his daughter, but she was asleep, breathing laboriously, wearing her Walkman. Laura was nowhere about and there were no signs of supper.

After some hesitation, Carter went into the living-room to see his own incarnation of God. He switched the light on. Closing the door and leaning against it, he looked at the Being who moved languidly in His tank.

'Well, Wednesday's almost over, O Lord, and it didn't have much to offer. I'm sorry I hurt You this morning by the way. That was a really disgusting performance.'

'I'm touched by your penitence, Carter, but you should learn to control yourself.'

Sighing heavily, Carter went over to the window and drew the curtain.

'Isn't that part of Your job? You made us, after all.'

'You see, that's what makes me so absolutely fed up. You humans whine and winge for autonomy. You get it. I give it to you. Then when anything goes wrong you blame me. Every time. How do you think I feel? Grow up, will you?'

'So what about Judy, then? Is she going to be fit enough to go back to school tomorrow, or isn't she?'

'I'm the Creator, Carter, not your family doctor.'

'Surely You must be bored out of your wits in that tank—'

'—In these multitudinous tanks, Carter—'

'—not getting through to humanity, preaching, just performing a minor conjuring trick now and again. Why don't You try a really major miracle for once? It might improve Your morale as well as everyone else's.'

'What precisely do you suggest?'

'You see, You've got no imagination . . .'

'So what do you suggest?'

'I wish I had Your job!'

Next moment, Carter found Himself dispersed among a myriad tanks, staring out at the whole of humanity. In the background, joy, illumination, trumpets, and the thrilling tintinnabulations of galaxies.

Countless representatives of humanity stared back at Him, aware that something inexplicable had happened. For once, everyone's attention was centred on God.

Carter spake. 'All is well. And all is eternally well.'

What else could He have told them?

He was to find that even omnipotence had its limits.

Afterword

It's an honour to be asked to pull together a new collection of Aldiss short stories to mark my father's centenary year. When I began, I knew I would be mining from a full and rich seam. I thought I would be able to read all the short stories he had written quickly and pick the 'best' easily. In fact, the experience was quite different. There were even more stories than I had realized, and I found that after almost every one I needed to take more than a moment to reflect on it and process the complexity and message.

Some I could remember from reading them when they were first published, such as the fantasy 'Intangibles Inc.'. Others I came to for the first time, like 'In the Arena'.

Inevitably the 'Best of' could include far more than we had space for here. It may be that you would have chosen others as your 'Best of'. I was grateful for the suggestions of the favourites of others. In the end I chose a selection that I thought would appeal to first time readers as much as to avid followers of Brian's work. There's a mix of dark and light, long and short, optimistic and more pessimistic. Many are full of humour; all are full of humanity.

The stories range across the span of his professional writing life (I write 'professional' because he was writing stories from the age of three and would later scare his boarding school friends with horror stories at night). 'Not For an Age' was written in the fifties, long before *The Truman Show*; 'A Tupolev Too Far' is from the eighties, right through to

'Something from the Turkish', which was early 2000s. He was still writing on his 92nd birthday, adding to his extensive journals.

Finally, there is the story that may have the greatest title of all time: 'Softly, as in an Evening Sunrise'. As in a number of Brian's stories, the protagonists are observed, or at least listened to, by others; in this case from the artificial moon in its geostationary orbit. If my dad is now regarding us from some other planetary system, I hope he will look favourably on this choice. I hope too that you will enjoy this collection as much I have enjoyed pulling it together.

—Wendy Aldiss, 2025

—*Multi-headed beast by Brian Aldiss*

Publication history

'Not for an Age' – *No Time Like Tomorrow,* published by Faber & Faber, 1959

'Supertoys Last All Summer Long' – *Harper's Bazaar,* 1969

'Conviction' – *Space, Time and Nathaniel,* Faber & Faber, 1957

'All the World's Tears' – *Nebula Science Fiction 21,* 1957

'Intangibles, Inc.' – *Intangibles Inc. And Other Stories,* Faber & Faber, 1969

'Breathing Space' – *Science Fantasy,* 1955

'Softly – As in an Evening Sunrise' – *Interzone,* 1992

'In the Arena' – *The Second 'If' Reader,* 1968

'Working in the Spaceship Yards' – *Punch,* 1969

'As for Our Fatal Continuity . . .' – *New Worlds Quarterly 3,* 1972

'Psyclops' – *New Worlds Magazine,* 1956

'Never Let Go of My Hand!' – *New Worlds SF,* 1964

'You Never Asked My Name' – *The Magazine of Fantasy & Science Fiction,* 1985

'Juniper' – *Seasons in Flight,* Grafton, 1986

'Confluence' – *Punch,* 1967

'The Under-Privileged' – *New Worlds Science Fiction,* 1983

'Something from the Turkish' – previously unpublished

'Poor Little Warrior!' – *The Magazine of Fantasy & Science Fiction, 1958*

'How the Gates Opened and Closed' – *The Secret of This Book,* HarperCollins, 1995

'The Worm that Flies' – *The Farthest Reaches,* Trident, 1968

'A Tupolev Too Far' – *Other Edens III,* 1989

'A Romance of the Equator' – *The Birmingham Science Fiction Group (Novacon #10),* 1980

'A New (Governmental) Father Christmas' – *Avernus,* 2002

'Last Orders' – *S.F. Digest #1,* 1976

'Bill Carter Takes Over' – *Twenty Houses of the Zodiac,* New English Library, 1979